RECKLESS KING

EMPTY KINGDOM

BOOK 2

L.M. DALGLEISH

Cover Design by Wildheart Graphics

Photography by Rafa G Catala

Editing by VB Edits

For all the readers who love seeing the playboy finally fall—
and fall hard—this one's for you.

CHAPTER ONE

VIOLET

I swear, the ancient espresso machine hates me.

Planting my hands on my hips, I squint at the frustrating lump of metal, trying to ignore the bead of sweat tickling its way down my spine.

To the right of me, a small line of customers has formed at True Brew's pickup counter. Although there haven't been any complaints so far, I can sense the infamous New Yorker impatience building with every foot shuffle and watch glance. "Sorry for the wait," I call out, hoping my smile doesn't look as frazzled as I feel. "We'll have your coffee ready in no time!"

I inch closer to the machine, peering around to make sure no one is in earshot before I whisper, "If you won't do it for me, do it for Dad."

I clasp my hands together and hold my breath, almost believing it might hiss into action at the mention of its late owner. Unfortunately, it doesn't look like I'll be adding machine whisperer to my resume anytime soon, since it stays obstinately silent. And now, short of frantically tapping the temperature gauge, I'm officially out of ideas.

Jarrod steps up beside me, nudging me away with his shoulder. "Let me look at her," he says. "You can take over up front."

Brushing a loose tendril of hair out of my eyes with the back of my wrist, I give him a grateful smile. "You're a lifesaver." Jarrod's been working at True Brew for a couple of years and has developed an uncanny ability to keep the temperamental machine running. But regardless of his magic touch, there's no denying the truth. It's going to have to be replaced sooner rather than later.

Leaving him to tinker and hopefully get everything running again, I head to the front counter. There's only one customer waiting, a young, harried looking mom with a fussy toddler on her hip. The little girl, who has a glorious mop of red curls on her head, looks hot and cranky and about ready to explode.

I smile at the mom and take her coffee order. After ringing her up, I point at the jar of giant fluffy marshmallows we keep on the counter. "Would she like one?"

The woman's face brightens. "She'd love one." She turns to her daughter. "Wouldn't you, Molly?"

The little girl hides her head in her mom's shoulder, before peeking out at me and nodding.

I smile to myself as I lift the lid of the jar and use a small pair of tongs to pull out a pink marshmallow. "Here you go, sweety."

The little girl holds out her hand and I drop it onto her palm. She pulls it into her chest and stares down at it rapturously.

"Thank you so much," her mom says. "She's had a long day. We both have."

"Well, I hope she enjoys it. And I hope you enjoy your coffee. It sounds like it's well-deserved."

She gives me one last smile before she heads to the pickup counter. I even get a wave from Molly over her shoulder.

Unfortunately, there aren't any other customers lining up behind her, and my shoulders sag as I scan the space. The small rustic coffee shop with exposed brick walls looks more dull than cozy, and almost every one of the wood-topped tables is empty.

For a split-second, I flash back to another time. One when True Brew was packed to the rafters and filled with the sound of happy chatter, the grinding hiss of the espresso machine, and the clink of cutlery. Rising above it all was my dad's booming laugh as he joked with the customers lining up to enjoy pastries baked in-house, simple, tasty meals, and a range of ethically sourced artisan coffee.

I let out a sigh. That was then, and this is now.

Twenty months ago, a heart attack took Dad from us. With his passing went the heart and soul of True Brew. And after the manager my brother Mark and I made the mistake of hiring to run the place mishandled it, the shop is no longer the bustling community hub it used to be.

That's why, when Mark called five months ago to tell me we might need to sell, I'd known what I had to do. I quit my job working for a Maine-based non-profit and came home. True Brew is all we have left of Dad. There's no way I'm going to be the one to put a *For Sale* sign on his dream.

"Got her going, boss," Jarrod says from behind me.

I turn to him; hit with a familiar wave of gratitude that he's still working here. He's only twenty-five, the same age as me. He could have easily moved on to another job when things started going downhill. But he stuck around. I'm sure his familiar face is what's kept our few remaining loyal customers coming back. Although, now that I've convinced

True Brew's long-time specialty coffee supplier, Jose, to renew our supply agreement—a casualty of one of the previous manager's cost-saving measures—I'm hoping I'll be able to draw more customers back in.

I just need to keep the place going until that happens.

I smile up at Jarrod. "Thank god that machine loves you."

"She should." His hazel eyes sparkle. "My relationship with her has lasted longer than any I've had with a real live woman."

With a laugh, I move out of his way so he can take his place at the counter. "That's because your charming smile gets you in trouble," I tease.

He tilts his head, one corner of his mouth ticking up. "You think I'm charming?"

I wave my finger at his face. "That's exactly what I'm talking about. Don't think I haven't seen the girls who come in here batting their lashes at you."

With his dark hair, cheeky grin, and that dimple, I can see the appeal. Even if I don't get butterflies when he turns that smile on me.

I give him a pat of thanks on his arm, then after tightening the elastic tying my long hair back, I turn my attention to clearing the small backlog of coffee orders.

Soon the rush is over—although I'm not sure I should call the slow trickle of people a rush—and our part-time waitress, Sarah, heads home for the day.

I'm making a coffee for Jarrod and myself when the bell over the door jangles and my best friend Anna strolls in. She's fresh from her job as a personal trainer, still in her yoga pants and tank top. I round the counter and give her a hug. "What are you doing here at this time of day?"

"Would you believe my last two clients canceled? I took it as a sign that I should visit my very favorite person."

"Perfect timing, then." I grab her hand and lead her toward a small table at the back. "Jarrod and I were about to have a coffee together."

Anna's dark brows arch up, and an excited smile spreads across her face. "Don't let me interrupt."

I roll my eyes, even as I suppress a smile. "You know it's not like that."

"Hmm, if you say so."

I lower my voice and angle away from where Jarrod's cleaning up. "Just because we work together doesn't mean there's something going on between us. Besides, I'm his *boss*."

"As if that means anything," she scoffs. "Haven't you read a romance novel lately? Besides, I've seen him looking at you. And have you looked at *him*? There's no way he wouldn't be fun in bed. He could be just what you need to get you out of your rut."

Across the room, Jarrod wipes down the counter, the muscles in his forearm flexing in a way that even I can appreciate.

I turn away and nudge her toward a seat. "He looks at everyone that way. Including you. But please don't try to find out for yourself if he's as fun as he looks. The last thing I need is any weird tension between my best friend and my best employee."

Anna sits, crossing her forearms on the worn wooden tabletop. "He's cute, and I'm sure he'd be fun, but he has too much golden retriever energy for me. I'm more of a BDE kind of girl." She gives me a shameless wink.

I can't help but laugh. Big dick energy, indeed. Anna's

taste in men has always trended toward the alpha variety. Guys with a bit of an edge. I'd take a sweet guy over an arrogant lady killer any day. They're all charm and swagger until you fall for them. Then, once they've gotten what they want, and have you tangled up in all kinds of emotions, they let the mask slip, and their true selves appear.

"Anyway," Anna nods toward the counter. "You've been working too hard. Go grab your coffee and come sit with me. Because if Jarrod's off the table, then I have a suggestion."

I shoot her a curious look, but she merely grins and says nothing.

"Do you want a coffee too?" I ask.

"Well, since you're offering, I'd love one of your single origin lattes."

A few minutes later, I'm placing Anna's cup in front of her. She grins down at the latte art cat I decorated her coffee with. It's a technique I've finally mastered after many, *many* failed attempts, which Jarrod used to teasingly call my latte artrocities.

Then I take my own cup and settle into the opposite seat. "Okay, what's this suggestion then?"

She leans forward and regards me seriously. "I want you to hear me out before you say anything."

I give her a small nod. "Of course."

"Do you remember about a year ago I told you about this guy I was seeing? Older, handsome, *wealthy*."

I was still living out of state at the time, but I remember the phone conversation we had about Richard and some of the things he was into. "Oh yes, I *definitely* remember. He left, though, didn't he? Is he back?"

"He's still in California. We agreed on a clean break

when he moved, and we haven't spoken since then. But do you remember me telling you about how he took me to that club?"

Her cheeks turn a little pink. Anna and I have been friends since junior high. Talking about relationships and sex isn't new for us. And she isn't exactly the bashful type, so the blush she's sporting makes me wonder exactly what she and Richie Rich got up to at that club.

"I remember, but you didn't go into detail."

She takes a sip of her coffee, studying me over the rim of her cup. "It's hard to describe. Let's just say it was, uh, liberating."

I raise one brow. "That's all you have to say about it?"

"Well..." She shoots me a sly smile. "I don't want to give too much away, because I think you should experience it yourself."

My stomach swoops, and I bobble my coffee, righting it just before it spills. "You want me to go to a... a *sex* club?" I whisper that last part. "I'm sorry, have you met me? That's a terrible idea."

She pouts, even as her dark eyes sparkle with amusement. "You promised to hear me out."

Pressing my teeth into my lower lip, I nod. I did, though I'm not sure I want to know where she's going with this.

"I know what you're thinking. I thought the same thing when Richard suggested it. But this place isn't seedy at all. It's super exclusive because it caters to a lot of very rich, very famous people. Members are vetted, and masks are required to enter, so everyone is anonymous."

She scrutinizes my expression, then grimaces. Probably because it's obvious she isn't selling me on the idea. "Look. They take security seriously there. Background checks are mandatory, even for guests. The masks are to ensure anonymity, but I promise it's not freaky." She grins a little. "Actually, it's pretty damn sexy. Just think, it's a once-in-a-lifetime opportunity to mingle with the rich and famous while they're getting their sexy on. *And...*" she pauses for effect, "if you decide you want to, it's perfect for some no-strings attached, anonymous, safe, stress relief. Which you, my friend," she points at me dramatically, "desperately need after everything you've gone through the last couple of years."

I try to wrap my mind around what she's suggesting. I know she's not just talking about True Brew, or even my grief over Dad and my guilt for not being here when he died, although I've struggled with both those things. She's also talking about my cheating ex, Eric. Anna's the only person I told about what happened with him, since I didn't want to burden Mark with the fallout from my bad choice in men. Not when I only have myself to blame for being so blind to all Eric's red flags. That means Anna's the only one who knows why I've been so reluctant to open myself up to another relationship.

That doesn't mean I haven't missed a man's touch. I might have my trusty battery-operated boyfriend at home, but there's no replacing that human interaction and skin-on-skin connection. Could this be the answer? One night with no names, no expectations, no numbers exchanged. No hurt feelings because the question doesn't even get asked. And no awkward morning after.

Anna studies me, a crease between her brows. "I don't want to push you or make you uncomfortable. But it would be good for you to let go, even if only for one night. A little distraction from everything you've got going on." She puts her hand over the top of mine on the table and squeezes.

"And there's no pressure at all. You can do as little or as much as you want. The front area is almost like a normal nightclub, so when we get there, we can just drink and dance. It doesn't have to go beyond that. But if you do meet someone you like, then, you know, you can explore that."

My heart rate ratchets up. Could I do it? At the very least, it could be an item I can cross off my bucket list. Not that *go to a sex club* is on there. But who hasn't added a task to a list just so they can have the satisfaction of crossing it off? And the prospect of doing something so out of character, so wild, is oddly appealing. It's been a long time since I've felt carefree or acted in a way that even resembles spontaneous. Maybe it's crazy, but a night of pure escapism actually sounds... good.

Not to mention it would be a big *fuck you* to Eric.

I take a deep breath. "Okay, let's say I'm considering it. Richard invited you, right? How would we get in if he's not around?"

Anna's eyes light up, and she sits a little straighter. "Before he left, he paid for a membership for me. Called it a parting gift. But to be honest, I haven't been interested in going back without him." She brings her coffee to her lips and takes a small sip before continuing. "The membership is due to expire in a couple of weeks. It would be a shame not to use it at least once. Especially since they're not cheap. And because I'm a member, I can bring you as a guest. We'd just have to submit your details for a background check first. Once it's processed, you'll be allowed in with me." She leans forward. "But you don't have to decide now. Think about it and let me know."

I could think about it. *Or* I could put on my big girl panties, give myself permission to have a night off from being Violet, struggling coffee shop owner, and do something bold for the first time in a long time.

I finish my coffee, put the cup down and give Anna a grin—one that probably looks far more confident than I actually feel. "So what should I wear?"

CHAPTER TWO

TATE

The polished wood of the bar gleams under the glitter of chandeliers, and the air is a little too heavy with the mingled scents of cologne and perfume, courtesy of New York City's elite filling the ballroom behind me.

I tap my finger on the rim of my now-empty glass. The bartender gives me a knowing look and reaches for the Macallan 25.

"Are you trying to break a record with this one, Tate?" he jokes. It's a testament to how many of these events I've been to recently that I'm now friends with the bar staff. This is the fourth charity gala I've been to in six weeks.

"Just trying for a personal best." I bring the lowball glass to my lips, inhaling the warm, oaky aroma before swallowing. The whiskey's smoky burn is a welcome respite as it courses down my throat.

I've completed my networking duty as chief of marketing for my family's company, the King Group, and mingled for what feels like several monotonous hours talking up all our latest real estate developments. Now I'm taking a well-earned break at the bar. At least, *I* think I've earned it.

The Blue Planet Benefit is a high-profile event for environmental conservation, meaning the ballroom is full of power players and social climbers, all pretending to care deeply about the cause while eyeing each other's net worth. And since my net worth is one of the largest here, there are a lot of eyes on me.

"How much longer before we can leave?" my older brother Cole asks in a low voice from next to me, echoing my own thoughts.

Blowing out a relieved breath, I turn to him, only to discover he isn't talking to me at all. He's addressing the pretty dark-haired woman he has tucked into his side.

Delilah, his fiancée, looks up at him, her green eyes bright with amusement. "We've only been here for an hour."

Fuck. I could have sworn it was longer than that.

Even with that unpleasant revelation, I have to suppress a grin as Cole dips his head so his mouth is near her ear and grumbles that he'd rather be at home making her scream his name.

"Cole," she hisses, slapping him lightly on his tuxedo-clad chest as a faint blush tints her cheekbones. My gaze lingers on the two of them for a moment. I never thought I'd see my brother in love. Surprisingly enough, it suits him. Since being with Delilah, his smiles are more easily earned and his laughs more frequent. He's constantly touching her, or she's touching him. From subtle caresses to the possessive way his arm circles her waist—Cole seems to soak it all in. As if he can't get enough of it. As if he can't get enough of *her*.

"I need to stay at least another hour," Roman, my eldest

brother, states bluntly, interrupting my thoughts. "And if I need to be here, so do you."

I can't resist poking the bear. "Don't tell me the big bad CEO of the King Group needs his hand held at a party. If that's the case, I'm sure there are any number of women here who would volunteer for the job. Although," I cock my head, "it might not be your hand they want to hold..."

He pins me with his cool gray eyes, and this time I can't hold back my smirk.

"*Hand* holding isn't what I need from you," he says. "What I need is for the King Group leadership to put up a united front. Not my chief of operations running home with his fiancée, and not my chief of marketing disappearing into a dark corner with the nearest bored socialite for the rest of the night."

Schooling my expression to avoid showing the spike of irritation his words cause, I hold his gaze and take another sip of whiskey. I can't argue with his assessment. Until recently, that has been my standard procedure at events such as this. But it's been months since I've pulled that kind of stunt, and he knows it, even if he's not prepared to acknowledge it. "Don't worry. The *bored socialites* of the world are safe from me tonight."

With nothing more than narrowed eyes and a nod, he turns back to the ballroom, where New York's richest and most obnoxious are in full see-and-be-seen mode.

When Delilah pulls away from Cole to stand next to me, I glance at him and grin at the dark expression on his face. Our relationship has improved significantly over the last year and a half, but I'm not sure he'll ever fully forgive me for my brand of "helping" when he was about to screw up the best thing that ever happened to him.

Speaking of, I turn back to Delilah. "Have I told you

already how beautiful you look tonight?" I ignore the growl that comes from my brother.

The corners of her lips tip up. "You did, thank you." She touches my arm. "Cole showed me your marketing ideas for Genesis-1. I love them. You're highlighting all the sustainability features while still showcasing the luxury high-rise lifestyle." It's not empty praise coming from her, since she's one of the architects who've been working on the project—her second for the King Group.

I nod my thanks at her recognition. To be honest, Genesis-1 almost sells itself. State-of-the-art architecture, cutting-edge technology, unparalleled luxury, and a carbon-neutral footprint—it'll be a game-changer in New York's real estate market once it's built. Construction is still months away though. In the meantime, it's my team's job, *my* job, to secure as many pre-sales as possible and to make sure cash-flow stays steady and investor confidence remains high.

As I scan the crowd, a tall, willowy blonde catches my attention. Mainly because she's staring directly at me. Her mouth curves in a slow, seductive smile, and her gaze flashes with an all-too-familiar hunger as she brings her champagne flute to her lips.

She's not the first woman to try to capture my attention tonight. And not long ago, I wouldn't have hesitated to take her up on her unspoken invitation. She has the look of a woman who'd enjoy being fucked up against a wall and given an orgasm or two to get her through the night. But things have changed. The reputation I've gained over the years hasn't necessarily reflected well on the company. And since my brothers and I took over after Dad's arrest eighteen months ago, the last thing I want to do is jeopardize its future. Particularly since my relationship with Cole, and to a lesser extent, Roman, is improving again. At twenty-nine,

I finally want to stand side by side with my brothers and know I contributed as much as they did.

It's why I've been doing my best to prove I'm reformed. Not that anyone would know, judging by the increasingly ridiculous articles that have been printed about me recently. It's as if, in the absence of any real scandalous behavior on my part, the tabloids are determined to make up the craziest stories they can. Like the one from two weeks ago. Someone snapped a photo of me standing next to a recent divorcée and her twenty-year-old daughter, both of them smiling up at me, which apparently meant we were moments from indulging in a threesome. I may have done some crazy things in my life, but tag teaming family members is not one of them.

So I merely give the woman a polite smile and continue taking in the scene of glittering excess in front of me. Unfortunately, the next blonde who comes into view is approaching fast, and suddenly, I wish I'd escaped to a dark corner with the first one when I had the chance.

Mom sweeps to a stop in front of us, gracing us all with an icy smile. She's decked out in a dress as cold a blue as her eyes—and probably her heart.

"Roman, Cole, Tate," she says, acknowledging our presence. "Delilah." She hesitates briefly, then continues. "It's nice to see you again, dear." It's interesting that her future daughter-in-law gets seven more words of greeting than her sons. Not that I blame her. Delilah is probably worth more than all three of us put together. Cole did mention a while ago that he thought not having Dad around might soften her a little. Maybe it has, and I'm just struggling to see it.

I take another sip of whiskey as Mom makes small talk that even she's having trouble feigning interest in. Her focus is on the crowd, ensuring we're seen by her society friends.

In the circles we operate in, appearance is everything. And Mom has always liked the world to think the King family is united, even during the times we've been anything but. It's even more true since she divorced Dad following his conviction for insider trading. Not that I blame her for that. Their marriage was never in more than name anyway. Considering how many affairs Dad had, I'm surprised she waited for his imprisonment before she signed the divorce papers.

Though she's hardly innocent herself. Both my parents screwed other people throughout their marriage. Although, as far as I know, Dad never made the mistake of leaving permanent proof of his indiscretions.

I'm faced with the proof of Mom's every time I look in the mirror. While Cole and Roman both have light eyes like Mom and Dad, mine are a distinctive golden brown. Dad passed his dark hair on to both my brothers, and while I could have gotten my blond hair from Mom, hers is a cool platinum, while mine is a warmer, tawnier shade. Even my skin tone differs, holding a natural tan that lingers, even during winter. Despite what it says on my birth certificate, we all know the truth. Not that we ever openly discuss it.

"I hear your father is giving interviews now." Mom's words interrupt my train of thought.

"Dad likes attention almost as much as you do," I throw out, giving her a too-wide smile when she glares at me. My ability to control my mouth around her seems to decline the older I get.

As always, she doesn't react beyond a sharp look. A reaction would require her to care what I think about her. She merely clears her throat and continues on as if I said nothing at all. "I have no idea what he's hoping to gain, apart from drawing attention back to his misdeeds and dragging the King name through the mud again."

"You know what Dad's like," Cole says. "Watching us taking over the company and elevating it to new heights is probably driving him crazy. He just wants his name in lights again."

I snort. "He's in prison for insider trading, not a string of armed heists. He's not going to have people lining up to listen to him tell sordid tales about his life of crime."

"What's with the attitude tonight?" Roman's voice is steeped in irritation.

I stare down at my glass, swirling the amber liquid around the bottom of it. I'm honestly not sure. Normally, I'm better at putting on an act at these events. Maybe it's because, in my quest to become a responsible, committed member of the King family, it's been months since I've gotten my dick wet.

"Late night last night." I shrug.

Mom sniffs. "I only hope the details won't appear in the tabloids tomorrow."

I paste on a smirk. "Don't worry, Mom. I made sure to screw the photographer who took my photo while I was shooting up in a back alley with those three hookers. I think she'll say nice things about me in the article."

From the flare of her nostrils, I've legitimately horrified her.

I take a moment to relish the satisfaction that brings as I down the last mouthful of my drink. "Excuse me, I see a woman across the room with my name on her."

With a wink at Delilah, I leave them, navigating through a sea of immaculate tuxedos and flowing evening gowns. People approach me as I pass through the crowd, shaking my hand and attempting to curry favor, or in the case of many of the women, flirting and angling to secure a night in my bed. Not that my bed is ever on offer. Give me any other flat surface, though, and I'm good to go. Or I was, anyway. Despite what I said to Mom, there's no woman here that interests me enough to stop my forward progress.

My phone beeps in my pocket, and I pull it out, using it as an excuse to step away from the curvy brunette currently trying to maintain my attention. It's a message from my business partner, Reid.

I hope you're planning to visit soon. We have matters to discuss.

I grin. Every message from Reid comes across sounding a little ominous. Maybe that's because he's a little ominous himself. Or at least that's the impression he likes to give. He's so tight-lipped about his past I wouldn't be surprised if he did have some not-so-squeaky clean connections. But it *has* been a while since I've been to Onyx, the club we co-own. And the idea of talking business over a drink suddenly seems a whole lot more appealing than being here.

I scan the room, taking in all the people focused on me, *wanting* something from me. Fuck it. Roman might have something to say about it if he finds out I left early, but for tonight at least, I'm done caring. Securing his good opinion may be a pipe dream anyway.

Buy me a drink tonight and I'm all yours.

If you're lucky, I'll stretch to two. But you better put out.

With a chuckle, I slide my phone back into my pocket, loosen my tie and head toward the exit.

CHAPTER THREE

VIOLET

I take in my reflection in the mirror as I dab at my red lipstick. When was the last time I got this dressed up? Having to ask myself that question guarantees it's been too long. But it's not going out for the first time in a while that has me jittery tonight; it's *where* I'm going.

From the moment I agreed to go with Anna until now, I've avoided really thinking about the whole concept of visiting a sex club. It was easier just to leave it as an abstract idea. Now that I've been approved as a guest and I'm preparing to step firmly outside my comfort zone, nerves are practically vibrating through me.

Anna, though, is untroubled. She dances over with two glasses of white wine and passes one to me. Her expression is soft when she meets my gaze in the mirror. "You look beautiful."

I smile back. "You do too." Her glossy dark curls and espresso-brown eyes are a vibrant contrast to my wavy brownish-blond hair and blue eyes. My coloring is an echo of my mom's. I don't remember her, since she died when I was a toddler, but the fact that I take after her is obvious based on the family photos Dad used to keep on the wall, as well as the one I have on my nightstand now.

I eye Anna's outfit. She's wearing a plunging red halter top and skin-tight leather pants that highlight all of her curves. I arch a brow at the pants. "I don't know much about sex clubs, but I assumed the easier the access, the better."

She laughs. "True. But I'm not planning on giving anyone access tonight."

I swing around to face her. "I thought you were going to be, you know, doing stuff. It's your last chance, right?"

She shrugs. "Tonight's about you. I don't intend to do more than drink, flirt and dance."

"And people really do that there? Just that?"

"Of course. It's still a place to connect with people and have fun. But that fun can progress to the X-rated variety if you want. You know, for that stress relief." She gives me a grin.

I wrap my arms around her, breathing in the light floral perfume she always likes to wear. "Thank you for being such a good friend." My vision goes blurry as she squeezes me tightly. I might be a little emotional, but it's moments like these that make me beyond grateful that Anna chose to sit next to me on our first day of junior high.

"You'd do the same for me," she says, stepping back and holding me at arm's length. "I want you to feel good about yourself again. That cheating asshole had no right making you feel like less than the amazing woman you are. I wasn't there to stand by you then, so the least I can do is help you shove him firmly in your rearview mirror now. And what better way to do that than by getting your freak on with a hot, rich man you never have to see again?" She releases me, then slaps me on my ass, making me yelp. "Now come on.

Let's finish these drinks and get going. Once you're there, you'll feel a lot more relaxed."

"Okay." I tip my wineglass back and take a big gulp. A little extra courage never hurt anyone, right? With one last run through of my hair with my fingers, I turn and face the bed where my mask awaits. Anna ordered it for me. According to her, the masks they wear at this club aren't the frilly, lacy kind that barely conceal anything.

The one she chose for me matches the small butterfly tattoo on my back—the result of a spur-of-the-moment decision after I broke up with Eric and realized how free I suddenly felt. Cliché, I know, but I love it anyway. The mask itself is expertly shaped from a thin layer of supple leather and is painted in vibrant shades of blue and purple and black. When it's on, it covers my face from the bottom of my cheeks to the top of my forehead, the edges sweeping up from the eyeline to emulate wings. Each one is scattered with tiny jewel-colored crystals that catch the light and shimmer iridescently. The only parts of my face that will be visible once I put it on will be my jaw, my mouth, and my eyes.

Anna gently takes the mask from my hands. "I'll put it on for you. We need to be wearing them when we arrive."

Another wave of nerves cascades over me. I wet my suddenly dry lips, then give her a nod and turn so she can tie the silk ribbons. Then I do the same for her mask, which is designed to resemble peacock feathers. The leather is dyed in a beautiful gradient of blues, greens and golds. Like mine, it's adorned with crystals for added sparkle.

When I'm done, we stand side by side in front of the mirror.

"Wow," I breathe. The result is breathtaking—and strangely intoxicating. The anonymity provided by the masks eases some of the tension that has been plaguing me for the last few days. I can be anyone I want with this on. And as I study my reflection, I think I might just be a woman who's finally ready to breathe life back into the banked sparks of her desire.

THE UBER PULLS UP outside a discreet entrance nestled between two unassuming buildings in a quieter part of Manhattan. There's no indication of the club's presence other than a man in a tailored black suit standing outside a plain black door. Rather than the stereotypical big, burly bouncer, this guy is compact and neatly put together. The intensity with which he scrutinizes Anna and me as we approach, though, makes it clear that he knows how to take care of trouble.

Anna hands him a matte black card, which he scans with a small device he pulls out of his pocket. When he holds it out to her, she presses her thumb against it. I raise my brows, baffled at this whole secrecy thing. Not to mention the idea that my friend is a part of it.

The machine beeps, and he hands her card back. He stares down at the screen, then up at me, probably confirming my identity against the photo identification I had to provide with my details.

With a small nod, he pockets the device again. "Enjoy Onyx, ladies."

The door clicks open, and I follow Anna inside. The scene I'm confronted with isn't at all what I expected. Not that I know what a high-end sex club looks like. But the long, dark, quiet corridor we've stepped into throws me. A beautiful red-haired woman stands at the far end, wearing a serene smile.

"Good evening, ladies," she says as Anna leads me toward her. "If you would like to leave your purses here, you can go right in."

"Don't we need those to pay for drinks?" I whisper in Anna's ear.

"No." She gives me a slight shake of her head. "It's a tab system. Before we leave, we'll pay for anything we've purchased."

Once our purses are secured behind a locked panel with a keypad, the woman hands us each a black bracelet with a silver four-digit number on it.

I slip mine on with a frown, darting a glance at Anna, then at the woman.

Obviously sensing my confusion, she addresses me. "If you'd like to order drinks, or certain *activities*, just scan your bracelet. It's been coded with your details, and anything you purchase will be charged to your account. It saves you from having to worry about your belongings if you choose to indulge while you're inside. Also, please be aware, there's a limit of three alcoholic drinks per person during your time here at Onyx, to ensure your ability to consent is fully maintained."

"Oh yes, of course." I plaster a bright smile on my face to hide how out of my depth I feel.

She returns the expression with a reassuring smile of her own, as if she can see right through the pretense. "The first time is always a little intimidating. But give it a chance, and I think you'll enjoy your evening. How it unfolds is completely up to you. Please remember that."

Swallowing past my increasingly dry throat, I nod. "Thank you."

With that, she presses a button, and a door unlocks. Anna leads me through, and a moment later, we're stepping into the club itself. I stop just past the entrance and scan the space. At first glance, it appears like any super-exclusive nightclub. Or what I imagine a super-exclusive nightclub might look like, anyway, since I haven't been to any. Apart from the strobe lights over the packed dance floor, the lighting is dim. A long, curved bar extends down one side of the room, and in the far shadowy corners are a number of booths and alcoves with seating.

But with a longer look, I take in all the details that distinguish this club from others. The most obvious being that everyone is wearing a mask, even the bartenders—although while most of the guests have donned detailed, elaborate face coverings, theirs are plain black. The anonymity lends an edge to the scene that, like Anna said, makes the atmosphere more mysterious and just that bit sexier. The music isn't a recent hit, as far as I can tell, but it has a low, seductive beat that pulses behind my sternum. The rhythm pulls my attention back to the dance floor. As I examine the crowd, I realize it isn't only singles and couples dancing, but groups of three, four or even more people of all sexes rubbing up against each other.

Biting my lip, I continue my perusal. It's then that I notice what's going on in the seating area. In one of the booths, a man has pulled down the top of a woman's dress, and he's bending over her so he can... Oh, wow.

With a wave of heat washing over me, I glance away, only to find myself focused on a couch where another woman is straddling a man's lap. She's wearing a dress, but his hands are kneading her ass. I can't tell whether he's moving her or she's moving on her own, but with the way her head is thrown back, there's definitely more than making out going on over there.

I swallow hard and turn to Anna.

Her smile is amused. "I'm pretty sure I had that same expression on my face when Rich brought me here."

"Uh, yes. It's a lot to get used to." I let out a nervous laugh as I fan myself. "Although, I actually expected it to be more..." I hesitate, my mind a little too jumbled to find the word I'm looking for.

She arches a brow. "Debauched?"

"I guess. Not in a bad way," I hurry to clarify. "Like... I don't know, people getting tied up and whipped, or something like that."

She grins and points to a spot behind me. "See that doorway over there?"

On the other side of the room, there's an opening in the black-painted wall, and through it, the start of another darkened corridor. "Yes."

"That leads to the back area. Lots of smaller spaces for different *activities*." She uses the same word as the woman out the front. "There are private rooms as well, with all kinds of equipment. That's where most of the stuff you're thinking about happens."

"Oh." My shoulders ease a fraction. I wasn't sure what to expect, but the possibility of walking into the middle of an orgy has crossed my mind a time or two. Apart from the action happening in some of the darker corners, though, it's easy to pretend this is just a normal club.

"Do you want a drink?" Anna asks.

With a deep breath in, I give her an enthusiastic nod. "God, yes."

We move to the bar, which, fittingly, appears to be made

from backlit onyx. The slight concave curve to it means everyone standing at the bar can see and be seen. A bartender soon approaches, and after he scans our bracelets, we order—a Manhattan for Anna, and a Cosmopolitan for me. As soon as the drink is in my hand, I take a long sip to calm my remaining nerves. Then I turn so I can take in more of my surroundings. The whole place drips with decadence. The dim lights reflect off the black glass panels lining the wall behind the bar, the liquor bottles arrayed on the attached shelves and the crystal chandeliers hanging from the ceiling.

The masks worn by the other guests are similar to mine and Anna's, though in an assortment of designs. There are animal masks, demon masks, cute masks, beautiful masks, masks meant to scare or intimidate. The women are dressed in varying degrees, from near-nakedness to skin-tight bodysuits. I thought I was daring when I put on my sexiest outfit for the occasion—a little black dress with a low neckline, an even lower back, and a skirt that flares out at my hips and flirts with my upper thighs. But Anna and I are among the more conservatively dressed women here.

In contrast, many of the men are wearing suits, which throws me a little. I assumed there'd be more skin on display. But maybe that's the point. Maybe for many people, it's the power imbalance, or at least the illusion of it, that turns them on.

"See anyone you like?" Anna asks.

I blink, then focus back on her. "I'm not really sure what I'm looking for. Or what I want. Or even *if* I want."

"That's okay, there's no rush. Let's finish our drinks and then go and dance. And Violet..." She touches my hand, what I can see of her expression earnest. "Remember what I said. There's no pressure. If all we do is dance the night away, then that's okay. Right?"

It's been too long since I've given myself a night to forget all my cares and just dance and have fun. She's right. I take a deep breath and will the last of my jitters to disappear. Finally, the tension fully leaves my body, and I smile at her. "Right."

CHAPTER FOUR

TATE

I lean against Onyx's bar as Reid orders two whiskeys from one of the masked bartenders. After talking business upstairs, he invited me to join him down here for a drink. On our way out of his office, I snagged a mask from the collection he keeps on hand. It's made of leather dyed a red so dark it's almost black and has devil horns that curl up over my forehead. I'm sure Mom would find it a fitting choice for me.

Once we have our glasses in hand, we stand with our backs to the bar and survey the club. Onyx was Reid's dream, but he didn't have the capital to get it up and running on his own. At the time he approached me, he was merely an acquaintance of an acquaintance. But over drinks, he sold me on the idea of this place—a club that would fulfill all the desires of New York's richest and most powerful while allowing them to stay out of the spotlight.

A mass of bodies writhes on the dance floor before us, caught up in the thrill of anonymous hedonism. It's something I'm familiar with. As one of the richest men in the country, it's a feeling I've craved many times. The freedom that anonymity gives you can be intoxicating. I'm used to being the focus of most rooms I occupy. It can be a heady sensation, but sometimes, being the center of all that attention leaves me feeling more alone than anything else. At least here, when I catch the attention of others—and I do—it's only because of the way I carry myself. It's curiosity about what pleasure might be found under my hands, not interest in my money or power.

Reid takes a sip of his whiskey. "Are you sure you'll only stay for one drink?" he asks. "I know you said you were toning things down, but that doesn't mean you have to be celibate."

He's right. There's no reason I shouldn't indulge. This is the one place I can guarantee that what I do won't end up splashed all over the tabloids. Except when I look around at all the women filling this place, most of whom would be ready and willing to do anything I ask of them, the anticipation that used to hit me like a shot of adrenaline isn't there. After restraining myself for so long, I should be dying to let loose. And yet, the interactions I used to seek out, emotionless fucking, mindless pleasure seeking, leave me empty these days. I shake my head. "Just this one, and I'll head home."

As we sip our drinks, we talk more about the potential for Onyx's expansion, adding a few other cities to the list of possible future locations, and Reid asks about Genesis-1. He's one of our first buy-ins, so he has an interest in the project's development. I've almost finished my whiskey when my attention is caught by a woman stepping through the club's entrance.

She's with a friend, but I barely notice the other woman. I'm too absorbed by the one in the short black dress and butterfly mask. She's frozen just inside the doorway, her head turning one way, then the other, like she might bolt back outside at any moment. It's glaringly obvious it's her first time here. But when her friend leans in and speaks to her, she smiles and appears to relax.

She follows her friend to the bar, the hem of her dress brushing the tops of her toned thighs with every step, and for some reason, I can't tear my eyes away.

They settle a little way down from where Reid and I are and order drinks. Then her dark-haired friend in the peacock mask leans in with a grin, and butterfly tilts her head back, her fingertips lightly brushing her chest as she laughs.

Something niggles at the back of my mind, as if the movement is almost familiar. I study her, taking her in from head to toe, getting momentarily distracted by the dip of her waist and the curve of her hips. But apart from that one gesture, nothing else triggers a sense of familiarity.

Not from this distance, at least.

Reid lets out a low chuckle. "So *not* one drink and then you're leaving?"

I drag my attention away from the woman, who's now sipping a cocktail as she looks out at the dance floor. "I'm leaving. Just admiring the view while I finish my drink."

"Just so you know, you're not the only one enjoying that view." He gestures with his almost-empty glass toward two men farther down the bar, their heads turned toward the women as well.

It shouldn't matter whether another man is considering making a move. I'm not staying, after all. And possessiveness over a woman—any woman, let alone one I haven't even spoken to or touched—is a foreign concept to me. There are more than enough fish in my sea that I don't have to worry about getting caught up with just one of them.

But when the men leave their position and park themselves next to the pair, a strange tension grips me. The woman in the butterfly mask stiffens as the taller one rests his forearm on the bar behind her.

Normally, I wouldn't intervene, but considering how nervous she was when she arrived, I don't like that he might be making her feel more uncomfortable.

I down the last of my drink and set it a little too hard on the bar. When I turn to Reid, his dark eyes behind his mask are full of amusement.

"You heading off now, then?" he asks, one side of his mouth tipping up in a smirk.

"Something like that." I don't bother to say goodbye as I stride away. He knows exactly where I'm going, as evidenced by the laugh that follows me as I move toward the woman and her friend. I couldn't explain my motives if I tried. I'm just going with my instinct.

And right now, my instinct is telling me that tonight, the woman in the butterfly mask is all mine.

CHAPTER FIVE

VIOLET

I angle away from the man in the Phantom of the Opera mask who has his arm on the bar behind me. He's standing so close the fabric of his shirt brushes my bare shoulder blade. I'm trying not to make a big deal about it because he hasn't actually done anything wrong other than stand too close. And regardless of how normal this place appears, it's still a sex club. Getting physical quickly is probably normal here. It's just not normal for me.

"First time?" He slides another inch closer, clearly not reading my body language.

I give him a small, polite smile in return. "That obvious?"

He laughs. "Fresh meat is easy to spot."

I recoil in response to his words and this time he notices.

"Sorry, bad joke. I just meant you have this whole baby deer thing going on. If you let me buy you a drink, I can help you get past that." He tips his head down and runs his tongue over his lower lip as he rakes his gaze over my body.

This time, it's a shudder that works its way through me. Being more forward here might be a thing, but there has to be a better way to do it than this. His demeanor isn't intense or aggressive, but whoever he is—and assuming he's a member here, there's a good chance he's *someone*—he has all the charm and tact of a gorilla.

Anna intervenes, putting a hand on my forearm. "Actually, we're just going to have a couple of drinks and a dance, relax and have some fun out there. You know?"

Phantom's friend lifts his chin, clearly getting the hint. "Come on, man. Let's head to the back and catch some action. There's supposed to be a shibari demonstration happening in one of the rooms."

I have no idea what a shibari is, but I'm grateful that they're going. I don't want to be rude, though, so I smile at Phantom. "Thanks though. Enjoy the…" I've forgotten what the other guy called it. "Demonstration," I finish, a little lamely.

Instead of moving away, he edges closer, making my hackles rise. "You could come with us. Shibari is—"

He doesn't get to finish what he's saying, because a man wearing a devil mask comes out of nowhere. He stops next to Phantom, practically looming over him, since he's several inches taller.

"I think the ladies have made themselves clear." His voice is low, but it's laced with steel.

My gaze darts back and forth between him and the men we've been trying to let down easy.

Phantom frowns. "I was just trying to be friendly."

"Then you should probably practice being friendly in the mirror, because what you're doing isn't it. Take the very polite hint you've been given and walk away."

Phantom looks at his buddy, then shakes his head. "No problem. We're leaving."

And without another word, they're gone. Now it's just

Anna and me and the man in the devil mask. He's tall, like I already noticed, and well built. The way his impeccably tailored white dress shirt hugs his broad shoulders and chest leaves no doubt as to the presence of muscles beneath. He's not wearing a tie, and his top button is undone, revealing a small V of smooth tanned skin.

Out of nowhere, an image of pressing my lips against it flashes through my mind, and heat instantly smolders to life inside me.

Shaking away the thought, I drag my attention back to his face. Or, at least what I can see of it. A strong, smooth-shaven jaw and full lips with a seductive curve. In the dim light, the hair curling around his ears looks dark blond, and his eyes, shadowed by the mask, appear to be a light brown. It's hard to tell. Regardless of their color, the amused gleam in them is unmistakable.

The amusement is no doubt due to him having just caught me blatantly checking him out. I flush and avert my gaze.

"Thanks for that," Anna says.

I take in a steadying breath and focus on her to distract myself from the man standing in front of us and the way my pulse has started to race.

She widens her eyes at me, silently urging me to talk to him. I guess she thinks this guy is a better option than the two he just scared off. Although a part of me wonders if he might not be more dangerous.

Still, being polite doesn't have to lead to anything more.

Unless I want it to.

I clear my throat, racking my brain for something to say. "Do you come here often?" I wince as soon as I say it. Could I have asked a more cliché question? Plus, I'm not sure I want to know his sex club attendance habits. I put up my hand. "Sorry, don't answer that."

His laugh is low, seductive. How is it even possible for a laugh to be seductive? "Let's just say I'm not exactly fresh meat."

I wrinkle my nose under my mask. "You heard that?"

"Unfortunately, Onyx can guarantee your physical safety while you're here, but it can't completely protect you from the idiots of the world."

"We were just about to have another drink," Anna jumps in. "Would you like to join us?"

Ugh, she's much better at this than me. I'm completely out of practice with flirting. The man in the devil mask diverts his intense focus from me to her, and I'm instantly hit by an unfamiliar pang of jealousy. Which is ridiculous. I don't know this guy, and he'd be beyond lucky to spend time with my best friend.

"Only if you'll let me buy," he says.

The smile Anna flashes has that little niggling worm of jealousy burrowing deeper. I turn toward the bar and force the emotion down. She's not trying to claim his attention. She's just being her friendly self. But she's so pretty. What man wouldn't be won over by her smile? There are plenty of other men here though. If I want to flirt—or do more—I'm sure I can find someone.

I'm pulled from that thought when a hand brushes my lower back, and then he's standing next to me. He bends his head and speaks into my ear, his warm breath on my neck making goose bumps erupt all over my body. "What can I get you?"

Can he tell how my body is reacting to his proximity? Somehow the thought that he can leaves me feeling strangely exposed. "I'd like a Cosmopolitan, thank you."

With a nod, he turns to the bartender that's materialized in front of us.

Anna presses close on my other side. "Oh my god," she whispers. "This guy is so hot. You have to go for it. If you don't at least kiss him, I'm going to cry."

"If you like him, you could—"

The sharp shake of her head stops me in my tracks. "Even if I wanted to, it wouldn't matter. The guy's been laser focused on you from the moment he walked up."

My stomach twists into a knot. A man like this, a member of this club, probably expects a woman who's happy to throw caution to the wind and get down and dirty in one of the back rooms. And as hot as this guy is, I'm not sure I'm up for that.

When a large hand appears in front of me holding my Cosmo, I take it and smile my thanks at him. He passes a Manhattan down the bar to Anna, then picks up his own glass of what looks like expensive whiskey.

While he takes a sip and studies me over the rim, I frantically search my mind for an interesting topic to discuss. Being anonymous makes it way more difficult to have a conversation. No asking names, no talking about what we do for work. What the hell *do* we talk about?

He doesn't seem to have the same concern, leaning his elbow on the bar and looking down at me with a hint of a smile on his face. "What brought you here tonight? If it's your first time, then something must have prompted you to come."

"Um, well, Ann—uh, my friend's membership is about to expire, and she asked if I wanted to come with her for her last visit."

His smile grows slowly. "So you're just doing your friend a favor?"

"No. I mean, that's not the whole reason."

"What are your other reasons, then? Because you don't strike me as the type of woman who spontaneously decides to visit a club like Onyx just because a friend needs company."

My shoulders stiffen. What type of woman does he think I am? A stick-in-the-mud who spends all her time working at a coffee shop and worrying about malfunctioning espresso machines? Of course, that's accurate, but that's not who I want to be tonight. I raise my chin and stare him straight in the eye. "I'm crossing it off my bucket list."

The mask hides most of his expression, but the way he rolls his lips together makes me think I've amused him. "What exactly was on your list? Just a visit? Or to actually partake?" His mouth twitches, his amusement clearer now.

Irritated by his reaction, I'm forced to respond. "I was going to see how I felt when I got here. Check out some of the, uh..." My mind spins until I remember what Phantom and his friend mentioned. "The demonstrations." I shrug, going for casual. "See if something takes my fancy."

A muffled noise comes from beside me. I've been so absorbed in this guy I almost forgot the two of us weren't alone. But when I turn to Anna, she doesn't seem annoyed at all. In fact, from the cheesy grin she's wearing and the way her eyes bounce from me to the man at my side and back again, it looks like she wishes she had a bowl of popcorn. I wrinkle my nose at her, and although I doubt she can see it under my mask, she gives me a wink in return.

"Really?" the man says. The disbelief in his tone makes it clear he knows I'm talking shit. "You were interested in seeing the shibari demonstration, then? What about it appeals to you?"

I should admit that I have no clue what shibari is, and

that I'm not planning to leave the relatively safe space of this open area, but his cocky attitude is needling me. I'm not normally easily riled up, but this man who doesn't even know me has figured out how to press buttons that haven't been pressed in years. I can't help but rise to the challenge. So I force my shoulders to relax and smile. "No, shibari doesn't interest me. I want to see what else might be available here."

His hand, which has been resting casually on the bar next to my shoulder, moves, his forefinger brushing featherlight against my skin, making my breath hitch. "You're not into rope play?"

Rope play? That's what shibari is? Rope play as in being tied down or something else? I may have had a fantasy or two in my life about being tied down and taken. But then, who hasn't? I shake my head, deciding not to display my ignorance by probing for more information. "Rope play's a little tame for my tastes."

This time, Anna chokes, and the two of us turn to her. She bangs her fist on her chest. "Sorry, swallowed my drink the wrong way."

I glare at her, but she just grins at me.

"So, something a little wilder than shibari," the man muses, rubbing his jaw. "Let me guess, then, and you can tell me if I'm right or wrong. Okay?"

I swallow back the nerves rising inside me and nod. I'm pretty sure I'm getting in way over my head with this conversation, but I won't back down now.

He grins, his white teeth flashing in the dim light. Paired with the mask, it gives him an almost predatory appearance. Angling closer, he brings his lips to my ear. "How about spanking? Does that interest you? Do you want to be bent over while your ass is reddened?" When he pulls back, there's a devilish glint in his eyes.

My cheeks flame, but I'm counting on the mask and the dark to hide my reaction from him. I shake my head. "I'm not a child. I don't need to be disciplined."

Now it's his thumb tracing small, hypnotic circles over my upper arm. The contact is making my head hazier than it has any right to. "You're definitely not a child, and spanking is about far more than discipline," he says. "But moving on. What about voyeurism? Are you here to see someone get fucked? Do you want to stand in the audience and watch a woman with her legs spread and pussy on display, made to come for your entertainment?"

My breaths are uneven, and I have to resist the urge to squirm at his words. None of my boyfriends have ever spoken to me like this, let alone a stranger. But I refuse to give him the satisfaction of knowing he's affecting me. "I'd rather do, not watch," I say, keeping my tone as flippant as I can manage.

"Really?" he almost purrs. "You're an exhibitionist, then? You want to be watched as you're made to orgasm over and over?"

There's a throb between my legs that I'm doing my best to ignore, even as it grows more insistent. I can only shake my head.

"No? Well, it's not for everyone." He rubs his finger over his full bottom lip and tilts his head as if he's thinking. "How about breath play?"

What the hell is breath play?

All I can do is blink at him in response.

One corner of his mouth kicks up. "Do you like the idea of giving control of your breath to another person while being fucked? Allowing them to cut off your oxygen until you're dizzy with pleasure and need? Is that what you're looking for here, butterfly?"

My throat goes dry. I'm going to have to tap out. I don't know what I was thinking taking part in this game. And a game is exactly what it is. He knows I have no idea what I'm talking about, and he's laughing at me.

I release a ragged breath. "Fine," I concede. "I don't plan to partake in anything like that. I just wanted a break from real life for a night. I wanted to get away from myself, and this seemed like a good way to do it. But I doubt I'd be comfortable with the stuff that goes on back there. I have no clue what shibari is, or breath play. And I'm probably incredibly naïve compared to you and everyone else here. Happy?" I cross my arms, annoyed that I was so easily caught out *and* by my slightly pouty reaction to that fact. What is it about this guy that makes my temper flare at the same time as my libido?

His eyes are still intent on mine, and a spark of excitement ignites in my belly.

Anna is the one to break the simmering tension. "You know, I think I might go and dance."

A confusing mix of relief and disappointment swirls inside me as I turn to her, ready to join her on the dance floor. But she stops me with a hand around my wrist.

"On my *own*."

When I open my mouth to protest, a big shit-eating smile grows on her face.

"Don't forget about stress relief, babe. That's the other reason you came, right?" She gives me a quick hug, lowering her voice so only I can hear her. "Ditch him and come get me if he's an asshole, okay? Otherwise, have some fun.

Remember, it's just one night." Then she winks as she spins away from me. "I'm going to find someone to shake my ass with."

I watch her go, then, almost reluctantly, turn back to the man in the mask. Not because I wish I'd gone with Anna, but because my pulse is hammering in my throat, and there's still that unfamiliar hum in my veins. Although this interaction has me on edge, I actually feel alive for the first time in a long while. And there's a part of me that really wants to find out how far this could go, be it another drink, a kiss, or something... more.

He's still watching me. When I wet my lips, his focus dips, and he tracks the movement.

"Stress relief?" he asks, his voice softer. "Are you stressed, butterfly?"

I let out a little laugh, not sure how convincing it is. "The last few months have been a little rough, that's all." Longer than that, but I doubt he's interested in the details.

"So that's why you're here? To relieve some of that stress?"

I roll my lips together and consider how to answer that question. "I told you. I came because my friend's membership is running out, and because I needed a break, to have fun for a night." Then I let out a breath and focus on that little triangle of skin at the base of his throat rather than his eyes when I concede. "And yes, to relieve some stress, if that's what ends up happening."

The corners of his mouth curl up, drawing my attention back to his face. "I've been told relieving stress is one of my greatest skills."

An excited little shiver darts up my spine. "Is that so?"

He dips his chin, his mouth still curved up. A mouth

that I'm suddenly staring at, wondering how it would feel on mine. Oh god, am I crazy for considering doing this? Is he even offering what I think he is, or am I getting ahead of myself? I don't know how to ask or how to proceed from here.

I raise my glass, desperate to ease my suddenly dry throat, only to discover it's nearly empty. I drain it a little too eagerly, then lick the remnants of the sweetly tart liquid from my lips.

Even in the low light, the way his gaze heats is visible. He takes the empty glass from me and places it on the bar. Then he gently slips his big hand under my chin and tilts my face up. He studies what he can see of it, his thumb drifting along my jaw. Tingles follow in its wake. "Come and sit with me," he says.

My stomach falls. This time it's definitely disappointment I'm feeling. "You want to sit down?"

The grin he gives me this time is almost wicked. "I want to get to know you better."

"Isn't the whole point of this place not to know each other?"

"I don't need to know your name or where you work. I don't even need to know how old you are since you wouldn't be here if you were underage. What I need to know is how I can help you relax, what will make those gorgeous lips part for me, what will make your pulse flutter at the base of your throat, and," he leans forward until his mouth hovers just over mine, "what's going to make that pretty pussy of yours wet."

My breath stalls, even as his words send desire flooding through me. God, I don't know how this happened so quickly. But I can't deny that his confidence is incredibly appealing. And I'm intrigued by what he's offering. It's been a long time since I've been touched with any kind of intimacy.

"Okay," I say before I can second guess myself.

"Okay?"

I let out a breath. "Okay, let's sit."

CHAPTER SIX

VIOLET

I expect him to smile in satisfaction, but he doesn't. Instead, his big body almost seems to draw tight. Then he's stepping into me and sliding his hand around to circle the back of my neck. The possessive hold has me sucking in a breath as my nipples tighten and rasp against the thin material of my dress.

He notices my reaction, of course he does, and that's when he finally smiles—although it's more of a primal baring of teeth than anything else. It sends a pulse of need through me.

"Come on, beautiful." He glides his hand down my spine and settles it at my lower back, then guides me through the club to a couch in one of the darkest corners. He keeps me in front of him, so I'll be closest to the wall once we sit. But before I can, he gently grasps my wrist to stop me and brushes the hair hanging loose down my spine to the side. When I glance over my shoulder, I find him focused on my back. With the ghost of a smile, he lightly traces my butterfly tattoo with his finger, causing every one of my nerve endings to crackle into life.

Then, without commenting, he lets me go. My shaky legs carry me the remaining step, and I manage to get my butt on the seat without them giving out on me. He sits next to me, his knee close to mine.

Here in this dim corner, just the two of us, there's nothing to distract me from him—from the angle of his jaw, the seductive curve of his lips. Even his scent invades my senses. He smells too good. Fresh, like I imagine a forest at night might smell. It fills my head, triggering a wild impulse inside me, and I'm suddenly tempted to crawl into his lap, just so I can experience his mouth against mine.

Maybe it's because of the mask, the anonymity it provides. Or maybe it's the darkness and the low pulsing beat of the music. Whatever the reason, I've never been so aroused with so little physical contact before. There's no doubt in my mind that this man, whoever he is, knows exactly how to make a woman feel good. He exudes confidence. It's in every line of his body, the way he talks, the way he moves.

And I'm woefully unprepared for dealing with him.

He leans back and stretches his arm out along the back of the seat so it's brushing my shoulders. "Why have the last few months been so difficult?"

I frown, a hint of the worry I can never quite seem to shake these days settling in my chest. "You really want to know?"

His mouth quirks up. "That's generally why I ask questions."

I pull my bottom lip between my teeth as I consider the best way to summarize the events of the last several months. "Work has been... difficult." I offer him a faint smile. "And before that, there was a bad breakup." I don't mention Dad's death. It seems wrong to talk about that, considering where I am.

He pushes my hair behind my shoulder, his fingers brushing against my neck. "I'm sorry to hear that. Can you quit your job? Find a better one?"

"I co-own a business, so no, quitting isn't an option."

He nods, his fingertips now running softly along my skin, back and forth, back and forth, making it hard for me to think. "And the breakup?"

I swallow past the residual anxiety that always hits when I think about Eric, then shrug as casually as I can. "Let's just say he wasn't who I thought he was."

His eyes are dark as he watches me, and I'm hit by a sudden surge of déjà vu, like someone's looked at me that way before. I blink, and the feeling dissipates. "Did he break your heart?" he asks, his voice low.

That question is the last I was expecting him to ask. I was under the impression that this conversation was leading to something physical, and now he's asking me whether Eric broke my heart?

Despite my confusion, I answer him. "I don't think I loved him, so I can't say he broke my heart in that way. But he hurt me, made me feel bad about myself. When I discovered he was cheating, it was an... awakening more than anything." But I don't want to think about just how badly Eric had fooled me. I don't want to think about Eric at all. So I take a deep breath, square my shoulders and look him straight in the eye. "I'm not here trying to get over a broken heart, if that's why you're asking. I already told you, there are lots of reasons I'm here, but that isn't one of them."

There's a long beat of silence as we study one another. Even the hypnotic pulse of the music seems to fade into the background. A muscle ticks in his jaw, and I shift on the couch, nerves fluttering in my stomach under the intensity of his scrutiny. Maybe he wasn't expecting such a thorough answer. In hindsight, I should have just said no and left it at that. I glance toward the dance floor. Should I call my first foray into breaking out of my comfort zone a bust and go hide in the crowd with Anna?

I'm surprised when he threads his fingers through my hair, bringing my attention firmly back to him.

The smile that curves his lips is as devilish as his mask. "That's good. Because if I'm going to relieve some of your stress tonight, I don't want your mind on somebody else."

My mouth is suddenly dry again. This man has me completely off-kilter, and it's kind of exhilarating. I may be filled with nerves, but I can't ignore the desire and anticipation building inside me.

I wet my lips, and his fingers tighten in my hair in response. "Are we going out there?" I whisper, glancing at the double doors and the shadowy corridor beyond.

He tilts his head to one side, and I do my best to breathe through the apprehension that's welling up inside me at the idea of taking part in some rope play or spanking, at the possibility that he might want something else entirely. Something even more intimidating.

"I don't think you're ready for that," he says.

Some of the tension leaves my muscles. "Then what?"

"I'm going to take care of you right here."

My pulse jolts, and I scan the darkened club. "Here?"

He tugs lightly on my hair, bringing my attention back to him. "If anyone looks, it's because they like what they see. But I'll make sure they don't see much. I promise."

My heart is trying to beat its way out of my chest. Flashes of the scenes I witnessed when Anna and I arrived hit me. While it was obvious what those couples were doing, I didn't really see all that much. And the people involved were unrecognizable anyway. Just like I'm unrecognizable right now. And tucked away in a corner like this, well...

My mind works overtime, uncertainty warring with arousal.

He watches me for a moment, then leans in close. "I'll take care of you tonight, butterfly. You just need to tell me yes or no."

CHAPTER SEVEN

TATE

The uncertainty in her pretty blue eyes morphs into desire. She's nervous. That's understandable. This is obviously not her scene. But she came here tonight for a reason, and from the moment she walked in, I wanted to be the one to give her what she needs. I haven't felt this much desire for a woman in a long time, and I can't even put my finger on the reason. From the little I can see of her face, she's pretty, probably even beautiful, and her body in that little dress is mouthwatering. But that's not what it is. I've been with plenty of gorgeous women who haven't caught my interest the way she has.

Most of the women I fuck know exactly what I'm capable of giving them and aren't afraid to ask me for it. It's always made things easy. I give them what they want and take what I want, then we both walk away satisfied. No seeking a connection, no looking back. That's how it's always been. That's how I've always *needed* it to be. But the easy gratification I used to seek has lost its appeal.

Maybe that's why she's having such an effect on me. Because this isn't about my gratification. This is all about her. About the stubborn tilt to her chin, and the fire that flashed in her eyes when she tried to convince me she knew what she wanted, about the way she almost forgets to breathe when I touch her, and the trust she's giving me, just by sitting next to me here.

That might be what I'm craving most of all—her trust. She's allowing herself to be vulnerable with me. Truly vulnerable. It's a rare thing in the world I live in, where every person I encounter is vying for power, even when it comes to sex. Trust may be an essential part of what goes on in this club, but even that is given within boundaries, tailored by rules put in place to make sure it's not abused. The people who come here to let go of their inhibitions know what they're signing up for when they walk through the door. But this woman? She doesn't know what she wants or what she needs. So she has no idea what rules and boundaries to set. I want to be the one she takes that leap of faith with. The one she trusts with her body and her pleasure. I want her to trust that I'll push her to the edge of her comfort zone, but not past it.

Not this time anyway.

I shake that odd thought away. Because there will only be this one time. I'll keep her safe and give her what she needs, then send her on her way. That will be it. No looking back for either of us.

"Yes or no, butterfly?" I prompt her again, itching to touch her. But I won't until she decides.

Her throat bobs in a swallow, and then she tips that stubborn little chin up. "Yes."

Those pretty lips of hers have barely stopped moving before I'm sliding my hand around to the back of her neck and my mouth is on hers. She tilts her head and, with only the slightest hesitation, opens for me. I groan at the taste of her—sweet and tart, like the cocktail she was drinking. My teeth tug on her lower lip and my tongue thrusts deep, possessing, taking, *claiming* her—even if it's only for tonight. And then I'm dragging my lips along her jaw until I reach the sensitive patch of skin beneath her ear. She smells like fucking peaches and cream. "How long since you've been touched?" I ask.

"Too long," she breathes.

I scrape my teeth over her sensitive flesh. "*How* long, beautiful? I want to know how gentle you need me to be."

She shudders and presses her soft breasts against me. "Over a year."

"You're right," I murmur. "That's too long for a woman like you to go untouched."

I tug on her hair, just enough to get her to angle her head to the side and give me access to her throat. She makes breathless little noises as I kiss and lick my way down the slender column, but those sounds turn into a moan when I flick my tongue over the rapid flutter of her pulse point.

"Don't... Don't be too gentle."

I pause and glance up at her. Her eyes, glazed by vulnerability, fix on mine.

"I just..." She exhales shakily. "I want to feel it. What you do to me. Really feel it. I doubt I'll ever do anything like this again, so..." She worries her lower lip with her teeth, as if what she's asking for might be wrong.

Fuck. She's killing me. "I'll make sure you feel it, beautiful. Every second." Then my mouth is back on hers, and both of my hands find their way to her hair as I take control of the kiss, angling her to get deeper, to taste more of her. She clutches at my shirt and tries to shimmy closer.

I release my hold on her hair, only to grip her hips. She gasps as I lift her and deposit her on my lap so she's straddling me, her pussy centered over the hard ridge of my erection. Her eyelids flutter shut, and she clings to my shoulders as I use my hold on her to rock her against me. Even with the material of my pants and whatever skimpy underwear she's wearing between us, the heat of her seeps through.

I force down visions of pulling down my fly, dragging her panties to the side and thrusting up into her. I want to. I fucking want to feel her wrapped around me. But this is about her gratification, not mine. And though I'm certain I could have her crying out as she comes all over my dick, that isn't what she needs. After the high of her orgasm, she'd remember where we are. She'd be embarrassed. That's the last thing I want.

So I won't fuck her. I'll give her what she needs, what she's asked for, but I won't take more than that.

With my lips on her throat once more, I drag my mouth along her satin-smooth skin, then suck lightly on the spot where her pulse is now hammering. Keeping one hand on her hip, I use the other to push inside the bodice of her dress and cup her breast. She's not wearing a bra, and the hard point of her nipple presses against my palm.

"Oh god," she breathes as I roll the tight little peak between my fingers. When I tug on it, she bucks against me, her lips parting on a whimper. For the first time, the anonymity of the club bothers me. I want to see her face. I want to see the pleasure written there as I touch her. I could take her to a private room. We could remove our masks. Hell, I could even ask her name. Tell her mine. Make sure it's the only word on her lips when she comes for me. But I've never done anything like that. Not here. That's not what this place is about. So I shove the urge aside and give her nipple one last pinch, enjoying her sharp gasp as she bucks against me. Then I drop my hand to her ass so I can gather her skirt and pull it up. Not too far. Not enough to expose her to the people nearby. The people likely watching. Just enough that I can slide my hand underneath to cup the cheek left exposed by her tiny thong.

I flex my fingers. But as incredible as her ass feels, I don't linger there for long, tracing the thin scrap of fabric over the curve of her hip straight to the heat between her legs. A sharp surge of lust flares up my spine when I find a spot that's already damp. I press my thumb against it. "Fuck, you're wet, butterfly," I grit out. "Soaking through these tiny panties for me."

She drops her head to my shoulder as if she's embarrassed. But I grasp her hair with my free hand and tilt her face back up.

"Do you need me to touch your pretty little clit? Fill that tight pussy with my fingers? Ease some of the ache?"

She swallows hard and darts a glance over my shoulder, probably looking to see if anyone's watching. I cup her jaw, focusing her attention back on me.

"They don't matter. All that matters is what you came here for. I'm going to relax you, beautiful, get rid of some of that stress you're under. And you're going to let me. We both know that's what you need." I press my lips to the corner of her mouth, then to the spot just below her ear. "If you tell me yes, I'll make you come so hard you'll be feeling the echo of it for days."

Her breath leaves her in a rush. "Yes. God, yes. Please."

"Good girl." I claim her mouth again while I slip my fingers under the edge of her thong. Her breath hitches as I dip lower, finding smooth, soft skin, then slippery heat. I can't help but groan as I press lightly against her already swollen clit.

I nip at her bottom lip and savor the way she gasps as I

move my hand lower and skim her entrance, then circle it. She's fucking dripping, more than ready to take me. She jerks at the contact, and I swallow the stunted cry she lets out when I slide one finger into her. Her hot, wet cunt grips me as I ease in and out, willing her muscles to relax enough that I can add a second. Once again, the urge to pull out my cock and drag her onto it lashes at me. She's so fucking tight, I'd need to work her down onto me. She'd like it, though; I'd make sure of it. I'd hold her wrists behind her back, make her take—

Fuck. I clench my eyes shut. That's not going to happen. My dick throbs in protest, and I grip her hip to get her moving against me again. Not too hard. Just enough that she rocks onto my finger and against my swollen shaft at the same time. Just to ease the pressure and let me claw back some control.

Soon, she's taking over the movement herself. I let go of her hip, and with a hand at her nape to hold her in place, I watch her. Fucking gorgeous. She looks almost drunk—her lids at half-mast, lips parted. Now that she's relaxed and found her own rhythm, I slide another finger inside her. Then I twist and stroke while pressing my palm to her clit. Those pretty blue eyes of hers close completely in response, and she whimpers as I move faster, arching her back and thrusting her chest toward me.

More than happy to accommodate her wordless request, I pull the neckline of her dress down to expose one perfect breast, ensuring it's the one that will be least visible to any observers. I resist the urge to suck on her flawless skin, mark her with my teeth, give her a memento to take home with her. Instead, I lower my head, take her tightly furled nipple between my lips and lightly bite down on it.

"Oh my god." Her hips jerk again, burying my fingers even deeper inside her.

I want more of those reactions. I want to hear her gasps and moans. To see her fall apart for me. I spread my legs wider to give myself better access, and then I drift my free hand down the cleft of her ass, push aside the tiny scrap of material and circle the tight little pucker between her cheeks.

She freezes, but I don't. I keep the hand between her legs moving, and after a few moments, she relaxes again, her rhythm picking back up. The way her body is tightening around me tells me she's close, so I curve my fingers until they press against her front wall with every stroke in and out. I find her clit with my thumb and brush lightly over it. The moment I give her more pressure there, she'll tip right over the edge, but I'm not ready to let her go yet. "Hands behind you, butterfly."

She hesitates for only a moment before she obeys. After one last tease between the cheeks of her ass, I use that hand to grip her wrists and hold her down on my fingers, hold her still. My dick is so hard underneath her it's throbbing almost painfully. Even my balls are drawn up tight. Every part of me wants to be inside her for what comes next. But unfortunately, only my fingers are going to experience it.

I add a third, and she inhales sharply at the stretch.

"Relax, you can take it. It's going to feel so good when you come." I tug on her wrists, forcing her back to bow and her breasts to push forward. Then I drop my head and draw her hard nipple into my mouth.

Jesus. She's strangling me. Her breaths are coming fast and heavy, interspersed by whimpers every time I suck on that tight little peak. I release her with a pop and look up at her, loosening my grip on her wrists just enough to let her move. "Ride my fingers."

Her hips work, rocking over my lap. A thin sheen of sweat coats her chest, and the tips of her hair cling to her damp skin. I give her clit a little more pressure with my thumb, then latch on to the tight point of her nipple again, sucking hard, making her body spasm around me. She's almost there. This pretty little butterfly's done so well for me. She deserves the orgasm I'm going to give her.

By now, she's so lost in the pleasure she no longer cares about where she is or who might be watching. The same can't be said of me. The thought of someone else—most likely more than one someone—watching her come apart for me has tension knotting the back of my neck. I should have taken her to a private room. Kept this moment all to myself.

Hindsight's a fucking bitch.

She's rolling her hips and grinding her pussy onto my fingers. Her muscles tighten further, and she drops her head to my shoulder again, as if she can no longer hold it up. Fuck. I suck in deep breaths, willing myself to keep it together. This is far from the first time I've finger-fucked a woman, but it's the first time I've been this close to blowing my load without having at least a hand working my dick in return. I'm done playing with her now. I need her to shatter for me.

I turn my head, mouth grazing the shell of her ear. "Your needy little clit is all swollen and wet, butterfly. Do you want to come now?"

"Yes," she moans. "Please, yes."

With a smile, I brush my lips against her jaw. "Just because you asked so nicely." Then I press my thumb to that sensitive bundle of nerves, make quick hard circles. Her legs tighten around my hips, and she buries her face in the crook of my neck to muffle the sounds she makes as she breaks apart. Her pussy clenches around my fingers again and again as she comes, her arousal dripping down my hand. I'm going to have the evidence of her orgasm on the front of my pants, and it only makes me harder.

"Good girl," I growl. "Such a good girl, leaving a mess all over me."

With one final spasm, she slumps against my chest. I can still feel where she pressed her mouth against my skin as she came. My fingers are still buried inside her. And even though this moment was all I intended to have with her, walking away without more than this small taste would be a travesty. Not looking back is what I do—what I'm best at.

But even as I remind myself of that, I know the truth.

I won't ask for more than this tonight. But I'm not done with her yet.

CHAPTER EIGHT

VIOLET

I'm boneless, slumped against him. A part of my brain, the small part that isn't buzzing from my first non-self-induced orgasm in over a year, is wondering how I can be so comfortable like this. People surrounding me, a stranger's *fingers* inside me. And a very large bulge underneath me.

Is it this place? Is it the much-needed relief of having an itch scratched? Or is it him? Is there something about this man that my body instinctively trusts?

Blinking away the arousal and satisfaction fogging my brain, I push myself upright. As I do, his fingers press into my sensitive flesh, and my still-pulsing clit brushes his palm. I jolt and suck in a sharp breath as an aftershock of pleasure ripples through me.

He eases his fingers free of me, and with his gaze fixed on mine, raises them between us and slides them into his mouth.

I inhale sharply. None of the men I've been with have ever done anything so erotic. Not one of them has ripped an orgasm from me with an intensity even close to what I just experienced. But the pleasure on his face as his eyes drift half-closed and he groans his enjoyment has me involuntarily rolling my hips against the hard ridge beneath me.

With a wince, he clamps both hands down on my thighs and holds me in place. Then those lips curve into a smile as dangerously potent as one from the real devil might be. "Unless you want to continue this in a private room right now, I'd advise you to hold still. It's been a long time since I've disgraced myself with a woman. I'd rather not do it tonight."

I let out a breathless laugh. There's a certain thrill that comes with the knowledge that my pleasure alone is enough to get him close to the edge. But the humor fades quickly, because I'm not sure what the next step is. Does he *want* to go to a private room? I don't know if I'm ready for that. But I need to offer him something in return. It wouldn't be fair for him to have gotten me off so spectacularly, only for me to up and run away without returning the favor. I reach for the button of his pants, fumbling to undo it.

Before I can slip it free, his big hand is closing around mine, holding it still. "That's not what I need."

Confused, I freeze and search his eyes, my heart still beating out of my chest.

What I can see of his expression softens, as if he can read my mind, and his thumb strokes slow circles over my wrist. "I won't ask you for more right now, beautiful. Not that I wouldn't enjoy your hand—or any other part of you—wrapped around me. But this isn't a quid pro quo arrangement. Seeing you come for me so prettily is enough."

He's so obviously aroused. Why wouldn't he want me to take care of him? It hits me then, a swift sting of hurt lancing my chest. Of course he doesn't want a hand job. That's not what he came here for tonight. There are plenty of women in this club who would be more than happy to step in once I'm gone and give him what he's really after. Whatever that might be—rope play, breath play, or even scarier-sounding activities.

I press my hand to my stomach and will the embarrassment twisting inside to abate, even as I berate myself. I've only just met this guy, and we're in a sex club, for goodness' sake. He probably comes here all the time to get his rocks off. While I'm not looking down my nose at him for doing it, particularly considering what he's just done for me, I don't want to date him. So why should I care that after I leave, he'll probably take his pleasure from another woman?

"Of course." I force a smile to my face and start to climb off him, but once again, his hands wrap around my thighs and hold me in place.

"Will I see you here again?"

The gravel in his voice surprises me. His *question* surprises me.

"Do you want to see me here again?"

He brushes his thumb across my bottom lip, his head dipping closer. "I'd say this was a teaser, wouldn't you? I'd like to experience more. I'd definitely like another taste of you."

Is he talking about kissing me? Or... other things? The thought of either has my pulse careening into my throat. Could I come back and do this with him again?

Biting my lip, I search his gaze. But then it hits me, and disappointment settles heavily in my chest. "I can't come back. I'm only here as a guest."

He gives an easy shrug of his broad shoulders. "I'll organize a membership for you."

I stare at him blankly. Anna told me how much memberships cost, and they're ridiculously expensive. Richard paid for hers, but he's a millionaire, and casual or not, they'd been seeing each other for months. This man is a stranger and... well, I guess he must be rich, since that's the type of person this place specifically caters to, but paying that kind of exorbitant fee for a woman he's never met before? That makes no sense.

I shake my head. "Why would you do that? You don't even know me."

One corner of his mouth kicks up in a smile that's just short of a smirk. "If you come back next Friday, then I will know you."

My mind spins at the prospect. "I'm not sure... I mean... My friend might not want to come, and I... I don't know if I should..."

"Butterfly." He interrupts my nervous rambling. "I'd like to see you here again next week. I'm prepared to pay for a membership to make it possible. But it's up to you if you use it or not."

Why? Why would he spend all that money on the off chance that I'll come back? "That's way too expensive a risk to take."

The sinful smile that grows across his face makes my stomach flip over. "Some risks are worth the price."

"Right." I don't know what else to say. I'm at a loss for how to handle this situation.

He removes his hands from my thighs and leans back against the couch. My legs are still shaky from the intensity of my orgasm as I climb off his lap, and I self-consciously brush my skirt down over my thighs, making sure I'm covered. Which is probably pointless considering what I just did in a public place, but I won't let myself dwell on that right now.

I take a step back as he stands, reminded once again of how much taller than me he is. With my chin tipped up so I can take in the height of him, I find myself wishing I could remove his mask and see what he looks like underneath it. Not that it should matter, but I can't help but want to put a face to his voice and his body and his touch.

"Let me help you find your friend," he says.

I shake my head, my chest suddenly too tight. I need a moment to breathe. To wrap my mind around what we just did. "I'll be fine. She's probably dancing or at the bar. She wouldn't go anywhere else without letting me know."

His lips flatten, but he doesn't argue.

"Okay..." I grind to a halt, because what the hell do I say now? How do you thank someone for giving you an orgasm in the middle of a sex club? "I really enjoyed... I mean, it was nice to... uh..."

The way he chuckles, low and deep, sends a wave of heat through my whole body. "It was definitely my pleasure."

I nod jerkily, my smile feeling a little manic. "Thank you," I finally force out, hoping he can hear the sincerity in my voice.

Letting out a breath, I turn and make my way through the crowd, barely registering the bodies moving together in my periphery as I try to process everything that's happened tonight.

Anna suddenly pops up in front of me, shooting my heart into overdrive and making me slap a hand to my chest. She grins broadly as she loops her arm through mine.

"So? Did Mr. Tall, Muscular and Devilish rock your world?"

I laugh, fighting the temptation to glance over my shoulder to see if I can catch another glimpse of him. "You could say that."

She lets out a little squeal and hugs me as she steers me

toward the exit. "I'm so happy for you. I kept an eye on you at the start, to make sure you were okay. But once it looked like you were, ahem, starting to enjoy yourself—"

I groan, my skin flaring hot again.

"*I* enjoyed a nice flirtatious conversation with a man with a sexy accent at the bar."

"I'm glad you had fun while I was... also having fun." I follow her out the door and into the long black corridor, already looking forward to getting home and taking this mask off. The soft leather is comfortable, but it's still a little stifling, especially after my recent... exertions.

The woman who admitted us is still standing behind the desk, watching us approach with a smile. When we reach her, Anna holds her arm out, and the woman scans her bracelet, then removes it, reminding us that our accounts will be charged for our drinks. When it's my turn, she scans my bracelet, but when the computer beeps in response, she frowns at the screen in concentration. A couple of key taps later, there's a whirring sound from under the desk. With a small smile directed at me, she reaches down, then places an item on the counter and pushes it toward me.

"You must have made quite an impression," she says.

I pick up the black card, still warm from the machine that just produced it. Surely, it can't be what I think it is. I half expected him to be all talk, and even if he wasn't, I never would have thought he'd work so quickly.

"He bought you a membership?" Beside me, Anna's eyebrows almost reach her hairline.

The woman places a small machine on the counter between us. "If you could place your thumb on the screen," she directs.

I do as she asks, and when the scanner is finished doing

its thing, she puts it away again and turns back to her computer. With a few keystrokes, she gives me another smile. "All set. Have a wonderful night."

"Thank you. You too." Avoiding Anna's gaze, I turn and head toward the door we stepped through what feels like forever ago.

She catches up to me outside, lacing her arm through mine. "You want to tell me what just happened?"

When I glance at her, the grin on her face stretches from ear to ear.

I'm not sure I could even explain it to myself. But maybe she can help me make sense of it. And decide what I should do with the card that's doing its best to burn a hole in my hand. "I'll tell you about it on the way home."

CHAPTER NINE

TATE

I stride into Cole's office and settle into one of the two deep leather chairs in front of his desk. "I've got the latest Genesis-1 numbers."

"Good," he says, looking up from his computer. "Roman should be here in a moment."

This is our regular Monday morning update meeting. Typically, we hold it in Roman's office, but since he's having some upgrades made to his IT system, Cole volunteered to host.

I hum to myself as I tap my fingers on the arm of the chair and take in the New York cityscape outside the floor-to-ceiling windows.

When I glance back over at Cole, his dark brows are arched high. "You're in a good mood this morning."

"I don't know what you're talking about. I'm always in a good mood."

"Hmm." His blue eyes narrow.

Luckily, he's distracted from probing further when Roman enters.

My eldest brother sits down in the chair next to me, braces his elbows on his knees and leans forward. "So, what are the numbers telling us?" There's no preamble. As always, he gets straight down to business.

"We're on track," I tell him. "Almost fifty percent of apartments have been sold already."

"What about the penthouses?"

"One sold, with strong interest in a second. I think it will go through."

Cole taps his pen on the desk, a frown on his face. "It would be good if we can get two or even three sold before we break ground. We can hold off on the last one to capitalize on the higher market value when construction is almost complete. But having a minimum of two confirmed sales will provide the proof of concept we need."

I nod. Ideally, we'll have investors clamoring to jump on board when we eventually take the concept for Genesis-1 global. We have a chance to corner a niche in a growing international market, particularly in Europe, where high-rises are traditionally renter dominated. If we make an early move, the King Group can establish itself as leaders in the luxury high-rise sector. Our UK office is about to wrap up a feasibility study for construction of a Genesis-1 in London.

"The team's working on it. We're already looking at expanding our usual marketing channels."

"Good." Roman still has his elbows planted on his knees, his focus fixed on the carpet in front of him. "Will you have an updated phased marketing plan available soon?"

"By the end of the week."

He grunts his acknowledgment, and we move on to other issues, including a minor change to the construction timeframe due to a hold-up with one of our planning permissions.

As we talk, I'm mostly on autopilot, thinking about what Cole said when I walked in. He's right. I am in a good mood. Have been since Friday night. And if asked why, I don't know if I could explain it. Having an unexpected taste of a beautiful woman, then walking away with blue fucking balls, isn't something I ever thought would put a smile on my face. But witnessing her come apart on my lap like that, all wide-eyed behind her mask, plump lips parted as she made those sexy little gasps and whimpers, had been incredibly satisfying.

Fuck. Even now, the memory has my dick swelling in my pants—not a reaction that typically happens when I'm sitting in my brother's office. As soon as she walked away that night, I found Matt, the bar manager, and gave him her bracelet number. All it took was a couple of taps on the screen of his tablet, and the concierge was alerted to her change in status. Considering I wasn't even planning to be with anyone at the club that night, I'm far more invested in seeing her again than I should be. I refuse to spend too long second-guessing myself though. One more night with her, just to have my fill, and I'll walk away like I always do. Then she'll have her membership, and she can do whatever she wants—with *whoever* she wants—for a whole year.

"Are you even listening?" Roman asks.

No. But I give him a lazy smile. "Of course. You were telling me what an amazing job I'm doing."

Behind his desk, Cole snorts. "Something like that." He tilts his head, a crease forming between his brows as he scrutinizes me. "What's going on with you?"

I shake my head. "Nothing. There's nothing going on

with me." Cole's right. I'm distracted, and that's not good for any of us right now.

Leaning forward in my seat, I mimic Roman and brace my elbows on my knees. "I'm here. Let's get this done."

With one more skeptical look, Cole taps on his computer and focuses on the screen. "Right, let's talk amenities."

BY THE TIME we wrap up an hour later, it's past lunchtime. I could get my PA, Sophie, to order in or pick something up. But since I have a rare break between meetings, now seems like as good a time as any to catch up with my college buddy.

I take the elevator down to the fortieth floor, where the lawyer's offices are located. If I know Mark, he hasn't had lunch yet either. It's been a while since we've spent any time together. Our jobs keep us both busy. Not to mention that he's been with the same woman for the last year, so our occasional post-work alcohol-fueled catchups have dwindled.

I find him in his office as usual. His door is open, and when I walk in, his serious expression lightens into a grin. "To what do I owe the pleasure of a visit from on high?"

"We all know the pleasure is dubious at best," I say, dropping onto the small sofa in the corner of his office. "Feel like grabbing lunch?"

He turns in his chair, his brows rising. "Taking a break for once?"

"Hey, a man's got to eat occasionally."

With a smirk, he leans back, crossing his ankle over his knee. "That's what I've heard. Not sure I believe it though."

I laugh. Mark's almost as much of a workaholic as Roman. I've known him since we were roommates at Harvard. The guy was there on a scholarship and busted his ass every day. I respected that about him, even if I was more inclined to enjoy the full range of college experiences. But on occasion, he'd take time off from studying, and we'd get drunk together.

I've confided in Mark in a way that I haven't with anyone else. We'd share a bottle of whiskey, and he'd talk about losing his mom when he and his sister were kids and how hard his dad worked raising them on his own. I'd tell him about my family, about how I was a part of it, but not really a part of it. I skirted the truth, even then, but he knew enough about my family's dysfunction that I joked that I'd have to hire him as a lawyer so all my secrets would be covered by attorney-client privilege.

And as soon as he passed the bar, I hired him to work for the King Group.

"I was planning to go to the coffee shop and see Violet," he says, glancing at his watch. "You want to come along and grab something to eat?"

"Violet's back in New York?" The last I'd heard, Mark's little sister was living in Maine. Though I suppose that was a year or so ago.

He stands and grabs his suit jacket off the hook on the back of his door. "Yeah. Didn't I mention it?"

I stand too. "No. What's she doing now?"

"She came back to take over managing True Brew after the previous manager screwed things up."

I grin as an image of Violet forms in my mind. I haven't seen her in years, not since Mark and I graduated. While we were in college, she would visit him now and then and stay the night at the apartment we shared. The thing I remember most about her—apart from her fresh-faced prettiness that was hard not to notice, even if she was my roommate's little sister—was that she was not impressed with me at all. Granted, our first meeting didn't go as intended. I'd forgotten she would be visiting, and I'd come back late after a night of partying—and not alone.

Mark, being the caring big brother he is, had let his sister have his bedroom while he slept on the couch. Unfortunately, his bedroom shared a wall with mine. So before even meeting me, Violet was subjected to the high-pitched screams of a woman begging me to fuck her hard. Not my finest moment, I admit. And the horrified expression she couldn't hide when I walked into the kitchen the next morning, half-naked, with not one, but two women in tow, told me exactly what she thought of me.

Of course, the only reason I'd been drunk enough to forget about her visit and to end up with two women in my bed was because of the news I'd received that morning. But since I hadn't told anyone about it—not Mark, not my brothers, and definitely not my parents—I wouldn't use it to justify myself to a woman I didn't even know.

I did try to work my way back into her good graces, considering she was my friend's sister, but she proved to be immune to my charm. And after a while, I realized I enjoyed the way she turned her nose up at me. So much so that after that discovery, I made a point of being extra cocky when she visited, just so I could see the sparks flaring in her eyes when I got under her skin. Immature, maybe. But strangely addictive, nonetheless.

After all these years, will she still look at me the same way? The possibility is more appealing than it should be.

"How's the coffee shop doing?" I ask as we make our way to the elevator.

He hesitates for a moment, his brows pulling together. "Violet's still working on building up the customer base again. I'm hoping things are improving. She's stretched pretty thin right now—physically and financially."

I stop short and regard him with surprise. "You're hoping? I thought you'd be keeping a close eye on her."

He winces, and his shoulders tense. "I'm trying very hard not to be *that* guy. I think half the reason she went to college out of state was because Dad and I were a little... overprotective while she was growing up. Now that she's back, I don't want her to think I don't believe she's capable."

"So you're not helping out at all?"

The sigh he lets out is one of defeat. "She's pretty adamant about doing this on her own. She's determined to prove she can handle it without her big brother waiting in the wings to bail her out." He grimaces. "Not that I can do much anyway. The next step is probably selling unfortunately."

"If finances are an issue, has she considered getting a loan?"

"We did discuss it. But even if we could get a loan, Violet doesn't want to saddle the shop with more debt. She said it would be like trying to put out fire with gasoline. But she's smart and determined, and she's a hard worker." There's a mixture of pride and concern on his face. "There's no reason she can't bring the coffee shop back to its previous standing on her own."

I nod, leaving it there. He's overprotective, just like he said. I knew it the first time he mentioned his sister. But from what I recall, their dad left the place to both of them. It seems strange to me that he wouldn't at least look over the coffee shop's numbers.

With a small shake of my head, I dismiss my thoughts. I

don't know what it's like to have a sister, and I've never been close enough with another person to feel the need to protect them—not as an adult anyway. I'm the last person who should be questioning him.

Once we're settled in my town car, Mark gives directions to my driver, Jeremy. Twenty minutes later, he drops us off outside a small coffee shop in Brooklyn. Most of the front window is covered in a sign that reads *True Brew* in large blue outdated script.

Two young women clutching to-go cups step outside as Mark and I approach. Their eyes widen as they pass, then they hunch close, whispering and giggling as they scurry down the sidewalk.

Mark smirks at me over his shoulder. "You've still got it, old man," he says.

I shake my head. "You're two months older than me, asshole."

The bell above the door jangles as he opens it, and I follow him inside. It takes a moment to adjust to the dimmer lighting, but when I do, I scan the shop. There's a quiet murmur of conversation, but though there are a few people seated around the compact space, more tables are empty than full.

Standing behind the counter is a young, dark-haired man wearing a smile. "Hey, Mark. Good to see you."

"Hi Jarrod." Mark steps closer and chats with him, but I tune out their small talk and take in the interior of the coffee shop more thoroughly. The shop isn't dirty or falling apart. Not at all. It's actually spotless. It's obvious that Violet and her staff take pride in keeping everything clean. But the signage is faded and out of date. The tables and chairs are mismatched, and not in the quirky way some places pull off. Even the pastry cabinet looks a little bare and sad.

"Violet's in the back," Jarrod says, drawing my attention to their conversation. "I'll get her for you. You want something while you wait?"

We both order a coffee, then Jarrod disappears through the door which presumably leads to the kitchen, while Mark and I take a seat at a table near the back.

Before I have a chance to do more than pick up the menu, the door swings back open, and Violet rushes out, a wide smile on her face aimed directly at Mark. I take a moment to look her over, from the hair piled on top of her head in a messy bun—the honey brown hue a little darker than when I last saw her, if I'm not mistaken—to her black tank top and black denim cutoffs. Even her Chucks and the little apron tied around her slender waist are black. In those shorts, her smooth, tanned legs look a mile long. The pretty, slightly awkward twenty-one-year-old woman I remember from years ago has morphed into a gorgeous-as-fuck woman.

As she emerges from behind the counter, her eyes find me. Her smile freezes for a split-second before she glances away. It's back again in all its brilliance as she approaches and gives her brother a hug.

I rub my hand over my mouth to hide my smile. Apparently, she still hasn't forgiven *or* forgotten.

Standing, I force her to acknowledge my presence.

Those clear blue eyes finally turn my way, giving my pulse a strange jolt. "Tate."

"Violet," I say. "It's been a long time."

Her full lips press together, then she tilts her head to the side and gives me a too-sweet smile. "Has it? I hadn't noticed."

The attitude sends a familiar kick of excitement through me.

I chuckle. "So it's safe to say absence doesn't make the heart grow fonder?"

She wrinkles her nose and turns back to her brother, dismissing me *and* my teasing. "Are you eating, or did you come to check up on me?"

The words are casual. Even her tone, for the most part. But there's a thread of tension underlying both. Interesting. Maybe she really does want Mark to give her space.

"Tate wanted to grab lunch, and I haven't seen you in a few weeks," he says. "I thought we'd kill two birds with one stone."

The hint of tension I swear I picked up on melts away. Now she just looks guilty. "I'm sorry I haven't visited more. By the time I get home, I'm so tired I just want to stay in, read a good book and have a glass of wine. I've been crashing early most nights. But I'll make more of an effort, I promise." She wraps her arms around his waist and squeezes.

Their easy affection tightens my chest. I've never had that type of relationship with anyone. Shit. I can't even remember the last time I hugged someone.

Violet releases her brother and smiles up at him. "You want your usual?" When he nods, she glances back at me, though she focuses somewhere around the knot of my tie rather than meeting my eye. "Are you eating too?" There's no missing how her tone flattens when she addresses me.

"I can't wait to try what you're serving up."

That gets her to focus on my face. I grin, and in response, she narrows her eyes, probably sifting through my words to find a hidden meaning.

"What do you recommend?" I ask.

She presses her lips together, then lets out a breath. "We don't have a large menu at the moment."

Her eyes flash with what might be embarrassment. Not that she has any reason to be ashamed. Considering what Mark said about her working to get this place back on its feet, having a small menu makes good business sense.

"But the grilled chicken avocado wrap is really good," she continues. "And the ham and cheese panini is always popular."

"I'll have the wrap, thanks."

She nods again, then turns to head back to the kitchen. Something catches my eye as she goes, and the sight sends ice sliding into my bloodstream. Because there, on one shoulder blade, is a small blue butterfly.

I pull in a long breath through my nose. It must be a coincidence—butterfly tattoos aren't exactly rare. She's gone too fast for me to get a good look, but my heart hammers against my ribs anyway. Because my body, if not my head, is sure of what I just saw. I traced over those delicate blue wings only a few nights ago. I can still feel her silky skin under my fingers. Fingers that then buried themselves in her tight little pussy and fucked her until she came all over them.

A lance of guilt spears through me, and my gaze shoots straight to Mark, who's wearing a proud grin on his face. Shit. I have to fight the urge to wince as I imagine how he'd react if he knew what I'd done to his sister.

Possibly done. There's no point in getting ahead of myself. I need to get a closer look.

Mark and I sit back down, and I focus on slowing my racing pulse while trying to concentrate on what he's saying. But it's pointless. My mind is filled with images and memories from last Friday night as I work to reconcile the woman who was writhing on my lap with the one who was just standing in front of me, expression full of familiar disdain.

I drum my fingers on the table as I wait for Violet to return with our food, my attention constantly drawn back to the kitchen door. Jarrod is back behind the counter, handling the few customers that trickle in, while a young blond woman serves the seated ones. When she drops our coffees off, I thank her absently.

I only snap out of my distraction when I take a sip of the hot beverage. The instant I register the taste, my eyebrows shoot up.

Across from me, Mark chuckles. "Good, huh?"

I take another sip and give a low hum. "Very good."

"The beans are all sourced from small sustainable farms. Costs more, but it's worth it. Ethically, and for the taste."

"I'd agree with that." This time when I take a sip, I close my eyes to savor the flavor. "With coffee that tastes like this, why isn't this place packed?"

He sighs. "It used to be. But like I mentioned, I made a mistake with the previous manager. He had great referrals, but he was used to working for large franchises, not small, community-focused shops. I should have been keeping a better eye on things, but..."

"We've been keeping you busy."

He shrugs. "It's not a good excuse for dropping the ball. But it's the only one I've got."

"Not worth suing, I suppose?"

He shakes his head. "His actions wouldn't be considered gross negligence or deliberate misconduct. It was my mistake anyway. Hiring someone who didn't understand Dad's vision for the shop." Grief shadows his expression for a moment before he shakes it off. "He always wanted it to be a community cornerstone, where every cup served not only tasted amazing but represented a commitment to ethical sourcing. Unfortunately, Violet was out of state, and I didn't check in enough to notice all the little changes the manager was making." He sighs. "I should have realized sooner, but it was hard... coming back here with Dad gone, you know? I kind of avoided it." He studies his coffee cup for a long moment, but when he looks back up again, he's smiling. "Violet will do it. I have no doubt."

He has so much belief in his sister. It's obvious in his every word and in the way he looks at her.

In my whole life, has anyone ever had even half that belief in me?

My thoughts are interrupted by the kitchen door swinging open and Violet re-emerging with our meals.

I watch her every move as she makes her way toward us. The club was dark, but from what I can tell, the color of her hair and eyes matches the woman I was with. I take in the rest of her—breasts, hips, legs. The *shape* of her matches too.

Fuck, the *shape* of her. A jolt of arousal hits me with so much force that I inhale sharply. I'm bombarded with the mental image of my hands on her body. My fingers *inside* her. I will the hot rush of lust spreading through me to dissipate as she places our plates in front of us. I still don't know for sure it's her. Not 100 percent.

I'm still studying her, cataloging the angle of her jaw and the curve of her lips, comparing what I see to what I remember, when she says, "Is there something wrong with the food?"

Her question snaps me out of my thoughts. "It's fine," I say, picking up the wrap in front of me and taking a large bite. It tastes as good as it looks, but I don't get a chance to tell her that, because before I can swallow, she aims a final warm smile at her brother—and a tight-lipped one at me—and heads back to the counter.

"Are you okay?" Mark asks as I track her retreating form. There's no doubt in my mind now. It's exactly the same tattoo, in exactly the same position.

"Yeah. All good. Looks like Violet's all grown up."

What the fuck kind of observation is that?

I should be engaging him in some kind of work-related conversation, then getting the hell out of here, not focusing on his sister.

Mark frowns, watching me a little too intently, as if he can sense a deeper meaning he won't like behind my words. "It's not like she was a kid the last time you saw her."

"No, she wasn't." I busy myself with my wrap so I can avoid his gaze. "She just looks different."

"Yeah." He sighs, glancing back at the counter where she's talking to Jarrod. "She had a rough time after Dad died. Withdrew a bit. I'm glad she's back in New York. I was worried about her for a while."

"It's good that she has you." I'm only half listening, because I'm distracted by the way Jarrod is smiling down at her.

He touches her arm, and she laughs up at him, as if he's made a joke, the dimple in her left cheek flashing. Then she turns to head to the kitchen. I narrow my eyes as he watches her go. Is he looking at her curvy ass in those little shorts as she walks away?

As he turns back to the counter, his attention snags on me. Surprise flashes across his features before his jaw tightens and he returns my stare. I get the feeling he's sizing me up the same way I'm doing to him. I don't know why the thought of there being something between this guy and Violet bothers me. From the little she told me at Onyx, it doesn't sound like that's the case—not at the moment, anyway. Regardless, I don't have a claim on her. And more importantly, I shouldn't care.

Jarrod finally looks away, and I turn back to Mark and my lunch. This time, I deliberately steer the conversation away from his sister and back to work. But as hard as I try, I can't stop replaying that night in my head. Suddenly Violet's no longer my college friend's little sister—who I enjoy riling up way too much—she's the sexy-as-hell woman I made come in the middle of the club.

And I bought a membership for her. Invited her back.

Biting back a groan, I scrub my hand over my mouth. Now that I know it's her, I can't return. She'll never forgive me for what I did, even if I didn't know it was her at the time. Compounding the issue by doubling down would probably be grounds for my murder if she ever found out. The only logical solution is to avoid Onyx for a while. Not that I've been there much lately, but still.

Though if she does turn up looking for me this weekend, and I'm *not* there, she could end up on some other man's lap—or under him. Unbidden, my fingers clench into a fist. With a deep breath in, I force them to uncurl. She's a grown woman. As much as I don't like the idea, if she wants to indulge with another man at Onyx, she has every right.

I don't linger after we finish our meals. While Mark says goodbye to Violet, I don't even throw a smart-ass comment her way. I merely tip my head at her. The close-mouthed smile she gives me in return is the reinforcement I need. I'm doing exactly the right thing by not dragging out this mistake.

But even as Mark and I return to the office, I can't stop

thinking about the way she felt as she moved against me, the heat of her breath on my skin, and the press of her lips to my neck. Then I'm hit with a wholly different vision. Violet moving over another man. Her breath on *his* skin. Her lips on *his* neck.

Fuck.

CHAPTER TEN

VIOLET

"I'm proud of you." Anna is lying stomach down on my bed, knees bent and her bare feet kicking back and forth in the air over her ass.

Shaking my head, I suppress a smile as I smooth down my sparkly blue dress. "Proud of what? That I'm apparently too horny for my own good, so I'm hoping a masked stranger might give me my second man-supplied orgasm in over a year?"

"Uh, yes. Exactly." She pushes herself up to sitting and swings her legs over the edge of the bed. "Eric was an asshole who manipulated you and abused your trust. You needed time to get past that. But now you're ready to take back control of your life. What better way than to have some anonymous sexy times with a hot, rich stranger? No pressure, no expectations, just fun, and hopefully many, many orgasms."

This time, I can't stop the grin that tugs at my lips. "Well, when you put it that way."

"So, are you ready?"

Nerves suddenly swarm my stomach, but I nod anyway. "I think so."

"Great. Let's go." Anna leaps to her feet and slides on the heels she left by the side of the bed.

I take a deep, settling breath. I have no idea if this is the right decision. Will I even be able to go through with doing anything more than I did last week? And what if I show up and he doesn't? Even worse, what if I show up and he's with someone else?

"Don't talk yourself out of it now, Vi." Anna wraps her arms around me from behind and rests her chin on my shoulder, regarding my reflection in the mirror. "Whatever's going on in that pretty head of yours, ignore it. If he's not there, or whatever, then screw him. You and I can have plenty of fun on the dance floor. Or we can find another McHottie for you to get your freak on with."

I let out a laugh. Even when I'm at my lowest, Anna knows how to cheer me up. It's why she's the only person I told about Eric. At the time it happened, I was feeling so low. I knew confiding in her would help me dig myself out of the hole I'd been wallowing in. If I'd spilled everything to Mark, he would have defaulted to full protective mode and gone ballistic, potentially getting himself into trouble in the process. Particularly since Eric's boss is a state senator *and* his uncle. There was no way I'd let my big brother potentially risk his career for my sake.

Anna's right. Tonight isn't about a man. Not really. It's about remembering what it's like to enjoy myself, rediscovering the old me, the woman who's gotten a little lost over the last twenty months.

I give my friend a firm nod. "Yep, let's go and have fun."

Half an hour later, we're pulling up outside the familiar unassuming building. We've both donned the same masks we wore last week, but this time, it's me scanning my membership card. It still seems so bizarre.

Inside, we pass off our purses. The woman stationed at the desk is not the same one from last time, but she's just as friendly and professional. Once the check-in process is complete, we make our way into the club. I know what to expect now, but watching all the masked men and women mingling in the dim light is still surreal.

Tamping down my nerves, I search the crowd for a devil mask. When I don't spot one, I tell myself not to be too disappointed. After all, he might not be here yet, or he might be in a section of the club I can't see. I smile at Anna. "Let's get a drink."

One slowly sipped Cosmopolitan later, that disappointment has gained ground. After another, I've decided I got my hopes up for nothing. Anna pulls me onto the dance floor, and I'm about to write all of this off as something I'll laugh with her about later—much later, after the sharp edge of disappointment dulls a little—when a man in a Roman soldier mask approaches.

"Ladies," he says, his voice deep, but not quite as deep as the man from last week. "May I join you?"

Uncertain, I glance at Anna, who grins at me in return.

"Um, sure?" I don't get any flutters in my stomach when he trains his dark eyes on me, but I let him wrap a muscular arm around my waist and pull me back against his chest.

I do my best not to compare the feel of his body to my memory of another one. That man invited me here tonight and, just like I feared, has left me hanging. Why should I pine after him? He's practically a stranger, after all.

A stranger who had his fingers inside me. A stranger who, just with those fingers, made me come harder than any man before him.

That doesn't mean he owes me anything though. Or that I owe him. Even if he did buy a very expensive membership for me, that was his choice. And he didn't give me the caveat that I could only use it to see him again.

I will myself to relax into the body behind me, despite that it doesn't feel quite right. Anna catches my eye, cocking her head in a subtle gesture to check that I'm okay. When I nod, she smiles and focuses her attention on another masked man loitering to the side of us. Needing no more encouragement, he's soon grinding away at her back.

The man behind me grips my hips in his big hands and pulls me back tighter against him. I try not to tense when his hard length presses against my ass. He's not being shy about pushing that thing into me either. Which makes sense, I suppose, considering where we are.

The ambience of this part of the club makes it easy to forget about its deeper purpose. Obviously, that's deliberate. After all, the place is meant to cater to almost any and all activities the rich and famous are interested in—be that enjoying a casual drink, a sexy dance or full-on kink indulgence—all while ensuring anonymity.

I can't help but peek over at the doorway Anna said leads to the private—and not so private—rooms. My stomach flips. When I pictured coming back here tonight, I wondered whether I'd be daring enough to pass through that door. I may have even gotten a little worked up thinking about it. In no way did I imagine doing it with another random stranger though. From the way this guy is breathing hot and heavy in my ear, I can sense the question coming. Would I even consider it?

My answer comes an instant later when the man presses a wet, open-mouthed kiss against my neck. My heart jumps into my throat, and I instinctively shudder. Nope.

I'm not feeling it at all. I try to pull away, but he's holding on to me too tightly.

I throw a glance at Anna in the hopes that she'll know what to do. Only she's not looking at me. She's focused on something over my shoulder, her eyes wide and her lips parted slightly.

A second later, I find out why. The hands gripping my hips release me so quickly I almost stumble forward. With a gasp, I spin around, only to find a tall form wearing a familiar devil mask looming over the man I've been dancing with.

He bends down so they're almost nose to nose, and from here, his growled *she's mine* is impossible to miss.

Those two words, said in that low, gravelly tone, send a flare of heat up my spine. My physical response shocks me. After Eric, I didn't imagine I'd find any level of possessiveness a turn-on. I guess I've been proven wrong. At least where this guy is concerned.

The man in the Roman soldier mask puts both hands up in the air. "Sorry, sorry. I didn't think she was collared."

My eyes almost bug out. *Collared?*

"She's not a sub. Doesn't mean she's not mine." His tone is uncompromising.

Anna's at my side now, grasping my arm. The guy she was dancing with has disappeared, though the grin stretched across her face below her mask makes it clear she doesn't care.

"*That* is hot as hell," she whispers in my ear.

I'm too stunned to formulate a coherent reply.

In the next moment, a large bouncer in a black suit appears at our side. "Is there a problem here?"

Roman soldier shakes his head. "No problem. Just a misunderstanding."

The bouncer looks between the men, then does a double take. He focuses on the man in the devil mask. "My apologies, sir. Is everything okay?"

A wave of confusion washes over me. In this place, which is literally filled with VIPs, why does this guy get special treatment?

He nods. "Everything's fine. This gentleman was just finding somewhere else to be."

With a shake of his head, Roman soldier guy disappears into the crowd. I don't notice whether the bouncer fades away as well, because I'm too busy scrutinizing the visible parts of the man standing in front of me, trying to figure out who he is.

Unease flickers to life in my chest as I examine him. The line of his jaw and the shape of his mouth trigger a thrum of awareness that I don't remember from last weekend. I step closer, angling my face up toward him. If I can get a better look at his eyes, then maybe it will shake loose the nagging sense of familiarity.

The truth is hovering just under the surface of my conscious mind. Without thinking, I reach up and drift my fingertips along his jaw, the faint rasp of stubble sending a tingle down my arm. A muscle leaps under my touch, and he gently takes my wrist and pulls it away from his face.

"Violet," he says, his tone low, almost like a warning.

With a gasp, I snatch my hand back and clutch it to my chest. Not because he shouldn't know my name, but because the moment it fell from his lips, the connection clicked into place. How did I not see it before?

"Tate?" I whisper.

He inclines his head, and my heart plummets. How could this happen? Tate King, arrogant bastard, playboy extraordinaire. And last week I let him... He had his fingers in my...

I press my hand to my stomach. "You knew?" A wave of humiliation and betrayal crashes over me, making my face flame. I back away from him, but he stops me by taking hold of my arm, his grip firm but not painful.

"I didn't," he says. "Not then."

Rigid in his hold, I shake my head. Even if he's telling the truth... "You came tonight though. Expecting what? To go even further? To have *sex*?"

Anna steps closer to me. "What's going on? Do you want me to have security come back?"

Based on the interaction only a moment ago, security knows exactly who he is, so I'm not sure that will be any help.

Tate's jaw clenches. "Let me explain, Violet."

Now I know why the prickly irritation that hit me last weekend felt so familiar. It's the same reaction I used to have when I visited Mark at college and had to spend time with his infuriating roommate—one of the few people who could get under my skin, and who seemed to enjoy it far too much. I cross my arms over my chest, eyes narrowed. "Go on, then. Explain."

CHAPTER ELEVEN

TATE

The anger and betrayal are practically rolling off her.

I quickly survey the crowded dance floor, noting the people still eyeing us after the disruption. The disruption *I* caused. My reaction to seeing that man's hands and mouth on her might have been a little over the top. It's far from my usual response when it comes to women. "Not here," I say to her. "Come to one of the private rooms."

She tugs her arm back, and I release my grip. Holding on to her right now isn't going to help.

"You think I'd go to a *sex* room with you?" she hisses, glaring at me through slitted blue eyes.

I can't help it. I almost smile at her outrage. She's recovering her equilibrium, and there's fire in her gaze now. The way my dick twitches probably makes me a little twisted. "Not for sex. So I can explain in private."

She lifts her chin and with those still-narrowed eyes, her expression is so familiar, I can't believe I didn't recognize her last week. This is the look she'd give me during her visits to Mark, when she couldn't help but argue with me. The one she'd hit me with just before a snarky comment would pop out of her mouth.

Before she can refuse, I casually shrug, knowing it will rile her up. "Of course, if you think you won't be able to control yourself alone with me..."

Her full lips press together. "Fine. But you only get fifteen minutes, and then Anna and I are out of here." She turns to her friend, who's watching in avid interest. "Right?"

"Right. Fifteen minutes," Anna replies, tapping the slim watch on her wrist. "I'll be timing you."

It's wrong, and it will only serve to piss her off more, but I can't help myself from leaning close and whispering in Violet's ear. "Are you giving me a time challenge? Because I'm *very* good at performing under those circumstances."

She snorts, turning her head just enough to meet my gaze from the corner of one narrowed blue eye. "I'm not surprised, considering all the *practice* you've had. Of course, that's with women who are actually attracted to you."

"You certainly seemed attracted to me last week."

The way her jaw drops before snapping shut again tells me the reminder probably wasn't welcome.

I take a step back. If I don't stop pushing my luck, I'll lose the opportunity to explain. With a deep breath, I rein myself in. "Come on," I say. Without thinking, I reach down and thread my fingers through hers.

I half expect her to jerk away, and I wouldn't blame her if she did.

But she doesn't.

She looks over at her friend. "Will you be okay?"

Anna nods. "I'll shake my booty for another fifteen minutes, then we're out of here. You can explain," her gaze flicks to me, then back to Violet, "*everything* on the drive home."

Not waiting for Violet to change her mind, I lead her off the dance floor, weaving through the writhing bodies. It's only when we reach the entrance to the back area that she hesitates. I stop and turn to her.

"I—uh," she stutters, focusing on anything other than my face. "I haven't been back here. Is there going to be... *stuff* happening?"

"You know what kind of club you're in, right? I can guarantee there's plenty of *stuff* happening."

She sucks in a breath, her big blue eyes meeting mine, then darting away again. "I'm not sure I want to see it."

Her uncertainty makes my chest pinch. This woman is such a fucking contradiction, going from fiery to vulnerable in the blink of an eye.

I step toward her, take her chin between my thumb and forefinger and tip her face up to mine. "These people are here enjoying themselves, just like you did last weekend."

She bites her bottom lip and looks away again. No doubt because I've reminded her of what we did together.

I use my thumb to gently tug her lip from between her teeth. "The guests here aren't ashamed of what they're doing, just like you shouldn't be ashamed of what we did." I study her, trying to read her expression under the mask. The anger she was exuding before has been temporarily muted, replaced by nervousness and embarrassment. "We're going to walk down these corridors. You can look or you can stay focused on me. It's completely up to you. Okay?"

After another brief hesitation, she nods. I'm still holding her hand, and when I start forward again, she comes with me, walking close by my side. Even though she doesn't particularly like me, she trusts me enough to do this, and that thought warms me in a way I don't want to examine too closely.

Unlike Violet, I'm familiar with this area, so I don't bother looking into the rooms we pass. I only care about finding privacy so that I can explain why I showed up tonight. Though considering I was determined not to, I'm not 100 percent sure I know the answer to that question myself. Except that when I was sitting at home in my penthouse, drinking whiskey and staring out at the lights of New York spread out beneath me, I couldn't get the vision of her here without me out of my head.

I imagined her searching for me, then eventually giving up and letting another man—or god fucking forbid, multiple men—touch her, give her pleasure, hear her gasps and feel her come apart for them.

Before I knew it, I was out of my seat and grabbing the mask I'd held on to from last week.

And yeah, that makes me an asshole, because despite what Violet might think, I don't intend to take any of those things for myself. I just don't want anyone else taking them either.

The sounds of moans saturate the hallways we walk down, interspersed with the occasional loud cry of pain or pleasure—or both. The distinctive sounds of slapping flesh, or the sharp crack of a paddle or cane, emanate from a few of the rooms we pass. People are gathered outside the rooms that haven't been screened for privacy, watching the activities. I can't help but glance over my shoulder at Violet, to see whether she's letting herself look. Sure enough, her eyes are wide and fixed on what's taking place behind the window we're passing—a fully dressed man pleasuring a naked woman with a magic wand while she's strapped down, helpless to do anything to resist him.

My hand tightens around Violet's as the image morphs in my head until it's her strapped down, and me wielding the toy, making her come over and over again until she begs me to fill her with my cock.

Lust hits me like a punch to the gut. With a deep breath, I force it down. That's not what I should be thinking about when it comes to Violet. And it's certainly not what she wants from me.

When she faces forward again, she ducks her chin, making it impossible for me to read her expression. And the mask she's wearing means I can't tell if her cheeks are flushed. If this situation were different, if I wasn't the man she can't stand, and she wasn't Mark's little sister, I'd press her up against the wall, slide my hand into her panties and check for myself whether what she'd witnessed had turned her on. If things were different, maybe I'd take her to another room and do exactly the same thing to her.

Except in that little fantasy, I wouldn't allow anyone to watch. No. I'd keep that experience all to myself. Not that it matters, because it'll never happen. I just have to convince my dick about that before Violet sees the bulge it's making in my pants.

With the turn of a corner, we approach the room I'm after. Compared to the others in the club, it's plain. That fact is why it's not used as often. I lead her in but don't close the door behind us. Not yet.

She takes several steps inside, her head turning as she examines the space. Her focus is quickly stolen by the enormous bed. The heavy wooden headboard and footboard are studded with metal bolts that can be used for tie points. But that's about it. It's probably Onyx's least kinky room, making it the most suitable for our conversation.

I flick the switch next to the long window facing the

corridor, rendering the smart glass opaque for privacy, then turn to Violet. "We'll need to close the door if we want to take our masks off." It's her choice. If she's more comfortable with the door left open, we'll keep our masks on. But I'd rather be face to face for this conversation. And this particular mask won't do me any favors when it comes to convincing her I'm innocent either.

Not that innocent is a word that's often used to describe me. But in this case, at least, it's true.

To my relief, Violet nods and turns to close the door herself. Once it clicks shut, I pull the mask off over my head. For a moment, she only examines me from across the room, but finally, she removes hers as well.

Her hair is tousled, and her cheeks are pink. Maybe because of the mask or maybe in response to what we just walked past. Or it could be due to this situation she's found herself in. Regardless, she looks as sexy as hell standing in front of me in her shimmery blue dress. Her chin is angled up to meet my gaze, exposing the smooth column of her throat and the deep V of her cleavage. I'm suddenly having trouble remembering why I shouldn't lay her down in the bed next to us and make her feel good all over again.

I'm reminded soon enough. She glances away, rakes her fingers through her hair, then crosses her arms, her butterfly mask dangling from her fingers. "Explain, please."

I toss my own mask onto the bed and rub a hand over the back of my neck. "I was here last week because I'm co-owner of this club. My business partner and I were talking at the bar when I saw you come in. And the honest to god truth is, I didn't know who you were then. Just like you didn't know who I was. It's been years since we've seen each other, and even before that, you only visited Mark a few times each year. It's hardly a surprise that with these masks on, in this place, neither of us recognized the other."

She tilts her head, silently assessing me.

"No matter what you think of me personally, Violet, I wouldn't lie about that."

She nods, almost reluctantly, but still doesn't speak.

"When Mark invited me to have lunch at your shop," I continue, "all I thought was that it would be good to see you again."

That has her brows arching up. "Why?"

"I don't know." I search for the words to explain my anticipation. "To see how you were doing? To see whether you still disliked me as much as you did back then? Believe it or not, I always enjoyed your visits."

Her arms drop to her sides. "We'd bicker the whole time I was there."

I take a step toward her. "And I liked it. It was refreshing."

"You mean it was a nice change from all the women throwing themselves at you?" She doesn't physically roll her eyes, but I hear it in her voice.

My lips quirk. "Something like that. Anyway, the take-away is that Mark invited me along, and I was curious enough to say yes. And then..." I step forward again. This time when I do, I'm close enough to touch her shoulder.

When my fingertips brush her bare skin, she inhales sharply.

Doing my best to ignore the way her pulse flutters at the base of her throat, I turn her just enough to reveal the tattoo on her back. "I saw this." Barely making contact, I trace the outline of the blue and black wings, the same way I did that first night.

Goose bumps erupt all over her skin in response to my

touch. I inhale deeply, flattening my hand so it covers the entire tattoo. Then I close my eyes and imagine sliding it down the length of her spine until I can fill my palm with the curve of her ass.

After one long heartbeat, I force myself to step back.

Violet turns to face me. Her cheeks are flushed again, her nipples pressing against the thin material of her dress. She might not like me much, but there's no disguising that her body likes my touch.

It's obvious she knows it too, when she quickly crosses her arms again and clears her throat. "And tonight? Why did you come back?"

This is the tricky part. "I wasn't going to. After I saw you at the coffee shop, I planned to leave well enough alone. But..." I decide on a half-truth. "I didn't like the idea of you waiting for someone who never showed up. I didn't want you to think that I didn't come because I didn't want to see you. So I came here to tell you the truth, and then I was going to leave."

For a second, her expression softens, but then her brow furrows. "But why did you chase off that other guy? Why tell him I was yours?"

Even now, I have to resist the urge to curl my fingers into fists at the memory of that douchebag touching her. It's a completely irrational response, considering who she is and who I am, but I can't help it. "I didn't want you doing something with him you'd regret, just because your feelings might have been hurt."

Her eyes widen for a moment before her delicate jaw clenches.

Clearly, that was the wrong thing to say.

"Let me get this straight. You only came tonight because you thought you needed to save me from myself? Because you assumed I'd be so devastated by your absence that I'd throw myself at the next man to come along, then end up regretting it because he wasn't you?"

I really shouldn't be turned on right now. But fuck, when she looks at me with those sparks flashing in her eyes, all I can imagine is pinning her to the bed and playing with her body until that fiery antagonism turns into a completely different but equally incendiary emotion.

I don't think she'll appreciate me mentioning that though. Not when she's still on a roll.

"I'm more than capable of making my own decisions, Tate. Just because you made me come once doesn't mean I would have fallen apart if I hadn't seen you again. Not to mention, you gave me a *year's* membership. Did you think I wouldn't use it to enjoy other men once you were inevitably done with me?"

Whether she means it or is reacting out of anger, the thought makes my blood pressure spike. Teeth gritted, I pin her with my gaze. "That was before I knew who you were."

She lets out a cute little growl. "So once you discovered who I was, you regretted what happened between us, and now you feel guilty. But if you still thought I was a stranger, then you probably would have come here tonight and screwed me, then walked away, like you do with every woman. Would you even have cared what I did, or who I did it with, after that?"

The answer should be no. I've never cared who—or what—my sexual partners do before or after me. I expect the same courtesy from them. What Violet doesn't know is that her very presence here now is unusual. I don't invite women back because I haven't had enough of them. I don't pay for memberships so I can see them again. Since finding out who she is, I've been racking my brain and picking apart every detail of our interaction. Did some deep, subconscious part of me recognize her that first night? Was that why I couldn't keep my eyes off her from the minute she walked into Onyx? Why I needed to be the one who took care of her?

I can't tell her what I would have done after, because I don't fucking know.

She takes my silence as agreement. "Oh my god. You are so egotistical. You came here to rescue me because you thought I'd be so heartbroken if you didn't show that I'd lose all ability to reason and allow myself to get taken advantage of." She steps forward and pokes me in the chest. "I'll have you know, Tate King, I'm a grown woman, and I can, and will, sleep with whoever I want, wherever I want, *whenever* I want. Your friendship with my brother doesn't come with the obligation of protecting me, and it doesn't give you any say in the matter." She shakes her head. "I think we're done here."

Before I can formulate a response, she pulls her mask over her face, whips around and stomps from the room—quite a feat in the heels she's wearing. I don my mask as well before following her out. I don't care what she says. I won't let her wander around back here by herself. Not that she's in any danger. Reid designed this place with safety in mind, but I don't want her being propositioned in the corridor by a random man.

And I don't want her to do something stupid just to prove a point.

I walk far enough behind her to let her feel like she's making a dramatic exit, but close enough to intervene if necessary. She walks briskly down the corridor, briefly glancing into each room as she passes. At one in particular, her steps slow. She doesn't stop completely, but she definitely shows more interest there than she has the others. Then she shoots a look over her shoulder, sees me and hauls ass again.

I don't bother hiding my grin. And when I draw even with the window she was so interested in, I can't help but take a moment to check out what caught her attention.

A woman, skin sheened with sweat, is flat on her back on a bench, arms and legs tied, leaving her helpless to move. A man kneels between her spread thighs while she tosses her head, her eyes scrunched closed.

Does Violet like the idea of being held down? Made helpless and forced to endure more pleasure than she thinks she can take?

Fuck.

When I find her again, my gaze lingers on the sway of her hips. I shouldn't be thinking about that. I shouldn't stare at her ass and remember the way it filled my hands. I shouldn't imagine having her at my mercy and fucking all that fire out of her until she's warm and limp and pliant underneath me.

And what I definitely shouldn't do is catch her arm just before she and her friend walk off the dance floor to leave—or slide my hand around the nape of her neck. But I do it anyway. Then I lean in close and lower my voice so only she can hear me. "If I'd known it was you last weekend, I would never have touched you. But if you think for one second that I regret experiencing the way you came all over my fingers, then you're mistaken."

Her lips part on a gasp, and her pupils flare in response to my words. I'm so damn tempted to say fuck it, forget the fact that she's Mark's sister, and kiss her, prove to her she doesn't dislike me quite as much as she likes to think she does. That she never has. But I restrain myself. I've been irresponsible too often in the past, and I'm determined to do things differently. Knowingly kissing my friend's—and lawyer's—little sister in the middle of a sex club is the definition of irresponsible.

I may have made her come a week ago, but kissing her like this wouldn't be about anonymous sex. It would be something else—something more. And that's one thing I never let myself do.

So instead, I allow myself a single brush of my thumb along her jaw.

Then I let her go.

CHAPTER TWELVE

TATE

First thing Monday morning, I saunter into Roman's office and throw myself onto the leather couch next to Cole. Stretching my legs out and lacing my hands together over my stomach, I arch my brows and look from him to Roman, who's sitting across the coffee table from us with an expression even more severe than usual on his face.

"What's the emergency?" I ask.

The second I stepped foot in the office this morning, my PA, Sophie, informed me that Roman needed to see me immediately.

He leans forward, his elbows on his knees. "Something's happened." From the frown on his face, it's not a positive something.

With a groan, I tip my head back. "Why does it feel like we're always putting out fires around here?"

"Because people keep starting them," Roman snaps.

His tone has me straightening and side-eyeing my other brother, who's also looking a little too serious for my liking. "What's going on?"

Roman rubs his forehead, then glances at Cole. "You tell him."

Cole presses a button on the laptop sitting on the table in front of him and angles the screen toward me so I can read it.

I frown down at the headline, which screams out at me.

Royal Flirt? King Caught Cozying Up to UK Envoy's Queen!

Beneath it is a photo of me with a familiar red-haired woman. Serena Worthington, former supermodel and current wife of the British ambassador to the US. She's also a woman I fucked once. It was years ago, long before she met her husband, and I haven't touched her since. Not that anyone could tell that from the photo. No, in the image, Serena appears to be pressed up against me, her hand on my arm. Our faces are turned toward each other, only inches apart. It would be easy to assume that we were moments away from kissing.

"What the fuck?" I growl.

"Please tell me it's not what it looks like," Cole says, his voice tight. "Because you realize the ambassador's brother sits on London's Planning and Development Committee, right? Piss him off, and our upcoming London developments could be faced with any number of unnecessary delays."

Ignoring the tension that knots my back at his lack of faith in me, I shake my head. "It's not what it looks like."

"Then what the fuck is it?" Roman asks.

I scrub my hand over my face. "This was at the British art exhibition at the MET the other week. The one you insisted I attend. We were just talking. She told me she had information on one of the European real estate conglomerates looking to sell off some of its holdings.

When I asked her for details, she said she'd prefer no one know she gave me the information. Then she leaned in and whispered it in my ear. It was completely fucking innocent."

"That's not how it looks." Frustration colors Roman's tone. "Especially given your reputation."

I narrow my eyes, the tension transforming into aggravation. "My reputation? You mean the one everyone keeps throwing in my face, even though I've spent day after day proving that's not who I am anymore?"

"It's not?" he asks. "Then you wouldn't mind telling us where you disappeared to two weekends ago when you should have been at the gala, would you?" His gaze pierces into me.

I take a deep breath in through my nose and focus on keeping my composure. "I got bored and left. I've gone to every single event you've pointed me at over the last few months, so excuse me for wanting to have an early night for once."

"And you're telling me that night didn't end with you balls deep in a woman?"

I temper the shit-eating grin threatening to spread across my face, so he doesn't get suspicious. "Hand on my heart, I didn't fuck anyone that night."

He scrutinizes me, brows pulled low, but I don't let my eye contact waver. I'm not lying, though he doesn't need to know the details about what I *was* doing. And it's not like what happened with Violet was my plan when I left the gala.

He lets out a harsh breath and pinches the bridge of his nose. "I'm sorry. I know you've been stepping up and taking the hits when it comes to these events. But unfortunately, it takes more than a few months of being discreet to repair a reputation you've spent years cultivating. The tabloids don't forget that easily."

Now I do feel a little bad. This is the first time he's apologized to me in years. Hell, the last time he did was probably when we were kids. And the worst part is that he's right. This is my fault. I've spent too many years caught up in my own issues to give a damn what was reported about me. Now it's coming back to bite me in the ass.

"We'll get them to post a retraction tomorrow," I say. "I'm sure she'll be refuting the claims as well."

But Roman shakes his head. "The lawyers are already on it. But I'm not convinced that's going to be enough. We can respond, and so can she, but the tabloids are going to keep going after you, because they see you as an easy target—you're the King Group's wild card. But we can't afford to keep *putting out fires*. Especially after what happened with Dad."

Frustration rips through me. "There's nothing I can do about what they decide to print."

"I think there is."

With every one of my brother's words, my dread deepens. "What are you suggesting?"

"You need a buffer."

I raise my brows and wait for him to clarify.

"A girlfriend," he states. "You need to find yourself a girlfriend."

I bark out a laugh. He can't be serious. After what happened with Cole, I would have thought he'd learned his lesson. "Thanks, but I'll pass. Your matchmaking services haven't exactly received rave reviews."

His jaw tightens, and what looks like regret flashes across his face. He doesn't back down though. "This isn't matchmaking; this is damage control. You're chief of marketing. You should know how these stories can keep snowballing. We can't afford to lose investor confidence again."

"And as chief of marketing, I can come up with another way to handle things if needed. But a fake girlfriend? Come on, you can't really think that's necessary."

"Normally, I wouldn't agree with Roman," Cole speaks up.

I scowl at him. *Traitor*.

The corners of his lips quirk up, as if he can read my mind. "This could be a good solution, Tate. The King Group really doesn't need more scandal so soon after Dad's conviction. Even fake scandals. If the tabloids see you with one woman on your arm for a few months, hopefully they'll get bored and focus their attention elsewhere. After you break up, you'll have proven you're no longer New York's biggest playboy. And it's not like you have to actually do anything with whoever she is other than go out together in public and pretend to only have eyes for her."

Dammit. He has a point. A girlfriend is the last thing I want or need. But apart from my mistake with Violet, I've been doing my best not to fuck around anyway. Would it really hurt to act the part of a taken man for a few months? Not only could it help me prove I'm just as serious about the King Group as my brothers, but it could help me to finally shed my reputation. With our current focus on Genesis-1, the last thing the King Group needs is made-up reports about my antics overshadowing one of our most significant projects.

Roman clears his throat. "I'm not going to force you," he says, his gaze flicking to Cole for a split-second before returning to me, "but if we can find a woman who'll be on board with this plan, then no one will get hurt, and it will hopefully get the tabloids off your back. Once everything has died down, you and the woman you choose to do this with can go your separate ways."

"Right," I say, but I've stopped listening, because one detail of my previous train of thought has gotten stuck in my head.

"What are we thinking?" Cole scoots to the edge of his chair. "A professional actress?"

Roman roughs a hand down his face. "That will look too obviously staged, though a model might do. Whoever she is, she'll need to be content to take the money and attention that will come along with it and sign an NDA to keep quiet about the arrangement."

My brothers continue hashing things out, but I'm too busy turning an idea over in my head to contribute. An idea I should have dismissed the instant it materialized. But I can't. Because, according to Mark, *Violet* needs money for True Brew. And she doesn't like me at all, even less so now than before, so there's no risk of her becoming emotionally attached. I could sell this to her as the business arrangement it is. A scenario where I can side-step any number of potential future scandals, and she gets the financial boost her coffee shop needs. All she has to do is pretend to be crazy about me for a few months. That thought has my lips curving up. The idea of watching her try to do that appeals in a way it probably shouldn't.

"We'll get our legal team to draw up a contract," Cole's saying. "Ensure the terms are clear so there aren't any misunderstandings."

"Yeah," I murmur absently, my mind still on the logistics of getting Violet to agree to this arrangement.

"Do you have someone in mind?" Cole asks, squinting at my obvious preoccupation.

I focus my attention back on him. "Maybe."

"Great." Roman stands from behind his desk and buttons his jacket. "I've got a meeting with the lawyers in ten minutes to discuss getting the article retracted." He zeroes in on me. "Whoever you're thinking of, lock her down and get her details to the legal team as soon as possible."

I nod, another thought occurring to me. If Violet agrees to this—and it's a big if—there's no way to avoid Mark finding out. He's a member of our legal team, after all. He admits it himself—he's overprotective of his sister. So there's a chance he'll be adamantly against the proposal. But I'll cross that bridge when I come to it. First, I need to get her to agree to this plan.

And I don't think it'll be easy.

CHAPTER THIRTEEN

VIOLET

"Argh." I'd be tempted to kick the stupid espresso machine if it wouldn't hurt my foot, and if it wasn't sitting on the countertop, meaning I'd likely fall on my ass if I tried it.

Jarrod steps up next to me and crosses his arms. "I don't know how much longer I can keep her going."

I put my hands on my hips and let out a sigh. "I know. I'll check the books again tonight. See where I can find some money." A commercial espresso machine costs thousands of dollars. But maybe I can find a second-hand one for slightly less.

"I can put something toward it. I have some savings," he says.

I drag a tired but genuine smile onto my face. "Thank you, Jarrod. That's sweet of you. But I'll figure it out." The last thing I want is him risking his money on what might very well be a sinking ship. Though just the thought of that being the case makes my chest hollow.

He opens his mouth, as if he's going to protest, but the bell over the door rings, signaling we have a customer.

"If you get that, I'll try and keep her going a little longer," he says.

I pat his forearm. "What would I do without you?"

He winks, and I give him a smile, then turn to the person who's just come in. My smile drops, along with my mood, as I register who the *customer* is.

The grin Tate is wearing only spreads—I'm assuming in recognition of my dismay. As he saunters toward me, his body encased in an impeccably tailored business suit, his eyes glittering, it's almost impossible to ignore how sexy he is. Annoyingly, I have to admit that a look like that from Tate King would make most women weak in the knees. Considering what I know of him, and what he now knows about me, my own knees stay strong.

Mostly.

With a brush of my hands down my denim-clad thighs, I meet him at the counter. "Tate."

His smile grows even wider at my terse tone. As if he actually likes it. It's annoying. *He's* annoying. "Violet."

I look over my shoulder at Jarrod, then turn back to Tate and lower my voice. "I wasn't expecting to see you." The *again* is implied.

He leans casually against the countertop, assessing the empty coffee shop a little too knowingly. "Busy day?"

I grit my teeth and will away the irritation that sparks to life in my chest at that simple sentence. "It will pick up soon."

"Until it does, do you have time for a cup of coffee?"

I frown. "With you?"

"Yes, with me." He chuckles. "We need to talk."

I huff out a breath and cross my arms. "I can't imagine we have anything to talk about."

"That's where you're wrong. We have a lot to talk about."

If he thinks I have any interest in rehashing the events of last Friday night—or the one before—especially here, he's very wrong. "I don't think—"

"Violet." His voice is low, and those unfairly gorgeous golden-brown eyes of his pierce into me, sending a jolt of adrenaline through my veins. "Stop arguing and just spare me a few minutes of your time."

I swallow. For a moment, I'm transported back to that first night at Onyx. To the way he looked at me when he told me he'd make me come so hard I'd feel it for days. The horrible part is that I did. I *still* do. The memory of how good he made me feel with just his fingers has haunted me since that night. Even more so after I found out he was the man in the devil mask. I hate knowing that before I found out who he was, I got myself off to the memory of him touching me. I hate even more that I've had to force myself not to fantasize about it again in the days since.

My skin warms, and I hope to God he can't tell where my thoughts have gone. But apparently, my curiosity as to what Tate could possibly want to talk to me about is stronger than my embarrassment. I let out a breath and turn to Jarrod, finding him already watching us, a quizzical look in his eyes. "Could you coax two cups of coffee out of the machine and bring them over to us?"

He gives me a smile. "Sure thing, boss."

When I turn back to Tate, he's focused on Jarrod. I can't quite read his expression, but a moment later, his attention is on me again. He gestures toward the back of the shop, and I round the counter and follow him to a table in the corner.

When we get there, he surprises me by pulling my chair out for me. I slip into the seat, stumbling over my thanks, and his mouth tilts up in amusement as he slides into the seat opposite.

"Why are you here?" I ask. I'd rather not drag this out any longer than I have to.

Rather than answer straight away, he merely leans back in his chair and extends his long legs out under the table. I move my own out of the way when he brushes against them.

"I have a proposition for you," he says.

My brows scrunch up, as well as my nose. "What kind of proposition?"

"One which will be mutually beneficial for both of us."

Considering how different our worlds are—how different *we* are—it's hard to believe any type of proposition could benefit us both. Even so, he's piqued my curiosity. "Okay, what is it, then?"

Instead of spilling the details, he falls quiet and watches over my shoulder. A moment later, Jarrod appears carrying two cups of coffee. He places them in front of us, and after we thank him, he gives me a smile, nods at Tate, and heads back to the counter.

Only once he's out of hearing range does Tate speak. "I need your help with a problem. And in return, I can help you with this shop."

I flinch. Is it that obvious that I'm struggling? "Why do you think I need your help?"

His brows rise, and he glances around, drawing attention to the emptiness in place of what should be the bustle of customers. "Don't you?"

"It's just a bit slow right now."

"I've been in twice now, and it's been slow both times."

I shift in my seat and wrap my hands tightly around my mug. "I'm working on getting things back on track."

"And I can help you do that far more quickly and efficiently than if you keep trying on your own."

I look away from Tate's too-perceptive gaze. "I don't need a handout."

"It's not a handout. It's a business arrangement."

I shouldn't listen to him. I should tell him to enjoy his coffee and then go out the back and move some money around so I can buy a new espresso machine. Except I'm terrified that there isn't any money *to* move. Our contract with Jose isn't cheap, and I've only recently been able to start serving the coffee he used to supply us with again—the quality coffee that Dad built this place around. Not only am I banking on bringing people back in with it, but if I have to cancel the contract, Jose won't give me another chance. It wouldn't be fair to expect him to.

Other than the contract with him, the shop's budget has no wiggle room. Cutting costs anywhere else is impossible. A business arrangement with Tate has to be better than admitting defeat and either risking a loan or losing the place altogether.

"Okay. What's the arrangement?"

A hint of a smirk curls his mouth. "I need you to pretend to be in a relationship with me."

I raise a brow and wait for him to laugh and tell me what he really wants.

But he merely takes a sip of his coffee, his full attention locked on me. Finally, I realize he's not going to laugh. "You can't be serious."

"I'm absolutely serious. I want you to pretend to be my girlfriend for a few months." His smirk broadens. "Bear in mind, you're the first woman I've ever asked to date me, so don't break my heart by saying no, butterfly."

He's joking. He has to be. Because what he's asking

makes no sense. But still, the way he says *butterfly* in the same low tone as that first night at Onyx has my stomach involuntarily flipping.

If I were smart, I'd get up and walk away. Instead, I ask the single question gnawing at me. "Why on earth would *you* need a fake girlfriend?"

He rubs his hand over his chin. "There are some things being printed about me in the tabloids that have the potential to be detrimental to the King Group."

Why does that not surprise me? This is Tate I'm dealing with, after all. I should have known it would be something like that.

"Don't tell me you screwed someone you shouldn't have." My mind flashes back to the first time I met him. "Or two someones."

Surprisingly, the near constant amusement in his gaze fades. "Not two someones. Not even one someone. These are photos being taken out of context. Unfortunately, the tabloids are relentless, and we need to start managing the narrative before it begins to negatively affect the company."

My brain ticks over. "And you think a fake girlfriend will somehow convince the world you're now responsible and committed?"

He nods, eyes still fixed on me. It's disconcerting, but then I've always found being the focus of Tate's attention a little too disconcerting for my liking. "Why me? There must be any number of women who would be more than interested in dating you."

"Because I don't need a real girlfriend. I need a fake girlfriend. A woman I already have a connection with so that it won't appear to come out of the blue. A woman for whom this will be a simple business transaction." He arches one brow, his amusement returning. "Maybe a woman who doesn't even like me, who won't catch feelings."

I scrunch up my nose. "Because you're such an amazing guy that any woman would fall for you if they spend more than one night by your side?"

He laughs, completely unfazed by my tone. "Something like that."

That I'm still sitting here has me questioning my sanity. Pretending to date Tate is a terrible idea. But I can see the logic. Kind of. "So how long do you think it will take to *manage the narrative*?"

He shrugs. "It's hard to say. A couple of months. Maybe more. We could add a term extension into the contract if needed."

A contract. Right. And I've yet to discover what the other side of this arrangement would entail. "Explain to me what I would get for pretending to be certifiably insane for two or more months."

His mouth twitches like he's fighting a smile. "Insane?"

"How else would you describe someone who would actually fall for your..." I wave my finger in his direction.

"Charm? Good looks? Sexual prowess?" he offers.

I cock my head and give him a sweet smile. "Huge ego."

He tips his head back and laughs, and it's impossible to stop myself from staring at the strong column of his throat. Memories of pressing my lips there as I writhed on his lap force their way into my head. I squeeze my eyes shut and will them away. Still, my cheeks burn, and arousal coils low in my belly. When I focus on Tate again, he's no longer laughing. His gaze is hot and intent and fixed entirely on me.

How red is my face right now? Does he know why?

"For pretending like you can't get enough of my huge...

ego." His smirk returns, and I roll my eyes. "I'll give you fifty thousand dollars."

My heart stalls, then shoots into overdrive. Before I can open my mouth to respond, his next words shut me up completely.

"Per month."

I sag back in my chair, my racing pulse making me light-headed. One hundred thousand dollars minimum. More if the fake relationship continues for longer than two months. That would be life changing. I could invest it all back into True Brew. Buy new equipment, hire additional staff, get the place back to the way it should be.

It seems too good to be true.

A niggling suspicion makes me sit upright again. I grip my fingers together. "Mark isn't behind this, is he?" I know he'd like to help, but regardless of how well the King Group pays him, I refuse to drain his savings in the event that I can't make this work.

The corners of Tate's eyes crinkle, as if he's suppressing a smile. "If you think he would willingly suggest you date me, fake or not, you don't know your brother very well."

A laugh reluctantly breaks free. "You're right. I don't know what I was thinking."

"You know he warned me away from you before we even met?"

"He did?"

"Sat me down and gave me a very serious talking-to about how his baby sister was off-limits."

Warmth spreads through me, and I can't help but smile. "That sounds like him." Which begs the question. "How do you think he'll respond to this arrangement?"

Tate leans forward, scanning my face. "Does that mean you're agreeing to it?"

"I..." Glancing around the quiet coffee shop, I remember how it looked a few short years ago when Dad was still with us. Back when it buzzed with energy and was filled with the chatter of happy customers. I look back at Tate. "I have stipulations."

The wolfish grin that spreads across his face has nervous butterflies taking flight in my stomach.

What am I getting myself into?

CHAPTER FOURTEEN

TATE

After my surprisingly successful meeting with Violet, I head back to the office. Now that she's agreed to go along with this plan, I need to talk to Mark. Initially, she wanted to be the one to inform her brother about the arrangement, but I convinced her to let me speak to him. Considering how she feels about me, I'm not confident she'd have done a good job of selling him on the idea.

Though Mark isn't likely to take it very well coming from me either, even if the relationship will be completely fake. I wasn't kidding when I told her he'd warned me away from her before we'd even met. Not that I would have considered messing around with a friend's sister, especially when I had a whole college of women to have fun with back then. But Mark wasn't taking any chances, and I respect that.

I'm not prone to procrastination, especially when it comes to unpleasant situations, so when I make it back to the King Group, I head straight up to the legal floor and make my way to Mark's office.

He's on the phone when I get there, but when I step inside, he wraps up the conversation.

After hanging up, he leans back in his chair with a grin. "Two visits in two weeks. What did I do to get so lucky?"

He won't feel quite so lucky in a moment. I pull up a chair opposite his desk. "I need you to write up a contract for me."

With a nod, he sits up again, picks up a pen and makes a note on a pad. "Okay. What's this contract for?"

"A relationship."

He looks up from his pad with his eyebrows raised. "A relationship? Like an NDA? Since when did you start dating?"

"I didn't. This is for PR purposes only."

"Is this in response to that photo of you with Serena Worthington? Your brother met with general counsel about it this morning."

"That and all the other crap that gets printed about me."

His grin is a little too broad. "I have to say, I never thought you'd go the fake girlfriend route."

I snort. "Neither did I. I guess Roman's more convincing than I gave him credit for."

"Well," he drawls, obviously enjoying this. "I can't wait to see how you do with that." He looks back down at his pad. "Okay, what are you thinking for terms?"

I run through what I've already discussed with Violet, and he jots the details down on his notepad, making suggestions of his own here and there. A crease forms between his brows when I tell him the payment amount, but he doesn't comment.

"Okay," he finally says. "I'll get this drafted and back to you for review. Once you're happy with it and you've found the woman, we can finalize it."

I clear my throat and sit a little straighter. "I already know who it's going to be."

Surprise flashes across his face, and he picks up his pen again. "You work quick. So, who's the lucky lady?"

"Violet."

He scratches the name onto his pad. "Last name?"

I almost laugh. He didn't even blink. He's that sure I wouldn't be talking about his sister. "Sinclair."

His head snaps up. "What?"

"Your sister."

He drops his pen on his desk. "No."

I lean forward, keeping my eyes fixed on his. "Why not? This is strictly business, and you already know it'll benefit her significantly."

"Because she's my sister, Tate. And you're... you."

I school my expression so he can't see the way his words hit. "And she's a grown woman making a smart business decision. I have no intention of screwing her over, regardless of what you apparently think of me."

Mark winces. "That's not what I meant. I know you won't deliberately hurt her. But you know how charming you are. Women can't resist you. And you can't even turn it off. It's just who you are. What if she falls for you? It's been like a year since she dated anyone, and I get the feeling her last relationship didn't end that well." He frowns for a moment, then shakes his head and continues. "Getting swept up in the excitement and glamour of dating Tate King might be too much for her."

I can't help but smirk. "I think you underestimate your sister and just how *not* charming she finds me."

Mark's frown doesn't let up. "What about all the publicity? She's not used to that kind of scrutiny. She could be put in uncomfortable situations."

I don't particularly like that possibility either. "I understand your concerns, and I'll do everything possible to make sure the media don't go overboard. We'll keep the relationship low-key. My hope is that it looks as though this is an ongoing secret romance that has just come to light. A relationship I want to protect from the press."

"Will you be able to play that? How long has it been since you've been with a woman? You have to know that if someone else comes forward and says she was with you after this relationship supposedly began, it would hurt Violet."

I resist the urge to say that the last woman I was physical with was Violet. He definitely doesn't need to know that little fact. And I understand his worries, even if they grate on me. "I haven't been with another woman in months. Whether anyone else is willing to acknowledge it or not, I've been working to adjust my image for a while now." I smooth down my tie. "I'll do everything in my power to make sure Violet doesn't get hurt, and I'll compensate her well for her time and effort. I've spoken to her, and she's on board with all of this. And with all due respect, Mark," I lean forward and pin him with the full weight of my stare, "I'm going through this with you out of courtesy and because you're my friend. But the final decision is up to your sister. The reason I want you to write the contract is because I know you'll have her best interests at heart and will make sure it's fair to her. But if you don't want to handle it, I'll have one of our other lawyers do it."

He narrows his eyes, and for a long, drawn-out moment, tension hangs heavy in the air between us. I'm probably an idiot for forcing the issue with one of my very few real friends. But out of the many people I associate with, I trust hardly any of them with more than the surface of me. Mark's one of those I do.

Finally, he looks away and picks up his pen again. When he meets my gaze, his eyes shine with concern. "You're right. I should have more faith in you. And Violet's a grown woman. She can make this decision herself. But I worry about her. She went quiet on me after Dad, and it's only since she's been back in New York running the coffee shop that she's seemed more like herself. I don't want anything to jeopardize that." He sighs. "Just... take care of her, okay? That's all I'm asking for."

I nod. He's not exactly enthusiastic, but at least he's on board.

"One last thing," Mark says. "What's the exit strategy?"

"Exit strategy?" And then it hits me. How will we get out of this relationship when the time comes? It will have to be in a way that doesn't invite more scandal and won't make either of us look like the villain. Particularly Violet. I tip my head back and mentally run through scenarios. "We can say that we've known each other for years, and that after reconnecting and spending time together, we've decided that we're better off as just friends. We can be seen together amicably a few times after the split is official, to make it clear there's no blame on either side. Then that will be it. Done. Violet goes her own way, and I go mine."

"That sounds believable." Mark rubs his chin, brow furrowed, then nods sharply. "Okay, let me get this drafted. I'll call Violet, make sure I cover all of her concerns, and send it up to you when I'm done."

I stand and straighten my jacket. "Include whatever she needs in the contract. Her comfort is the priority. I'll work around her."

He studies me, hands clasped on the desk in front of

him. "She'll need to be able to tell her best friend, Anna. It's not fair to ask her to lie, and she might need the support."

I consider it for only a second. "Include it in the NDA."

Mark's shoulders relax almost imperceptibly, as if I've passed some kind of test. "Okay."

Just before I walk out the door, he calls out to me. "Look after her, Tate. She's the only family I have left."

All I can do is nod. And as I head back to the elevators, I reassure myself that all the reasons I have for making Violet my co-conspirator in this are logical and have nothing to do with the memory of her lips pressed against my neck as she came on my fingers.

CHAPTER FIFTEEN

VIOLET

Mark slides the contract to me over the highly polished wooden table.

As I take a sip of the water that an assistant brought for me, the ice clinks against the glass in response to the slight tremble of my hand. Since agreeing to Tate's proposition in principle, the process has moved quickly. Two days ago, I received a tense phone call from my brother, where he laid out his concerns, and I reassured him that I knew what I was doing. This morning, I was summoned to King Plaza, the King Group's headquarters building in Manhattan.

The high-rise is intimidating, from its marble-floored foyer to the impressively silent and swift elevator that carried me to the fifty-third floor to this huge conference room with an incredible view of New York City. I've never visited Mark at work before. I've never had a reason. Or particularly wanted to. Not knowing he worked for his annoyingly arrogant college roommate. It's kind of ironic. Or maybe that's not the right use of the word. Honestly, who knows?

I rein in my scattered thoughts and force myself to focus on the contract in front of me.

"Take your time," Mark says. "I'm here to answer any questions you might have."

I glance around the big empty room. "Shouldn't Tate be here?"

The moment the words leave my mouth, I wish I could take them back. Of course he doesn't need to be here for this. And it doesn't matter to me whether he is or not. Soon, I'll have to see far more of him than I ever planned—or wanted. It's not like having him here would be reassuring anyway. Mark is with me, and he's all the support I need. And yet, there's a heaviness in my chest that seems to be more than just nerves.

Mark checks his watch. "He's in a shareholder meeting with his brothers. He said he'd try to make it."

With a nod, I focus back on the contract and start reading through it. I'm unfamiliar with some of the legal terminology, but a few things jump out at me:

The term of this Agreement will continue for a period of no less than two months, with a potential extension period of up to six months, in accordance with the provisions outlined in Section 23...

In consideration of the services rendered under this Agreement, the Second Party shall receive a sum of fifty-thousand dollars per month, payable at the end of each month directly to the designated account...

Both parties acknowledge the highly confidential nature of this arrangement...

The Second Party agrees to accompany the First Party to a minimum of three public events per month, which may include a combination of scheduled and spontaneous appearances...

Both parties shall refrain from entering into any romantic relationships outside the scope of this Agreement...

While the nature of this Agreement implies a romantic relationship in the public eye, both parties acknowledge that their interactions are purely for appearance and hold no real romantic intent. There will be no physical intimacy between the two parties...

Any changes to the terms of this Agreement must be mutually agreed upon in writing by both parties. No verbal modifications will be considered valid until—

Wait.

I scan a few lines up, then look at Mark. "No physical intimacy? Did Tate ask you to include that?"

He shifts in his chair, his jaw tight. "I added that in on your behalf. Tate said to include anything that would make you feel more comfortable."

I give my head a little shake. In theory, I don't mind there being a limiting clause, since the last thing either of us wants is to... expand on what we've already mistakenly done, but I assumed we would have to act like a real couple in public, at least to some extent.

"If Tate and I are going to convince the world that we're

in a relationship, don't you think we might need to, I don't know, kiss in public at some stage?"

Mark rocks forward in his chair. "You've never been Tate's biggest fan, so I didn't want you to feel like you owed him anything more than your presence at his side."

"For fifty thousand a month, I should do more than just show up. I might not be his biggest fan, but he's paying me for a service, and the least I can do is make it believable."

Mark presses his lips together, then huffs out a breath. "You want me to change it?"

Halfway through his question, the door swings open and Tate walks in, followed by two dark-haired men just as tall as he is.

"What are we changing?" he asks, his gaze sweeping over me with an intensity that dries my throat.

I cringe inside. Talk about timing. Why did he have to walk in just as we were discussing the physical intimacy clause? Mark regards me, brows raised in question.

With a sigh, I nod.

Dragging the contract back across the table, he addresses Tate. "Violet wants me to add in kissing."

My mouth drops open at the same speed my stomach plummets. Why the hell did he say it like *that*?

An irritatingly smug grin grows on Tate's handsome face. "She does, does she?"

A wave of heat creeps up from my chest to my face. "I just thought it would be unrealistic otherwise. If we're supposed to be dating, wouldn't we have to maybe... I don't know, sell it or, you know...act like we're..."

The more flustered I get, the wider Tate's smile grows.

I grind to a halt and narrow my eyes at him. "But on second thought, maybe we should leave in the no phys—"

"No, no." He holds up both hands. "I think changing it

is an excellent idea. In fact, maybe we should specify exactly how many kisses we should—"

"I don't believe that's necessary," Mark cuts in with a pointed look at Tate. "I'll include a phrase along the lines of including the minimum amount of physical intimacy required to establish the nature of the relationship. And that it will be at Violet's discretion."

Tate chuckles, his gaze meeting mine. The devilish curve to his lips sends a little shockwave through me, and instantly, my mind goes in a direction it shouldn't. To memories of exactly how those lips felt against my breasts, how they might feel against other parts of my body. I quickly shake that thought away. I'm sure there are plenty of women out there who could tell me exactly how they feel. Just like any other man's, I imagine.

His fingers didn't feel like any other man's...

God, why can't I stop thinking about that night?

Luckily, I'm distracted from that train of thought when one of the dark-haired men behind Tate steps forward. He leans across the table and extends his hand. "Cole King. Nice to meet you, Violet." Ah. I'd assumed they were more lawyers, but these must be Tate's brothers.

I stand and slip my hand into his. "It's very nice to meet you too."

The second man holds his hand out next. "Roman King."

I take them all in as they stand side by side across from me. While Cole and Roman both have dark hair and light eyes, Tate is blond, with golden eyes. They're both as good looking as Tate but seem far more reserved. It's hard to see the family resemblance between them.

All three men take a seat at the table. "We appreciate you doing this, Violet," Cole says.

"I appreciate the compensation you're giving me to do it."

A smile quirks the corners of his mouth, but Roman's serious demeanor doesn't crack. His icy gray eyes assess me, though it's impossible to tell whether he approves or whether I've come up wanting.

As we run through the rest of the contract, Mark and sometimes Tate or one of his brothers answer my questions. I fight the self-consciousness that creeps in. With the three imposing King brothers sitting on the other side of the table, all focused on me, the scrutiny is overwhelming. Apart from the intimacy clause, the agreement doesn't need many changes. To my relief, they've even included a section that gives me permission to talk to Anna about this whole situation. Thank god, because I may have already spilled the beans to her.

What eases my nerves the most is that Mark put the contract together. There's no way he'd screw me over, even if he does work for the King Group.

A question hits me then. Did Tate have Mark handle this to give me that extra layer of reassurance?

I glance up at him, only to find his eyes already on me. He looks far more serious than I think I've ever seen him—at least, without a mask on. A spark of awareness crackles through me, and I quickly look back at Mark, who's gathering up the pages of the contract.

"Give me a minute to make the changes, and we can get this signed," he says as he stands. With a smile to me and a nod at the other men, he disappears out the door.

Cole and Roman stand too. "It was nice to meet you, Violet," Roman says. "I'm sure we'll be seeing more of you in the future."

I smile a little stiffly at the reminder.

As Roman strides out of the room, Cole leans down and murmurs in Tate's ear. Tate's eyes find mine, and he shakes his head, though a small smile plays at the corners of his mouth. Cole straightens and claps Tate on the back, then tips his head at me one last time before the door closes behind him.

And suddenly Tate and I are alone.

"Are you ready for this?" he asks, his voice pitched low. "The moment you sign that contract, you become my girlfriend."

A single, rogue butterfly takes flight in my stomach. "Your *fake* girlfriend."

He lowers his chin in acknowledgment, but that smile returns. "How are your acting skills?"

"Isn't it a bit late to ask that question?"

"Probably." He leans back in his chair. "Let's hope you can pull off kissing me, then, since you were the one who insisted on having it in the contract."

Too-familiar irritation flashes through me. Ugh, why does he have to be so smug. "I think I can feign being into you for a few seconds at a time."

"Is that so?"

The way one of his brows arches has me pulling my shoulders back and raising my chin. "Yes."

He stands suddenly and rounds the desk. I turn in my chair and follow his movement, a sudden flurry of nerves taking over from the one rogue butterfly. What is he doing?

He stops a foot in front of me. "Care to put that claim to the test?"

My heart thunders as I stare up at him. "What do you mean?"

He reaches down and grasps my hand, then tugs me to my feet. "Maybe you should prove you're up to the job before we sign. It would be the smart thing to do, wouldn't it?"

Slowly, he takes me in, his gaze sweeping over every inch of my face before finally landing on my lips. He's good at this faking it stuff. If his expression alone was all I had to go by, I might actually think he *wants* to kiss me.

"Mark will be back in a second." I try not to wince at the way the words come out as a breathless whisper.

"Let's see how you perform under pressure, then." With one big, warm hand curved around my nape, he uses his thumb to tilt my jaw up. "Are you ready?"

When I force myself to focus on him, there isn't even a hint of the amusement I expected to find on his face. Instead, his eyes burn into me with a heat that sends my internal temperature skyrocketing.

I nod, my whole body humming under his touch. But he doesn't lower his head, and he doesn't kiss me. Instead, he ghosts his thumb over my mouth. And god, why does this feel so real? It shouldn't. We're minutes away from signing the contract that spells out the terms and conditions of this relationship. Not to mention, Tate is the last man I should want to kiss. And yet, when he lowers his head until his lips hover over mine, and I inhale the clean masculine scent of him, anticipation shivers over my skin.

"Show me what you've got, butterfly," he murmurs.

He's not going to make it easy on me. Or maybe he wants me to prove exactly how committed I am to this arrangement. Either way, I won't back down from this challenge. Not when True Brew is at stake.

I go up on my toes and slide my hand into the soft strands of hair at the back of his neck. My pulse kicks into high gear and excitement skitters up my spine. Just as I'm closing the space between us, Mark's voice sounds from outside the room.

I leap away from Tate and turn to face the windows behind me just as the door swings open.

Tate's low chuckle scorches my skin, but I don't dare look at him.

"Okay, I've made those changes—"

I turn to my brother when his words cut off abruptly.

He squints at me where I'm standing at the window, then narrows his gaze further when he shifts his attention to Tate, who is standing suspiciously close by. I'm too scared to look at Tate, afraid that this time, I'll see the amusement he was hiding before, so I keep my attention focused just over Mark's shoulder, willing my still-hammering pulse to slow.

"Everything okay?" Mark asks.

"Everything's fine," Tate says. "Violet was just demonstrating her excellent acting skills."

His voice is casual, almost flippant. Probably because he actually was acting when he all but dared me to kiss him.

And now the heat in my cheeks has more to do with embarrassment than anything else. I feel like I've been played. It's ridiculous, because pretending to be attracted to him is exactly what I signed up for. But I didn't expect to lose track of that within the first few minutes. We haven't even signed the damn contract yet.

I close my eyes and exhale. I'll do better from now on.

Finally composed enough to face him, I shoot Tate a quick glance. Just as I expect, he looks completely unruffled. That cool, slightly amused expression he always wears is even more grating than usual.

I look away. Now that I know how easily he can fall in and out of the act, I'll make sure to remain just as detached.

Mark has a little crease between his brows, as if he doesn't quite believe Tate. He'd be smart not to.

But I reassure him anyway. "Just working out some of the logistics of playing a misguidedly doting girlfriend. It might be a struggle to make it believable, but I'll manage."

"I'm happy to help you practice anytime you need," Tate says.

I don't turn toward him or acknowledge his comment. I also ignore the quiet laugh he lets out.

Keeping my focus straight ahead, I sit back down in my chair. Mark does the same. Instead of going back around the table, Tate surprises me by pulling out the chair next to me. His leg brushes mine, but I swivel away a fraction.

"Better not do that once we've signed," he murmurs while my brother is preoccupied with separating the documents. "You're supposed to be crazy about me, remember? We don't want to see any tabloid articles about there being trouble in paradise."

This time, I turn my narrowed gaze on him, and the corners of his mouth curl up. He's enjoying himself. I get the horrible feeling I've just signed up to endure months of Tate King having too much fun at my expense.

But if I can save True Brew, then it will all be worth it.

With a sigh of resignation, I turn away from his too-handsome face and pick up the pen. "Let's get this over with."

CHAPTER SIXTEEN

TATE

"That's it from me. Any questions?" I ask the room.

I wrap up my daily meeting with my marketing team by going over the few issues they raise and possible solutions to them. We're on track to launch the second stage of the Genesis-1 marketing plan, and we're getting more interest from buyers as we near the first stage of construction.

My team is working overtime on the project, but it'll all be worth it. The room is abuzz with excitement. This development has the potential to be a huge success for the King Group, and every person here knows it.

Once the room has cleared out, I make my way to the elevator. When I exit on the top floor, I go right and head toward Cole's office instead of going left toward mine.

Cole's PA, Samson, nods at me as I pass his desk. I don't bother to knock before opening the door and walking in. Samson would have stopped me if Cole didn't want to be interrupted. And about the only reason my brother would care about me walking in unannounced is if Delilah was in here with him.

He's on his phone when I enter, and he waves me toward a seat.

He hangs up a moment later and straightens in his chair. "That was the UK office," he says. "They have the results of the feasibility study, and it's positive. It highlighted a growing interest in owning luxury high-rise properties in London among affluent professional and international buyers, specifically with a focus on luxury *and* sustainability. That's good news for us, since it's exactly what we're offering with Genesis-1. If we move fast, we can corner that market before our competitors catch up."

"It'll be about marketing it correctly." I cross an ankle over my knee and lean back. "We're selling an exclusive lifestyle. A chance to be part of something groundbreaking. Have they started looking at potential sites?"

Cole doesn't answer. He's picked up his phone and is staring down at it.

My brows rise. "Cole?" I prompt him.

"Yes, sorry. What?"

I cock my head. It's rare for Cole to tune out like that, especially during work discussions. "Something on your mind?"

He rubs the back of his neck. "Sorry. I'm just... distracted." He slumps back in his seat and drums his fingers on the arm of his chair. "Delilah and I had an argument this morning, and it has me on edge." His brows pull down. "I don't like when she's angry at me."

I hide my smile. It's hard to believe this is the man who spent years being cold as fucking ice to everyone around him before he met her. "What did you argue about?"

He picks up his pen and fiddles with it. "She was making suggestions for the new King International hotel. And I got distracted by... something." He glances at me, then quickly away. "I lost track of the conversation. She accused me of not caring about her input, and I may have responded by telling her that I wasn't interested in mixing business and pleasure right then, and that if she wanted to talk business, she should make an appointment at the office."

A lungful of air escapes me, and all I can do is stare at him. "You told your fiancée to make an appointment to talk to you?"

Cole grimaces. "I wasn't thinking clearly at the time. She was wearing this little low-cut—" He shoots me a glare, as if it's my fault he was half a second away from describing what had the power to make him so lust-drunk he told Delilah to schedule a time to talk with him about work. "And to be honest," the smallest of smirks curves his lips, "I like when she comes to the office to see me."

I bet he does. I eye the desk between us, which has no doubt seen a lot of action. They've probably done it on every surface of this office by now. Suddenly overly conscious of what might have occurred on or around the chair I'm sitting on, I edge forward, minimizing my contact with the possibly contaminated leather. "Not the most tactful way to request some afternoon delight, I would imagine."

His smirk disappears, and he runs a hand through his hair. "She was less than impressed."

I can't help the laugh that escapes me. Delilah may be a sweetheart most of the time, but she doesn't hesitate to call Cole out on his bullshit. And clearly, that's what happened this morning. Her ability to ruffle Cole's feathers never stops being amusing.

She's good for him. Since they met, he's less the guarded COO of the King Group and more the brother I remember from our childhood. And by childhood, I mean the years before the three of us discovered what a farce our family actually was. Before we found out that the ties that bound us together were made up of money, power and our shared bloodline, with no room for love, and definitely not for affection.

We were brought up to believe that the King name and the wealth and influence associated with it were the only things that mattered. Dad made sure to drill that into our heads from the minute we could understand the concept. Of course, without ever saying the words, he made sure I was aware that none of his blood runs in my veins. I could probably credit that for why I took all his lessons with a grain of salt.

"How are you feeling about your first public appearance with Violet?" Cole asks.

Tomorrow night is the annual Save the Rainforest charity ball, and our first appearance as a couple. "What should I be feeling?" I ask, ignoring the kick of anticipation that tightens my muscles. "All we have to do is show up and make sure the photographers get a few good shots of us."

The corners of Cole's mouth twitch upward. "Just make sure your girlfriend doesn't look like she wants to strangle you while they do it."

I laugh. After our almost kiss two days ago when we signed the contract, Violet was anything but the warm, loving girlfriend she was supposed to be portraying. She barely looked at me as we signed, and she rushed out before the ink had a chance to dry. Considering we weren't on display at the moment, I wasn't particularly bothered.

"Delilah's going, isn't she?" I ask Cole.

"She'll be there. Hopefully after having forgiven me." His expression shifts into a smug grin. "Multiple times."

I groan. "I don't need to hear about your plans for makeup sex. Just don't do anything stupid to make things worse. I want to introduce her to Violet. I'm sure Delilah will be happy to have another woman to talk to instead of having to deal with your possessive ass hovering over her all night."

Cole's brows draw together. "I don't hover."

"You absolutely do. And you glare at any man who even considers coming near her."

He doesn't argue that point. "You're just lucky I let *you* get anywhere near her."

I grin. "You don't have to worry about me. I'm a taken man now, don't forget."

He eyes me for a long moment. "You sound way too happy about it, considering how reluctant you were to begin with."

I shrug. Not that I'd admit it, but maybe I am looking forward to this arrangement. The thought of spending more time with Violet is appealing in a way it shouldn't be, considering how she feels about me. "There's no reason I can't make the best of the situation."

"No reason at all." His expression is a little *too* bland for my liking.

I scrutinize him, searching for his angle. Is it some kind of strange payback for when I interfered in his relationship? Regardless, I don't have time to figure out what he's insinuating, so I do what I do best and ignore it.

I push myself up from the chair. "I look forward to seeing you and Delilah tomorrow night, then. Delilah more than you, obviously."

Then I'm gone, heading out the door with a smile on my face. Not long ago, our interactions were nothing more than curt emails about work. They say every cloud has a silver lining, and if Dad's arrest was the cloud that had hung over our company and our lives, then my improved relationship with my brother is the silver lining. Roman might still be a work in progress. He's completely consumed by his role as CEO, but hopefully, given time, I'll see some changes there as well.

With a glance at my watch, I pull out my phone and find my short text conversation with Violet.

Are the stylists there?

I organized a team of stylists to go to her apartment and help her choose a dress and shoes to wear to the gala tomorrow, as well as some outfits for other events we'll probably have to attend during our arrangement.

Her response is immediate and short.

Yes.

Have you found a dress for tomorrow night yet?

Not yet.

The responses make it clear she's still disgruntled. Her annoyance, strangely, makes me smile. The funny thing is, I've never seen Violet be anything less than friendly and sweet, except with me. I get under her skin, and I like that I have that power. I like getting a reaction from her. What we did at Onyx can't ever happen again, but that doesn't mean I can't take advantage of my new role in her life. I grin to myself as I tap out another message.

Looking forward to our first date, butterfly.

There's no immediate response this time, and I can imagine her studying the message, wondering if there might be some other meaning to my words. The funny thing is, there isn't. For the first time in a long time, I *am* looking forward to attending one of these events.

When Violet's response finally comes in, I have to laugh.

It's not a date. And you need to stop calling me butterfly.

I quickly type out my reply.

Yes, it is, and not a chance. See you tomorrow, butterfly.

Still smiling, I slide my phone back into my pocket. Tomorrow night will be interesting, to say the least. I can't wait to see how well Violet acts the part of my girlfriend under the scrutiny of cameras and the public. I get the feeling she'll keep me on my toes. This time, I embrace the thrill of exhilaration that sparks through me. I have no idea what to expect from her, and that's exactly what makes her so damn intriguing.

CHAPTER SEVENTEEN

VIOLET

The makeup artist and hair stylist that Tate organized for me left twenty minutes ago, and I'm staring at my reflection in my bathroom mirror. I've never looked like this before, so polished and put together. The shimmery gold material of the dress I chose yesterday clings to my curves and falls to the floor in a perfect drape, the neckline dips just low enough to show the swell of my breasts, while almost all of my back is left exposed. My eyes have been beautifully painted to make their blue color pop, my lips are a subtle, glossy pink, and my hair has been styled into gentle waves that tumble down my spine and over my shoulders. A few strands are loosely braided along the sides and meet at the back, where they've been woven together and pinned to add a whimsical touch. I look like me, and yet not me.

Finally forcing myself to look away, I pick up my phone from the bathroom counter and check the time. Tate will be here to pick me up soon, and my stomach is roiling with nerves. Part of me wishes that our first appearance as a couple could be more casual, more subdued. It would relieve some of the pressure tightening my chest if we were going somewhere a little less high profile. But then, being seen together is the whole point of this arrangement.

I give myself one final inspection, then head to the front room to wait. My nerves get the best of me, so rather than sitting patiently, I head straight for the window. When I move the curtain aside and peer out, there's no long black car parked outside yet. Though I should have expected that. Tate will probably call me when he's near so I can meet him downstairs.

Letting the curtain fall, I turn and pace back across the small room. I shouldn't be this nervous. It's not like I'm incapable of making small talk with strangers. Spending almost every day at the coffee shop talking to customers means I've had plenty of practice. And thanks to Tate arranging the dress, and my hair and makeup, I look as much the part as I can.

When my phone beeps, I pull it out of my clutch. It's Anna. She stopped by earlier to hold my hand as I got ready, but since she has a date of her own tonight, I sent her home after an hour so she could get ready herself. In typical Anna fashion, she found it incredibly entertaining that I ended up in this situation. Thank god the NDA allows me to discuss it with her. Even if I hadn't already told her about it, there was no way I could have successfully lied about my sudden change in feelings toward Tate. Not after I went into detail about my less than stellar opinion of him when we left Onyx the other night.

I swipe open her message.

Is he there yet?

Not yet. I think I'm wearing a hole in my carpet.

Relax, Vi. You looked stunning in that dress. He won't know what hit him.

Thanks. But also... Why did I agree to do this again?

For all the free food and wine?

Ah yes, I remember now.

Seriously, you're going to dazzle him tonight! Just remember, it's for a good cause! Plus, maybe he's not as bad as you think. You might even have fun!

I'm in the middle of typing a reply about her overuse of exclamation marks when a knock on the door startles me.

Tate came all the way up here to get me?

Ignoring the nerves that tumble through me, I delete my message and tap out another quick one, letting Anna know he's here. Then I rush to the door, unlock the bolt and swing it open. My heart does a little unwanted spasm in my chest at the sight of him in a tuxedo. The black jacket stretches across his shoulders, making him look even taller and broader than usual, and his crisp white shirt molds to his—

The item in his right hand distracts me entirely from my perusal.

Because the man is twirling the stem of a single, delicate violet between his fingers.

When I drag my focus back up to his face, his golden eyes are fixed on me. Emotion rises in my throat, but I choke it back. God, what would it be like to have a man show up at my door like this for real? A man who isn't a playboy who's only in this situation because of his well-earned reputation for *not* taking women on dates.

Still, when one corner of his lips curves up and he holds

the violet out to me, I can't help but smile as I take it. "Did you steal this out of someone's garden?"

He chuckles and rocks back on his heels. "How did you guess? I even had to trample over their petunias to get it."

I shake my head at the vision of Tate in his tuxedo clambering over a fence to pick a flower for me. "Why do I find that very hard to believe?" Stepping back, I hold the door open for him. "Do you want to come in for a moment? I just need to grab my purse."

He follows me inside and pushes the door closed as I swipe my clutch off the counter. With it in one hand and the flower in the other, I turn to Tate. "I don't think there's a small enough vase in existence for this."

He closes the distance between us and takes the flower from me, his fingers brushing mine as he does. Then he reaches up and tucks it into the braid over my right ear. His gaze sweeps my face, then drops down the length of me before meeting my eyes again. "Beautiful," he says softly.

It's not just one butterfly that takes flight this time, it's a whole kaleidoscope. A tiny breath escapes me. One I hope he doesn't notice. He's good at this. I have to keep reminding myself of why that is. He's had a lot of practice seducing women over the years. Hell, the first time I met him, he'd sweet-talked *two* women into bed with him. And I had to experience the whole damn event through the walls of Mark's bedroom. I shudder at the memory of holding the pillow over my ears to mute the moans and squeals of ecstasy. Not to mention, as much as I'd like to forget, I've already succumbed to his charms once myself. I refuse to let that happen again.

Being another notch on his bedpost is the last thing I want. So I merely give him a tight smile and step back. "We should go."

He holds his hand out, gesturing to the door. "After you."

Though he doesn't touch me as we leave my apartment, he might as well. I can *feel* his presence like a warm shiver against the exposed skin of my back as I lead him to the stairs. Neither of us speaks as we descend, the silence causing my nerves and apprehension to ratchet higher. How is this possibly going to work if I'm this on edge after only a few minutes in his company?

I force my shoulders down from around my ears and slow so we're walking side by side. "Tell me what I need to know about your family before we get there."

His lips quirk. "Delilah, Cole's fiancée, will be there. She's great. She'll take you under her wing. Cole will do his best to include you, but don't expect him to be overly chatty. Roman? Well, if you get more than a smile and a few words from him, then consider yourself fortunate."

"Will your mother be there?"

His response to that question is a clipped "yes." His expression, when I peek up at him, is unreadable.

"Your brothers obviously know this is fake, but what about Delilah and your mom?"

"They both know. Cole would tell Delilah regardless. And it was better to make Mom aware. Otherwise she'd be the most vocal in questioning my sudden change in relationship status."

His tone cools at the end. Obviously, his mom isn't his favorite topic.

At the bottom of the stairs, he opens the door and holds it for me.

"Such a gentleman," I say, looking up at him as I pass.

"Only on the streets." He winks.

I groan. "Does that line actually work on anyone?"

He chuckles. "No."

Despite my best efforts to remain unaffected, I can't stop the laugh that bubbles up. During our limited interactions over the years, he's always remained cocky and arrogant, but something seems different now. He's still those things, of course, and he's still clearly aware of the effect he has on women, but aside from all his flirtatious charm, he doesn't seem to take himself too seriously, and though I hate to admit it, that quality is... disarming.

My laugh dies quickly when he splays his big hand over my lower back and guides me toward the car. The unexpected contact has a silent breath shuddering out of me. I'm really going to have to get used to his casual touches when we're out in public.

Tate's driver is already waiting as we approach and is holding the back door of the limo open for us.

"Violet, this is Jeremy," Tate says.

I hold out a hand. "Hi, it's nice to meet you."

Jeremy's brows shoot up, and his eyes flick to Tate, as if he's surprised, but then he focuses on me, his face splitting in a grin. He takes my hand, giving it a little shake. "Good evening, ma'am."

Once he's stepped back behind the open door, Tate helps me slide into the car. He follows, sitting close but not too close, and a moment later, the car pulls away from the curb.

Hit with another wave of nerves, I run my fingers back and forth over the silky material of my dress, concentrating on the texture against my skin.

Tate covers my hand with his, the heat of his palm grounding me. "You have nothing to worry about."

I swallow and nod my thanks at him. He removes his

hand, and a small part of me wishes he'd left it there, if only because the warmth of it was reassuring.

Sooner than I'd like, we arrive outside the venue. There's a red carpet with the press lined up along it, just like in the movies. A glamorous-looking couple walk toward the building's entrance, and camera flashes explode as they pass. It takes a moment to recognize the man as one of cinema's hottest stars, but when I do, all the air rushes from my lungs.

I turn to Tate and force myself to take a breath. "Just a casual Friday night for you, then?"

He focuses on the actor and his date, who have almost reached the end of the carpet, and his gaze narrows. "I can introduce you later if you like. Just don't get any ideas. You're too crazy about me to flirt with anyone else, remember."

Even though I have no intention of flirting with anyone, I tap my lips with my pointer finger and hum. "I don't remember a no-flirting clause in the contract."

The corners of his mouth curl up. "We'll amend it on Monday."

"So, until then...?"

He grips my chin, tipping my face up to meet his hot stare. "Until then, butterfly, you only have eyes for me. That's the agreement."

My pulse kicks into high gear, blood rushing in my ears. With another forced breath, I will my heart rate to steady. He just said it himself—his attention, his words and actions, are all about the agreement.

It isn't until he smooths his thumb across my lower lip, tugging it out from between my teeth, that I realize I've been staring too long. When I blink back to reality, there's something dark and potent flickering in his gaze.

"You with me?" His voice is low, his fingers still warm against my skin.

I let the breath I've been holding in a little too long trickle out, then take another one to steady myself. This is just us getting ready to perform for the press. I summon my brightest smile. "Yes."

He angles his head down, gaze flickering to my lips for the briefest of moments. "Good girl."

Instantly, a memory flares to life inside me: *Such a good girl leaving a mess all over me.* The sudden ache low and deep inside me has me pressing my thighs together.

I turn my face away to hide the flush creeping up my neck, and his fingers drop. An instant later, Jeremy's opening the door and Tate's climbing out of the car. Then he's offering his hand to me. I accept it, clinging a little tighter than I normally would as I climb out after him. The last thing I want is to face-plant on the red carpet in front of a crowd of photographers.

With his hand on my back again, Tate leads me toward the entrance. As camera flashes erupt around us, I focus on keeping a serene expression on my face and avoid looking directly at them.

"Tate!"

"Mr. King!"

"Who's your date tonight, Tate?"

All the way down the carpet, voices call out around us, but Tate keeps us moving until we're past them and inside the expansive foyer.

"Shouldn't you have introduced me as your girlfriend?" I ask.

He looks down at me with that devilish grin of his. "Got to keep some mystery going to pique their interest. Plus, if we shove it in their faces right off the bat, they're bound to be suspicious. I'd rather not make it obvious that this is a PR stunt."

"Makes sense." I refuse to acknowledge the burn in my chest at his words.

We make our way through the throng of beautifully dressed people. The atmosphere reeks of money and power. It's so potent the air is thick with it. Crystal chandeliers drip from the ceiling the way diamonds drip from the necks and ears of most of the women here.

Finally, we approach what is obviously our table. I recognize Cole and Roman, and smile at them as they both push back their chairs and stand.

"Tate." Cole nods at his brother, then turns his attention to me. "Violet, it's nice to see you again."

"You too," I say.

Roman runs his gaze over me, his attention appearing to linger on where Tate's hand is resting on my waist. It's hard to know what the eldest King brother is thinking. His aloof expression and cool eyes give nothing away. He's in on the plan, so it's not like he disapproves of Tate's "girlfriend" being here, but I'm also not convinced he agrees with me as Tate's choice.

I smile at him anyway. "It's good to see you again too, Roman."

To my surprise and reassurance, his mouth tilts up. "We're glad you could join us."

A beautiful woman with dark hair and green eyes appears at Cole's side.

Immediately, he loops an arm around her. "Violet, I'd like to introduce you to my fiancée, Delilah."

The possessive way he holds her close to him and the way his expression softens when he looks down at her sends a small pang of longing through me.

What must it feel like to be loved like that? I always imagined it was how Dad loved my mom. With how protective he was of me, it's hard to believe he wasn't the same with her. The pang of longing is replaced by the familiar ache of loss. One I always get when I think about my mom. I may not have memories of her, but I have hundreds of the way Dad used to talk about her. I can only hope that one day I'll be lucky enough to be loved the way he loved her—the way I can already tell Cole loves his fiancée.

The woman in question steps forward and envelops me in a tight hug. I'm taken aback by the reception, but before I can find my bearings and hug her back, she lets me go and grasps my hands.

"I'm so happy to meet you," she says, her smile bright and genuine. "I'm looking forward to having another woman to spend time with at these things."

Her warmth immediately puts me at ease. It must be tough for her to be surrounded by these three imposing men all the time.

I smile back at her. "I'm glad I can do double duty as Tate's girlfriend *and* as company for you."

She keeps my hand in hers and tugs, signaling for me to sit in the chair beside hers.

Tate pulls out the chair next to mine and unbuttons his jacket with one hand before settling into it. "Where's Mom?" he asks Roman, who's across the table from us.

"She's sitting with the Jensens tonight."

"Actually," Cole says, "don't look now, but she's on her way over. She must have spotted you coming in."

Nerves dance in my stomach at the thought of meeting Tate's mom, and I force myself not to swivel in my seat to watch her approach.

A tall, striking blond woman glides up to the table, her

gaze sweeping over everyone before landing on me. Her eyes are cool, assessing.

"Mom, this is Violet," Tate says. "Violet, my mother, Beverly King."

She offers me a nod, her expression unchanging. I guess now I know where Roman gets it from.

I smile brightly and clasp my suddenly sweaty hands in my lap. "It's a pleasure to meet you, Mrs. King."

"The pleasure is all mine, I'm sure," she says, although I'm not sure her tone backs that up. "I've heard about your arrangement with Tate. What an inventive solution to his problem." Her words are edged with a subtle sharpness. "I trust you're finding it to your... benefit?"

My skin prickles at the implication, but I maintain my composure. "I hope it's mutually beneficial."

Tate clears his throat. "You may find it hard to believe, Mom, but Violet's doing me a favor. Not everyone wants to spend their evenings drinking overpriced wine and mingling with the rich and bored." His tone is light, but there's no missing the thread of sarcasm.

Mrs. King's gaze flicks toward her youngest son, an unreadable expression crossing her face. "As long as you both get what you need from this... partnership. I hope you enjoy your evening, Violet. As well as your time with the King family."

With that, she gracefully moves away to mingle with other guests. My shoulders sag a little after she's gone.

Delilah leans over and gives me a reassuring smile. "Try not to let her bother you. That's Beverly King in all her glory. You get used to it."

"I suppose I won't really have to worry about getting used to it," I respond.

She cocks her head. "I suppose not. How are you doing,

by the way? I know it's not easy being thrust into this kind of environment."

Relief that she's aware of the situation and I can talk to her about it washes over me. "It's a little nerve-racking. I'm not sure that I'll fit in, and I can't help but worry that people will see straight through us. I want to do a good job; I just don't know if I can."

"You'll do just fine. In fact, a little discomfort probably works in your favor. It's obvious to everyone that the women Tate has let himself be with weren't ever going to capture his heart. It's more believable that he'd fall for someone outside his usual circles, a woman who challenges him to think and feel differently than he has before."

I can't help but look at Cole on her other side, his arm draped over the back of her chair, hand brushing her shoulder, as if he can't abide not touching her. Is she talking from personal experience? I stifle my curiosity. Even if she is, she isn't talking about reality here. She's discussing the believability of our act.

I smile at her. "That's good, then. Now Tate and I just have to make it convincing that we like one another. If we can do that, then we should be good to go."

Her brow furrows. "You don't like Tate?"

"Oh, no, no. Um..." I cringe inside. Why did I say that? He's her future brother-in-law, after all. I glance at Tate, relieved to find him busy talking to his brothers. "Dislike isn't the right word. It's more... I don't really have anything in common with him. And I guess he didn't make the greatest first impression. That's all." I almost stumble over my words in my hurry to reassure her, just in case she thinks I'm not taking this seriously. "It doesn't mean I'm not fully committed to helping him with this situation."

She tilts her head, her lovely green eyes assessing. Then

she smiles a small, almost knowing smile. "Considering it's Tate, I can only imagine what kind of impression he made." She leans forward, lowering her voice. "Just... don't let a bad first impression color your opinion too much. If you can let go of that, then I think he'll show you the kind of man he really is." Her knowing smile turns a little wicked. "Of course, that doesn't mean you shouldn't give him hell if he's being obnoxious."

I grin back. "I think I can manage that."

Delilah turns the conversation to other topics, and after a glass of a deliciously crisp white wine, which Tate pours for me, most of my misgivings have dissipated. This isn't so bad. Delilah is sweet and funny, and the conversation between Cole, Roman and Tate about their latest venture, Genesis-1, is intriguing. I'm engrossed in the discussion about their marketing strategy, and wondering if I can pick up any tips that can be translated to True Brew, when Tate casually leans back in his chair, drapes his arm over the back of mine and starts playing with a tendril of my hair.

Instantly, my breath catches, and I freeze. I should have been expecting it, but it takes me by surprise anyway. Maybe it's the nonchalant way he did it. As if touching me like this is the most natural thing in the world.

I school my features into something I hope resembles serenity, not wanting to give the game away to observers by looking shocked that my boyfriend is being affectionate. In fact, I go one better and lean farther back so his arm is basically around my shoulders.

He turns to me, and I give him a smile that says *see? I can play this just as well as you.*

His lips quirk up, but without a word to me, he merely joins in with the conversation again. Except a moment later, he cups my neck and traces circles with his thumb on the sensitive skin just below my ear.

Oh god. If I didn't know before now that the spot he's caressing is an erogenous zone, I do now. The slow circles he's drawing have goose bumps erupting over every inch of me, and before I can help myself, I shiver. Unfortunately, he catches my reaction, his thumb pausing for a fraction of a second before starting up again, even slower and more sensuously this time. He knows exactly what his touch is capable of.

I grit my teeth as my pulse quickens and my nipples tighten and rasp against the material of my dress. Willing myself to ignore the sensations he's drawing out of me, I focus extra hard on the conversation.

"The higher profile the groundbreaking ceremony, the better," Tate is saying. "The media buzz and social media posts will get people talking. We can bring in key stakeholders. Even invite celebrities and maybe a few dignitaries. Make it a day-long event. We've already got the team working on VR tours based on the architectural renderings. We could have booths set up to allow people to check out the finished product at the actual site."

Roman, mouth fixed in a skeptical frown, drums his fingertips on the table. "Don't you think that's a bit gimmicky?"

"A few years ago, yeah," Tate responds, lounged back in his chair, his arm still draped across mine and his thumb still moving, threatening to distract me completely. "But in this day and age, gimmicks sell, especially to younger age groups. If our primary target is the younger, more socially conscious demographic, then this is how we attract them. We can't underestimate the impact of social media these days."

"I'm not underestimating it. I just want to ensure we're staying on brand," Roman continues, his tone measured. "Genesis-1 is about luxury and sustainability, not just flashy events."

"We don't want to put off our secondary target markets either," Cole says. "Affluent professionals and international buyers might not look favorably on a media circus."

Tate's thumb stops moving, and his hand tightens around my neck as he leans forward. I don't hear the words he speaks to his brothers, though, because the grip he has on me sends heat flaring up my spine.

Before I can wrap my head around *that* reaction, Delilah breaks into the conversation. "Why don't we shelve the work discussion?" she asks, though it's more of a strong suggestion than a question. "You can do that at the office on Monday. There are dozens of people here waiting for a moment to talk to one of you. Plus," she lowers her voice, "I thought the whole idea was for Tate and Violet to be seen together."

Roman scrubs his hand over his chin. "You're right. I saw Carl Masters when I got here. He's been wanting to discuss increasing his investment in the King Group. I should catch up with him. He and his wife never stay long at these events." He stands and regards Tate and me like he has something to say, but he just nods at us, then walks away.

I lean toward Tate. "Is he always so... intense?"

"That's one way to describe him. Roman is all business all the time. Ever since his divorce. More so since becoming CEO."

I can't help the small gasp that escapes me. "He was married?" It's hard to imagine the aloof eldest King brother having a wife.

Tate tracks his brother's departing back. "When he was younger. It didn't last long."

"He's not dating anyone now?"

Lips turned up, he shakes his head. "Wining and dining women is pretty low on his list of priorities."

I hit him with a faux innocent smile. "Must be a family trait."

Eyes glittering, he brushes his thumb against my pulse point and leans in close. "I'm sure you'd agree that some of us have developed far more enjoyable skills when it comes to women."

His focus drops to my lips, but before my heart can hammer more than twice, he turns his attention over his shoulder toward the ballroom behind us. "Delilah's right, we should socialize. Make sure people see us together."

I inhale, taking a moment to center myself. I'm here for a reason, and I'm determined to do a good job, despite his deliberate attempts to ruffle my feathers.

"Okay."

When he stands, I follow his lead.

Delilah looks up and mouths, "Good luck."

"Thanks," I mouth back. Then I take a deep breath and follow Tate as he leads me into the crowd.

CHAPTER EIGHTEEN

TATE

When I put my hand on Violet's lower back, it's easy to tell myself it's what the act calls for, but I'm self-aware enough to know that it has more to do with how much I enjoy touching her. Sitting next to her, stroking her silky skin while she chatted with Delilah and occasionally joined in my conversation with my brothers, felt far better than such a simple thing should.

The way she shivered under my fingertips had all sorts of dirty thoughts spiraling through my head. She's so fucking responsive. If she were really my girlfriend, I'd tease her like that all evening, knowing that at the end of the night, I'd take her home and make good on that teasing until the sun came up.

I'm starting to understand why Cole can't keep his hands off Delilah.

With my focus on the crowd we're approaching, all of them sizing up each other with glittering eyes and razor-sharp smiles, I bend down and murmur to Violet. "Ready to dive into the shark tank?"

Her laugh comes out on a nervous breath. "As long as I don't get bitten."

I can't help it when my attention drifts to the swell of her breasts in that sexy-as-fuck dress, but I have enough respect to fight the urge to imagine marking her creamy skin with my teeth.

Violet's body presses close to mine as we navigate through the crowd, her head moving from side to side as she takes it all in. Her eyes are wide, and there's a nervous tilt to her full lips.

"Lesson one in high society," I say close to her ear. "Always smile, even if you can't stand the people around you."

"You mean like this?" She gives me the same too-sweet smile she used to give me whenever she visited Mark.

I chuckle. "Not sure I believe you still hate me, butterfly."

Her brows pull together. "I—I never hated you—"

"So your nose just wrinkled every time I walked into the room because...?"

Her nose wrinkles again, proving my point. "Because you always had some poor deluded woman trailing after you, desperate for a night in your bed."

"Don't be so judgmental. Those women knew what they wanted and weren't afraid to ask for it."

She rolls her eyes. "And you were more than happy to give it to them."

With a hum, I take her in from head to toe. "Much like a recent night at Onyx."

She huffs, but her cheeks turn pink. "We should have made a stipulation that we aren't allowed to mention that night."

I smirk. "Too late now."

She crosses her arms. "Verbal addendum."

Damn, I love when she gets fired up like this. "Doesn't count unless it's signed."

Her lips purse and her eyes narrow. "We can add it on Monday."

"Sure, I'll just email your brother and ask him to add in a line about not mentioning the night I finger-fu—"

"Fine." She shoots me a dirty little scowl. But a heartbeat later, that scowl transforms into a huge, beautiful smile.

My breath stalls in my chest. Damn. I don't think Violet has ever smiled at me like that. It's a breathtaking sight.

She pats me on the chest. "Thanks for the lesson. I think I'm getting the hang of it." Then she turns away.

I can't help the low laugh that rumbles out of me. When she looks back over her shoulder, her eyes sparkling and a little smile of satisfaction playing on her lips, it hits me almost like a blow to the gut. I could get used to those smiles. The genuine ones. The ones she gives me when she lets her walls down.

Like some kind of lovesick puppy, I follow her to the bar, unwilling to let her get too far away. Not when she looks like that. I don't even have to scan the crowd to know that every man in our proximity is watching her. When I get to where she's waiting for me, I brace my hands on either side of her shoulders—not too close, not crossing any lines. Although right now I don't just want to cross those lines, I want to erase them completely. But we have a contract, so this will have to do.

"You should be more careful, butterfly," I say in a low voice so no one else can hear me.

"Why?"

Her pulse is throbbing erratically at the base of her

throat. The sight of it triggers a memory. A sensation. The feel of it under my tongue.

My dick swells in my pants. If I pressed a few inches closer, she'd feel it. Instead, I hold myself still while I answer her. "I could get addicted to the way you smile at me."

Her eyes widen and her lips part. The satisfaction that hits me is short-lived though. Before Violet can come up with a retort, we're interrupted by the clearing of a throat from behind me.

I hold Violet's gaze for a beat longer, then turn, tempering my expression so it doesn't show my annoyance.

"Hello, Tate," the familiar blond-haired woman purrs. "It's been a while."

Amy's a socialite whose family moves in similar circles to mine. The heir to her mother's makeup empire, she spends her days dipping her toes into whatever job takes her fancy. "Amy, how are you?"

"I'm wonderful now," she coos, fluttering her lashes at me. The predatory glint in her eye is unmistakable.

"This is Violet," I say, resting my hand on the small of her back.

"It's nice to meet you," Violet says with a smile.

Amy rakes her gaze over Violet, her eyes narrowing slightly. "Delighted." That single word is clipped, an obvious dismissal. Then she turns her attention back to me.

I grit my teeth at her rudeness. "Violet's my girlfriend."

Amy's eyes widen, and she turns back to Violet, this time scrutinizing her more thoroughly. "Girlfriend?"

"That's right."

She touches my arm and trills a laugh. "Now I've heard everything."

"So, what do you do, Amy?" Violet asks, far more graciously than Amy deserves, considering how she's acting.

I'm tempted to cut this conversation short and take Violet out on the dance floor, but Amy's one of the biggest gossips in this room. If we want news about our relationship to spread, and spread quickly, this is the way to do it.

And there's a part of me, one that's growing stronger by the minute, that wants to see how far Violet's willing to go to sell this act. Fake or not, I know what I'd do if a man started flirting while I was standing by her side. There wouldn't be the faintest doubt that Violet was mine. But I signed on the dotted line, agreeing that physical intimacy between the two of us is at Violet's discretion. And fuck if I don't want to know what exactly it will take to get her to kiss me.

"I'm a fashion designer," Amy says, a hint of smugness in her tone. So that's what she's trying out these days. "And you?"

Violet keeps her chin tipped up. "I own a coffee shop."

"A coffee shop? How cute."

I swear I can hear Violet's teeth grind together, but her composure doesn't waver.

"Violet's shop sells the best coffee I've ever tasted," I say.

Violet's surprised gaze meets mine, and I quirk a brow at her.

"Is that so?" Amy asks, giving me an overly enthusiastic smile. "Maybe you can take me to try it one day."

I'd laugh at the absurdity of her behavior if she wasn't insulting Violet. She's acting as if there's something between us when, in fact, there never has been. I'm pretty sure she slept with my dad, although that's never stopped her from making a play for me or my brothers. I won't look down on someone for having daddy issues, not when I have plenty of my own. But I draw the line at being anything more than civil to a woman who knowingly slept with a married man and now wants to complete the father-son set.

As she continues to attempt to flirt with me, Violet's gaze flicks between us. I'm not encouraging Amy. Not even a little. The woman is flat-out ignoring my blatant disinterest and Violet's presence all on her own.

My fake girlfriend has gone quiet beside me, but the waves of irritation radiating from her are palpable. I turn my full attention on her, willing her to read my mind. Because if she doesn't do something soon, I'm going to.

Come on, butterfly. I'm yours now. Stake your claim before I break the terms of our agreement on the first fucking night.

CHAPTER NINETEEN

VIOLET

Whoever this Amy is, her attitude is really grating on me. I'm standing here right next to Tate, yet she's blatantly ignoring my presence. Even after Tate told her I was his girlfriend, she's continued to flirt with him.

I move closer to him as irritation rolls through me. In response, he glances down, his eyes glinting with what I assume is amusement at my frustration. I'm tempted to walk off and leave him to it. After all, this whole thing was his idea. What's the point of posing as his girlfriend if women are just going to disregard me anyway?

He turns back to the beautiful blond woman, his arm brushing mine. She's talking about some party she's hoping he'll attend. I don't think I'm included in that invitation.

"I hope you'll come," she says, squeezing his bicep a little too familiarly.

Have they slept together? The question gnaws at me. Not that it matters if they have. For all I know, Tate's slept with half the women here.

Even so, the thought that he might have had his hands on her pricks at my chest.

"Violet and I will have to check our schedule," Tate says.

Amy's gaze darts to me, then back to him quickly, her smile faltering for an instant. "Well, you don't both need to be there."

Tate doesn't physically react, but the air around us grows thick with tension at her words. "Why would I want to go to a party without my girlfriend?"

Now Amy's eyes are ping-ponging between us. Her hand flutters to her chest. "You're actually serious? You're... dating?" Her tone is heavy with disbelief.

Tate fixes his eyes on me. "I'd be stupid not to lock her down when I had the chance, wouldn't I? It took me a while to convince her, and she had very stringent *terms and conditions* when it came to agreeing to be with me, but I finally wore her down."

Oh god. It hits me then. That stupid clause in the contract. Physical intimacy is at my discretion. *I* need to initiate it.

He lifts one brow, as if he knows I've finally caught on and he's daring me the way he did in the conference room when we signed the contract.

Yes, I put the clause in there, but can I follow through with it? I glance again at Amy, who still has a hand splayed across her chest, as if shocked—or possibly horrified—at the thought that Tate might actually be dating me. That's all it takes for me to make up my mind. "I'm still deciding if I was crazy to say yes, but so far, the benefits haven't been too unpleasant."

Without overthinking the move, I rest my hand on his hard chest, go up on my toes and press my lips to his cheek. At least that's my intention. Only, Tate turns his head at the last moment. Just a little. Just enough so my mouth brushes the corner of his. As if he's been waiting for exactly this, he slides his hand around my waist, drags me to him, and brings his lips to my ear. "Took you long enough."

"What are you doing?" I whisper back.

"She's still watching. And I'm not sure she's convinced." His eyes flick between mine, then zero in on my mouth. A wicked grin tilts his lips. "Yes or no, butterfly?"

My heart hammers against my rib cage. I can do this. I can kiss Tate for show and not feel anything. I know *he* won't.

I swallow hard and murmur, "Yes," doing my best to ignore the way my stomach twists. It's nerves, not anticipation.

Tate doesn't hesitate, dipping his head and brushing his lips across mine. At first, I think that's all it's going to be. But I should have known a man like Tate wouldn't half-ass things. He captures my chin, his fingers warm against my skin. Then he presses his mouth firmly to mine.

Out of sheer instinct, my eyes flutter shut, and I open for him. He pushes his tongue into my mouth, and instantly, the kiss becomes harder, hungrier. Tingles course over my skin, and the noise of the ballroom around us fades as, without thinking, I kiss him back. My pulse races and I can barely restrain myself from moaning when his teeth tug on my lower lip and his tongue strokes deeper. With one hand keeping me close, he slides the other down to collar my throat, and I press my thighs together as my core clenches in response.

That involuntary reaction snaps me out of the haze I've drifted into. I've completely lost track of where I am and what I'm supposed to be doing. I pull back, trying not to let my embarrassment show. Because once again, I let myself get swept up in the pretense. But when I try to step away,

Tate tightens his hold on me. He looks back at Amy, who, for reasons unknown, is still standing there.

"As you can see, I find it hard to keep my hands off my girlfriend," Tate says.

"Yes, well, how... nice." Her lips are pursed, and she's obviously uncomfortable. After a half-hearted comment about hoping to see us both soon, she rushes away.

She's quickly replaced by another person though, so I don't have time to think about the kiss and how it affected me. Or maybe I don't *want* to think too hard about it. Tate keeps his arm wrapped around my waist, and I get so used to having it there that I even begin to enjoy the weight of it. After a delicious dinner, where I chat with Delilah and have a surprisingly enjoyable conversation with Tate and his brothers, we spend more time mingling. Tate's arm is around me again, and I find myself melting into his hold a little too easily.

Finally, the night is over. We say good night to Tate's brothers and Delilah, but he doesn't bother to seek his mom out before we leave. It's only when we're safely ensconced in his limo, away from the music and the wine and the people, that I can no longer distract myself from thinking about his lips on mine.

For some reason, I was expecting this role to consist mostly of Tate pointing at me and telling people I'm his girlfriend, with the occasional chaste hug or peck on the cheek to be convincing. I wasn't expecting him to put so much effort into making our relationship appear real. And I definitely wasn't expecting to find it so overwhelming being the focus of his attention that way.

Now, as we sit in the back of the car, I have to fight the worry creeping in. This playacting Tate's girlfriend was supposed to be easy. The opinion of him I established years ago should have ensured there was no possibility of developing real feelings. But in the short time we've spent together, that opinion is already changing. He might be a playboy, but apparently, even I'm not immune to his charm when he lays it all on me.

Our ride home is silent. He's as lost in his thoughts as I am in mine. I don't mind the quiet. I've been indulging in small talk most of the night, so it's a welcome reprieve. I do wonder what's filling Tate's thoughts though. I could ask him, but I'm not sure I want to know. Maybe I wasn't as good at playing the part of his girlfriend as he hoped. Maybe he's wishing he'd chosen someone else. Or maybe he's not thinking about me at all. His mind could very easily be fixed on his work after how often it was brought up tonight.

Jeremy pulls up outside my building, and a moment later, he opens the car door for me. As I step out onto the sidewalk, I turn back to Tate to say goodbye, only to find him already climbing out behind me.

"You don't have to get out," I say.

"What sort of boyfriend would I be if I kicked you out on the side of the road?"

A laugh escapes me. "A fake one?"

He steps closer, his big form crowding me, forcing me to look up at him. "I don't care if this is fake or not. You signed up to be my girlfriend, so I'll treat you exactly the way I would if you were actually mine."

I swallow past my dry throat. That's not the first time he's used the word mine. I should hate it far more than I do.

With a shake of my head, I make one last effort to resist. "You don't need to—"

He tucks a loose strand of hair behind my ear, stopping me mid-sentence, and cups the back of my head. "Don't argue with me, butterfly. It's going to happen one way or the other. Either we walk together like a civilized couple, or I'll sling you over my shoulder and carry you up there." He pulls back, that devilish look dancing in his eyes. "To be honest, I'm not sure which option I'd prefer."

I'd laugh it off if I didn't think Tate would do exactly what he'd described without a second thought.

Deciding to save my energy for another battle I'm sure to have to wage against him, I step back and fish my keys out of my purse. "Come on, then, Prince Charming. See me safely home."

Silently, we take the stairs up to the third floor. I unlock my door and step inside, then turn to face him. When I do, my pulse immediately races. God, he's gorgeous. He undid his bow tie in the car, and the way it hangs loose around his neck is so undeniably sexy. As if he's in the middle of stripping his clothes off. As if his next move will be to take me to bed and ravish me.

A man like Tate probably wouldn't even make it to the bedroom.

The thought has desire snaking its way through my veins. I can only hope he can't see the direction my mind has gone. "I hope you're not expecting your fake boyfriend benefits to extend to me inviting you in for a drink."

He props his shoulder against the doorframe, a smirk pulling at the corners of his lips. "If I was going to push for the full boyfriend experience, it wouldn't be a drink I was coming in for."

A slow wave of heat rolls through my body, leaving my skin flushed in its wake. "Well, since the full boyfriend experience isn't on the table, I guess this is where we say good night."

He straightens, unruffled. "I guess so." He steps forward, focused a little too intently on my face. "Thank you for tonight, Violet." His voice drops low. "You were very... convincing."

The way he's looking at me feels too real. It's been a long time since a man's attention has caused my skin to tingle and butterflies to take flight in my stomach. It's all wrong for this situation.

"You'll call me when you need me?" The breathiness of my voice makes my words sound far too suggestive.

Instead of teasing me about it, his gaze flickers to my lips. Of its own volition, my tongue darts out and wets them.

His eyes darken to a molten bronze. Does he want to kiss me again? Do I *want* him to?

Maybe it's all the wine I've had tonight, but the line between what's real and what's fake is rapidly blurring in my head, and I can't risk that. This thing we're doing is supposed to be safe for the very reason that I'd never mistake it for real.

So I inhale shakily and step back, breaking the tension that flares between us.

Tate scrubs his hand over his mouth, then drops it and smiles. "I'll definitely let you know when I need you. And when I do, I have no doubt you'll come."

My jaw drops at his obvious insinuation. Before I can think of a retort, he takes a step back of his own. "After all, that's the deal, right? You come when I need you. To play my girlfriend, that is."

I shake my head and bite back a smile of my own. I'm reading too much into Tate's behavior. He's just being his typical flirtatious self. I'm not sure if I'm relieved or disappointed that he's just messing around, but I know which one of those I *should* be. I take hold of the door handle. "Good night, Tate."

With a dip of his head, he regards me from beneath his lashes. "Good night, Violet."

Almost reluctantly, I swing the door shut between us, then drop my forehead against the smooth wood. I've got a horrible feeling that keeping this professional might be more difficult than I thought.

CHAPTER TWENTY

VIOLET

"Now ladies, transition into downward dog."

With a huff, I force my body to surrender to the instructor's command. Why did I let Anna talk me into an early morning yoga session? It's been so long since I've had the time or motivation to exercise, and my body is rebelling. All I can do is hope I'll appreciate it after the torture is over.

"You kissed him?" Anna whispers to me from where she's effortlessly folded in half.

A bead of sweat trickles down my temple. "I had to make it believable."

"And it had nothing to do with this Amy woman making a move on your man?"

I try to glare at her, but my trembling arms almost buckle, and I quickly concentrate on my wobbly form. "He's not my man."

Thank goodness the instructor leads us through a cooldown next.

As we finish, and I'm sprawled on my mat on my back in savasana pose, Anna whispers, "You know that, and he knows that, but she didn't know that. Which meant she was being completely disrespectful."

I sigh. "She was."

The instructor shushes us, and we quickly close our eyes and relax for the next few minutes. But if I thought the conversation was over, I was wrong.

"So when are you seeing him again?" Anna asks as soon as the instructor releases us with a parting namaste.

Wiping the sweat from my forehead with my towel, I heave myself to my feet. "I'm not sure. He said he'll let me know."

Anna casts me a look. "You almost sound... disappointed."

"*What*? No. I just wish there was more of a schedule, you know? So I'm not waiting around for a phone call and putting my social life on hold."

"Vi. I love you, but your social life sucks. I can't imagine you'll have to worry about canceling any big plans when he calls."

She's right. And the smug look she's giving me says she knows it.

"Okay." I might as well admit it. She'll drag it out of me eventually anyway. "Maybe I'm a tiny bit disappointed. I enjoyed last night more than I expected."

Anna's smile is a little too big, and I know what that means.

"Don't get excited. It's still just business."

"Why can't it be business with benefits? If I was lucky enough to be fake dating a hot-as-hell billionaire, I'd be taking advantage of *all* the perks."

I clamp down on the teeny, tiny irrational ball of jealousy that pings around my chest at the thought of Anna in my place. Tate probably would have been better off asking her to enter into this arrangement with him. Not only would she likely be able to pull the role off better than me, but she'd give him a run for his money in the seduction stakes too. But I don't particularly like imagining his lips on hers the way they were on mine last night. Or the perks they might take advantage of.

"Seduction is basically Tate's middle name," I mutter. "It comes as naturally to him as breathing. The last thing I want is to develop any kind of connection with him, just to have him walk away at the end."

A crease forms between her brows as she regards me. "Maybe he wouldn't walk away."

I laugh and shake my head. "Tate has spent his adult life walking away from women. I can guarantee this won't be any different. Being anything less than businesslike with him is guaranteed to hurt me in the long run."

"Hmm. You might be right."

I nod, satisfied that she's seeing my point of view.

"But—"

That one word brings a frown to my face.

"I saw the way he was with you at Onyx—*both* nights. And I don't know. That kind of reaction is the opposite of what I'd expect from a playboy."

I roll my eyes, going for flippant even as my stomach knots. "Whose side are you on?"

She cocks her head, a grin teasing her lips. "I didn't know I had to pick a side. But now that I do, obviously, I pick yours."

"Good."

"Although," she says, her smile getting wider. "I hear team 'maybe leopards can change their spots' has a growing number of supporters."

I throw my towel at her chest while holding back a

laugh. "Men like Tate don't change their spots. They have no reason to."

"Okay." She holds up her hands, finally conceding defeat. "But the next time you go out, I want to hear all the juicy details first thing the next day."

"I'll call you, but I guarantee the details will be drier than that chocolate cake you baked that we never talk about."

Her mouth drops open. "You broke the rule," she whispers in mock horror.

I smirk. "That will teach you to consider changing sides."

She snickers, but the amusement in her expression fades quickly. "Look, babe, I know you're not Tate's biggest fan. But don't let that stop you from enjoying this situation. You're dating a billionaire. A *hot* billionaire. A hot billionaire who, for the next few months, is going to pretend to be crazy about you. I understand that you don't want to let your feelings get involved, but there's nothing to stop you from having fun with it."

I chew on my bottom lip. She's right. I agreed to this arrangement. I might as well relax and enjoy it. "Fine. From now on, I'm going to have fun being Tate King's fake girlfriend. I'll enjoy *some* of the perks." I ignore Anna's disappointed pout. "And regardless of how charmingly flirty he is, I won't let it get to me."

Anna grins. "Exactly. Relax and have fun while Tate King wines and dines you for the next few months."

My mind flashes back to last night. When he told me he'd developed far more enjoyable skills than wining and dining women. There's no doubt he's right about that, but I get the gut-sinking feeling that if he puts his mind to it, he might end up being good at all of it.

Which means I need to be even more careful not to fall.

CHAPTER TWENTY-ONE

TATE

"Mr. King? Tate?"

I look up and find half the meeting room staring at me. Damn it. "Apologies, I got distracted. Can you run through that again?"

I try to concentrate on what Rebecca, my head of marketing, is saying. She's providing an update on the VR tours we're designing around the 3D renderings we've received from the architectural team.

"We're still working on some of the glitches, but they should be ready for the groundbreaking ceremony."

"Thanks, Rebecca. Let me know if any other issues crop up." I scan the marketing team assembled around the conference table. "If that's all, we'll wrap it up here. Thank you, everyone."

There are the usual murmurs and sounds of chairs pushing back, but I stay seated. Usually, I'd be the first one out the door, since I'm the kind of guy who likes to keep moving. But today seems to be the exception.

I wait for everyone else to leave. Then, with a glance at my watch, I finally rise from my seat and head out.

Cole catches up to me as I stride down the hallway. "You want to join me for lunch?" he asks.

Normally, I'd say yes. It's been nice getting to know my brother again after years of almost-estrangement. But I've got something more important to do today. "Rain check?"

"Of course," he says. "Or we can grab a drink after work."

"Sounds good. I'll let you know when I'm done for the day."

He nods and peels off to enter his office, while I continue toward the elevator, giving Jeremy a call as I go.

"Where to, Mr. King?" he asks once I'm seated in the back of the town car.

I tell him where I want him to take me, and he nods. Once we're headed toward True Brew, I settle back against the leather. I hadn't planned to visit Violet at work, but since she did such a good job at the gala on Saturday, I've decided to see if I can give her some marketing advice for her coffee shop.

Although maybe that's just the excuse I'm giving myself to see her again.

I had more fun on Saturday night than I've ever had at an event like that. It was so enjoyable, in fact, that I didn't want it to end. After that kiss, the one that had me wishing we were somewhere else—somewhere without witnesses—I was hard pressed to think about anything but doing it again. For the rest of the night, I kept her close to me, conscious of the avaricious eyes wandering over her.

Considering our relationship isn't real, it shouldn't have bothered me that she was attracting so much attention. In fact, I should have been happy. After all, the whole point of what we're doing is to draw attention to my newfound commitment. What better way than to have a beautiful woman on my arm?

But instead, I spent the whole night wishing I could keep her to myself. The urge to take her somewhere private and taste her again was difficult to resist. Luckily, I was able to. I doubt that's a boundary she wants to cross.

It's one I shouldn't want to cross either.

Twenty minutes later, Jeremy pulls over just down the street from the coffee shop. I don't get out right away, giving myself a minute to take in the shop front. What I see makes me smile. Since the last time I visited, Violet has made some changes. There's a chalkboard sign out front that's been decorated with a drawing of a steaming cup of coffee and a couple of pastries. The weekly specials are listed on it, and down at the bottom, there's a social media handle for the shop. I make a mental note to follow the account.

In addition, she's scraped off the old-fashioned painted shop name and replaced it with a bright cursive decal that fits her personality far more than the old one.

"You want a coffee?" I ask Jeremy.

He grins at me over his shoulder. "I wouldn't say no to one."

As we approach the shop, I peer through the windows. Even with the changes Violet has made, the place is still mostly empty. Violet and Jarrod are standing close together in front of the ancient espresso machine. A stab of irritation hits me in the chest when he puts his hand on her back, rubbing it as if he's reassuring her. Has she told him that she has a boyfriend?

The bell jangles as I push the door open. Violet looks over her shoulder, surprise flashing across her face when she sees me. It's soon replaced by a smile, but I'm too far away to tell whether it reaches her eyes.

"Grab a seat," I tell Jeremy, though I don't look away from Violet.

She turns back to Jarrod, and he looks over at me too, his brows arching. I give him a steely smile, and by the way he drops his hand from where it was still resting on her back, he got the message I was sending with that expression loud and clear.

Violet squeezes his arm, then heads toward me. Her honey brown hair is pulled back in a ponytail, her black tank top stretches over the swell of her full breasts and her tanned legs look insanely long underneath her denim cutoffs and apron.

She looks fresh-faced and gorgeous, and I don't take my eyes off her, even as I sense Jarrod's scrutiny.

The question of whether he knows about us beats too urgently through my veins.

What is she going to do when she gets to me? Will she give me a hug? A kiss? Or will she keep me at arm's length? An unfamiliar and completely irrational jealousy smolders to life inside me, and I have no idea how to control it. Then again, should I have to? To everyone in this room, she's my girlfriend. Why wouldn't I want them to know she's mine?

As always, once I make a decision, I don't second guess myself. The moment she reaches me, and before she has a chance to speak, I curl my fingers around the back of her neck. "Yes or no?" I ask quietly enough that only she can hear.

Her brows draw together, but her confusion is quickly replaced by a flare of understanding. "Um." Her throat bobs in a swallow. "Yes, but—"

It's all I need to hear before my mouth is hard against hers. Her lips part on a gasp, and I take the opportunity to slide my tongue inside. She tastes sweet, as if she's been sampling the pastries on display, except she's tasted just as delicious each time I've kissed her. It's all her, and fuck if it isn't addictive. If *she* isn't addictive.

She's hesitant at first, but then she turns pliant, her tongue meeting mine. I know what I asked of her—what I'm doing to her—is inappropriate at her place of work. And maybe if there were more customers in the shop, I wouldn't have done it. Or maybe that's a lie and I wouldn't have cared who was here to witness me kiss her.

I pull back before I'm ready, leaving her breathless in front of me, her already plump lips swollen from the pressure of mine.

In a daze, she brushes her fingertips over the evidence of how I've claimed her. It isn't until a couple of young women sitting at a small table at the back give us a round of applause that she startles and her eyes refocus. As if suddenly remembering where we are, her gaze darts around the shop. When she makes it to the women, one of them lets out a whoop and shouts, "Go girl!"

I don't bother looking back over at Jarrod. If he didn't know we were together before, he does now. Like a magnet, my hand finds the small of Violet's back as I walk her toward the counter. "Jeremy and I felt like a coffee and thought we'd drop in." I remember what she was doing when we came through the door. "Is the machine working?"

She sighs. "It's on its last legs. Thankfully, Jarrod's incredible at keeping it going. That'll be my first purchase when—" Her eyes find mine, widening slightly, and I know what she stopped herself from saying. She's waiting for the money from our arrangement to come through at the end of the month.

She rounds the counter and leans on it, cocking her

head, her expression curious and a little wary. "So you felt like a coffee and decided to come all the way out here?"

I give her a thorough once-over, not bothering to hide my smirk. "I had a very compelling reason."

The faintest of pinks stains her cheeks. "Oh yeah, what's that?"

"Someone told me this place serves the best coffee in New York."

The way her shoulders sag a little sends a surge of satisfaction through me. It means she isn't completely immune to me, regardless of how adamantly she'd argue that fact if I called her on it.

"And that I wouldn't be able to keep my eyes off the woman serving it."

That brings a subtle curve to her lips. "Did that person tell you that the woman serving it is taken?"

I frown at her, feigning disappointment. "That's too bad. I was hoping to ask her out on a date."

"Good thing I told you, then. Now you can save yourself the embarrassment of asking."

With a chuckle, I tap my knuckles against the countertop between us. "Thanks for the warning. It sounds like her boyfriend is quite the catch. It's obvious she's crazy about him."

Her responding eye roll is accompanied by a huff of laughter. "More like being *driven* crazy." She tilts her head. "Seriously though. Why are you here?"

"I'm here for coffee, and I'm here to see my girlfriend."

She purses her lips and scrutinizes me, her eyes filled with skepticism.

Grinning, I lean closer. "And I thought we could work through some marketing ideas. Maybe I can offer some insights."

Her expression brightens. "I've been thinking of some already. Your conversation with your brothers on Saturday night inspired me."

"Oh yeah? Do you have time to go through some of them now?"

"Absolutely." She turns to Jarrod. "Could you make three cups of the new blend, please?" When she addresses me again, her eyes are lit with excitement. "I'll grab my notebook and be right over."

I pull out my black Amex, and when she shakes her head, I put it down on the counter and slide it across to her. "I'm paying."

She puts her finger on it and pushes it back, focus fixed firmly on my face. "No, you're not."

"Do you really think it's good business sense to refuse a customer's payment?" I shouldn't provoke her, but I can't help it. I enjoy the thrill of it too much to stop.

She leans forward, bracing her hands on the countertop and narrowing her eyes. "Do you really think it's a good idea to cross your girlfriend and insult her in her place of business?"

Fuck. My dick instantly stands at attention. I don't know whether it's the fire blazing in her eyes or hearing her call herself my girlfriend with that heat in her tone. Either way, I'm rewarding her for it.

I snag my credit card from the counter. "You're right. This is your business, and if my *girlfriend* wants to treat me, who am I to argue?"

She presses her lips together to hide a smile, but the dimple in her cheek gives her away. "That's right. Don't you forget it."

She disappears through the door that leads to the back, and I make my way over to a table near where Jeremy is sitting, though I'm sure to pick one that isn't too close. He raises one dark brow at me, a slow, knowing grin crossing his face. I ignore him. He isn't aware of the contract between Violet and me, so he's probably delighted by the way my supposed girlfriend just bested me.

A few minutes later, Violet returns, a notebook clutched in front of her. She settles in opposite me and places it on the table. "You probably didn't notice, but I made some changes to the front of the shop."

"I did notice. It looks great. Much more you."

"I—Oh." She looks adorably flustered. "Um, thank you. I should have done it before, but it still looked the way I remembered from when Dad was here." She swallows hard, her eyes misting over. "I think maybe I've been holding back on making changes because I didn't want to lose that."

Without thinking, I cover her hand with mine across the small table. "I'm sure your dad would have wanted you to make this place your own."

She regards my hand with a little crease between her brows, then glances up at me. "That's what I told myself. It's just hard to make changes sometimes. It's hard to erase those fond memories, you know?"

I casually draw my hand back. I *don't* know. I have very few fond memories of my childhood. Playing with my brothers when I was younger, maybe. Before we all drifted apart, or before the truth of our family drove us apart, anyway. I don't need to go into all of that with Violet though, so I nod, encouraging her to go on.

"Anyway, I finally bit the bullet. And it might not look like it right now," she says, surveying the almost-empty space, "but I've already noticed more new customers."

"What other plans are you working on?" I like the enthusiasm radiating from her. And even more than that, I like the way we're actually talking to each other normally and not trying to bait one another.

As much as I enjoy it when she gets fired up, seeing this side of her, the happy, excited side, warms me in a way I'm not used to. I like that she's opening herself up to me—trusting me with this thing that means so much to her.

We're interrupted by Jarrod, who, after dropping off a coffee for Jeremy, sets two steaming cups on our table.

"Thank you," Violet says, smiling up at him.

"You're welcome." He returns her smile, shoots me an unreadable look, then leaves.

I take a sip of the hot beverage and close my eyes in appreciation. Bad coffee is definitely not one of the issues here. It's rich and vibrant. Possibly the most perfect cup I've ever tasted.

When I open my eyes, she's watching me with a shy smile that I somehow feel in my gut. "Good?"

"Fucking delicious. Who's your supplier?" Maybe I can get them to supply the coffee shop in the foyer of King Plaza. Even better, the one we plan to install in Genesis-1.

"An old friend of my dad's. He and his wife spend their days traveling the world and sourcing incredible coffee. It costs extra, but people used to flock here for our range of single origins and specialty blends." She taps a fingernail on the tabletop. "I just need to remind them of why they used to come and get others interested in giving us a go instead of going to the closest chain." She sighs. "The cost does eat into the profits. But it's the heart of this place, and I don't want to change that."

"Okay." I rest a forearm on the table, pushing away thoughts of her supplier. "What ideas have you come up with to increase profits?"

She flips her notebook open. "I've updated the shop's

social media presence and uploaded pictures of the coffees and baked goods. I'm thinking about recording videos to share as well. Maybe some behind-the-scenes stuff. The art of coffee making, that kind of thing."

"That's smart." I take another sip of coffee, hit all over again with the bold flavor. "Visual content is a great way to engage people. Have you thought about collaborating with local influencers or food bloggers? They could help amplify your reach."

"That's a good idea too." She catches her lower lip between her teeth as she makes a note.

I focus on my coffee once more to keep myself from getting distracted by her mouth. The one I've just tasted. The one I'm already thinking about tasting again. What we're talking about is important to her, so I need to focus.

"I worked out a loyalty program, too, with tiered rewards to encourage people to give us a chance," she continues. "Once they've discovered how good our coffee is, that will be an incentive to return, even if we're a little out of their way."

"What incentives are you talking about? A free coffee for every ten bought is pretty standard."

She nods. "It is, but I want to do something different. I've done some *market research*," she gives me a little smirk, "focusing on what our returning customers have in common. What I discovered is that outside of the few remaining regulars who live close by and come here because of their loyalty to Dad's memory, the two types of consistently returning customers are the connoisseurs, who want to check out the coffees we have available on any given day, and the environmentally conscious people who appreciate our sustainable practices. The ones who will go out of their way to support an eco-friendly, community-focused business."

I can't help but smile. She's put some thought into this. "What sort of rewards are we talking, then?"

"For the people that have been coming here forever, they get every tenth cup free, but for the connoisseurs, I'm considering hosting early tastings of our new coffees once we receive them, or small events where we introduce seasonal specialties and new menu items to go with them. It can be a reward for our returning customers and generate buzz on social media at the same time."

I rub my chin and nod. The idea definitely has merit. There's nothing people like more than feeling like they have exclusive access. That exclusivity is exactly what the King Group focuses on, so it makes perfect sense to me. "That has the potential to be effective. What about the third group you identified, the ones interested in your eco-friendly status?"

She flips over a page. "Each time we introduce a new coffee, we showcase it with a story—about the farmers, the land, the harvesting and production processes, the farm it came from and the efforts that make their farming sustainable. It will fuel that feeling of connection—from the farmer who grew the beans to the person enjoying the final cup. People love the storytelling aspect. I think it could bring back some of that community feeling my dad cultivated."

I'm impressed. All these ideas have the potential to rapidly gain traction if Violet can get her ideas in front of the right people. "Why haven't you implemented any of this already?" She obviously has all the right ideas, she just hasn't put them into practice.

Violet sits back in her seat and rubs her forehead. "Honestly, I haven't had the time, energy or money to do anything other than keep my head above water for the last five months. The manager we hired after Dad died canceled our arrangement with Jose, our supplier. After I came back, it took me over a month just to convince him to put True Brew back on his books. It was a challenge. Not because he didn't want to help, but because he's a businessman, and he didn't want to risk the arrangement falling through again."

I can understand that, even if I don't like the stress that negotiation must have added to her plate. "How did your dad get into this industry anyway?"

Her brows pull together, and she searches my face a little skeptically. As if she's unsure that I'm really interested in the story. That doubt pricks at me. I *am* interested in her, and not just because of this arrangement. I want to know what's made her into the woman she is today. I want to know what makes her smile and what makes her sad. For my entire adult life, I've made a habit of avoiding those things with women. But apparently that doesn't apply when it comes to Violet.

After a moment, her gaze softens, and a little smile appears on her face. "Before my parents met, Dad traveled a lot, backpacking mostly. He loved discovering new places. On one trip, he spent some time working on a small, family-owned coffee plantation in Brazil. He used to say that's when he fell in love with the process of brewing coffee. The sourcing of the beans, roasting them to bring out the flavors —every part of it. When he met Mom, and they settled down to start a family, Dad decided he wanted to open a coffee shop. And that's how True Brew was born."

I watch her face, intrigued by the different emotions that play over it as she talks—happiness, wistfulness, a touch of sadness—just as much as what she's telling me.

"He researched and studied the coffee industry and

discovered how the little farms, like the one he'd worked at, were getting beaten out by large commercial farms. Typically, the kind that treat their workers unfairly and trash the environment. He wanted to do business with the farmers who cared for their workers and the land, so he tracked down the suppliers that source specifically from those farms. That's how he and Jose met. His dream was to educate customers about the importance of sustainability in coffee production while providing fantastic-tasting coffee. And that's exactly what he did."

"He sounds like an amazing man." No wonder Mark and Violet are both so honest and hardworking.

"He was." Her smile is warm, if not a little sad. "He put his heart into True Brew. After Mom died, it was just Dad, Mark and me. Dad had to juggle a lot, but he always made time for us."

That knowledge is bittersweet. It's hard not to compare her relationship with her parents to mine. I wouldn't wish the pain of losing her mom and dad on her, but I'm glad she knows what it's like to be loved. "You were lucky to have each other."

"Yeah, we were." She swallows, her voice turning husky. "Losing Dad... it hit us hard. I wish I'd come back sooner, looked after this place better, but..." She takes a shaky breath and looks down at her notepad.

"You were only, what? Twenty-three? Taking over a business when you've just lost your dad and when you're still struggling to find your feet would have been incredibly difficult. Don't beat yourself up, Violet. You're here now, giving it everything you've got. That's the only thing that matters."

She's watching me now, her eyes a little glossy, her expression so open and vulnerable that it almost makes me wish that what we're doing could be real. That I could pull her onto my lap, kiss her, take away the pain. But that's the last thing she'd want from me, so I take another sip of my coffee to wash the urge away.

"Thank you, Tate," she says softly. Then, with a deep breath, she picks up her pen and smiles a little too brightly. "I guess we got a little off track. I know you're busy, so, um, am I missing anything?"

She's right, I'm getting distracted, and I do need to get back to the office. Clearing my throat, I sit a little straighter and force myself to focus on why I came here in the first place. For another few minutes, I rattle off a few ideas I think are worth trying. Things like leveraging social media for teaser campaigns and adding a Google Maps interior view of the shop to attract people who are searching for a new place to visit.

Violet notes my suggestions while I take my last sip of coffee. As I put my cup down, I catch sight of Jarrod. He's at the counter, laughing with a customer as he takes their order. I do need to go, but I'm strangely reluctant to leave. When I do, Violet will be here all alone with her too-handsy barista. Not that it should matter. According to our agreement, neither of us can engage in other relationships while we're together. And on top of that, I don't see any interest in her eyes when she looks at him. Even so, I don't like the idea that while she's here, he's the one helping her run the place. He's her shoulder to lean on.

For the first time in my life, I consider what it would be like if *I* were someone's shoulder to lean on.

What would it be like if I were Violet's?

CHAPTER TWENTY-TWO

VIOLET

"You kissed him again?" Anna gasps.

I've got my phone pressed to my ear, and I'm hustling down the street toward True Brew. I should be there already. Jarrod has probably started opening procedures, but I should be there as well. I don't like being late under any circumstance, and now that we're getting a little more traction during the morning rush, I hate the idea of losing customers because I couldn't get my ass in gear this morning. I blame that damn kiss for all my tossing and turning. "We have to make it believable," I repeat what I told her last time.

"And a full-on make-out session in the middle of your coffee shop is what's going to sell it?"

An excited little shiver darts up my spine at the memory, but I ignore my body's misguided reaction. "I didn't know it would turn out that way."

"But you didn't stop him?"

I clear my throat. "I may have gotten a bit carried away."

Anna giggles. "That good, huh?"

I give her a noncommittal hum, hoping she won't call

me on it. I shouldn't be losing sleep over Tate. Then again, the Tate I imagined I'd be fake dating isn't the Tate who keeps showing up. Yes, he can still be arrogant, and that smirk of his still gets under my skin. But then there are the other things, like his kindness and his sincere words, that make my heart flutter.

And that kiss yesterday. God, I shouldn't have let him kiss me in the middle of True Brew like that. But the way he was looking at me, like he wanted me, like he wanted to claim me, made it impossible to keep my wits about me. And damn it, in that moment, I'd wanted him to claim me too.

I can't get into that with Anna right now though. I have to focus on work. "I'm almost at the shop," I say. There's an unfamiliar delivery van parked in the loading zone in front of the shop. The sight stops me in my tracks. Jarrod's there, like I knew he would be, and he's talking to the delivery man, gesturing broadly. "I have to go," I tell Anna. "I'll call you later."

After we hang up, I approach the shop. "What's going on?"

Both men turn to me.

"Are you Violet Sinclair?" the delivery man asks.

"Yes."

"I have a delivery for you." He holds out a clipboard. "Just need you to sign here."

I shoot Jarrod a look, but he just shrugs.

After I've signed, the man rounds the back of the truck and returns with a large box on a trolley.

As he comes closer, the name on the box becomes visible, sending a jolt through me. "Did you order a new espresso machine?" I ask Jarrod. Shit. We need it, but a decision like that isn't one he has the authority to make. And there's no way we can afford it.

"Nope. You didn't?"

"No."

"In here?" The delivery man makes his way to the shop door.

With a nod, I pull the unlocked door open for him, then follow him in.

He unloads the box behind the counter, then dusts his hands on his pants. "Would you like me to install it for you?"

"Um. Give me a minute, please." Rubbing at my forehead, I inspect the box and pull it open. Sure enough, there's a brand-new top-of-the-line commercial espresso machine inside. I only know one person who would do something this outrageous. But why? My first payment from him is set to hit at the end of the month, and with it, I could have bought this myself. Not this one, of course. Because I've priced the machines more than once, and this particular one must have cost at least fifteen thousand dollars.

I turn back to the delivery guy. "I'm sorry, can you wait just a little longer?" When he nods, I take a few steps away and dial Tate's number.

He answers on the second ring. "What a pleasant surprise."

Despite his words, he doesn't sound surprised to hear from me at all. "Did you buy a new espresso machine for the shop?"

"I did."

I lower my voice and move farther away from Jarrod and the delivery person. "Why? You didn't need to. You're already paying me."

"You were having problems with your old one. And I

didn't want you to have to wait. This way, Jarrod won't have to fix the machine all the time."

I frown, surprised he even remembers Jarrod's name, let alone that he's always fixing it. "I appreciate the gesture, Tate, but—"

"It's not a gesture, it's a gift. One I'm giving to my fake girlfriend for being so believable. Consider it a bonus."

"I'll pay you back when the first installment comes through. I—"

"You're not paying me back. And I instructed the company to not accept a return, so if you don't want it, then you'll have to find some way of getting rid of it yourself."

His tone is pure satisfaction now. I roll my eyes and huff out a breath, though I'm not as annoyed as I should be. I might even be... touched that he cares enough about my business to help me out. Even if a fifteen-thousand-dollar espresso machine is probably overkill for my little coffee shop. "Well, thank you. Jarrod and I appreciate it."

The noise he makes in response almost sounds like a growl. "Let me make this clear, Violet. I don't care if Jarrod appreciates it. I only care if *you* appreciate it."

Though they shouldn't, those words elicit a warm flutter in my chest. One that tells me I'm taking his comment in a way I probably shouldn't. "Okay. *I* appreciate it," I say softly.

"Good." His voice drops. "You can show me just how much you appreciate it on Friday night."

A sudden vision hits me and my breath falters. It's a vision where Tate makes me show my appreciation in ways that I should *definitely* take offense to, but according to my body's reaction to what I'm imagining, I apparently do not.

Based on the low laugh that comes through the phone, my silence must be telling. "While there are all sorts of enjoyable ways you could thank me, all I'm asking is for you to join me for dinner at Trio's on Friday night."

I screw my face up. Apparently, he can read me like an open book, even over the phone. "I knew that's what you meant."

"Of course you did. So, are you available?"

Desperate to recover my mental and emotional footing, I make my voice as nonchalant as possible. "I'll have to check my calendar."

"*Violet.*"

Oh. Oh wow. The grit in his voice when he says my name sends an involuntary quiver through me. Thank god he's not here to see it.

"Fine. Yes. I suppose it makes sense to be seen in more intimate settings as well as big events to make our relationship believable."

"Exactly," he says smoothly.

"Then yes, I'm available."

When we end the call, I turn back to Jarrod and the delivery man. "Thank you for waiting. And yes, it'd be great if you could install it."

He nods and sets to work while Jarrod joins me, a frown on his face. "Did you find out where it came from?"

"It was Tate."

Behind Jarrod, the delivery man quickly and efficiently adds the machine to the existing plumbing.

Jarrod's brows arch. "Your new boyfriend sure knows how to make a splash."

"He's just trying to help. He noticed that we were having trouble with the machine the other day, and he didn't want us to have to worry about fixing it all the time."

"I bet that's what he was worried about," Jarrod murmurs.

I turn to him. "What do you mean?"

He shakes his head, a smile flickering at the corners of his lips. "Nothing. But since we now have a shiny new espresso machine, let's practice using it by making ourselves a pre-rush coffee."

I smile. He's being optimistic, considering the rush isn't all that much of a rush. Not yet anyway. But it will be soon. I know it.

CHAPTER TWENTY-THREE

VIOLET

Anna plops down on my bed with a sigh. "I'm feeling a tad bit jealous right now. I've wanted to have dinner at Trio's for ages."

Ducking my head, I smooth the satiny material of my red dress down over my hips. "Does this look okay?"

"You look fabulous. You'll have Tate tripping over his own tongue."

I laugh, but my heart sinks a little. "Believe me, with the women Tate has been with, the only thing he'll be tripping over while in my presence is his limp dick."

"Pfft." She swats at me from where she's curled up on the mattress. "Tate would have to be blind not to see how gorgeous you are."

Gingerly, I bend down and give her a hug, careful of the expensive dress I've just slipped into. "What would I do without you?"

"You wouldn't be going out to Trio's tonight, that's for sure."

A laugh bubbles out of me. "You're taking credit for all of this?"

She arches a brow. "Of course. If I hadn't invited you to Onyx, none of this would have happened." Her smirk turns into a genuine smile. "But seriously, I'm happy for you, Vi. You deserve to be spoiled a little."

"Thanks. I'm looking forward to it."

"Even though your date is your least favorite billionaire?"

Is he my least favorite? When Tate came to see me at True Brew, he was genuinely interested in the shop and why it's so special to me. Then he went and bought me an espresso machine. Just the memory of how well he's treated me since we started this fake relationship has a lick of warmth spreading through me.

"Tate isn't the worst company."

"Wow." Anna's brows jump to her hairline. "That's praise I never thought I'd hear from you. What happened to *Tate King is such a manwhore*?" She parrots back the words I may or may not have said to her after that second night at Onyx.

"Well, he's still a manwhore. But I guess maybe there's more to him than *just* that."

"So you're saying that maybe your opinion is a bit outdated?"

I screw up my face, but I can't lie. "Maybe I've held on to my bad first impression of him for too long."

"It's a distinct possibility." Her straight face is belied by the amusement in her voice.

I pick a cushion up off my bed and throw it at her.

She ducks, laughing as it misses her. Then she checks her watch and hops off the bed. "Okay, I'd better go. Lover boy is going to be here soon."

"Fake lover boy." I correct her, even if the nervous anticipation dancing in my stomach doesn't feel all that fake.

I see her out. Then, to make this evening feel more like the business transaction it is, I grab my purse and my keys and leave my apartment. With the way my pulse races every time I think of him lately, meeting Tate downstairs feels safer. I stand at the bottom of my apartment block steps and pull my phone out to scroll while I wait.

I've just opened True Brew's Instagram account when Tate's big black town car pulls up. I drop my phone into my clutch and head toward it. Tate is out of the car before Jeremy has even rounded the hood.

He stalks toward me. "Why are you waiting on the street?"

I blink at him. "I didn't want you to have to come upstairs."

He threads his fingers through mine, sending a tiny electric shock up my arm. "I have no problem coming to your door, Violet. It's dark out, and this isn't the safest neighborhood." Hand still tight around mine, he leads me toward the car. The whole way there, I fight the warmth spreading through me. The neighborhood really is a relatively safe one, but even so, that he cares about my safety when there's nothing in our agreement that says he has to is way too endearing.

By now, Jeremy is holding the door open for us. "Evening, ma'am."

"Good evening, Jeremy." I barely have a chance to smile at him before Tate bundles me inside.

I slide over, and he follows me in. As Jeremy pulls the car into traffic, Tate watches me with enigmatic eyes that drop to take me in. A smile curls his lips. "You look beautiful."

"Thank you." Those butterflies are back. I mentally tell

them to go away. This is Tate. Being charming comes naturally to him. It doesn't mean anything.

Even so, I'm conscious of his proximity the whole ride to the restaurant. My attempt at small talk is way more stilted than it should be, and Tate's amused gaze tells me he knows why. I'm pretty sure he enjoys knowing he disconcerts me.

When we pull up outside Trio's, there's a line of people waiting to get into the uber-exclusive restaurant.

"How did you get a reservation last minute?" I ask him.

"I'm a silent investor. It gives me some privileges."

"So you invest in more than just sex clubs?"

He lets out an easy laugh. "Only one sex club. But I have multiple restaurants."

"Which do you visit more?" The question is out before I think it through. I sound like I'm interrogating him. Like I'm more interested in his sexual habits than I should be, considering I don't have any romantic interest in him. Since I can't take the words back, I smooth my expression, hoping that I come across as mildly curious and nothing more.

No such luck. The wicked grin that grows on his face has my cheeks flaming.

"Violet, if you want to know how often I experience what you and I did together at the club, you just have to ask."

"That's not what I—"

"Never."

My mouth snaps shut and I tilt my head. "You've never been with someone at the club? That doesn't seem likely."

A muscle pulses in his jaw. "I've been with women at the club. Not as often as you probably think, and not recently. Except for you."

I digest that information, caught between confusion and relief. "Then what do you mean never?"

"The club has always been an easy way to scratch an itch when I don't want to deal with being recognized. That's not what it was about when I was with you. I had no intention of being with anyone that night. I was there strictly for business. But when I saw you come in, I couldn't resist." His eyes darken, his voice lowering, becoming rougher as he continues. "I wanted to know about you. Why you were there, how I could help you relax. What I could do to make you mine for the night. *That's* never happened before."

My heart beats wildly. It pounds so hard against my ribs I'm sure he can hear it. *Why* do his words affect me so intensely? Part of me wants to write off his confession as a line he'd give to anyone, but I can't. What reason does he have to lie? And if he's lying, then why is he watching me with such an unwavering intensity?

Tate's familiar smile—the one I've always considered cocky but am beginning to realize screams of justified self-confidence—is slow and knowing. He sees exactly what he's doing to me. Before I can unscramble my brain and come up with a coherent response, Jeremy opens my door for me.

Outside the car, the patrons in line are staring and murmuring, probably wondering if a celebrity will appear. While I wait for Tate to join me, I shuffle my feet and keep my face averted. Somehow, this moment is worse than when the photographers were lined up along the red carpet at the gala. As if the scrutiny of my peers is more meaningful than the impartial camera lens.

When Tate takes his place by my side, his too perceptive eyes sweep over me, then move to the line of hopefuls waiting to get a seat in the restaurant.

He cups my jaw, and his seductive lips curve up. "They're staring at you because you look stunning. Hold your head up, butterfly. Show them what you're made of."

I lick my lips and nod, suddenly fixated on his proximity rather than the people watching.

He brushes a thumb over my bottom lip, following the path my tongue just took. For a moment I struggle to draw in oxygen, and I'm hit with a new worry. Will I have to kiss him again tonight? The possibility makes my knees wobble.

When he clasps my hand, I can't help but examine where we're connected. My hand looks so small wrapped in his, and I like the sensation far too much. I must be starved of affection from a man if such a simple gesture feels this good. Or maybe it's the strange sense of security that winds its way through my chest at his touch. Something I'm beginning to realize I haven't felt in far too long. It was completely missing in my relationship with Eric.

Just another warning sign I missed.

Side by side, we make our way into the lavish restaurant. The kitchen is open to the dining area, allowing patrons to view chefs skillfully preparing gourmet dishes. A staircase at the far end leads up to the attached bar that has its own street-facing entrance to allow people to enter without passing through the restaurant.

A pretty hostess meets us, a big smile on her face. "Mr. King. We're so glad to see you back here again."

She leads us to a booth at the back. The table is covered in a white tablecloth, and flickering candles add to the already warm atmosphere. Tate finally lets go of my hand so I can slide in. But instead of settling into the opposite seat, he slides in right beside me.

CHAPTER TWENTY-FOUR

TATE

Confusion flashes across Violet's face. "What are you doing?"

I sit close, draping my arm along the back of the booth so that my sleeve brushes her bare shoulders. "People come here to see as well as be seen. And what I want them to see is that I'm so crazy about my girlfriend that I can't handle leaving any space between us."

She rolls her eyes and lets out a disbelieving laugh. But she also doesn't move away, so I take it as a victory.

A waiter appears next to the table and hands us menus. "Can I offer you a drink before ordering?"

I look at Violet. "Do you have a preference, or would you like me to choose a bottle?"

"You can order."

"A bottle of *Charmes Chambertin Grand Cru*, please," I say to the waiter.

His face lights up. "Very good, sir. I'll be back shortly to take your order."

Violet is studying the menu, but since I could list each item on it without looking, I study her instead. She looks beautiful. Her hair is loose around her shoulders, which are bare except for the thin red straps of her dress. The one that clings to her body in a way that makes me want to peel it off her so I can run my hands along the bare curves beneath. With her eyes cast down, her long lashes almost brush her cheekbones. And those full pink lips of hers? They look as soft as they've felt under mine every time I've kissed her. Before I can stop the direction of my thoughts, I'm imagining how they'd feel wrapped around my dick.

Fuck. The organ in question swells and jerks as more imagined situations and sensations flare to life in my mind: the heat of her mouth on me, the silken slide of her tongue, her body writhing under me, damp with sweat after I've teased her for hours, the way she'd clench around my cock when I finally let her come.

Jesus.

When those clear blue eyes meet mine, I do my best to force the fantasies out of my head.

"There aren't any prices?" she asks.

My voice when I speak is rough. The mental imagery still has me in a stranglehold. "How can patrons show how much money doesn't mean to them if they're worried about prices?"

She lets out a laugh. "That's ridiculous. What about the people who come here who aren't millionaires like you?"

"Billionaires," I correct her automatically.

She looks at me blankly for a second before scrunching up her nose. "When you get to a certain point, surely the extra zero doesn't make that much difference."

"Sometimes that extra zero is what keeps you on top."

Her head tilts. "On top of what?"

"The people who enjoy looking down on others."

With a furrowed brow, she gives a little shake of her

head. "Has anyone ever looked down on you way up there where you're sitting?"

I let out a wry chuckle. "In my world, people will use any chink in your armor as an excuse to prove they're better than you. It's best not to give them that opportunity."

She searches my gaze, a little line still etched between her brows. But there's concern in her expression now, not disbelief. The candlelight reflecting in her eyes makes her irises look like twin blue flames. "That sounds... exhausting," she says softly.

That simple observation makes my chest draw tight. "Sometimes you have to step away from something to realize just how exhausting it is." And being here with her is exactly like that—a break from putting on a mask it feels like I've been wearing for far too long.

She hesitates for a moment, then touches my arm. "Do you get a chance to step away from it?"

My gaze drifts slowly over her face, lingering a moment too long on that plush mouth of hers. "Sometimes."

There's a subtle shift in the air between us, and the slender column of her throat moves in a swallow.

But when I don't expand on what I said, she rolls her lower lip between her teeth, then nods. "I know what you mean. I've spent so long concentrating on nothing but keeping True Brew going. I didn't realize how all-consuming it's been until now."

I raise my brows. "Now?"

"Sitting down and enjoying a meal with an attract—uh, I mean, with a man."

My slow smile has her delicate jaw tightening, but she manages to keep the rest of her expression even.

Rather than teasing her about her slip up, I move the hand still resting behind her to the back of her neck and stroke lazy circles over her skin with my thumb. "I'm enjoying it too." My attention drops to her lips again for just a second. "Far more than I ever anticipated."

Sparks flare in her eyes and she stiffens, apparently taking my words as an insult. "You were the one who came to me."

I shake my head, still smiling. "I don't mean you. I mean pretending to be in love."

Those pretty eyes of hers soften, along with her body. I'm still stroking the warm skin of her neck, and consciously or not, she allows herself to lean back into it slightly, as if she's enjoying my touch as much as I'm enjoying touching her.

"Is that what we're doing?" she asks.

I cock a brow in query.

"Pretending to be in love. We're pretending to date. But I didn't know we were pretending to be in love."

I sift my fingers through her hair and a tiny shiver works its way through her. "Are you worried your acting skills aren't up to the job?"

The softness in her eyes disappears and they narrow in that look of irritation I'm so familiar with. "You should probably be more concerned about your own acting skills. Have you ever even been in a relationship?"

I suppress a grin, but before I can reply, she shakes her head, her full lips tilting down. "I'm sorry, that was uncalled for."

I go back to stroking her neck. It feels a little too good under my fingertips to want to stop. "Since when has that stopped you?"

Her brows pull together, and she gnaws on her lower lip, but the waiter appears next to us before she can tell me what's obviously bothering her.

He cradles a bottle of wine in his hands, presenting it to me.

Once I've given him a nod of approval, he expertly uncorks the bottle and pours a small amount into my glass. With my spare hand, I pick it up and take a sip.

"Perfect, thank you."

With a polite smile, he fills both glasses, then sets the bottle on the table. "Are you ready to order now, or would you like some more time?"

Violet squeaks and picks up her menu again. She barely had a chance to look at it before I distracted her. With her lip caught between her teeth, she scans the page, no doubt searching for what she hopes is the least expensive option.

"Can you give us a few more minutes?" I ask the waiter. When he's gone, I resume the small circles I've been rubbing on Violet's neck but will myself not to be distracted by my growing obsession with touching her. "Butterfly," I say softly. "Get whatever you want. I promise I can afford anything on that menu."

She arches a brow at me. "Just because you can afford it doesn't mean you should have to. You're already paying me to be here. Not to mention buying me gifts you absolutely don't have to."

"Turns out, I quite like buying my girlfriend gifts. I'd like to buy you a meal you'll remember."

Confusion is written all over her face. "Why?"

Does she really not understand that I like spending time with her? That I want to make the experience special? "So that maybe after this agreement is over, when you're happily married to some lucky guy, you'll think back to this night with me. Even if it's just because the meal was the best you've ever had."

Violet stares at me, and once again, something shimmers

in the air between us. Something fragile but almost tangible. A connection that tugs at my chest. That urges me to close the distance between us.

She wets her lips, then looks down at the menu. With a soft exhale, she closes it and smiles up at me. "Okay. I'll have the house-made black truffle ravioli with the brown butter and sage sauce."

"Good choice."

"And Tate?" She places her hand on my thigh. "Thank you. I doubt I'll forget this night. Or any of the other things you've done for me and True Brew." She takes a deep breath. "I... I'm sorry I wasn't very nice to you when you and Mark were in college." Sincerity shines from her eyes.

Is that what's been worrying her? "Don't apologize for that," I say. "I didn't exactly put my best foot forward when we met. And after that first visit, it might have even been on purpose."

"Are you saying you were deliberately provoking me?" She's trying to fight a smile, but she's doing a terrible job of it.

I laugh. "I enjoyed seeing that fire in your eyes when you would snap at me."

She sits back in her chair and shakes her head. "Here I was thinking I was bringing you down a couple of notches. And all the while, you were having fun."

"More fun than I would have ever admitted to you—or your brother."

She cocks her head in question. Before she can voice it, though, the waiter is back.

Violet watches me through her lashes the whole time he's there. Certain she'll ask why I didn't want to admit anything to her brother, I remain silent after he takes our order and leaves, waiting her out. But she doesn't ask, and for an instant, a sensation that almost feels like disappointment wells up inside me. It's gone a moment later, when she turns our conversation to something a little less personal.

The food is incredible, as expected. Violet and I try one another's dishes—the black truffle ravioli for her, of course, and the Chilean sea bass for me. The act of sharing food is surprisingly intimate. As Violet mentioned at the gala last weekend, I don't exactly make a habit of wining and dining women. This is a different experience for me. But sharing a meal with her, listening to her moan as she enjoys the flavors, then watching a smile light up her face as she answers my questions about her life and True Brew, has me captivated. I'm not sure if she notices the way I steer her away from questions about my family. If she does, she's gracious enough not to let on.

We've mostly kept the conversation light, but when she mentions her ex-boyfriend, Eric, in passing, and her shoulders tense, I probe for more information.

"How long ago did the two of you break up?"

She hesitates, then lets out a sigh. "Just over a year ago."

"Can I ask what happened? You mentioned at Onyx it was a rough breakup."

Her wide eyes shoot up to mine. Is it because I mentioned that night at the club? Or is it because I'm asking about her relationship?

"You don't have to tell me if you don't want to."

She studies me again, her mouth twisting a little. I expect her to brush me off, but maybe because the wine we're drinking is quite strong—or because she's finally relaxing around me—she doesn't. "No, it's okay." She takes a sip from her glass. "We met at a community event in Augusta. I was hosting an information booth for the non-profit I was working for, and Eric was there with his uncle's political campaign."

"His uncle's in politics?"

She nods. "Yes. Senator Rawlins. Eric is his fundraising manager. Or he was when we were dating anyway. Though he was angling to be the finance manager. I guess he might have worked his way into that position by now."

Well that answers the question about whether they're still in touch. I didn't think so, but now I know.

Violet gives her head a little shake, as if she's gotten distracted. "Anyway, he was good-looking and charming, and when he came past our information booth and started flirting, I was flattered. So when he asked me out, I said yes."

I'm already irritated by this guy. The thought of Violet being so impressed by him that she *wanted* to date him when she was so reluctant to even give me the time of day has an unfamiliar emotion eating at me.

"We dated for a couple of months," she continues, her thumb rubbing over the rim of her wine glass as she speaks. "But I realized something just didn't feel right. I'd been debating breaking it off. But then..." Her voice catches and she blinks a couple of times. "Then Dad died."

I brush tendrils of hair away from her face and stroke my thumb over her cheek. "You okay, butterfly?"

For a heartbeat, her lashes flutter shut and she leans into my touch. That small act triggers a tightness in my chest.

"I just miss him," she says. "And I hate that I was so far away when he died."

I slide my hand under the silky fall of her hair and cup the back of her neck, squeezing lightly until her eyes, glossy with unshed tears, meet mine. "I saw you and your dad together when you came to Mark's graduation, and it was obvious how close you were—how much you loved him. That knowledge would have been with him at the end, even if you couldn't be."

I hold her gaze until she gives me a nod, then I lean back, waiting for her to continue.

"When I got back after the funeral, I was a mess." Her laugh doesn't hold much humor. "Dad had always been my anchor—him and Mark. I felt... untethered. I should have moved back home to be with Mark, but... I struggled with the idea of being here when Dad wasn't. Being back in Maine didn't feel right either. Everything felt wrong. Including Eric. I tried to break it off with him, but he refused to accept it. He kept coming around, bringing me gifts, ordering in food on days when I'd barely eaten. On the surface, he became the perfect doting boyfriend. But in hindsight, he was ignoring my wishes and already trying to control me. I fell for the act though. I ignored that little niggling voice of doubt because it was better than feeling so alone." She inhales shakily.

There's a pressure growing behind my ribs as she talks, and I flex my hands to loosen them, only realizing then that they've been clenched. "It's not always easy to see past the masks people show us."

She smiles, but it doesn't reach her eyes, as if she doesn't quite believe me.

"Tell me what he did, Violet."

"It started small. So small I didn't notice. Little criticisms. The shade of lipstick I was wearing was too bright, or my dress didn't fit quite right. All said in a way that made it sound like he was just trying to help me. And I listened." She shakes her head. "Every time I did something he didn't like, he'd let me know in subtle ways that I'd let him down. When we went out, he'd get jealous.

Accuse me of flirting with any single man who spoke to me. And instead of realizing what was going on and leaving him, I just tried harder to appease him. And if I did question his reactions, he'd twist it all around. Make me doubt my own mind." She glances at me before quickly looking away. "It makes me feel so stupid when I say it out loud."

"Hey." I turn her chin, so she's forced to meet my gaze. "You aren't stupid. You were alone and grieving, and he took advantage of that. He caught you when you were vulnerable and knew exactly what to say to make you believe he was on your side—so you'd trust him. But you figured him out. That's why you're here now, working hard, bringing True Brew back to life. You walked away from him."

Her eyes close as she lets out a sigh. "Yes, but only after I found him balls deep in one of his interns." The laugh that escapes her is tinged with bitterness. "He used to accuse me of flirting with just about every man who looked in my direction, but he was the one screwing around on me. And considering all his interns were young and pretty, I'm sure she wasn't the only one."

Anger simmers hot beneath the surface of my skin. I want to track this Eric asshole down and punish him for not treating her the way she deserves to be treated—for making her doubt herself. "What did he do when you ended it?" I ask. From what she's revealed about him, I can't imagine he'd let her go easily once he sank his claws into her. I've met plenty of people like him in the business world, and in my social circle. Narcissistic manipulators who don't care about anyone but themselves.

"He called, but I didn't answer. So he left messages. At first, he apologized and asked for another chance, then he started blaming me. Told me it was my fault that he cheated. That's when I blocked—"

"Wait," I growl. "He blamed *you*?"

Her gaze darts to mine and she pinches her bottom lip between her teeth. "He said he wouldn't have had to turn to someone else if I'd been able to... to satisfy him."

My shoulders tense with the need to take some kind of physical action. To find a way to hurt this guy the way he hurt her. I have to pull in a deep breath to calm myself down. Then I cup her cheek so she can't look away. "Tell me you know that isn't true, Violet. Tell me you know he was just trying to cover up his own inadequacies."

She stares up at me, eyes shadowed by residual hurt, and lets out a ragged breath. "I do. I do know that. I may have let it—let *him*—get in my head for a while. But I got past it. With Anna's help of course." She gives me a lopsided smile.

It's not enough though. I need to make sure. "Just the small taste I got of you at Onyx had me wanting so much more. There's no way being with you wouldn't satisfy any man."

"Tate," she whispers.

I realize my mistake. She doesn't want me talking about that night. She doesn't want to remember what I did to her —regardless of how much she enjoyed it. It makes sense to me now why she was there—what she was looking for—consciously or not. I'm glad I was able to give that to her. Even if she wishes it had been someone else.

Just that thought alone—of another man being the one to give her what she needed—has my jaw clenching.

I force myself to let her go. There's something I know about myself now that I didn't before. I don't like seeing those shadows in Violet's pretty blue eyes. I like when they're flashing fire at me, I like when they're shining with happiness, or when they're hazy with arousal. I don't fucking like when they're filled with pain. I think I would do a lot to make sure I don't see them that way again.

Violet's cheeks are flushed, and she takes a gulp of wine.

"Wow," she says. "Sorry, that was probably way more than you wanted to hear." She lets out a little laugh. "Probably not what you were planning to talk about when you invited me to dinner."

"I asked because I wanted to know. I'm just glad you felt like you could tell me."

She hesitates and her eyebrows knit together.

"What?" I ask.

"Other than Anna, you're the only person I've told."

I still as I take in what that means. Mark mentioned that Violet withdrew after their dad's death. I'd forgotten his comment about not knowing the reason behind it. Yet she trusted me enough to share something so personal. That knowledge steals the oxygen from my lungs, and I have to siphon in a slow breath to replace it.

She gives me a flustered smile, then pushes her plate away. "I'm so full," she says, changing the subject. "That was delicious though. Thank you."

The waiter returns just then to take our plates and ask if we want dessert.

"I couldn't," Violet says, "but if you want to, please go ahead."

I shake my head, but I'm not ready for the night to be over. "How about we go upstairs for a drink?"

She glances over at the stairway to the bar, then back to me. At first, I'm certain she'll shut me down, but instead, she holds my gaze and nods. "I'd love to."

CHAPTER TWENTY-FIVE

VIOLET

As I wait for Tate to pay for our meal, I mull over my decision to tell him about Eric. What is it about this man that has me dropping my walls so easily? He's so different from what I expected—from what he was like when he was in college. Could I have misjudged him even back then?

The memory of that first morning hits me. The first time I ever laid eyes on him, he was sauntering out of his bedroom in just a pair of boxer briefs with two women following him. His hair was tousled from what I could only assume was two sets of fingers running through it, and there were literal scratch marks on his chest. His eyes widened when he saw me at the breakfast bar, and then he quickly sent the women packing, despite their obvious desire to stay.

I push the memory away. What Tate chose to do back then, probably still chooses to do, is up to him. It doesn't make him a bad person, and the knowledge that I treated him as if he were because of his personal choices has guilt weighing heavily on my chest. Tate having consensual sex with anyone he wants to is absolutely none of my business.

I try to ignore the sharp twinge of jealousy behind my ribs. It's only because he's pretending to be mine at the moment that I don't want to think about him with other women.

After signing the bill, Tate slides out of the booth, and I follow. As always, he puts his hand on my back to guide me between tables. On our way up the stairs, he walks behind me, and I'm suddenly self-conscious. Is he staring at my ass? Is he *not* staring at my ass? Which one would I prefer? No. I shut down that train of thought. It's better if I don't know the answer to that question.

The bar is crowded and far louder than the restaurant below. As Tate leads me forward, I swear people make way for him, as if they know he's one of the most powerful men here. Or maybe it's just my imagination. Though the way women's heads turn as we pass is definitely *not* my imagination.

We reach the bar, and miraculously, considering how many people are clustered around it, a bartender immediately appears, ready to take our drink order.

Tate raises a brow at me, silently signaling for me to go first.

"I'll have a Cosmo."

His eyes drop to my mouth. Is he remembering the first time we kissed the way I suddenly am? Is he imagining the taste of vodka and cranberry juice on my lips at the club that night?

He nods at the bartender. "A Cosmo and scotch on the rocks, thanks."

As the bartender sets about making our drinks, Tate turns to face me. The crowd on either side is pressing close, and when someone jostles me from behind, Tate slides his arm around my waist and tugs me in until I'm pressed against the hard wall of his chest.

The sensation has crazy impulses scattering through my head. As fervently as I've willed myself to forget, the feel of him against me, and the memory of what he did to me at Onyx, has a throb centering low in my abdomen. It might be the wine we had with dinner, but the thought of him touching me—of doing more than touching me—has invaded my thoughts tonight. Especially now, when he's standing so close I can smell the fresh, masculine scent emanating from him.

Maybe my expression gives me away, or the way I keep staring at that little triangle of tanned skin at the base of his throat where his top button is undone, because he dips his head closer to mine. "What's going on in that pretty head of yours?"

My stomach sinks. There's no way I can admit that after only two official dates, I'm edging closer to succumbing to his charm. It's the wine. It has to be.

Luckily, the bartender chooses that moment to place our drinks on the bar. Quickly, I pick mine up and take a long sip to avoid the question.

When I work up the nerve to peek up at Tate, the familiar amused glint in his eyes makes it clear my actions answered for me.

I rack my brain for a safe topic that will douse the heated tension simmering between us. "How are sales for Genesis-1 going?"

The corners of his lips turn up, but he answers. "They're going well. Past our initial projections, so I'd consider it a success so far."

I nod a little too enthusiastically. "That's good. Is it because of your marketing?"

He tilts his head and watches me, his gaze moving lazily over my face. "The sustainable features are a big draw. The luxury market in New York is always hungry for innovation. We're interested in whether we can replicate the same interest in other markets."

He raises his glass to his lips, his throat working in a way that's far too sexy as he swallows.

I must be watching a little too closely because he lets out a low laugh. "Are our sales of Genesis-1 really what you're thinking about right now? Or do you have something else on your mind?"

I wet my lips because, god, every word out of his mouth only makes mine go drier.

His pupils flare in response, and he brings a hand up. He leaves it hovering a fraction of an inch away from my cheek, as if he's deciding whether he should touch me. The heat radiating from his palm warms my skin and sends my pulse skyrocketing.

"Maybe you're thinking the same thing I am," he says.

My breathing quickens next, almost matching the speed of my pulse. "What are you thinking?"

His eyes are locked on mine. "I'm thinking about how you felt when you came on my fingers. I'm thinking that I want to feel it again."

"Tate," I breathe. His words triggering an ache deep inside of me.

Finally, his hand makes contact, hot against the side of my face. Then he slides it into my hair, tangling his fingers in the strands and tugging just enough to send sparks racing over my skin.

Angling in, he brings his mouth so close that his lips graze the shell of my ear. "If I were to pull the hem of your dress up and slide my fingers underneath your panties, would I find you wet?"

Frozen to the spot, I let out a shuddery breath. Even though I was thinking about this just a few seconds ago, acknowledging that I'm attracted to him, that I want what he did to me before, that I might want more, leaves *me* vulnerable. Not him.

"Should I find out?" he murmurs.

I think I whimper out loud, but it's so noisy in here I'm not sure.

But the way his lips curl up at the corners and his eyes darken further tells me I must have, and he obviously heard it. His hand barely skims my hip, touching but not touching. "If you'll let me, I could make you feel good again, butterfly."

"Tate, my man." A loud voice close by has me almost jumping out of my skin. "Fancy seeing you here."

When the owner of the voice appears beside us, Tate lowers his hand casually and turns to the intruder, wearing a smile that would have a more observant man backing away in a hurry.

"Aaron. What a pleasant surprise." His icy tone contradicts the sentiment.

The man's beady eyes run over me, snagging on my cleavage, and he licks his lips. Then he turns his attention to Tate. "We're here celebrating a win. We took over Paladine Construction today."

From the ruddiness of his cheeks and his overly bright eyes, it's obvious that he's been celebrating a little too enthusiastically.

"This is the first I've heard of it."

Aaron puffs his chest out, looking smug. "We wanted to keep it under the radar until it was done."

"I guess congratulations are in order, then," Tate says, looking perfectly composed, even as tension radiates off him.

"Indeed." Aaron grins. "Maybe I can buy you a drink later."

Tate's expression is less than inviting. "Maybe."

When Aaron moves on, Tate leans close to me again, but the heat from a few minutes ago has cooled. "I need to make a quick call. Do you want to come with me or stay here?"

"Oh, uh..." I'm still disoriented from the moment we shared before Aaron interrupted, so it takes me several seconds to formulate a response. "Do you want to leave, or...?"

He ghosts his fingers down my arm, leaving sparks in his wake. "I'm not sure I'm done with you yet."

My heart accelerates again, pounding out a staccato rhythm against my breastbone. "If you're not going to be long, I'll just stay here."

He nods and half turns so he can address the bartender. "Another Cosmo for the lady, please." He leans closer, filling the space around me with his scent as his jaw brushes my cheek. "I'll be back, butterfly."

The bartender pours the drink in front of me, and when he slides it across the bar, I smile my thanks and pick it up. As I take a slow sip, I survey the crowded bar. Halfway through, I unintentionally catch the eye of the man who was just talking to Tate. I look away quickly, but a moment later, he's back at my side, as if taking that second of eye contact as an invitation to chat.

"Tate gone to find out if I'm telling the truth?" he asks, flashing me an obnoxious smirk.

I shift uncomfortably and play dumb. "I'm not sure what he's doing. But he said he'll be back soon."

"You know." He licks his already wet lips in a way that sends a tendril of disgust through me. "I've always admired Tate's taste in women. And you're no exception, beautiful." He presses forward as he says it, and I step back, avoiding contact. Clutching my drink close to my chest, I scan our surroundings in hopes that Tate is on his way back, suddenly wishing I'd gone with him instead of staying here on my own.

Aaron edges even closer, his breath hot on my skin. "I may not be a billionaire," he says, that last word almost a sneer, "but I bet my dick can give you just as good a ride as his. When he's done with you, why don't you take it for a test drive?" He clamps a hand down on my waist and squeezes.

I leap away from him with a shudder. "Don't touch me!"

His eyes go wide then, and he takes a step back.

CHAPTER TWENTY-SIX

TATE

I finish the call to Roman after giving him the information Aaron just foolishly boasted about. Several of Paladine Construction's investors have been wary of a takeover. Now that we know it's happened, Roman will want to get on the phone to them ASAP. See if they want to invest in a larger and more stable option instead.

Before I make my way back to Violet, I take a moment to clear my head. I let myself get too carried away with her tonight. With her soft body pressed against mine and her peaches and cream scent filling my senses, it's been too easy to forget what this is and what I promised Mark—that I'd take care of his sister. I'm pretty sure taking care of her doesn't include offering to make her come again.

I'll go back, we'll have one more drink, and then I'll take her home.

I'm returning through the crowd to the bar when that thought flies out of my head. That asshole Aaron is back at the spot where I left Violet.

I don't like the slimy expression on his face, but the trepidation and disgust on hers have me speeding up and shouldering people out of the way.

A heartbeat before I make it to them, Violet jumps back, holding her drink in front of her with both hands, as if it will shield her from that piece of shit.

Anger blazes through me. In two strides, I'm there. "Get your hands off her," I bark.

His eyes go wide, but he quickly tries to hide his shock by laughing. "Come on, Tate. No need to be greedy. We both know she'll be warming someone else's bed tomorrow. It might as well be mine." He leers at her again, his tongue slicking out to wet his lips. "Maybe we could tag team her."

When he reaches out as if to touch her again, that protective urge I felt before rips through me. He thinks he has a right to lay a hand on her? That I'll give her up tomorrow and he can make a move? He's wrong, and I'll make sure he gets that through his head.

I grip his wrist so hard he lets out a pained grunt. "Touch her again, and I'll break your arm." I let him go with a shove that sends him stumbling back.

He cradles his wrist, eyes wide, then lets out an incredulous laugh. "You can't be serious. I know you, Tate. Everyone knows you. There's no way she's more than a one-night good time—"

I take a step closer, fisting my hands at my sides. Red washes my vision, and the need to make it clear Violet is off-limits pummels me. "Keep a civil tongue in your mouth when you're talking about my future wife."

Aaron's jaw goes slack, and his beady eyes dart between Violet and me. "Your future *wife*?"

Violet clutches at the back of my shirt. "Tate, what are you doing?" she hisses. Her voice is just loud enough for me to hear over the music.

I hook my arm around her waist and pull her to my side. The truth is, I don't know what I'm doing. I'm operating on sheer instinct. And what my instinct is telling me is that I brought Violet into this. Now I need to protect her, and this is the best way. "I don't plan to let her go." The words are for Aaron, but I'm looking at Violet.

Her lips part, and her eyes go wide.

Come on, butterfly. Just go along with it.

She blinks and swallows, then turns to Aaron. "That's right. Tate asked, and I said yes." She looks back at me, her big blue eyes full of uncertainty. "When you know, you know, right?"

Even though she's saying it for Aaron's benefit alone, warmth blooms in my chest.

"Yeah, I bet you knew as soon as you saw his bank balance," Aaron sneers.

I'm in motion before I realize it, my fist meeting his cheek with a satisfying crack. He reels backward, and there's a shocked scramble of people moving out of the way. They don't have to worry about there being a fight though. Aaron doesn't have it in him. I stalk forward, grab him by the lapel and yank him toward me.

When I speak, it's loud enough for the people nearby us to hear. "Insult my fiancée again, *touch* her again, and a punch will be the least of your worries."

I let go of him, and he slumps back against the bar. Then I find Violet's hand, slide my fingers through hers and stalk off, taking her with me.

"Tate," she whispers. "Is your hand okay?"

I barely feel it, adrenaline and something else pumping through my system.

"What if he files assault charges?" she asks.

I let out a humorless laugh. "He has too much riding on

our company. He's not stupid. If he wants to watch me get locked up, he'll see his net value fall dramatically."

She falls quiet then but squeezes my hand. That simple gesture and what it conveys—that even though my actions just now were incredibly impulsive, she's still with me—are more than I can take. I pull her around a corner, and once I'm sure we're alone, I back her up against the wall, my large body dwarfing hers.

She looks up at me, eyes a wide stormy blue. "We shouldn't have said what we did."

"It's a verbal amendment to the contract," I say. "We'll formalize it first thing on Monday."

"But Tate—"

Curving my hand around her slender neck, I use my thumb on the angle of her jaw to tilt her face up to mine. I don't want to talk about the contract right now. I don't want to talk about terms and conditions. For a moment, I want to forget this is an arrangement. I want to believe what she said before. *When you know, you know*.

I slide my hand into her hair and pause there. She knows what I'm going to ask. How can she not with the way I'm staring at her mouth?

"Yes," she whispers, though I haven't asked the question.

With a groan, I crush my lips to hers.

She opens, letting me in, and her taste engulfs me again, pulling another groan from deep within my chest. Her mouth is hot, soft and so fucking sweet. I cup her jaw, tilting her open even more. The needy sound she makes in response sends a bolt of lust straight to my cock.

I nip her bottom lip, then take her mouth again, tasting her over and over, skating my hand over her hip and waist, drifting it over her throat and the swell of her breasts.

She shivers, then arches into me.

Satisfaction floods my veins. For now, she's my fiancée. Mine. And she's responding so perfectly to me, wanting me as much as I want her.

"Tate," she gasps in between kisses.

I can barely hear her over the blood whooshing in my ears. Desire has a stranglehold on me. My fingers rake up her thighs, sliding under her dress, seeking the hot, wet center of her. I stroke my thumb over the satin of her panties. She's damp, the material clinging to her sex.

A breath shudders out of her as her hips pulse against my hand.

I could get her off right here. It wouldn't take long. I could slide my fingers inside her and relish the way she clamps down around them. Just like she did that night at Onyx. I could prove to her what a liar Eric was when he told her she couldn't satisfy him. I could show her what hearing the shit Aaron said about her did to me.

And yet, after one more taste of her mouth, I force my hand out from under her dress. With my forehead pressed to hers, I smooth the material down over her thighs.

"Tate?" This time, her tone is tentative.

I pull back and survey her. She blinks, her lashes sweeping over the uncertainty in her gaze.

"I want you," I say. Not for a second do I want her to think that I don't. "It's taking all my willpower not to make you come right now. But I won't touch you again unless I know you're completely on board with it."

I don't want her regretting it tomorrow like she did when she found out it was me at Onyx.

The hot, glazed look in her eyes fades a little, even though her cheeks are still pink, her mouth still swollen from my kisses.

I can't stop myself from dusting my thumb over her bottom lip.

Her eyelids flutter shut, and her head drops back against the wall. "Right." She inhales a shaky breath. "Because us being together is an act."

I grit my teeth. She's right. It is. So why do the feelings she evokes in me seem so much more real than anything else in my life?

She peers up at me from under her lashes. "We don't really need to amend the contract, do we?"

I force my spine not to stiffen and breathe through the sharp sting in my chest. "Not getting cold feet now, are you, butterfly?" I brush a strand of hair from her flushed cheek.

"Surely that man won't say anything about it, right?"

A huff escapes me. "I can guarantee the news has already spread. Hell, the whole thing was probably caught on video by more than one person."

"Of course." She lets out a breath, her shoulders slumping. "I guess being engaged won't change things too much, right?"

Her eyes search mine for reassurance, but I'm not sure she'll find it. Because deep in my gut, I know things are already changing. I've never had someone of my own before, someone who's mine to care for, to protect.

With sudden clarity, the truth hits me in the face—fake or not, now I do.

CHAPTER TWENTY-SEVEN

VIOLET

I gnaw my bottom lip as my phone continues to light up with Mark's name. He knows. I can sense it. I don't know how a ring tone can sound urgent sometimes and not others, but right now, my ring tone sounds exactly like overprotective brother.

With a sigh, I swipe to answer it. "Hi, Mark."

"Please tell me the message I just got from Tate is a joke."

I lean forward and prop my elbow on the food prep bench in True Brew's kitchen. "It's not a joke. It's also not a big deal."

"How can you say that?"

"Because it's true. Apart from having to call him my fiancé now, there really isn't any difference. I guess we might have to come up with another reason for us to split at the end." Just the thought stings, but I ignore the irrational pain and continue on. "But I'm sure you can come up with something using that big lawyer brain of yours." I smile, even though he can't see it, because my big brother is a

Harvard-trained lawyer, and I'll never not be hit with a surge of pride when I'm reminded of that.

Clearly not sharing the sentiment, he lets out a frustrated huff. "I'm concerned that this is snowballing. If you're not careful, then before you know it, you'll end up..."

He hesitates and I fill in the gap. "Married?" I laugh. "I can guarantee Tate will never let it get that far."

He snorts. "Believe me, I know that."

It stings, even though I know it's true.

His tone gentles. "I was going to say *hurt*. I'm worried you'll end up hurt."

Of course that's what he'd be worried about. So why did I immediately jump to the thought of marrying Tate?

"I know what this is, Mark. This is me saving Dad's legacy. It's about keeping True Brew. You don't have to worry about me falling in love and getting my heart broken."

He sighs. He and I both know there's nothing he can do anyway. "Okay. I'll amend the contract and courier it over to you first thing Monday morning."

"Thank you, Mark. It will all work out, I promise."

"Just take care of yourself, okay?"

I smile, warm with affection for my brother, even if he is overprotective. "I will."

After we end the call, I go back to wiping down the bench, and I'm instantly lost in my thoughts. I may have fudged the truth there at the end. Just a little. But I can't tell Mark that his concerns might be valid. That I'm worried that spending all this time with Tate, touching him, *kissing* him, is going to start tearing down my walls. That *I'm* worried I'll get hurt. Because telling him won't help either of us. The truth remains the same whether I'm Tate's girlfriend or fiancée. I have no intention of backing out of the agreement, so I'll double down on my efforts to remind myself that it's all an act. One Tate happens to be very, very good at.

I ignore the niggling voice in the back of my head that reminds me that there was no audience for the kiss we shared last night. That was just a result of the adrenaline from everything that led up to it—that man trying to touch me, Tate's out-of-the-blue announcement that we're engaged, and his protective instincts kicking in. Adrenaline makes people do crazy things. Like kiss their fake girlfriend—sorry, *fiancée*—like they can't get enough. Like they won't be able to take another breath if they don't.

Yes, I've judged Tate too harshly. I admit that under all his polished charm, he's actually a good guy. But that doesn't mean who he is, and what he wants, has fundamentally changed. It means he's a good guy making the best of a bad situation. And after this is over, he'll go back to his playboy ways, and I'll go back to focusing on True Brew. I doubt we'll ever see each other again after that.

The squeeze in my chest at the thought is evidence enough that I've already let myself get too swept up in this. It's time to rein this whole thing in and get back to treating it like a business arrangement. The way we should have been doing all along.

Pulling in a breath, I straighten my shoulders and head to the front to check on Jarrod. Before I get a chance to suggest he take his break, the bell over the door jangles, and a small crowd of people push their way inside. The smile of welcome that spreads across my face automatically at the sound of that bell falls when I see the raised cameras.

"Violet, congratulations on your engagement. How did you get one of New York's most eligible bachelors to propose?"

"Violet. How did you and Tate meet? Did he come in for coffee?"

"When's the wedding, Violet?"

Heart pounding, I take a step back. "I—um..."

I throw a startled look at Jarrod, whose eyes are wide with shock. I haven't mentioned the engagement to him. He's probably wondering what they're talking about.

I grimace, and in response, he shakes his head. It's all the confirmation he needs. It only takes a moment for him to collect himself and pull his shoulders back. He runs his hand through his hair and glares at the group, who I'm guessing are tabloid reporters. "If you're not here for coffee, you can leave."

The man at the front fishes his wallet out of his jacket. With a smug grin, he pulls out a few bills. "I'll have an Americano." The men behind him follow suit, digging out their wallets as well. Unbelievable.

One of them brings his camera up and snaps a shot of Jarrod and me. Spots dance in my vision, and I put up my hand. "No photos inside, please."

"There are dozens of photos on each of your shop's social media pages," he protests. "Just think of this as free publicity."

The shock and confusion that hit me when they came in have now turned to irritation. Gritting my teeth, I take a step closer to the counter. "I think you should leave."

The man puts his hands up. "Okay, no photos. I'll take a coffee and a Danish."

So maybe the confusion hasn't completely gone. What am I supposed to do now? And does my change in status from girlfriend to fiancée really warrant this kind of reaction? I'm considering ordering them to leave anyway when the door swings open and another group charges in.

My stomach sinks. This is ridiculous.

Jarrod turns to me, his brows lowered. "Go hang out in the back. If they can't get to you, they'll leave."

He's right. And I need a minute to collect my thoughts and figure out how to handle this situation.

As I turn, he grabs my wrist. "Call your fiancé. He got you into this. He can sort it out."

With a stunned nod, I push through the swinging door into the kitchen. I was not prepared for this. I haven't had a lot of time to think things through, and it didn't even occur to me that the announcement of Tate's sudden engagement would be a huge deal.

Jarrod's right though. I need to tell him. Hopefully, he can advise me on how to proceed from here. Should I give them a prepared answer? Should I kick them out?

I pull my phone out of my pocket, tap on Tate's name in my list of contacts and wait for him to pick up.

CHAPTER TWENTY-EIGHT

TATE

"Nice of you to join us," Mom says as I take a seat next to her at the dining table.

I'm a bit late arriving at the family estate in Westchester County for our monthly King family lunch—another event that's all about appearances. One that's become more bearable since Dad's no longer around and Delilah's far lovelier presence has taken his place. Although she's not here today. According to Cole, she isn't feeling well.

My phone blew up all morning with calls from my brothers, and even one from my mother, but I ignored them, preferring to wait for lunch so I could have a single conversation rather than hash out the details with each of them separately. Now that we're all together, the confrontation can commence.

Roman pinches the bridge of his nose. "What the hell, Tate? Getting engaged was not part of the agreement. How did this happen?"

I reach for my glass of wine and take a long sip to collect my thoughts. Then I lean back in my chair. "I didn't plan it.

But Aaron was insulting her. I wasn't going to let him get away with it."

"And your solution was to propose? You realize an engagement is far harder to extricate yourself from than just a relationship, don't you?"

I shrug, going for unaffected. "We'll work it out. Violet backed me up, and I won't leave her high and dry. I'll fix this for her."

Cole chuckles from where he's sitting across from me. "If it makes you feel any better, Roman, Aaron isn't pressing charges."

"Surprise, surprise." I can't mask the contempt dripping from my tone.

Roman glares at me. "Don't be too smug. The tabloids are running rampant with this story. Do you know how many photos of you decking the CFO of Avalon Inc. are floating around out there? And—What the hell are you smiling at?"

I school my expression, even if the memory of the satisfying sound of my fist hitting Aaron's face is far too enjoyable. I lean forward and rest my elbows on the table. "Look, did I act rashly? Yes. Do I regret it? Not really. And this could work well for us. The tabloids are all over our crazy love story. People are eating it up. No one's doubting my ability to commit now."

"And will they eat it up when you break the engagement in a few months? What about Violet? Does she get to be your jilted fiancée when this is all over?"

I clench my jaw. "I haven't thought through all the details yet," I admit. "But I won't let her get hurt. I'll figure it out."

Silently, Cole assesses me, his expression speculative.

I raise a brow at him. "What?"

He rubs his hand over his mouth. "At the start of this, I thought it might be hard for you to convince everyone that you were in love. But you seem to have taken to the role of dedicated boyfriend, or should I say *fiancé*, with remarkable ease."

I shoot him a smirk. "Maybe I just copied the prime example of pussy-whipped man I see in front of me."

"Language, please, Tate," Mom interjects. She sounds as bored as usual, like she's just going through the motions.

Cole's lips twitch in response.

Roman clears his throat. When I focus on him again, he's frowning at me.

It takes everything in me not to roll my eyes. "Trust me when I say I can handle this. I'll make sure the King Group is safe from scandal and look after Violet at the same time."

Roman searches my face and drums his fingers on the damask-covered table, then nods. "I do trust you. Just... try not to be quite as *rash* with this arrangement going forward. You signed a contract for a reason—so the terms are clear, and so no one gets hurt."

He doesn't give me a chance to respond before moving on to the next topic—unsurprisingly, it's work.

"The marketing plan you put together seems to be working well. We're at sixty-five percent already. I—"

The shrill ring of my phone interrupts him, and he snaps his mouth shut. Since everyone who's been calling me this morning is sitting in this room, I pull it out of my pocket. When I see Violet's name on the screen, apprehension tightens the back of my neck. She's only reached out to me once before. And that's when she was asking about the espresso machine.

I push back my chair and stand. "I need to take this." Without waiting for a response, I stride from the room, hitting the answer button as I do. "Violet, is everything okay?"

"There are reporters at the coffee shop," she says, her voice hushed.

Fuck. I scrub my hand over my face. My actions last night all but guaranteed this, but I didn't expect them to track her down so quickly. "Are they causing issues?"

She lets out a shaky laugh. "Well, a few of them bought coffee, so at least they're giving me their money. But at the moment, I'm in the back, and Jarrod and Sarah are handling the front. I don't like not being out there to help, but they keep asking me about you and how long this has been going on and how I managed to tie you down."

She's trying to make light of it, but if she called me, then I have no doubt that she's shaken.

I check my watch. "Stay where you are. I'm calling our security company. Their offices are closer to your shop. They'll take care of the reporters. I'll be there as soon as I can."

"You don't have to do that. I just thought you should know that they're here. Jarrod won't let anyone get to me."

I grind my teeth and hold back a growl at that last comment. While I'm grateful that he can keep those bloodsuckers from her, that should be my job. Our engagement may be fake, but I won't let anything happen to her. She's mine to protect.

I keep those thoughts to myself though. "Someone from Pinnacle Security will be there within twenty minutes. I won't be far behind them."

She lets out a sigh, probably realizing there's no point in arguing with me. "Okay. Thank you."

The moment we disconnect, I dial Pinnacle. Once they have the information and assure me they'll head that way immediately, I stride back into the dining room. "I have to go. Violet needs me."

"What's wrong?" Cole asks, the tension stiffening his posture probably a reflection of mine.

"Reporters. And not the good kind." I don't need to say more. We've all had enough experience with the tabloids to know what that means.

He half stands. "You need help?"

"I've got it handled. A security team is on its way."

With a nod, he slowly sits again.

"Call us if you need anything," Roman says.

I nod my appreciation at him, strangely touched by his terse offer. Then I shoot a glance at Mom, expecting her to be wearing a look of irritation. She won't be happy that I'm cutting lunch short. Instead, she's watching me, the tiniest of creases between her Botox-frozen brows. I raise my own at her, waiting for the inevitable comment about my priorities.

But she waves her hand in the air. "Go, go. The last thing anyone needs is those leeches lurking around."

The surprise that hits me is etched onto my brothers' faces as well. I don't have time to unpack her out of character response, so with a silent nod, I head out the door, my mind back on Violet.

The urgency pumping through my veins right now is mostly unfamiliar, and it's got nothing to do with work, or the company, and everything to do with the woman I convinced to participate in this ruse with me.

I've gone through life doing my best not to care too deeply about anyone. It's safer that way. But within a few short weeks of meeting Violet again, I find myself caring more than I should. I don't quite know what to make of that knowledge. Maybe it will turn out to be nothing. Maybe it's just a side effect of the parts we're playing. But regardless of the why, the outcome is the same. The urge to protect her as if she were really mine is too strong to ignore. And I'll do whatever it takes to ensure she's safe. Even if Violet doesn't like what I'm going to propose when I get to her.

Twenty minutes later, while Jeremy is navigating standard NYC traffic, I get a call from Pinnacle. They're at Violet's shop, and they've evicted all the reporters. Although they're apparently still loitering outside. At least now Violet can come out from the back.

It takes another twenty minutes to get there. From down the street, the crowd gathered out front is easy to spot.

I shake my head. Fucking vultures. They're welcome to come after me. After all, I've been making news in the tabloids for years, but they can stay the fuck away from Violet.

"Do you want me to take you around the block, Mr. King?" Jeremy asks.

"No. Let me out here. I'll deal with them."

As soon as the car has come to a stop at the curb, I swing the door open and step out. I've barely straightened to my full height before the reporters have surrounded me.

"Mr. King, is it true that you and Violet Sinclair are engaged?"

"Tate, where did you and Miss Sinclair meet?"

"What made you decide to finally put a ring on it?"

For a long moment, I stand my ground and stare each reporter down. Only when the whole crowd has fallen silent do I speak. "I'm only going to say this once. Yes, Violet and I are engaged. Yes, I've known her for a while. This is not out of the blue. The time was just right for both of us. Now, let me make myself very clear. My fiancée is an extremely hardworking small-business owner. She doesn't need you descending on her and making her life difficult just because you have an unhealthy fascination with my relationship status. I would appreciate it if you give her the privacy she's entitled to and don't interfere with her business. That's all I have to say on the matter."

More questions are thrown at me, but with Jeremy by my side, I make my way through the throng of people and into the shop. With Pinnacle still on the scene, they don't bother trying to follow me inside, though several take photos through the window.

Inside, two burly bodyguards stand conspicuously next to the counter. I sigh to myself and head for them first, shaking their hands and thanking them for coming on such short notice. Then, because I don't see Violet, I tell Jeremy to wait for me here and make my way around the counter.

When I push through the door to the back room, I find Violet at the bench, slicing bread. Jarrod is standing next to her, his hand on her shoulder, his head lowered close to hers as he talks.

She looks up as she registers the sound of the door opening. My shoulders are tense in anticipation of how she'll react to seeing me. She has every right to be angry that I put her in this situation. But instead of irritation or outrage, her eyes fill with relief. She drops her knife on the cutting board, dusts her hands on her apron and starts toward me.

Jarrod steps back, a stony expression on his face. Yeah, he has a right to be pissed at me. Hell, I'm pissed at myself. I should have had security in place from the moment we started this thing.

I give him a nod, acknowledging his help. It's the least I can do. But that concession doesn't mean I'll allow him to take over my role in her life.

So I step forward and pull her into my arms, relaxing

when hers go around me and she lets me hold her. "Are you okay? Did they upset you?"

She shakes her head. "They just asked a lot of questions and took photos of the shop. I asked them to stop, but they just kept asking about you—about *us*. I wasn't sure how to handle it, so that's why I—"

"You did exactly the right thing. I want you to call me."

"Thank you for sending those men. Once they cleared the reporters out, I told them they could go, but they insisted on staying until you got here. They're scaring customers away though, so if you could ask them to leave, I'd appreciate it."

I stroke her loose hair away from her face. "I'm not sending them away."

"What do you mean?" Jarrod speaks up before Violet has a chance to.

I shoot him a look that has him ducking his head and picking up where Violet left off with slicing the bread.

I turn my attention back to her. "You need the protection. I should have had them here from the start."

She steps back and shakes her head. "They'll scare away all the customers."

With a gentle tug, I pull her back into my chest. I lower my head and murmur into her ear so Jarrod can't hear me. "I made a promise. That if you helped me with this, it would help your business. I won't let you be harassed because of it, and I won't scare your customers off."

She looks up at me and keeps her voice low, like mine. "Then what are you suggesting?"

"These guys are experts. They can blend in, act like customers. Give one of them a laptop, a corner table in the back, and a supply of your incredible coffee, and no one will notice him."

"You don't think I overreacted about it all?"

I shake my head. "Absolutely not."

Behind her, Jarrod gives me another skeptical once-over, but then he heads out front with the freshly sliced bread.

"You don't think they'll go away now and not bother coming back?" This time, she pulls away a step.

Another shake of my head. "They'll be back. They only care about the story, and the black sheep of the King family's unexpected engagement is a story they'll milk for as long as they can."

She wraps her arms around her waist and studies the floor between us. I should do the right thing and tell her she can back out of the agreement if that's what she wants. She didn't sign up to be my fiancée, and she has every right to reject the change. We haven't signed the amended contract yet, so she'd be within her rights to refuse to continue. But I won't bring it up. Because the truth is, I don't want this to end. Having someone to care about is strangely addictive. I don't want to stop pretending Violet is mine just yet.

She looks back up at me and straightens her shoulders. "Okay. I'm not thrilled about it, but I won't turn down security if this is going to keep happening. I just..." She sighs and rubs her forehead, then gives me a tired smile. "I guess I just wasn't prepared for... well, any of this. But I suppose it's all part of it, right?"

I smile benignly. "I'm glad you're being logical about it, because you'll also be moving into my penthouse with me tonight."

CHAPTER TWENTY-NINE

VIOLET

I stare at him, holding my breath, while my brain processes his words. "Um, what?"

He smiles down at me, eyes glittering. "When I called Pinnacle and had them send a team here, I also instructed them to swing past your apartment block. There are reporters loitering around outside there as well. I'm not going to let you get harassed at home, so you're moving into my penthouse for the duration of this... agreement."

A tremor runs through me at the thought of being with Tate in his penthouse, night after night. Spending time with him here and in public is one thing, but spending every evening in each other's company? After the night at the club and the kisses we've shared since? It's a terrible idea. "I appreciate the sentiment. But I really don't think it's necessary."

"You don't, huh? You like the idea of making your way through a crowd of reporters every day just to get in and out of your building? I've seen the security at your apartment block. It's nonexistent. Do you really want to deal with that? Do your neighbors? Your landlord?"

"I could always st—"

He cuts me off with a shake of his head. "If you're about to suggest staying with Mark or your friend, don't bother. We're engaged remember. How would it look if people find out you're staying anywhere other than with me?"

I grit my teeth and force down my frustration. He has a point. "Fine. But only until the press loses interest."

Tate cups my jaw and tips my face up to his. "Hate to break it to you, butterfly, but they won't lose interest in you until this arrangement is over. After all," a hint of that familiar smirk creases his cheeks, "you're the woman who stole the heart of New York's most notorious playboy. They want to know everything about you."

Unease coils in my stomach. I never considered that the press would care about me. That they might dig into my life or follow me around.

A line etches itself between Tate's brows. "I'll keep you safe. I promise."

I let out a shaky breath. "I believe that. It's just... overwhelming." I'm in over my head. I've thought it before, but it's even truer now. Still, if I just keep my end goal in mind, if I can just remember that I'm doing this for True Brew, then it will all be worth it.

Tate's expression softens, and his thumb brushes my cheek. "I'll make it as easy on you as I can, okay?"

"Okay."

He nods and drops his hand. "Can you leave with me now?"

I go up on my toes and peer out through the window in the swinging door. The security guards are still standing like twin mountains by the counter, and from what I can see, the shop is mostly empty. "Jarrod and Sarah can finish up and close without me."

"Let's head out. We'll swing by your apartment so you can pick up necessities for tonight, and then I'll have someone pack up your clothes and anything else you need tomorrow."

I don't particularly like the idea of a stranger rummaging through my stuff, but I'm too drained to argue. With a nod, I untie my apron and throw it into the hamper by the back door. "Let's do this, then."

Out front, I check in with Jarrod and Sarah. While I confirm details with them, Tate instructs the security guards to stay here until the shop is closed and informs them that he'll be in touch with their boss to organize a permanent presence.

Jeremy exits the shop first to help with crowd control, but luckily, most of the reporters have departed. When I scan the sidewalk, I relax a little. Maybe Tate's mistaken. Maybe the flurry of activity following our engagement announcement won't last long. Surely the tabloids will find something more entertaining to fixate on soon. I can hang out at Tate's penthouse for a few days and then go back to my apartment.

The drive to my place from the shop is quick. When Jeremy pulls up outside my building, the tension that's just begun to ease returns. Because Tate's right. There are half a dozen more reporters camped outside.

"Wait here," I tell him as I push the door open.

But he gets out right behind me. "Nice try."

We're still standing beside the car when one of the men shouts Tate's name, and suddenly, every camera is trained on us. Jeremy gets out and hustles around to our side, shielding us with his bulk as well as he can.

"This is ridiculous," I mutter.

Tate wraps his arm around my shoulders and pulls

me against him, then guides me to the entrance. Considering he's the source of this problem, I shouldn't relax at the feel of his hard body against mine. But I do.

Tate and Jeremy wait in my living room while I pack an overnight bag. I look around at my small but comfortable bedroom, feeling homesick already when I haven't even left yet.

Our departure goes the same way as our arrival, with Jeremy leading the way and Tate shielding me from the questions and the cameras. I breathe a sigh of relief once we're back in the car.

We're quiet on the way to Tate's place. I'm caught up with the whirl of thoughts in my head. It feels like my life is veering out of control, and I don't know how to stop it. Tate seems to respect my mood. I catch his gaze on me several times, but he stays silent.

When Jeremy pulls the car over to the curb, I duck my head and take in the sleek, glass-walled high-rise we've stopped in front of. In the light of the setting sun, it's an extravagant beacon—so different from my little apartment block. Just seeing it from here makes this whole situation feel surreal.

Jeremy opens the door, and I step out. Tate follows, bringing my overnight bag with him. He slings it over his shoulder, then tucks me into his other side and leads me toward the expansive glass entrance. An immaculately dressed doorman tips his hat at us as he holds the door open. "Good evening, Mr. King."

"Good evening, Harold. This is my fiancée, Violet Sinclair. She'll be living with me from now on."

I open my mouth, ready to clarify that it will only be temporary, but I snap it shut again when it hits me. This is part of the act. If I was really his fiancée, this *would* be a permanent move.

"Good evening, Miss Sinclair. It's a pleasure to meet you," he says.

I smile at him. "It's nice to meet you too, Harold."

With that, Tate leads me toward the bank of elevators. When he veers toward the one on the right, he says, "This is ours. It only goes to the penthouse."

Ours. Why does that word make my heart do a silly little flutter?

The ride up is quick and smooth, and when the doors slide open, we step out directly into the penthouse. The large marble-floored foyer opens up into a sprawling open-concept space bathed in warm westerly light, thanks to the floor-to-ceiling windows that make up one whole wall.

The incredible view steals the breath from my lungs. From here, the New York City skyline stretches out in front of me, broken only by the green expanse of Central Park. On the terrace outside the windows, a lap pool shimmers gold under the late afternoon sun. I shake my head in disbelief. How many apartments in New York have an actual private pool? "This is... incredible, Tate."

He shrugs. "It's home."

I regard him for a second. Is he being humble or quietly smug? It's hard to tell with him. But this time, there's a hint of what I could almost swear is vulnerability in his eyes.

I wander farther into the apartment, turning my head from side to side as I take it all in. The décor is masculine. Hardly a surprise. Rich, dark woods contrasting with sleek, modern furnishings. The living room is centered around a minimalist fireplace. The kitchen looks state-of-the-art, with marble countertops, high-end appliances and an island large enough to host a dinner party around. There's a formal dining area next to it, with a huge table surrounded by plush chairs and lit by a modern chandelier.

It's not my cozy, comfortable one-bedroom apartment, and it's ridiculously large—not to mention it must be outrageously expensive—yet I like it. It fits Tate. Maybe I don't know him well enough to actually make that assertion, but it's hard to imagine another place that would feel more like him.

I'm running my fingers over the huge couch, savoring the buttery softness of the leather, when he clears his throat.

"Let me show you to your bedroom," he says, his voice a little gruffer than normal. It's probably as weird for him to have me in his home as it is for me to be here.

"Okay." I follow along as he points out all the different rooms: his office, a home gym, a couple of guest rooms. With each room we pass, I'm more confused. Why doesn't he put me in one of them? It isn't until we're near the end of the hallway that a disturbing thought occurs to me. Surely he doesn't expect me to sleep in his room with him, does he?

Finally, Tate stops outside a large set of double doors. "And this is my bedroom."

My throat dries, and I stare at him with wide eyes. "Your bedroom?"

A smile curves his mouth, and he takes a step closer. "My bedroom." His voice is low, gravelly. "Is that okay with you?"

"Well, I—uh." Why can't I string a sentence together? Is it because I'm shocked at his audacity, or is it because my mind has already provided a visual of what's bound to be a large bed, and what it might be like to share that bed with him? Does he sleep naked? Would he touch me? Do I want him to?

"And over there, butterfly," he says, using his fingers to

turn my head so I'm facing the opposite side of the corridor, "is your bedroom."

From the tone of his voice and his devilish grin, he knew exactly what I was thinking, and the bastard leaned into that misunderstanding. The prickle of irritation I used to feel around him, the one that's frustratingly been replaced by butterflies in my stomach, makes a brief return. "How nice for me that I get to be so close," I say dryly.

He cocks a brow. "Just say the word, and you can be closer."

It takes all my strength to keep from smiling, from showing him just how close I am to letting my walls fall. A woman can only take so much sexy, flirtatious billionaire before she throws all her convictions out the window.

He chuckles as if he knows anyway, but he leaves the teasing there and opens the door for me, revealing a guest room that's more luxurious than any hotel suite I've ever been in. A plush queen-size bed dominates the space, while the floor-to-ceiling windows look out onto the terrace. A cozy seating area in the corner looks perfect for curling up and reading a book.

"Wow," I breathe, forgetting my nervousness about being so close to Tate's bedroom. "This is incredible."

"My fiancée deserves the best. Of course, the best is my bedroom, so technically, this is second best. If it doesn't meet your expectations, let me know, and I can arrange an upgrade."

I shake my head, though I can't help but laugh. "You can't help yourself, can you?"

"Not when it comes to you, apparently."

Heart in my throat, I appraise him. He watches me too, his expression more serious than I expect, considering he's just been teasing me. I swallow hard and look away from the intensity of his gaze.

Tate, unfazed, hands me my bag. "While you get settled in, I'll get started on dinner."

My eyes shoot back to his. "You cook?"

He shrugs, still completely at ease. "On occasion. This seems like an occasion."

"Can I help?"

He nods toward the large walk-in closet. "Get sorted, and if you're done before dinner is ready, then I'll put you to work."

Once he's gone, I close the door, take a deep breath and survey the huge room again, shaking my head in disbelief. Then I snap myself back into the moment and begin unpacking. My hands shake slightly as I fold clothes and put them away or hang them in the spacious closet. The significance of what I'm doing—moving in with Tate—is not lost on me. I can't help but worry that this new arrangement will confuse my already dangerously confused emotions even more.

Once my things are put away, I head back to the kitchen, grinding to a halt when I round the corner. The air leaves my lungs in a rush.

Tate is standing there, partly turned away from me as he chops vegetables, wearing nothing but a pair of gray sweatpants.

My heart rate shoots through the roof as I take in the way his smooth golden skin moves over the hard planes and angles of his shoulders and back while he works. Even from this angle, I can make out the cut of muscle at his hip. If he were facing me, I'd no doubt get the full effect of that V leading my eyes directly down to the waistband of his sweatpants.

Heat spreads fast through my veins, and for just a moment, I allow myself to forget what this is between us. I imagine walking up behind him, sliding my arms around his chest and pressing a kiss to his warm skin. Maybe I'd let my hands trail down over his abs until my fingertips skimmed the low waistband, then slid underneath. Would he be commando? Would he be hard and ready for me? I'd grip him, stroke him from root to tip as he groaned my name. And then—

Shit. I jolt out of the almost-trance I've fallen into, pulse pounding and nerve endings tingling. I can't think these things. I can't succumb. Tate and I are too different. He might be able to indulge in physical relationships and not get attached, but I can't. There's no way I want to risk getting my heart broken by the biggest heartbreaker of all.

I take a fortifying breath and then clear my throat, as if I've just walked into the kitchen. "I'm done. What can I do to help?"

He looks at me over his shoulder. "Can you finish me off here?"

"W-what?" I stammer. Coming so soon after my illicit fantasy, his words have my mind going right back where it was before.

He cocks a brow and takes me in, no doubt noticing my flushed skin. "Can you finish this salad while I get the meat going? What did you think I meant?"

I shake my head, unsure if I heard what I wanted to hear, or if he was messing with me. I wouldn't put it past him, but since I can't be certain, I merely smile sweetly and step up next to him so I can take the knife he offers me. "What are you making?"

He points at two pieces of meat resting on a platter. "Steak with green peppercorn sauce, salad." He points at a bowl full of salad leaves and then toward a couple of peeled potatoes. "And pomme frites."

I arch a brow. "French fries?"

A smile curves his lips. "No one in the King family would ever deign to eat French fries. We eat pomme frites."

I laugh, the tension I'm still carrying from the incident at the coffee shop and my temporary move dissipating. Maybe this situation won't be as bad as I thought. Maybe it could even be fun. As long as I can get past this annoying attraction to him. Tate might not be real fiancé material, but maybe he could be friend material, if I let him.

I smile at him. "Of course. How silly of me. And I guess tomato ketchup would be too pedestrian. Are you going to serve them with gold-infused tomato puree?"

Chuckling, he leans against the counter behind him and crosses his arms over his broad chest.

It takes all my willpower to keep my eyes from drifting down over all those defined muscles on display.

"Unfortunately, I'm all out of sparkly puree, so we'll have to settle for plain ketchup."

I push my bottom lip out in a mock pout. "And here I thought I was going to get the full Tate King experience."

His eyes darken, and he steps toward me, until our bodies are only an inch apart. "Just give me the word, butterfly, and I'll happily give you the full experience."

His gaze drops to my mouth and it's as if I've been hit with a burst of static electricity. Heat flares over my skin, and my nipples bead beneath my top.

How is it possible for things to change so quickly? I only just decided to stop being so defensive around him, and within seconds, I can't stop myself from imagining what the full experience would be like.

The only way I'm going to survive this new arrangement is to be completely honest. I close my eyes and let out a breath. Then I meet his golden gaze again. "I can't, Tate. This," I gesture between us, "is already complicated. Anything more, and it will get too confusing. For me, at least. And I don't want to get hurt."

A muscle jumps in his jaw, and what looks like pain flashes in his eyes.

I replay my words, realizing the implication, and try again. Taking a small step forward to reassure him, I press my palm to his chest, instantly soaking in his heat. "I don't mean you'd deliberately hurt me. But you don't want anything more than the physical, and I'm not sure if I'm capable of separating the two." I swallow, gathering the courage to tell him the truth, hoping it won't come back to bite me. "So as much as I might find the idea enticing, we can't get any more involved than we already are." Realizing I still have my hand on his chest, I let it drop, but I hold his gaze, waiting for him to say something, anything, hoping he won't use my admission against me.

He nods slowly, as if he's considering my words. "I have no intention of hurting you, Violet. But I'm not going to deny that I want you in my bed. I haven't been able to stop thinking about fucking you since that first night at the club. But you're right. I can promise to give you more pleasure than you know how to handle, but I can't promise more than that. I'd like to touch you. I'd love to make you feel good. I want to be the man who wipes your ex from your thoughts and memories. But I won't lie to you either." His throat moves in a swallow, and he lowers his chin a fraction. "So let's agree on this. The terms of the agreement stand. Physical intimacy is at your discretion. If you decide you want me, I'll be here, in any capacity you need."

Why, why, why does he have to be so damn sexy? With

his wide shoulders filling my vision, and the way he's staring down into my face with such intensity, all it would take is a single kiss, and I'd fold. I'd throw out my misgivings. I'd take what he's offering while we're in this situation and deal with the consequences later.

His attention drops to my lips, and for a heartbeat, I think he might do just that, kiss me. But then he drags his gaze back up again and meets my eye. "The ball's in your court, butterfly."

Before I can formulate a response, he steps back and reaches for a potato.

As he starts chopping, I exhale shakily and turn back to the salad I'm supposed to be finishing off.

If the ball's in my court, then all I have to do is resist the temptation of Tate for the next few weeks, and I'll be home free. I'll have enough money to keep True Brew running, Tate will hopefully no longer be the tabloids' favorite target, and my heart will be whole and safe in my chest.

I can do that. I'm sure of it.

CHAPTER THIRTY

TATE

"This is really good," Violet says, her brows lifted in surprise.

I smirk at her. "You should know, I never overstate my skills."

She pauses, a small bite of steak dangling from her fork in midair and gives me a look that says *I know exactly what you're doing*. I hold her gaze over the rim of my glass as I take a sip of my wine.

I meant what I told her. It's up to her where things go from here. But I have no intention of hiding what I want. Violet thinks that if we fuck, I'll hurt her, when all I really want to do is make her feel good. I want to show her the kind of pleasure she deserves so that she'll never settle for a loser like her ex again. If she truly doesn't think she can handle it, then I have no doubt of her ability to resist me. She's stronger than she knows. After all, she walked into Onyx and rode my fingers until she came all over them. And fuck it. Even then, I was the one asking her to come back the next week, while she was fully prepared to walk away.

After our conversation in the kitchen, I was worried that she'd fall back into her normal state of keeping me at arm's length. And maybe I moved too quickly after she started teasing me back, but fuck, that smile she gave me did something funny to my chest and made it impossible not to push for more.

Cooking with her was surprisingly enjoyable. I've never cooked side by side with another person. As a rule, I don't bring women back here, and even if I did, I certainly wouldn't invite them to stick around for dinner.

Like I have with most of the people in my life, I've been content to keep the women I sleep with at a distance. I show them a good time and send them on their way. Up until recently, I haven't been much closer to my family. I'd see my brothers at the office, talk business, then leave and not talk to them again until the next time I saw them at work. I'm used to being on my own, even when I'm with other people.

So having Violet by my side in the kitchen, talking and laughing as she worked, and now sitting opposite me as we eat, is all new. I never imagined I'd like being in such close proximity to someone for so long, but with her, I do.

I focus on her left hand and her bare ring finger. "Tomorrow, we'll get your engagement ring. Too much longer without one, and there'll be questions."

"Oh." Violet inspects her hand, as if she only just realized she's not wearing one. "I didn't even think about that."

"We can go shopping first thing in the morning."

She puts her hand in her lap, out of sight. "It doesn't have to be anything expensive. Considering you've already bought me an espresso machine, you don't need to splurge on a ring that I'll only wear for a little while."

"You do realize I'm a billionaire, right? The espresso machine was pocket change. The amount of money you're potentially saving the King Group by helping me out is far more than the cost of an engagement ring."

She sighs, her shoulders sagging. "I'm not going to win this argument either, am I?"

I take a sip of my wine, then smile at her. "Definitely not."

"Fine, I'll give you this one."

"Oh, butterfly, this won't be the only thing you give me before this relationship is over."

She narrows her eyes at me. "Fake relationship." But she hides another smile behind her wineglass.

The warmth in her expression when she looks at me like that is enough to make me think she likes the banter as much as I do.

She takes another sip of wine, then worries her bottom lip. "Can I ask you something personal?"

"I've asked you plenty of personal questions. I think you're due one."

One corner of her mouth kicks up, but her smile fades quickly. "Do you visit your dad often? In prison, I mean?"

A pit forms in my stomach at the question. For a long moment, I roll the smooth stem of my wineglass between my fingers, keeping my attention focused on the movement. When I force myself to look up at her, there's a hint of nervousness in her expression, like she's worried that she shouldn't have asked.

As much as I don't like talking about my dad, I want her to know she can ask me anything she wants. "No. Our relationship has never been the best. I think we're both happier keeping our distance."

"I'm sorry," she says softly.

I shrug. "I'm used to it. He's not the kind of man who cares about being a good father."

"Still, it must have been hard for you and your family when he got arrested."

She doesn't understand our dynamic, and I don't blame her. In fact, I'm thankful. Because she received nothing but unconditional love from her dad. "It was a blessing in disguise. For us anyway. Once we navigated the company through the scandal, his absence was like a weight off all our shoulders. Still is. It's a cliché, but Dad only cared about two things. Money and power." Sex too, considering how many mistresses he's had over the years, but Violet doesn't need to know about that. "And the only lesson worth teaching us, in his eyes, was how to use the King name to gain more of those things. None of us were truly shocked about his arrest."

"It was for insider trading, wasn't it?"

I nod. "All the wealth he'd already amassed wasn't enough. Now he's locked away for another seven years. But I doubt he'll learn anything from his time in prison."

Sympathy shimmers in her eyes. "And your mom? She didn't seem to have the, um, warmest personality when we met."

I smirk. "Warm and my mom don't belong in the same sentence. She cares more about appearances than reality. Always has. As long as she can get us all in the same room and imitating a loving family, she's content. Regardless of how we actually feel about one another."

Violet's quiet for a moment, absorbing my words. Maybe even the ones I didn't say. "I can't imagine how hard it must be to not have a parent who wants to love and protect you. I'm sorry you didn't have that growing up, Tate. I wish things had been different for you."

I can't even begin to identify the chaotic mix of emotions that churns in my chest.

She's hurting for me, upset that I didn't have what she had growing up. But I gave up on the hope of ever having a loving parent long ago. Right now, all I want is her. I want the compassion in her gaze and the way she looks at me so openly when she lets her walls down—when she trusts me. I want her to trust me with her body and her emotions. I want her to believe I can keep her safe.

But I can't force her to believe my intentions. I can only show her the truth of who I am and hope it's enough for her to let me in permanently.

"I stopped wishing things were different a long time ago." I say. "Now I'm focusing on shaping the future into what I want it to be."

A smile plays on her lips now. "Scandal free?"

I chuckle. "I can only hope."

Determined to keep the atmosphere light, I change the topic, asking her what it was like growing up with Mark. We finish our dinner talking about her childhood, and I love watching her smile as she remembers all the little things her dad and brother did for her to made it special.

After we finish eating, I suggest a movie. But her eyebrows pinch together as she studies the big, soft couch set up in front of the flat screen TV, and she declines, saying she wants to go to bed early so she can curl up with a book.

I consider watching a movie on my own, but I'm too restless. So I get changed and go for a swim. The pool isn't large, but it's big enough to swim laps, expel a little of that excess energy. Before, I might have fucked it away, but the only woman I'm interested in doing that with isn't on the same page. Not yet anyway.

I power through the water, the repetitive motion calming my mind of all but one thing. One person. Violet. Violet and her pretty blue eyes. Violet and her long smooth legs. Her smile. Her laugh. Her touch. The way I imagine it on me. The way I imagine touching her.

I've had a small taste of her, but I want more. I want to feel her come apart for me again.

Fuck. This swim was supposed to settle me, but now I have a raging fucking erection. I turn and wade toward the edge of the pool so I can head inside and take care of myself. Hands planted on the concrete, I freeze. Because Violet is standing in her bedroom window across from me, holding the curtain back.

How long has she been watching? I slick my wet hair back from my face and, never breaking eye contact with her, haul myself out of the water. From here, it's impossible not to notice the way her gaze drifts over my chest and abs, then farther down.

I'm hard already, but her attention turns me to granite. With my heart picking up its pace and my blood heating, I reach down and give myself a rough stroke over my trunks. It's wrong, I know it, but I'm desperate to ease the deepening ache caused by having her eyes on me.

There's no missing the way she catches her lower lip between her teeth or the press of her nipples against the silky material of her pajama top.

We stand there a moment longer, surveying, studying. I fist my hands at my sides and heave in a breath, ready to storm toward her bedroom, to force her to admit she wants me the same way I want her, but before I take that first step, she spins away, and the curtain drops between us. I clench my eyes shut as a wave of frustration surges over me. Then, letting out a harsh breath, I head to my shower to take care of my throbbing dick.

CHAPTER THIRTY-ONE

VIOLET

I don't know what I was thinking last night. I heard the splashes, and I knew Tate would be out there, looking way too hot for his own good. A wet, almost-naked Tate is a temptation I should know enough to stay away from. I went and stood by the window anyway. I told myself I'd take a quick peek, just to assuage my curiosity about how Tate looks in a swimsuit. But once I drew the curtain aside and saw him powering up and down the length of the pool, skin slick, muscles working, I couldn't look away.

When he made his way to the edge of the pool, I should have been quicker to drop the curtain and step back from the window. But stupidly, I hesitated, entranced by his wet hair dripping down onto his broad shoulders, the drops continuing down over his muscular chest and chiseled abs. Of course he noticed me watching. How could he not? And instead of finally ducking out of sight, I just stood there, my heart pounding against my ribs while I watched him watch me. While I watched him stroke himself, eyes fixed on my face.

The hard length of him straining against his wet trunks,

and the rough jerk of his hand, spawned an insistent ache between my legs that finally snapped me back to my senses, and I jumped away from the window. But by then, it was too late to undo the damage. And it was too late to undo the lust curling and flexing inside me. The thought of that hard, muscular body moving over mine, the long, thick length of him pushing inside me.

I was flat on my back, my hand between my thighs, before I knew what I was doing.

The orgasm came hard and fast, satisfying and unsatisfying at the same time, because I wanted *him* to give it to me. But I didn't dare let him, either. I tossed and turned for hours after that, and when I did finally drift off, I slept fitfully.

The idea of facing him this morning had my stomach churning. Could he tell what I'd done after I darted away from the window? I was sure the guilt was written all over my face.

But he acted as if it had never happened. No pointed comments, no veiled innuendo, no teasing of any kind. Which is absolutely fine by me. I can write the whole thing off as a moment of insanity on my part and leave it at that.

After surprising me once again by serving up eggs and bacon for breakfast, Tate told me to get dressed because we needed to go ring shopping.

Now we're idling outside a jeweler on Fifth Avenue, and the anxiety that has been plaguing me all morning is multiplying. By looking at the elegant, understated exterior alone, I can tell it's just as exclusive as everything else in Tate's life.

I turn to him, willing my voice to remain steady. "This seems like overkill."

He smirks. "I told you. Only the best for my fiancée."

"Fake fiancée," I mumble. The reminder is more for me than him at this stage.

He quirks a brow. "That doesn't mean I'm going to buy you a fake ring."

"I told you last night—you don't need to do this." I gesture toward the jewelry store. I don't know why I'm so uneasy about the whole ring situation. It has to be done.

"I know I don't need to. I want to give you this." He eases close enough that he can tuck my hair behind my ear, his fingers brushing that spot on my neck that seems to have a direct connection to my sex. "I don't want you wearing a cheap hunk of metal on your finger."

"I guess that makes sense," I say, trying not to get distracted by the way his scent is invading my senses. "The last thing you need is some eagle-eyed jewelry expert figuring out that Tate King's fiancée is wearing a cheap ring."

"Hey." He grabs my chin and turns my head. "*You* deserve the best, Violet. Not Tate King's fiancée, *you*."

My heart flutters. He needs to stop saying such sweet things. Because with every passing day, it's getting harder to resist throwing caution to the wind and taking what he's offering. But for all his sweet words, and his protectiveness, and his impossible to ignore sex appeal, when this is over, he'll go back to his world, and I'll go back to mine. And the only time I'll see him is if Mark invites him along on one of his visits.

I hate that I hate that thought.

With a deep breath in, then back out, I push the worry out of my mind and smile. "Thank you. That means a lot to me."

When Jeremy opens the door, I get out and wait for Tate to climb out behind me. I've grown accustomed to the weight of his hand on the small of my back. And temporary or not, I can't resist indulging in at least some of his touches.

The moment we step inside the store, I'm struck by the dazzling array of diamonds and gemstones that sparkle under the bright lights. It's like stepping into a fairy tale. As I make a slow turn, taking in the glass cases and luxurious décor, I've never felt more out of place. While Tate is in a suit, I'm dressed in a pair of jeans and a simple cap-sleeved blouse.

A smartly dressed saleswoman with her hair pulled back approaches, her focus flicking between Tate and me with thinly veiled curiosity. "Mr. King, how wonderful to see you. What can I help you with?"

"We're looking for an engagement ring," Tate replies smoothly, wrapping an arm around my waist and drawing me toward him.

"Of course." With a small, professional smile, she leads us over to a glass case filled with stunning rings. Just like at Trio's, there are no prices. But based on the sheer size and glitteriness of the diamonds, I have no doubt each one costs more than True Brew makes in a year.

"What do you think of these?" the woman asks, hands clasped lightly in front of her.

The rings, set equal distances apart in the cream-colored cushions, are ridiculous, the stones so large they look like they could take someone's eye out. And if they don't blind a person in that respect, their sparkly brilliance will do the trick.

Guilt that I'm not more excited eats at me. The last thing I want is to seem ungrateful. "Um, these are amazing," I say. Which is true, even if I've never pictured myself wearing a ring like one of these on my finger. Though that could be because I never pictured myself getting fake engaged to a billionaire.

She beams. "Just let me know which one you'd like to try on."

"Okay." I survey them again. There's no sense in being picky. Big and flashy will only help sell this engagement. So I ignore the disenchantment that every one of these rings stirs in me and point randomly. "That one."

She straightens, and I swear her smile gets brighter. "Wonderful choice. That's a ten-carat princess cut diamond on a platinum band."

Despite my best efforts, I cringe. Ten carats. When does a symbol of commitment become more about the show than the sentiment?

Never mind. In this case, that's exactly what it's about.

As she removes it from the case and wipes it with a cloth, I glance up at Tate, who's been uncharacteristically quiet. His arms are crossed, and there's a crease between his brows.

The woman grasps my hand, drawing my attention back to her, and slips the ring onto my finger. "It fits almost perfectly."

I examine it, envisioning my hands as I work the espresso machine and wash dishes with this massive rock on my finger. "It's beautiful." Pressing my lips together, I turn to Tate. "I'll just have to take it off while I'm working."

"No," he says.

My heart lurches at the flatness of his tone. "Oh." I look down. "I'll be worried about damaging it, that's—"

"No. Take it off."

The woman and I both stare at him.

"Now," he growls.

I fumble to slide the ring off, my skin flaring hot in

embarrassment. The woman gives me a placating smile and covers my shaking hands with hers. She removes it with ease, and as soon as she has it back in the display box, Tate has me by the hand and is towing me out of the shop.

"Thank you," I call back over my shoulder.

We're silent until we get back in the car. Confusion settles heavily in my chest, making each breath a challenge.

Once Jeremy has shut the door behind Tate, I turn and search his expression for answers. His brow is pulled low and his jaw is tense, but I can't understand why.

"Was it too expensive? You could have just said something. I didn't care which one we got."

"That's the point," he says.

"What do you mean?"

His eyes pierce me, the golden hue gone molten. "Fake engagement or not, I want you to care about the ring on your finger. I want you to at least goddamn like it."

I blink at him, stunned. When I finally find my words, I stutter through them. "I-I'm sorry if it came across that I didn't like it. That wasn't the case. I swear. It was beautiful. Really. We can go back and—"

He takes my hand and strokes his thumb over my ring finger. The touch is gentle, despite the tension vibrating through him. Little sparks flicker over my skin, traveling up my arm. "Don't apologize."

I roll my lips together. "It's just that you seem angry."

A muscle leaps in his jaw. "I'm not angry at you."

"Then who are you angry at?" The words are tentative, soft. This side of him is still new to me. He always puts on such a charming façade, so seeing his anger, his pain, feels far more intimate than it would from anyone else.

"I'm angry with myself." With one more brush of his

thumb over my finger, he lets go. "Jeremy, can you take us home, please?"

My stomach drops. "We're not getting a ring?" I shouldn't feel sad about that. It's just one more indication of how easily I could lose myself in this fake relationship.

His only response is a simple "not here."

On the drive home, he busies himself with his phone. I, on the other hand, am reeling over what just happened. He sensed my discomfort and obviously doesn't want to force me to wear a ring that doesn't work for me. But the way he whisked me out of the store and shut things down so abruptly makes me feel a little sick. He said not here, but he didn't elaborate. And now we're going home. Not home. *His* place. I don't know what to think.

Fifteen minutes later, as we step into the lobby of Tate's high-rise, he's still quiet. I don't know how to break the tension, so the ride up to his penthouse is silent.

When we get inside, he turns to me. "I'm going to take a swim. Want to join me?"

Before I have a chance to reply, he's shucking out of his jacket. I'm frozen to the spot as he tugs his shirt out of his pants and begins to unbutton it. His fingers move deftly over each one, revealing his smooth, tanned skin. My mouth goes dry as I track the movement of his hands. I only stop when they stop.

"My eyes are up here."

I whip my focus up to his face, and an incoherent explanation spills from my mouth. "I wasn't... I mean..."

An amused half smile tilts his lips, and he shrugs the shirt off completely, revealing his muscled shoulders.

While I'm relieved that any tension he was holding on to seems to have dissipated, the sight of Tate shirtless does nothing to calm my libido. In fact, it does the opposite. It sparks an image of him standing by the pool last night, his attention fixed on me, his hand stroking his cock.

My knees wobble, and a breath shudders out of me.

When Tate moves his hand to the button of his pants, I force myself to look away. "You're not going to get changed in your bedroom?"

"Why? Am I making you nervous?"

I look back at him, studiously keeping my focus on his face. "No, of course not."

"No? So you'll come swimming with me, then? It's warm out there. It would be a shame to miss out on a refreshing dip just because you're worried you won't be able to keep your hands off me."

A niggle of annoyance joins the lust coursing through my veins. I huff out a breath. That cocky attitude has me riled up enough to clear away the fog in my mind.

Two can play the game he's started. I turn to face him fully and bring my hands to the top button of my blouse. "Actually, I'd love to get wet," I say, keeping my voice low and breathy.

His pupils blow wide as I slowly work the first button open, letting the material gape slightly.

Though the button of his pants is undone, the zipper is still up. His waistband sits low on his hips as he takes a step closer, his focus on where I'm toying with the second button.

I haven't thought through my plan, where I'll go from here or how far I'll take it. With Tate, I have a bad habit of acting first and thinking later. He's a master at throwing me off-kilter when what I desperately want is to feel in control. But it's virtually impossible to feel in control when he's standing in front of me with no shirt on and his pants undone.

"You need help with that, butterfly?" His voice has gone low. The hint of gravel in his tone makes my nipples peak.

I slip the second button free, revealing the lace of my bra. The responding heat in his gaze makes my stomach flip. But it has to stop here. If not, it would be too easy to get carried away, to let him *help*. To let him slip the thin material of my blouse from my shoulders. The desire to have his hands on me again is getting harder and harder to resist.

I'm wavering, torn between what my body wants and what my head is telling me. I'm fixated on the middle of his chest, unwilling to look lower and afraid of what I'll see if I look at his face.

My avoidance tactic is thwarted when Tate moves closer, forcing me to meet his gaze. His golden eyes move between mine, the barest hint of a smile on his lips. As if he can sense every thought racing through my head. "I just want to swim with you, beautiful. That's all."

Of course he does. Here I am, imagining all the ways I want him to touch me, and he's just being his usual flirtatious self. He knows that if we were to get physical, I'd end up wanting more. And more is the last thing he wants. I'm letting myself get confused again, swept up in his charm and kindness and inherent sexiness, forgetting that charming women is what Tate does best.

I take a step back, but he cups the nape of my neck, pulling me closer again, and lowers his head. "Please come for a swim with me."

Though my embarrassment lingers, I remind myself that Tate and I have to share this apartment for a while, so I might as well practice spending time near him, whether he's dressed or half-dressed, without losing my composure. With any luck, it won't be long before I barely notice how hot he is. We'll become like... like roommates. Roommates who occasionally kiss in public.

"Okay. I'll go get changed."

He lets go of me, and I spin away from him and take off for my room as he stoops to pick up the shirt he dropped during his impromptu strip tease.

Once in my room, I sort through my clothes. A woman dropped off neatly packed suitcases filled with my clothes and toiletries this morning, and luckily, she included my swimsuit. As I pull on the pretty turquoise string bikini, I wish I was the kind of woman who preferred one-pieces, or better yet, those old-fashioned bathing suits that would cover me from my knees to my neck. With this on, I'm guaranteed to feel more exposed than I'm comfortable with when in the presence of a man who probably regularly sleeps with supermodels.

Taking a deep breath, I leave my room and make my way out to the terrace.

As I approach the glass door, I watch Tate. He's in the pool, with his back to me. He has his arms resting on the edge, and he's looking out over the sweeping city view.

I slide the door and step out, nerves raging inside me despite the pep talk I gave myself the whole way here. At the sound, Tate turns and leans back against the side, giving me a long once-over.

I'm frozen at the edge, my body heating under his perusal.

"Better get in the water." That gravel in his voice is back.

With a darting glance at him, I lower myself down and slide in. The water is cool, but not cold. Refreshing on such a warm day, just as he promised.

I let out a sigh and fully submerge myself, letting the

cool liquid rush and bubble over my hot skin. When I surface, pushing my wet hair back from my face and blinking my eyes clear, Tate is watching me with a strange kind of intensity. "Are you going to come over here?"

"I'm not sure I want to get that close to the edge." I give him a self-conscious smile. I'm not scared of heights, not really. But just the thought of standing at the edge of an infinity pool on the side of a high-rise makes my stomach roll with nerves.

With a low hum, he wades toward me, and oh god, the way the sun reflects off the drops of water trickling down the sculpted muscles of his chest should be illegal. I look away, but when he comes to a stop in front of me, I can't ignore his presence. As I turn back, he reaches up and brushes his knuckles down my cheek.

The light contact pulls a shuddery breath from my lungs, making his lips tip up just a little.

"I thought I was the one who was going to have trouble keeping my hands off you," I say.

"I never said I wouldn't have the same problem."

The rush of blood in my ears is loud enough to drown out the water lapping against the side of the pool. If I were to touch him right now, slide my hands along his smooth, wet skin, I have no doubt we'd both lose control. The hunger in his eyes makes that clear. He must be going out of his mind with pent-up sexual desire, considering our agreement requires him to be celibate. As for me, I can't stop thinking about that night at the club.

I imagine him peeling my swimsuit off my body, his mouth on my breasts. His hands on my hips as he lifts me up and sets me on the side of the pool so he can spread my legs and taste me.

But as much as I want to, I can't make myself do it. This

thing with Tate is temporary, but if I'm not careful, it could very easily leave a permanent scar on my heart.

"I won't do anything you don't want, Violet." His thumb smooths over my jaw and he holds my gaze, his head tilting toward me. "Until you say yes, you have control here. Remember that. But when you do say yes—and you will," his voice drips with confidence, "then you give control to me. Okay?"

I suck in a shaky breath and nod. I don't know what he means by that, but it sounds a little too appealing.

He backs up a little, giving me space to take in more than the short, shallow inhales I have been. Then he settles beside me with his back against the side, looking out over the surrounding high-rises.

I'm still going over his words when he asks, "When's your first tasting night?" His tone and his posture are the epitome of casual, as if we didn't just talk about the conditions under which he's going to have his way with me.

It takes me a moment to recalibrate, to remind myself that I should be focused on the coffee shop and our endgame here. "Next month. We've been slowly building up our customer base. We're giving out free coffees now, as more customers are coming back. I think the amount of business we're doing has grown enough to justify hosting a special event."

"Can I come?" he asks.

I shoot him a startled look. "Oh, of course you can come. I didn't think you'd want to, but since none of this would be happening if it wasn't for you, then you're absolutely welcome to be there."

"Don't sell yourself short, Violet. All I've given you is time and space to breathe. The rest is all you."

My traitorous heart flutters once more, forcing me to

run through the increasingly short list of reasons sleeping with Tate is a bad idea.

I keep my composure through our conversation about the tasting night, and he asks question after question until the beep of his phone interrupts us. He pulls himself out of the water the way he did last night, all rippling muscles and bulging biceps, and picks it up from where he left it on one of the deck chairs. He reads the message and smiles. It doesn't look like the kind of smile I imagine any man would make when reading a work message.

That thought causes jealousy to prick at my insides. Is it a woman? I grit my teeth and force myself to look back out at the view. It's none of my business. He said he wouldn't humiliate me by being with another woman during our relationship, and he's never given me any reason not to trust his word.

Though if I really want to read into my feelings, I'd admit to myself that what weighs on me the most is the thought that while he's saying all these things to me, the sweet things, the dirty things, he might be saying them to someone else too.

"Come on, butterfly. Time to get out."

Rubbing at the ache in my chest, I turn toward his voice. He's standing at the edge of the pool, holding his hand out for me. I extend my arm, and in one fluid motion, he grasps my wrist and pulls me up out of the water. One handed.

Why is that feat of strength such a damn turn-on? Every time I have myself convinced I can remain unaffected, he makes the smallest gestures look sexy as hell. I stumble a little getting my feet underneath me, and he catches me under the arms. Our wet bodies press together so I can feel every hard line and angle of him against me.

My hands landed on his chest as I wobbled, and

before I can stop myself, I'm giving in to temptation and tracing lines over his smooth, water-cooled skin, reveling in the feel of him under my fingertips. The ridge of his erection presses against my abdomen, sending arousal curling through me. My nipples are tight and sensitive, and god, I so badly want to rub myself against him. I want to rip his swim shorts off and drop to my knees and see for myself just how big he is. I must whimper, because suddenly, his hands are in my hair and he's tilting my head back. My lips part, and I'm so ready for him to kiss me.

His eyes are ablaze as he searches my face, from my eyes down to my mouth and back up again. With a groan, he lets me go and steps back. I'm left feeling nothing but cool air against my flushed skin.

He pushes his hands through his wet hair. "You need to get dressed," he says. "You have an appointment."

I shake my head, disregarding the comment about an appointment I have no recollection of scheduling. All I can think is that, with all his talk of wanting me, he seems to have no problem pushing me away when I practically offer myself to him on a platter. I gather up my tattered dignity and hold tight to it, telling myself once more that just because Tate likes to play, doesn't mean there's anything more to it than that.

He snags one of the two towels stacked on the table and hands it to me.

"Thank you," I murmur, avoiding his gaze.

We dry ourselves off in silence, then I follow him into the house.

"Where am I going, and what should I wear?" My voice sounds flat to my own ears, and I give myself a mental slap. This is the very reason I didn't want things to get physical between us. And yet, even without that having happened, I still keep slipping.

I pull myself together. I'm stronger than this. I know I am.

"You're staying here, so dress casually."

Equally annoyed by his vague answer and curious, I frown. "What's the appointment for?"

The infuriating man only winks in response, and then he's gone, sauntering into his bedroom and closing the door behind him.

I wrinkle my nose and stick my tongue out, even though he can't see me. Then I go into my own room, jump into the massive shower to rinse off, and throw on a pair of denim shorts and a T-shirt, leaving my feet bare. Tate said casual, so that's what he's getting.

I'm running a comb through my hair when there's a knock on my bedroom door. "What is it?" I yell out rather than opening it. I'm not sure I want to face Tate just yet.

In response, the door swings open, but instead of finding Tate in the doorway, I come face to face with Anna.

"Oh my god! What are you doing here?" I rush to give her a hug.

"I got a personal invitation from your fiancé," she says with a grin.

I'd called her first thing after the shock of our sudden engagement, to much amusement on her part. But I wasn't expecting to see her here. "Wait. Are you my appointment?"

"Not quite. Come on." She bounces on her toes and grasps my hand. "Nice new digs, by the way."

"I suppose," I say, following her down the hall. "If you like luxury high-rise living."

She laughs, and so do I, because Tate's apartment is

ridiculously gorgeous. But we both go silent at the sound of another feminine laugh coming from the living area.

As we step into the space and Tate and the mystery woman come into view, my heart does a strange little palpitation. The jealousy I was feeling before sharpens its claws as I take in the way he's smiling down at the pretty woman who looks just a little older than him. Is this the person he was messaging by the pool?

I take a deep breath. Regardless of who she is, I need to get a grip. Tate isn't mine, and I'm not his. And I have no reason, or right, to be jealous.

"Hi," the woman chirps when she catches sight of me. "You must be Violet. I'm Isabelle. I'm so happy to meet you." She strides toward me with her hand held out.

I shake it, but eye Tate, hoping for an explanation. He merely gives me an enigmatic smile. When I turn to Anna, she just waggles her brows.

"It's nice to meet you too," I finally say. "But I'm not sure who you are."

She laughs again, that same tinkling sound that had my hackles up when it was directed at Tate. But now that it's directed at me, it doesn't sound flirty at all. And the excited smile on her face pulls an answering one from me. As if her delight is contagious.

"Sounds like your man is keeping secrets," she says.

I look over at Tate again, warmth kindling deep in my chest at the sound of her calling him my man. "Sounds like it," I murmur. I turn to Anna. "Do you know what's going on?"

"Yep. Your *man* told me everything."

"Come and sit at the table," Isabelle says. "And I'll pour some champagne."

Champagne? I seek out Tate again. Rather than smiling,

this time he merely nods toward the table, his expression inscrutable.

Giving up the fight to figure out what's going on, I wander to the dining area, where Isabelle has placed a large black box. From another, smaller box, she pulls out a bottle of champagne and two glasses.

Anna and I sit, and Isabelle pours us both a drink.

"You're not having one?" I ask.

She gives me a cheeky little smile. "I'd be skinned alive if I drank alcohol while handling the merchandise."

Before I have time to question anything more, she undoes the box and pulls back both sides. I blink, not only in surprise, but because I'm hit with dozens of tiny rays of light. The box is filled with rings that glitter under the overhead fixture. This selection is far more eclectic than what we saw at the store this afternoon. These rings don't just boast beautiful diamonds, but rubies, sapphires, opals, and other gems I can't name. Big and small stones, platinum, gold, rose gold bands.

With my hand pressed to my chest, I look up at her. "What is this?"

She smiles. "Your fiancé asked me to curate a selection of ethically sourced and unique rings, tailored to your day-to-day activities and style. All of these have been crafted with materials chosen for their provenance. The gemstones and metals are sourced from conflict-free economies. Their creation has had a minimal impact on the environment. And they were mined by people benefiting from fair and safe working conditions." Isabelle removes a cloth from the box and unfolds it. "Some of these gemstones are recycled or second-hand. They also range in value. Though from what I understand after my conversation with your fiancé, the source and wearability of your ring are of more importance than the value. And if you don't find one you love, I can come back with more."

Keeping my focus locked on the display box, I take a second, inhaling deeply to make sure the tears blurring my vision won't spill over my lashes. Then I turn, anxious to express my gratitude to Tate, only to find him gone. He probably headed to his office to work. My heart does an almost painful little stutter when I realize he won't be here for this.

This must have been what he was doing when he was sending and receiving messages on his phone on our way back from Fifth Avenue. He was arranging this appointment, and he managed to contact my best friend as well, so that she could be here with me as well. He went out of his way to make it fun for me, rather than stressful.

I absolutely love having Anna here, but I can't help but wish that Tate was helping me choose. That when I find the perfect ring, he'd be the one slipping it onto my finger. As if it actually means something.

As if this were real.

Anna squeezes my knee. She knows me too well. I have no doubt she can tell that my emotions have gone haywire. She smiles gently. "Your man knows what he's doing."

I swallow past the knot in my throat and nod in agreement. When she holds out her champagne flute, I let out a watery little laugh and tap mine against hers.

"Okay, ladies," Isabelle says. "Let's get started, shall we?"

An hour later, I've chosen a ring. Although I tried it on to see what it looked like and to check the fit, I'm holding it between my fingers now. Isabelle walked me through the selection, explaining the origin of each gem exactly how I explain the origin of True Brew's coffee beans. Although the ring I'm holding is far from the flashiest, I was immediately drawn to it.

According to Isabelle, its design was inspired by the Edwardian era, with a low-profile rose-cut diamond surrounded by recycled antique round stones, all set on a slim, rose gold band. Its low profile means I won't have to worry about constantly knocking it against things at work. And for some reason, it's become important to me that I do wear it at work.

Isabelle has packed up and gone. Anna followed shortly after. She oohed and ahhed over every ring I tried on, making me laugh as we sipped our champagne. It was fun. Like being kids playing dress-up with costume jewelry. Except these rings are anything but costume.

And now I'm sitting all alone, holding my pretty engagement ring. The dark-blue velvet box is sitting on the table, but I leave it where it is when I get up and head toward Tate's office.

CHAPTER THIRTY-TWO

TATE

At the tap on my office door, I jerk my head up. "Come in."

Violet pushes the door open and pads in.

I immediately look at her left hand, and when I find it bare, I'm hit by an unexpected surge of disappointment. "You didn't find one you liked?"

"I did." She watches me with soft eyes as she holds out her right palm to reveal a pretty diamond ring. Her cheeks are flushed, likely from the champagne and all the laughing she and Anna were doing.

I stand and round my desk, then pluck it from her hand. It's understated but beautiful, just like her. A part of me wishes I had been the one to help her find it. But from the moment we approached the glass case at the jeweler this morning, her smile was forced.

I decided then and there that I didn't want that. When she looks at her engagement ring, I want her to smile. A genuine one. Because she loves it. Because it speaks to her. Not because she has to wear it in order to sell an act. Not because she felt pressured by my expectation, or anyone else's. If I'd chosen a ring for her, or hovered over her while she chose, that's how it would be.

"Thank you," she says softly. "I love it. And thank you for doing that for me. For inviting Anna. We had fun. Isabelle was lovely too."

"She helped Cole pick out Delilah's engagement ring. And I'm glad you found one you like. Does it need to be resized?"

She lowers her chin and shakes her head. "Perfect fit."

"I guess it was meant to be, then." I'm watching her carefully, trying to read her expression.

Her eyes are a little glossy. She might be tipsy from the champagne, although she's definitely not drunk. The smile she gives me is the real kind, the beautiful, unguarded one that was missing at the jeweler.

"I guess so." She worries her bottom lip with her teeth. "Should I start wearing it now, then? Or do you want to do something more dramatic? You know, for the act." She lets out a small, uncertain laugh.

Frustration rasps my nerves. She's so determined to remind herself—and me—that this thing is fake. But I know she feels the connection between us. I never wanted a connection with anyone. Never sought one out. But now that I've experienced it with Violet, I'm not sure I want to let it go. I wasn't lying yesterday when I told her I couldn't make her any promises. She's still wary around me, still doesn't trust me completely, and until she does, I can't predict how this is going to play out. But even with those doubts, my hope that this thing between us could last past the expiration date of our agreement is growing stronger. I'll give her a little more time to get used to the idea that there might be more to us than an act. But I'm done treading carefully around her.

"Now, Violet. You start wearing it now."

Her gaze lifts to mine. "Okay. I wasn't sure how you wanted to play it."

She holds out her right hand for the ring, but I don't give it back to her.

Confusion mars her brow. "I thought you wanted me to start wearing it..."

"I do. But if you think I'm not going to be the one to put my ring on your finger, then you're mistaken. Give me your other hand."

Her lips part, and her eyes sweep my face. But she wordlessly extends her left hand to me. With it cradled gently in mine, I'm all too aware of how small it feels in mine. I hold my breath as I slide the narrow band onto her finger, and if I'm not mistaken, she does too. For a long moment, I study the symbol that will tell the world this woman is mine.

My control snaps.

A hot wave of primal need surges through me. Maybe this is why I've shied away from commitment for so long. I've never wanted to stake this kind of claim. I've never wanted to hold another person's heart in my hands or give them the power to hold mine. I know how easily seemingly unbreakable bonds can come untethered, and until now, I've never been inclined to take that risk. Or maybe it was just that I hadn't found the person I'd be willing to take the risk for.

Whatever the hell my problem was, it's gone now. Violet's wearing my ring, and all I want to do is pull down her shorts and bend her over the desk behind me so I can pin her wrists above her head and admire how it looks on her finger while I fill her with my cock.

With her hand still in mine, I tug her toward me. Before

she can react, she's pressed to my chest, and my lips are ghosting the shell of her ear. "Do you know what this means? You're mine, Violet."

A shiver racks her body, and I'm rock fucking hard in an instant. "Tate," she whimpers. "I—"

Before she can finish that thought, I cup her face and trace her cheekbones with my thumbs. I was prepared to give her time, to make her ask for it, but I need this. I'm holding on by the thinnest of threads. "Yes or no?"

"Yes." The word comes out on a ragged breath.

I crash my mouth down on hers, reveling in the effortless way her lips part under mine, in the needy little whine she makes at the back of her throat, the way she arches up against me, as if she wants to get closer. None of that is a fucking act. There's no one here but us.

My kiss is anything but gentle, my teeth tugging on her lower lip, my tongue sliding deep. But she doesn't seem to care. She's rubbing herself against me, moaning. I could have her here, right now. I could fulfill my fantasy from a moment ago and bend her over my desk. Spank her ass for holding me at arm's length for so long. She'd do it. She'd take everything I gave her. I can feel it.

That's why I force myself to stop, to pull back.

Her eyes are midnight blue, shallow breaths falling from between her swollen lips. It takes every bit of my willpower to let her go. She brings her left hand to her mouth, fingers pressing against it as if she's shocked, either from the kiss or its sudden end. Maybe both.

"Why did you stop?" she asks.

I rake my hand through my hair, then adjust the raging hard-on pressing against my pants. It's in vain, because as I do it, she follows the movement with her eyes, pulling her bottom lip between her teeth, making me harder, if that's possible.

"Because you said yes to a kiss, not to being fucked on my desk. And that's where this would have ended up if I didn't stop. When I fuck you, butterfly, you'll be the one asking for it, not me. I want you so fucking desperate for my cock that you'll get down on your knees and beg for it. That way there's no damn confusion as to whether this is an act. Got it?"

A surprising anger has flooded me. I'm furious that the first time I've ever felt more than passing lust for a woman, I'm in this damn situation. With this pretense hanging between us. And I'm furious that Violet's opinion of me is so low. And that it's my own damn fault.

"Do you understand what I'm telling you, Violet? If you want my cock," I grab her hand and press it against my aching shaft, fighting back a groan when her fingers instinctively curl around it, "you're gonna have to ask me nicely for it. Okay?"

"Okay." The word comes out on a shuddery breath.

I leave her there, eyes wide, pupils still flared with desire, and make for the door.

"Wait," she says. "Where are you going?"

I grit my teeth. "To my bedroom so I can jerk off imagining all the things I'm going to do to you when you finally give in to this."

And then I'm gone.

CHAPTER THIRTY-THREE

VIOLET

I sag against the edge of Tate's desk. What the hell just happened?

One minute he was slipping the ring on my finger, and the next I was almost begging him to do me on his desk. And the fact that he knew that there was an *almost* in that thought is what I can't stop focusing on.

He read me so damn perfectly. I wanted it badly. I wanted *him* badly. And yet that vestige of doubt still claws at me. It would be incredible. I have no doubt. He could wreck me. With the best intentions, Tate could take my body and my heart and break the shield I've put up around them. That fear lives on. That I'll give him my body, then my heart, and at the end of this, he'll still walk away.

But god, I'm so turned on. My whole body is buzzing, my nipples hard little peaks inside my shirt. I close my eyes and take a deep breath, then another, willing myself to calm down. Willing my mind to clear. It's impossible, because I'm assaulted by visions of Tate in his bedroom, his hand working his cock, head thrown back, stroking himself while thinking about me.

My knees almost buckle. God, do I want to see it. He was angry when he left here, and I'm almost dizzy at the thought of how hard he might thrust into his fist. I want to see him while he touches himself. I need to. I might not be ready to feel his body against mine, but that doesn't mean I don't want it. This might be as close as I ever get.

Before I realize I'm doing it, I'm walking down the hallway toward our bedrooms. I stop outside Tate's door. It's ajar, like maybe he knew I'd come. Or was it hope? Maybe it was neither. Maybe it was carelessness on his part. Though the more time I spend with Tate, the more I learn that nothing he does is careless, contrary to how it often appears.

I take a deep breath, but my hand is still shaking as I push the door open and step inside. He's not on the bed. Not in his bathroom either. It takes a moment to find him where he's reclined in one of the deep leather chairs in his bedroom's sitting area. And he's not touching himself, even though he's still sporting a large bulge beneath his pants.

He's stripped out of his shirt, and with his upper torso bare and golden, he looks like a lion in repose, and just as arrogant. His eyes are hooded as he watches me. "Did you come for the show, butterfly?"

I flinch, but it's true. "Yes," I whisper.

Tension visibly drains from his body. His shoulders lower, and his rigid abs relax a fraction. He licks his lips, hungry gaze roving over my body. "Yes or no, Violet?"

He's asking for far more than a kiss this time. But I can't say the word. I shake my head instead.

He doesn't seem surprised. His eyes stay focused on mine as he unzips his pants and slides his hand inside. "I told you. You have control. I'm not going to touch you without you asking me to."

His forearm flexes with the languid movement of his hand, and desire is a hard knot deep inside me. All it would take is one word, and he'd be on me, his almost feline laziness replaced in an instant by the wild creature lurking beneath the surface.

My body is alive and thrumming with need. Arousal beats through my veins, and my nipples are pushing through the thin material of my shirt.

Tate catalogs my body's reaction, his jaw going impossibly sharp. "Show me, then," he grits out. "Show me what I can't have."

I shake my head as confusion washes over me.

His voice comes out dark and dirty. "Slide those shorts and panties down your legs, sit in that chair," he nods to the one opposite him, "and show me what I'm missing out on."

A strange, wild heat surges through me. The need to drive him as crazy as he's driving me. Without looking away from him, I hook my thumbs in the sides of my shorts and slowly lower them, along with my underwear. The blaze of desire in Tate's eyes triggers a fierce tension low and deep inside me. It gives me the determination I need to shove my remaining inhibitions into a vault in my mind and slam the door shut. I can have this. I'm allowed to have it. It might not be all that Tate wants, but he's ceding control to me, and when it comes to a man like him, that is... freeing.

I move toward the chair, feeling his gaze tracing over me almost like fingers ghosting over my skin. Then I turn and sit. He's pulled his erection out, and he's gripping it hard. Even with how big his hand is, there are still several inches of shaft left exposed between his swollen tip and where he's got his fist wrapped around himself. I squirm, imagining the way it would stretch my body as he pushed it inside me.

"Sit farther back and put your feet up," he commands. "I want to see every inch of you."

With a shuddering breath, I do as he says, propping my heels on the edge of the leather seat.

He drops his head back and groans, but quickly jerks it forward again, as if he doesn't want to miss a single second. The reaction gives me a heady sense of feminine power, which drowns out my remaining self-consciousness.

"Fuck, Violet." He gives himself one long, hard stroke. Precum glistens at his tip, making my mouth water with the need to taste him. But that's not what's happening here. This is Tate controlling me, directing me. He might not be touching me himself, but he's still responsible for my pleasure.

"Hold your pussy open with your left hand," he says. "Let me see that pretty diamond on your finger when you come for me."

I follow his instruction, the stone glimmering as I do.

"Do you know what that ring means, butterfly?"

My heart trips over itself at the need emanating from him when he calls me butterfly. "What?" I whisper.

"Until it comes off your finger, it means that perfect little pussy is mine. Your body is mine. Do you understand?"

I'm too far gone to protest. Maybe when I come back to my senses, I'll have the wherewithal to deny what he's saying. But for now, his words only send my desire spiraling higher.

"Touch your clit," he says, his voice like gravel.

I find the swollen bud and gently circle it, once, twice, my hips arching against the pad of my fingertip. I'm already close, so close.

"That's enough."

Without thinking, I obey, pulling my hand away. The smile he gives me is pure wolfish satisfaction. I whimper as the impending orgasm begins to recede.

"I want to see how many fingers my fiancée can fit in her pretty pink cunt."

God, his filthy words send a rush of arousal between my legs.

Slowly, deliberately, I slip my hand down, bypassing my clit and gliding my forefinger and middle finger on either side of my entrance, extending our mutual torture a little longer.

"You like teasing me, don't you?"

"Yes." My voice is breathless.

"Slide those fingers inside and fuck yourself the way I did that night."

Fire licks up my spine, heightening the need washing over me. I do as he says, easing my middle finger into the slick warmth of my body and moaning. I'm already so wet a second finger slips in easily.

He hisses a breath. "I still remember how hot and tight you were."

I lick my lips, watching him as his eyes drift half-closed.

"Fuck, it was damn near impossible not to pull myself out just like this and thrust up into you."

With a desperate shiver, I slide my fingers out and circle my clit. Little sparks of pleasure sizzle out from my core along my nerves. I squeeze my eyes shut, wishing for more, even though I know we can't. We shouldn't.

"Are you imagining it's me touching you?" he asks, his voice deeper, rougher.

Eyes still closed, I nod.

"You felt so good that night. Your pussy tasted so sweet. Pretend your fingers are mine. Show me how you want me to touch you."

The tension that built between us that very first night stretches taut now. The memories flood through me. I want him to touch me like he did then, but I can't let him, so this is the next best thing.

I've been gentle so far, but I don't want gentle from him.

I thrust my fingers back inside myself and whimper at the feeling of fullness. With every thrust, my palm hits my clit, and soon, I'm bucking my hips against my own hand.

Harsh breaths fall from my lips, and my heart thrashes against my rib cage. I don't slow as I open my eyes, though I falter for an instant when details of the scene in front of me register. Tate King, hooded eyes fixed on my face while I take my pleasure, his full, masculine lips parted, his hand slowly working his straining erection.

"I wish it was your cock," I say.

His steady movement pauses for a beat. "Imagine it is." Then he's back to working himself over, his rhythm now matching my own so that we're in sync. I add a third finger, trying to emulate the fullness I know I'd feel with him inside me.

"That's it, beautiful." His voice has gone hoarse. "Imagine it's me fucking you. Imagine I'm stroking into you, my cock filling you, stretching you."

I'm panting, gone now, picturing it all. Wanting it all.

"Are you close, Violet?"

The waves of heat washing over me are so powerful now they're threatening to drag me under. "Yes."

"Then stop. Right now."

I let out a frustrated moan. I could just keep going. One more swipe, two, and I'd come undone right here in front of him. But the almost drugged pleasure on his face as he watches me is addictive. He's getting off on keeping me on the edge. It's its own kind of torture. But I'll follow his command if it means he'll keep looking at me like that.

"Good girl, that's it. Do it again. Fuck yourself. Make me jealous of your fingers."

He moves his hand faster, and I match his pace. The pleasure of it all has arousal dripping between the cheeks of my ass.

Even without touching my clit, I'm dangerously close to shattering.

"You want to come, butterfly?"

I bite my lip and nod. If precum wasn't leaking down the underside of his shaft at an impressive rate, I'd be embarrassed by the noises my fingers are making.

"Do you have any idea how much I wish I could be buried inside you right now? To feel you so hot and wet and tight around me. You have no idea the things I dream of doing to you."

"What do you want to do?" The question comes out as a breathless gasp.

His gaze sears into me. "I'll tie your hands together and your legs apart."

My body jolts at the thought of being restrained, and another rush of heat hits me.

"I'll pin you down with my hand on your back so you can't move, then shove my cock in that tight little cunt. I'll use a toy on your clit to make you come over and over until neither of us can take it anymore. When you think you have no more left to give, I'll untie your hands and make you use your fingers to come one more time. And only when you're spasming around me will I let myself fill you up."

"Tate, please!" I cry out. The image his words paint in my head has me balanced on the knife's edge.

"Touch your pretty clit, beautiful." His voice is a dark, bass growl. "Let me see my fiancée fall apart for me."

It only takes two swipes of my fingers over that swollen bundle of nerves before my orgasm hits me. My spine pulls taut, and a sob rips its way from my chest at the intensity of the pleasure rushing through me.

Tate jackknifes out of the chair, and in two strides, he's before me, dropping to his knees between mine. I'm too far gone to care that he's so close and completely focused on the view between my legs.

As the final spasm hits me, he lets out a feral groan. "You made such a mess on my chair, butterfly. What am I going to do with you?"

My cheeks burn as I take in the wet patch on the leather of the chair. On instinct, I squeeze my thighs together, but when Tate shakes his head, I let them fall back open.

He runs his fingers through the moisture, then smears it all over his cock. With one hand pressed into my upper thigh, he spreads me wider for him, while his other hand moves again, in short, sharp jerks.

I can't stop staring at him, at the way his shaft glistens with my arousal. I'm feverish, my skin hot and sensitive, my clit still swollen, still pulsing. I'm so close to saying yes, to letting him slide that long, thick cock inside me. Maybe it's stupid to resist at this stage, considering what I've just done —what we're both doing. But once I have it inside me, I don't know that I'll ever want another. And that's a terrifying thought when Tate's always been one and done.

His harsh breathing pulls me back to the moment. I focus on his movements again just as he angles himself down, gives one final rough stroke, and with a hoarse shout, explodes. A jet of cum spurts out of him, and disappointment fills me when he doesn't let it hit my overheated skin. He strokes again, and another stream shoots out, the pearly white streaks covering the wet spot I left. Another jerk, and more pools on the leather. I can't look away as he uses that big hand to milk every last drop from himself.

By the time he's finished, we're both sweaty and panting. And my emotions are in turmoil.

I knew reality would hit. I just didn't expect it to hit so soon. I let my feet drop to the floor, and Tate doesn't stop me. He's sitting back on his heels, dick still hard.

"Let me get something..." I take in the mess we both made on the leather of what I'm certain is a very expensive chair. If I expected him to be embarrassed, I couldn't be more wrong. He stands, towering over me, his eyes dark, a flush high on his cheeks, and tucks himself back into his pants.

He scoops me up with both arms and sets me on my feet, helping me avoid having to awkwardly maneuver around the evidence of what we did.

His big hands steady me as I wobble on shaky legs. For a moment, he rests his forehead against mine, and only the sound of our breaths fills the air between us. "I think coming with you has become my new favorite thing," he says.

"What was your old favorite thing?" I ask, still struggling to catch my breath.

"Jerking off while imagining what it would be like to come with you."

All I can do is sob out a laugh.

He cups my face and presses a kiss to the top of my head. "Come on, butterfly. My fiancée should get to experience my shower at least once. I promise you'll love it almost as much as you loved what we just did."

"You just can't help yourself, can you?"

"Not when it comes to you." Then he takes my hand and leads me to his bathroom.

CHAPTER THIRTY-FOUR

VIOLET

I flick through True Brew's social media, replying to comments on the photos I've posted over the last couple of days. We started off small, but our followers are growing, slowly but surely. Customers are even tagging us in their own photos, especially ones of our latte art.

My cheeks ache from smiling as I type out a couple of responses to people commenting on how delicious our coffee is.

"You're in a good mood." Jarrod grins.

"Things are looking up," I say.

And they are. The first injection of cash from my arrangement with Tate came through at the start of the week, and since I didn't have to buy a new espresso machine, I hired a part-time baker to make fresh pastries in the morning, and another part-time waitress. The help allows me more time to focus on managing the books and working on our marketing plan.

I've started a mailing list, and we've garnered quite a bit of interest in our tasting night. We're not exactly bustling all day every day, but there are far fewer empty tables now than there have been since I returned to New York.

Though the way things are turning around here isn't the only reason I'm smiling more. I study the ring on my left hand, and the smile is back. I'm still not used to seeing it there. And I shouldn't *get* used to seeing it there, since it won't be long before I'll have to take it off. But I'm starting to enjoy this act more than I should. I'm starting to think that maybe enjoying every aspect of it while it lasts wouldn't be the worst thing in the world.

Tate is... god, I can't wrap my head around him. I wanted to dislike him. Keeping him at arm's length was so much easier when all I saw when I looked at him was a playboy who only cared about money, power and sex. But there's so much more to him than that. What we did last weekend. I don't have words for it. I close my eyes as the memory of watching him come, of him watching *me* come, pulses through me.

I squirm a little just thinking about it.

I expected him to join me in the shower afterward, but he surprised me instead by laying out a thick, luxurious towel and a robe for me before disappearing. For a moment, I waffled between disappointment and relief. I settled on relieved. Because it would have been far too hard to resist him if he was naked in the shower with me. And I'm just not ready for that. Not yet anyway.

After having the most incredible shower of my life, I retreated to my room for the night. The sight of Tate frying up eggs and bacon the next morning did nothing to curb my attraction. Neither have the subsequent days. He hasn't pushed me for more, but he hasn't made things easy on me either. He makes a point of walking around without his shirt on more often than not and insists we cook together. He's letting me in, showing me who he really is, treating me like he cares more than he should. As if there's more to this. As if there's more to us.

Tonight, we're attending another gala—this one actually hosted by the King Group—so he'll be all dressed up in his tuxedo again. That definitely won't help matters. God knows my willpower can only take so much. Especially knowing just how good he can make me feel. With just his fingers. Without even touching me. And knowing I haven't had the chance to touch him yet.

Marie, our new server, gives me a wave to let me know she's going on her break.

With a nod to her, I pick up my phone so I can head to the counter and help out while she's gone. Before I can slip it into the pocket of my cutoffs, a new notification pops up. It's a comment on our latest photograph. Deciding to fire off a quick reply before jumping into serving, I swipe into the app. Then I freeze. Because I recognize the username. It's Eric's.

All the comment says is *Looking forward to trying this place out.*

It's innocuous, but it's far too much of a coincidence to not be deliberate. I scroll back through my feed, looking at the recent photos. I appear in a few of them, although I've been focusing primarily on our coffee, food and the story behind the shop and our coffee beans.

I broke off all communication with Eric after the messy way we ended, blocking him on my phone and social media accounts. Since then, I haven't seen or heard from him. And as far as I know, he still lives in Maine.

So this? This is weird.

I make a note to do an internet search later and make sure he's still working for his uncle. But for now, I slide my phone into my pocket, pick up a tray, load it up with plates and coffees and get moving.

As I make my way across the dining area and take in the new customers at several tables, any thoughts about my ex are pushed to the side. For the next thirty minutes, I remain busy, serving and chatting with several people. A few tell me that friends or family recommended us to them, or that they saw one of our posts and decided to try the place out.

I'm even asked to pose for a couple of photos with smiling customers holding up their cups of coffee. The interactions fill me with so much hope I practically float my way from table to table. These customers will go on to post on their social media pages, and in turn, word will continue to spread. Finally, I feel like I'm doing more than treading water.

At the end of the day, Jarrod and I close up, and as always, the Pinnacle Security guy waits patiently for us. I've learned to ignore their presence while I'm working, since they do their best to blend into the crowd with their plain clothes.

Once I've locked the front door behind us and said goodbye to Jarrod, my bodyguard steps up and gestures down the street to where one of the team's dark sedans is waiting.

I give him a smile and head that way. I'm not going to lie, I could get used to being driven to and from work every day. Not having to worry about catching the bus or walking in the rain is wonderful. No wonder Tate has Jeremy drive him around everywhere.

Tate isn't home when I step inside his penthouse. The little pang of disappointment that ricochets through me is hard to ignore. For all my protestations, I'm already far more invested than I should be.

I lay out the dress I chose from the selection the stylists provided me, then jump in the shower. Tate offered to have hair and makeup organized for me again, but I prefer doing it myself. It was good for that first event, when I was nervous and had no idea what to expect, but I don't particularly love the idea of having a team of people fussing over me every time we go out.

I'm fresh from the shower and wrapped in a towel when there's a knock on my bedroom door. Immediately, my heart rate spikes. I blow out a breath and lift my chin, grasping for what little composure I can conjure, then shuffle to the door.

When I swing it open, an involuntary shiver darts up my spine. Oh god, will I ever get used to the sight of Tate in a suit? He's still wearing his jacket, but his tie's been loosened, and his top button is undone. The sight is so damn hot I almost spontaneously combust.

His eyes darken as they trail over my exposed skin. When he meets my gaze again, that cocky smile that I'm actually starting to like—maybe much more than like—creases his cheeks. "Wanted to see how you're doing."

"Good." I sound far too breathless. "I just have to do my makeup and get dressed."

Without asking permission, he walks into the room. I step back to move out of his way, but he grasps my waist with both hands and pulls me against him. He drops his head, pressing his face against the crook of my neck and breathing in.

"Tate," I say gently, "What are you doing?" I smooth my hands over his back, uncertain of what's going on in his head. There's something almost vulnerable about the way he's holding me like this.

"You always smell so good." He straightens and trails his

fingers along my collarbone. The move sends goose bumps skittering along my skin and makes my nipples pebble against the towel. It would be so easy for him to hook his finger in the material and tug it loose. And it would take no effort at all to go up on my toes and press my lips to his.

Just as the thought crosses my mind, his mouth finds the sensitive skin below my ear. "I haven't been able to stop thinking about your pretty pussy all day. I was in a meeting with my marketing team, and all I could think about was how you looked when you came." He huffs a breath against my skin. "I got a fucking hard-on in the middle of a meeting I was supposed to be running because I couldn't stop imagining how hard you'd come with my tongue inside you while I press a toy to your clit."

Heat pools low in my belly and spreads outward. "Tate." It's a strangled whisper.

When he pulls back, his smile is lazy and sexy. Like he knows exactly what his words do to me. He cocks one brow and leisurely scans my body, pausing when he gets to my hands. "Where's your ring?"

I gesture over to the bedside table. "I took it off before I got in the shower."

He stalks over to it, swipes it off the top of the table and then stalks back toward me. He picks up my left hand, then slides the ring onto my finger. "That's better."

I stare at him, my heart tapping out an erratic rhythm against my sternum. In a million years, I never would have pegged Tate King as a growly, possessive man who doesn't like when his fake fiancée isn't wearing his ring. It makes me wonder how much of his true self he's been hiding behind his devilish smiles and smart-ass remarks, his flirtatiousness and love 'em and leave 'em attitude.

"I'm going to get changed," he says. "Otherwise, I'll take something my fiancée isn't ready to give me."

I let out a shuddery breath. "Tate..."

He cuffs the back of my neck. The warmth of him seeps into me, fueling the flames he ignited when he murmured those dirty words. "I told you, butterfly. The ball is in your court. But when you do ask," his fingers slide along my jaw, and his golden eyes are hot on mine, "I won't take it easy on you. When you beg me to take you, you're going to take everything I have to give."

My thighs clench against the ache deep inside. If Tate were to slide his hand up under the towel wrapped around me, he'd find me wet and ready for him.

"Get dressed, Violet. I want to show off my beautiful fiancée tonight."

And then he's gone, leaving me wondering if there's even any point in pretending I won't give in to what we both want.

I'm distracted as I do my makeup and blow out my hair. I'm still lost in my own thoughts as I pull on the gorgeous dress and zip it up.

When I check my reflection, I can't help but admire how the champagne-colored gown clings to my curves. Tiny spaghetti straps attach to the V-neck bodice that dips low enough to reveal the swell of my breasts. The dress brushes the tops of my glittery nude pumps, while a slit reaches my upper thigh, revealing a sliver of skin with every step I take. It's probably the sexiest dress I've ever worn, and I'm thankful that on the night I'm going to be paraded around as the future Mrs. Tate King, I look as put together as I do.

When I'm ready, I grab my matching clutch, mist on some perfume and leave my bedroom. Tate is already in the living room, looking incredible in his tuxedo. He glances up as I enter the room and is immediately on his feet, striding toward me.

"I don't think I can take you out looking like this," he says.

Disappointment hits me hard. I was sure I'd made a good choice with this dress. With a hand pressed over my stomach, I look down at myself, then back up at him. "I can change. I have other dresses."

He molds his hand to my waist, and with his head lowered so I can feel the heat of his breath on my cheek, he groans. "You're killing me, butterfly. I don't know if I can handle it if any other man sees you looking so fucking sexy."

The weight in my stomach morphs into a kaleidoscope of butterflies in an instant. I laugh a little breathlessly. "Lucky for you, I'm wearing your ring."

"I like that," he says. "A little too much."

My heart pangs, because as much as those words affect me, I can't help but wonder if he only likes it because he *knows* it's not permanent.

"Are you ready?" he asks.

I nod, and he threads his fingers through mine and leads me to the elevator. On the ride down, we watch each other's reflection, some silent communication passing between us. The intensity of Tate's stare promises pleasure I can only imagine, and by the time we reach the bottom, my pulse is racing.

It isn't until we're in the back of the limo, driving to the nearby King Group hotel where the event is being held, that I remember what happened earlier. "Something strange happened today," I tell Tate, shifting in my seat to face him. "Eric commented on one of True Brew's posts."

His brows lower. "What did he say?"

"Just something about looking forward to trying us out."

"Has he ever commented before?"

"No. I haven't heard from him or seen him since before I moved."

Tate's jaw is rigid, along with his posture. "Did you ever talk about True Brew when you were together?"

"Sure. But the last he would have known was that I was in Maine. Maybe it's just a weird coincidence? Or maybe..." I trail off. Maybe he saw an article about Tate and me that mentioned where I work.

His dark frown tells me he's thinking the same thing. I gnaw on my lower lip. Perhaps I shouldn't have said anything. "It doesn't matter. It was just an innocuous comment. I doubt I'll hear anything else from him."

He's silent for a beat, his brows drawn down, and I can't tell what he's thinking. "Let me know straight away if you do, okay?"

I put my left hand on his leg, my engagement ring glittering in the lights of the passing traffic. "I will, I promise."

Tate dips his chin and focuses on my hand, and the tension drains from him. His gaze roams slowly back up over me, coming to rest on my face. The flare of his pupils makes it clear he's flashing back to the same thing that's been running through my head for the last week. All thoughts of Eric are forgotten as my blood heats under his perusal.

If we weren't pulling up outside the hotel, I'm not confident I wouldn't have slid across the leather seat and climbed onto his lap. But we're still locked in one another's gaze when Jeremy stops the car at the end of the red carpet and the flashes start going off. This year's King Group gala is in support of funding sustainable developments in underdeveloped countries, and the guest list apparently includes a host of celebrities, politicians and titans of industry, so the press is out in force.

As Tate and I walk past the crowd of reporters and photographers, they call out.

"Violet, let us have a look at the ring."

"How did you propose, Tate?"

"Have you set a date yet?"

I peer up at Tate. When we started this thing, I had no clue it would become such a big deal. I thought I'd accompany him to a few events. That people wouldn't care about me as a person, just that Tate had a girlfriend. But now we're engaged, and this whole thing has gained a life of its own. Tate doesn't look bothered by the questions at all though.

"Tate," one of the reporters calls out, "when did you know she was the one?"

Tate dips his head, a sinful half smile on his face. "What do you think?" he murmurs, low enough no one else can hear. "Should I tell them it was when you gushed all over my fingers at Onyx?"

I narrow my eyes. "Maybe you could tell them the truth and say it was when you came to True Brew and begged me to be your girlfriend."

He just chuckles and leads me toward the doors without answering any of the questions thrown our way.

The foyer is huge and resplendent with marble and glass and chandeliers. From there, Tate steers me to the side, where we go through open double doors into a large, luxurious ballroom.

"Our table's at the front," Tate says.

"One of the perks of being the hosts?" I arch a brow at him.

"I don't know that I've ever been to an event where we weren't at the front."

I let out a quiet snort.

"At least it means everyone will get a good look at my gorgeous future wife."

I press my palm to my fluttery stomach. Why do I get a thrill when he says *my future wife*, even when I know it's not real?

As we weave our way through the crowd, person after person stops Tate to shake his hand and offer him congratulations on his engagement, as well as the gala. I'm quickly tired of smiling politely as they assess me, some with arch expressions that smack of disdain. But I don't say anything. I'm getting paid to stand by Tate's side, so that's what I'll do.

When we finally reach the table and Delilah comes into view, I sag in relief. She smiles at me, looking beautiful in a classy black dress.

"It's so nice to see you again," she says as Tate guides me into the empty chair beside her. She angles close, her green eyes wide. "Cole told me what happened with the engagement. Are you okay?"

"Define okay," I whisper.

Her smile is sympathetic as she glances at Tate, who's talking to Roman, his arm resting along the back of my seat, thumb absently stroking the sensitive skin of my neck just like he did last time. And just like last time, it feels way too good.

She lets out a little sigh. "The King men are hard to resist," she says.

I play with the stem of my wineglass and swallow past the lump in my throat. "They are."

"Can I see the ring?"

With a smile, I oblige, holding out my hand.

"That's beautiful." Her tone is sincere. "I've never seen one like it before. Let me guess, Tate called Isabelle."

I laugh. "He did."

She lowers her voice. "When Cole told me about this ploy they cooked up, I didn't think Tate could handle pretending to have a real emotional connection with a woman. A purely sexual connection, maybe. But to convincingly act like he was in love? I wasn't sure his heart would be in it enough to make it believable. But..." She peers over my shoulder, then focuses on me again. "It looks to me like his heart is 100 percent in it."

Face heating, I look away, only to catch Tate watching me. He gives me that smile, not the cocky one, not a flirtatious one, but the one that sends a slow pulse of desire through my whole body. I want to think she's right. Sometimes, especially over the last few days, I almost believe it's true. But I've been so wrong before, and it's hard to fully let go of that niggling fear. That my judgement is off. That I'll let someone in, only to find out that I was wrong all over again.

In a flurry of emerald satin, Tate's mom appears at the table. Those icy blue eyes meet mine, and her lips twitch into a tight smile.

"Violet. How lovely of you to join us tonight."

"I'm very happy to be here to support such a wonderful cause."

She lifts her chin. "Yes, of course."

Tate cuts in. "Since Violet is my fiancée now, Mom, you should expect to see her at all these events."

Beverly frowns, and her brows dip just a little, as if in question, as she looks between me and her youngest son. It's clear she's confused about his statement. She knows this is fake, everyone at this table does, but Tate has a knack for sounding way too convincing.

"Yes, well. I'll look forward to that."

There's so little inflection in her tone, and her face is so expressionless, it's hard to know how to take that comment.

Tate stands, turning to me and holding out his hand. I take it, and he wraps his warm fingers around mine, then tugs me to my feet.

"Well, Mom. It's been a delight, as always. But I think I'd like a dance with the future Mrs. King before being forced to make awkward small talk with you over lobster and caviar."

Beverly purses her lips, but there's no cutting comment in response. She merely sniffs and settles herself elegantly in one of the empty seats.

With a nod to the rest of our table, Tate tugs me toward the dance floor. He looks down at me as we go, his golden eyes dark. "I'm sorry about that. I told you, my mother doesn't have a warm bone in her body."

I tighten my hold on his hand as an ache forms behind my ribs. I may have lost both my parents, but I never doubted that they loved me. I barely remember Mom, but Dad kept her memory alive for me with his words and stories and the framed pictures that hung on his wall.

On the dance floor, Tate pulls me in and holds me close. "I'm sorry," he murmurs. "I shouldn't complain about my parents when you don't have yours."

I put my hand on his arm. "You can talk to me about anything. I miss my parents. I always will. But I know how lucky I was to have had them. It hurts that they're gone, yes, but I imagine it's a different kind of pain feeling like you didn't have them at all, even while you were living in the same house."

Eyes blazing, Tate tightens his hold on my waist and kisses me. It's the first time he's done it without asking. Not that I would have said no. I don't even care that we're on the dance floor of a ballroom filled with the rich and powerful. In fact, I welcome it. I want everyone to see how much Tate wants me. Because even though we're still in this arrangement, even though there's still an end date, our connection is real. It has to be. The heat searing between us, the way his lips claim mine. It might not be love, but whatever it is, it's real.

I tangle my fingers in his hair and press myself against him. When his hands drop dangerously, low, his fingers brushing the curve of my ass, I whimper into his mouth.

He breaks the kiss and drops his forehead to mine, heaving out harsh breaths. "What are you doing to me, butterfly?"

I hope he doesn't expect an answer, because I don't have one for him.

We stay like that, swaying until the song ends.

When the music fades, he steps back. "Want a drink?"

Still floating an inch off the ground, I smile up at him. "I'd love one. But I need to freshen up first." I have no doubt he's kissed all my lipstick off.

"I like this look on you." He drags his thumb over my bottom lip. "Freshly kissed. Makes me wonder how beautiful you'll look when you're freshly fucked."

I let out a shaky breath. I get the feeling he's going to find that out very soon.

Hand in hand, we exit the dance floor. We only go our separate ways when I make my way to the bathroom and he heads to the bar. The women's bathroom is just as extravagant as the rest of the hotel—hardly a surprise—and I take my time reapplying my makeup.

After returning to the ballroom, I work my way back through the crowd to the bar, only to jerk to a halt when I see Tate standing next to that woman from the first gala, Amy. She looks gorgeous, with a siren-red dress hugging every curve. Jealousy coils like a living thing inside me. It shouldn't, but it does. The wondering if Tate has slept with her, the wondering if, even though I have his ring on my finger, she's shared something with him that I haven't, scores bitter nails down my spine.

I force myself to move toward them. Tate has his back to me, and she's too busy batting her lashes at him to notice me. As I get closer, I can make out the sound of her silvery little laugh, then her words.

"I never would have believed it if I didn't see it myself. Tate King, permanently tamed." She reaches out and places her fingers lightly on his forearm. "I have to say, a coffee shop owner is not who anyone expected you to end up with."

I stiffen but relax again a moment later when Tate moves his arm from under her hand.

"I can't imagine you've spent that much time thinking about the woman I'd finally make mine."

"I suppose it's more that we just never expected you to make anyone yours at all. But of course, everyone is so pleased that you have."

I'm surprised she can't feel the intensity of my glare. If I squint any harder, I'm likely to singe her with my anger.

"I don't really care whether anyone is pleased, except for Violet," Tate says.

My heart thumps, and warmth spreads like treacle through my chest. He doesn't know I'm here, but there's not the slightest hint of a lie in his voice.

The flash of irritation on Amy's face is quickly replaced

by an artificially bright smile. "Of course, that's very sweet. But maybe, before you and your shop keeper ride off into the sunset together, you and I could meet up for a drink one night."

I grit my teeth. Does she really think Tate's stupid enough to take her up on her offer? I'm just about to stalk forward and make my presence known when Tate straightens.

"That's not going to happen," he says, the words so icy I'm surprised Amy doesn't shiver. "I wasn't interested before, and I'm even less so now. Particularly considering how fucking *in love* I am with my fiancée."

Amy's smile is frozen, but before she has a chance to say anything more, Tate turns and sees me standing there. The look he gives me is the complete opposite of the one he gave her. It lights me up inside and sends liquid heat pouring through my veins.

He pulls me toward him, tips my face up to his and brushes a kiss over my lips. "Come on, I need you in my arms again."

I run my hand up his chest, press it against his heart and go up on my toes so I can murmur in his ear. "I need you inside me."

Every muscle in his body tightens. With a sharp exhale, he turns his head so his lips almost brush mine. I have no idea whether Amy is still standing there watching, and frankly, I couldn't care less.

He slides a hand up my back and grasps the back of my neck. "Is that a request, butterfly?"

"Yes. And as soon as we're alone, I'll ask you prettily, just the way you wanted."

Tate takes a step back and scrubs his hand over his

mouth. Without taking his eyes off me, he says, "Excuse us, Amy. My fiancée wants to get me alone."

He wraps his hand around mine and takes off, towing me behind him.

"Where are we going?"

His only response is that devilish smirk. The one that used to make me crazy but now has every nerve ending in my body lighting up.

CHAPTER THIRTY-FIVE

TATE

As we approach the dance floor, Violet tugs at my hand.

She frowns, and a little crease forms between her brows. "I thought we were going somewhere we could be—"

"Alone?"

She nods, and the way she presses her teeth into that plump lower lip of hers has my dick swelling. Fuck, I'm already imagining how good it will feel having her mouth on me.

I pull her toward me, so she has no choice but to end up pressed against my chest. "I'm looking forward to hearing those pretty words of yours, butterfly. But it might reflect poorly on us if we left my family's gala early."

"Well." She blinks up at me. "Maybe not leave, but..."

I slide my hand down the satin-smooth skin of her back and dip my head toward hers, so my lips brush the shell of her ear. "You want me to take you somewhere and fuck you, butterfly? Maybe one of the service corridors or an empty meeting room? My family owns this hotel. I could take you up to one of the suites and give you a quick orgasm if you need it that badly."

She scowls and pushes against my chest. "When you put it like that..."

"You're not going anywhere, Violet. I've waited long enough. Now you can wait right alongside me for a little while."

Her throat moves in a swallow before that delicate chin of hers tips up. "Are you punishing me for not saying yes sooner?"

I move my hand lower, fingers ghosting over the swell of her ass. "I'm not punishing you. Hurting you is the last thing I want. But some things are worth waiting for." I brush my thumb against her lower lip and savor the sound of her indrawn breath. "What's going to happen between us tonight is worth waiting for. But if you're feeling needy, beautiful, let me tell you exactly what I'm going to do to you. So that while we're sitting at the dinner table with my family, making polite small talk, you can think about what's to come, all the while pressing those gorgeous thighs together. After all," I smooth my hands down over her hips, "you don't want to soak through your panties and make a mess of this pretty dress."

"Tate," she half whispers, half moans.

I can't help but smile. Not because I'm enjoying torturing her, but because the desperation shining in her eyes is one of the hottest things I've ever seen. There's no way I won't get addicted to it. Hell, I probably already am.

"As soon as I get you in the limo," I murmur, pushing her hair behind her ear, "I'm going to tell Jeremy to put the privacy screen up, because no one but me gets to hear the noises my needy fiancée is going to make. Then I'm going to slide my hand up the slit in your dress that's been tempting me all night. I'm going to feel just how wet your beautiful pussy is for me, and then you're going to straddle me. You're going to work that swollen little clit against me until you're dripping all over my pants. You're going to use my cock to come."

Hell. Describing all the things I'm going to do to her—picturing it in my head—is affecting me too. I'm so hard I have to pull her closer and press into her to ease the ache in my dick.

"That's just going to be a starter. When we get home, I'm going to make you come again and again until you're exhausted. Until your body is shaking with sensory overload. That's when I'll bend you over, fuck my way into your tight, hot, wet little cunt, and make you give me one more orgasm."

Violet is clutching at my shirt, her lips parted, chest heaving with each breath. Her pupils are vast pools of black. Fuck. If I were to slide my hand between her thighs right now, I can guarantee I'd find her drenched. She's practically a puddle in my arms, and I fucking love it.

I brush a kiss to her soft mouth and will my body to relax. Then, keeping her in front of me to hide the evidence of just how turned on I am, I guide her off the dance floor and back to our table. The way she squeezes my hand tight sends a pulse of warmth through me. I think I love that almost as much as her desire. Maybe more. But now's not the time to examine that emotion.

While we sit at the table and listen to the speeches and awards, I rest my arm on Violet's chair and brush my fingers back and forth across her skin, ensuring she doesn't forget for a second what I promised I'd do to her. Anticipation hums in my veins, but that will only make it all the sweeter when I finally sink into her.

As the conversation flows around me, I only offer brief comments when needed. But I'm attuned to Violet's every shallow breath, her every subtle shift in response to my touch. Delilah engages her in conversation, and Violet does her best to chat and laugh while trying to suppress the shivers that rack through her at odd intervals.

Mom's presence across the table from us, unfortunately, has the ability to dampen the mood. She's spent much of the evening scrutinizing me, then Violet, with an odd intensity —a contrast to her usual cool disinterest. She knows this is an arrangement, but I have the strangest feeling she knows I'm not acting at all.

The way Delilah keeps sending me beaming smiles makes me think my future sister-in-law is also aware of my not-so-platonic feelings for my fiancée.

Before the final speaker puts his microphone down, I'm out of my chair, pulling Violet up with me. "Cole, Roman, I'll see you at the office on Monday. Delilah, a pleasure, as always. Mom, it's been... something."

She dabs her lips with a napkin. "Tate, always with the humor. Violet, it was nice to see you again."

"Thank you, Mrs. King. It was lovely to see you too."

"Mm-hmm." Mom drops the napkin.

As we turn, Violet cuts her eyes at me and gives me a fake grimace.

I can't help but laugh. The good news is that my fiancée has no trouble handling her future mother-in-law.

Pressing a hand to her lower back, I brush my lips against her ear. "Jeremy's bringing the car around now. Let's go."

We weave our way through the crowd, anticipation hastening our strides. I'm itching to slide the hand I have on Violet's back lower, but I hold my position. For now.

Waiting has its benefits, I'm all about delayed gratification, but I've about reached my limit. Outside the hotel, we pass the remaining die-hard photographers, who start snapping away as we head for the car.

Jeremy is waiting with the door open, and once Violet and I are settled, he rounds the hood and slides into the driver's seat.

Smoothing a hand down the front of my jacket, I lean forward. "Please close the screen, Jeremy."

When it's closed and it's just the two of us, I turn to face her. Those big fucking blue eyes of hers are fixed on me, and her pulse flutters wildly at the base of her throat. I've already told her what's coming, but she still hesitates when I say softly, "Come here, Violet."

I wait, silent and unmoving, until finally, with a deep breath, she slides toward me.

"Do you want my words now," she whispers.

"Not yet, butterfly. I'm not giving you my cock yet. But I do want your lips."

I tangle my hands in her silky hair and capture her mouth with mine. It starts off slow, but I can only be patient for so long, and her taste is intoxicating. Our tongues twist together as I trace over her curves until I find the satin that covers her thighs, searching for the slit that's been taunting me all night. When I find it, I trail my fingers across her exposed skin, then under the material until my knuckles brush over the thin strip of lace covering her. I was right; her panties are saturated. Slipping past the edge of them, I gather the liquid proof of her arousal and gently massage it into her clit. She inhales sharply, then moans into my mouth.

Fuck. My little butterfly is going to make such pretty noises tonight.

I can't fight the smile that takes over as I pull back and take in her pink cheeks and swollen lips. "Remember what I told you was going to happen once we got in the limo?"

She blinks, then nods.

"Then get over here and rub that pretty pussy on my cock."

With shaky hands, she shimmies her skirt up until the creamy skin of her upper thighs is exposed. Then, with one hand on my shoulder, she straddles me. She hovers just above my lap and pulls her lower lip between her teeth.

Desire for her is a physical ache inside me. I can feel the heat radiating off her, but I'm dying to have her pussy pressed up against my already throbbing dick.

She tilts her head, eyes locked on mine. "Is this when I ask?"

I smirk at her and bring my palm to her cheek. "So impatient. I'll tell you when it's time. Until then, I want you rubbing that needy clit against me."

Finally, she sinks down onto my lap. The heat of her soaks into me, instantly tightening my balls.

I grip her ass, encouraging her to move, and she tentatively rolls her hips. "That's it. Fuck, I can't wait to have my cock inside you when you're moving like that."

She looks up at me through her lashes. "You can put it in now if you want."

With a chuckle, I bring her face down to mine so I can brush my lips against hers. "I want to. But I won't. I'm going to enjoy watching you get yourself off just thinking about how good my cock will feel inside you."

"Oh god," she breathes.

I drag the bodice of her dress down, revealing her fucking perfect breasts. Then I take her wrists and cuff them together behind her back with my hand, tugging down until she's forced to arch her back and thrust her chest out.

"Now make yourself come while I suck on these incredible tits."

She exhales shakily and rolls her hips again. Without the use of her hands to brace her, she has to rely on the muscles of her thighs alone to work herself against my length.

But she does it.

I bend down and take one of those perky pink nipples between my lips. It's the first taste of them I've had since Onyx, and it feels as if I've been dying of a thirst that's finally been quenched. I suck hard, loving the feel of it furling tight on my tongue, then I move to her other breast and bite down lightly.

She whimpers in response, and I smile against her heated skin. From there, her movements get more frantic. She drops her head back, thrusting her tits even farther forward. God, I'm dying to see them bouncing in my face as I fuck her. As I finally take what I've already claimed as mine with that ring.

"Such a good girl, rubbing that beautiful pussy against me until you come." I can't help but rock up into her, giving her more friction, rewarding her for doing such a good job.

"Tate," she whispers. "I'm so close."

"I know you are, butterfly. Do you need me to push you over the edge?"

"Yes." The word comes out almost as a whine.

I raise my fingers to her mouth and press them to her lips. "Suck."

She opens for me, and when I feed them to her, she swirls her tongue around them. Once they're nice and wet, I pull them out and release her wrists so I can drag the back of her dress up and rub my saliva-slick fingers against the puckered muscle between her cheeks.

She stills, her eyes widening.

"Trust me, butterfly. I'm just going to make you feel good. Keep moving those hips for me."

She obeys, picking up her rhythm again. I use her own movement to nudge the tip of my finger just inside her back channel.

Her lashes flutter. "Oh god, Tate. That's... that's so..."

"Keep moving, Violet. Don't stop. I want to feel it when you come."

She moans again, and I press deeper, then hold, letting her rock onto my finger, giving her control over how deep she wants it. As she gets used to the sensation, her movements get stronger.

"Seems like my fiancée likes having my finger in her ass," I murmur. I push a little farther in. "Imagine how good it will feel when I have my cock in here. Do you think you'll like that just as much? How about my cock in your ass and a toy filling your pussy? When you come, do you think you'll gush all over me?"

"Tate!" She's barreling toward release, each moan louder than the one before.

As much as I want to hear her scream, her sounds are only for me to hear. I bury my hand in her hair and drag her mouth down to mine. I slide my tongue against hers, and she's really moving against me now. Her motions become jerky, and she's tightening around my finger.

"Let me feel it, butterfly," I growl against her lips.

"Yes, yes, yes." Her chants are muffled. I've still got her mouth pressed to mine. Then she's there, toppling over the edge, dropping her head to my shoulder the way she did that night at Onyx, her hot panting breath washing over my skin. She grinds herself down on me, riding out the force of her orgasm.

I force harsh breaths into my lungs, so I won't disgrace myself by coming in my pants while her ass chokes my finger and her arousal soaks through the material separating us.

When she stills, I gently pull out of her and let her skirt drop back down.

"God, Tate," she says in a shaky voice, her eyes wide and dazed. "I never knew I could come like that. I never knew it could feel so good."

I bring her face to mine again and kiss her. "It's going to get so much better."

She laughs a little dazedly, as if she can't imagine it.

That response only solidifies my determination. I can't wait to show her everything. Everything her body can do. Everything mine can do. And exactly what we're capable of doing together.

Jeremy's voice comes over the intercom. "We're a minute out, Mr. King."

I press the button. "Thanks, Jeremy. Take us underneath, please."

"Yes, sir."

"You don't want him to drop us off out front?" Violet asks. Since she moved in, we've mostly come and gone that way, ensuring we're seen together as often as possible.

"Butterfly, unless you want the doorman and the concierge to see the mess you left on my pants, then skipping the foyer is the way to go."

A blush creeps over her cheeks and she raises herself up on her knees, as if she's going to climb off me.

I grip her hips and gently force her back onto my thighs.

"I want you right here until I have to let you go so we can get out of the car."

We stay that way, our mouths fused together, until Jeremy pulls into the underground garage and stops in front of the elevator. Just before he opens the door to us, I murmur into Violet's ear. "As soon as we're in the elevator, it's my turn."

CHAPTER THIRTY-SIX

VIOLET

For a moment after the door of the elevator whooshes shut, Tate doesn't move. The mirrors on the walls reflect our visages back to us from all sides as we stare at each other. Then, in the space of one heartbeat, he's on me, caging me with his arms, pushing me against the wall and thrusting his erection hard against my stomach.

A small moan escapes me as I throw my arms around his neck. His mouth consumes me, tongue licking inside, sliding against mine, exploring ruthlessly as he brands my lips with his. He slips his hand into my hair and grasps a handful, twisting possessively.

Then, without warning, he's letting me go and dropping to his knees. "Pull your dress up," he demands.

I grip the silky material and pull it up over my hips. Without hesitation, he drags my wet panties to the side and buries his tongue inside me. After one lap, then another, he unerringly finds my clit, lashing it with his tongue, pulling a squeal from me as two fingers push inside. It's urgent and dirty, and even though I already came in the limo, I'm still on edge enough that, before I know it, I'm already close.

As if he can sense it, he chuckles against my slick skin. "Give me number two before we get to the top, butterfly."

His tongue connects with my clit again, and he pushes his fingers deeper. My legs are shaking already. So are my hands as I clutch at his hair to anchor myself. There's no holding back. Already, I'm clamping down around his fingers.

"God... I'm so close."

"That's it, beautiful. I want to taste the moment you orgasm."

All it takes is one more curl of his fingers. Then I'm coming, my hips bucking into him, my breath rasping loudly in the confined space. He licks and sucks me through it until I'm trembling and weak.

He stands, and a moment later, the elevator dings and the door slides open into his foyer. Rather than pulling me through, he grips the side of my face and kisses me. He's covered in my arousal, his mouth and chin wet with me. On instinct, I pull back a fraction, ready to recoil, but his tongue swipes across my lips, and underneath the taste of me, is the taste of him, and I can't get enough of him. So I let him kiss me. I let him tangle his tongue with mine until I'm kissing him back just as hungrily.

The elevator doors remain open, the sensors telling it we haven't exited, while he takes possession of my mouth. I've come twice already, and that should be enough. It *should* be. But when he presses the hard ridge of his erection against me, my clit pulses with need. I'm empty, and I want him to fill me. I want Tate to fuck me. I want all of him.

He rips his mouth from mine and, chest heaving, watches me. His pupils are so dilated, his eyes are just a thin ring of whiskey around black pools.

"Tate," I shamelessly whimper. "I need you inside me."

"You've had me inside you. My tongue, my fingers..."

"No, not your fingers. Not your tongue."

"That's all you'll get until I'm ready."

He spins me and backs me out of the elevator, all the way to the huge dining table. Then he lifts me, depositing my ass on top of it. "Let me see you," he growls.

I press a palm to the smooth, cool surface and raise my hips so I can rake my skirt up again. Then I part my legs. The air is cool on my slick flesh. Once more, Tate drops to his knees, latching on to my clit over the black lace and sucking. The heat and suction, even through my panties, are enough to make me gasp.

"I can't get enough of your taste," he groans. "These are ruined though." He twists his fingers in the sides of my thong and rips, then tosses them to the floor. Next, he deftly undoes the straps of my heels. "Feet on the edge," he demands. "Keep your thighs apart. Let me look at you."

The thought is just as nerve-racking now as it was the first time we did this. But just like then, I'm too desperate for him to care. I brace my heels on the edge of the table, but looking at him looking at me is too overwhelming. So I lie down and stare up at the ceiling, my muscles already trembling in anticipation.

He doesn't dive right in. The warmth of his breath washes over me, but he stops there. For all the sense of urgency he had before, now he's playing with me. First, he eases my thighs farther apart, and then there's just the lightest of touches, skimming over my sensitive skin. He brushes a kiss to my leg, and another closer to where I need him. Then he licks a line up my inner thigh, stopping just short of the mark. His next move is a nip that has sparks shooting straight to my aching core and a moan escaping from my lips.

His responding chuckle is dark. "Does my butterfly like a hint of pain with her pleasure?"

I don't know. I've never experienced anything like this before. Certainly not with Eric, nor with any of the men I casually dated through college.

"I like what you make me feel," I say.

He pauses, his breath hot against my skin. "Fuck, Violet. You don't know what you do to me." He bites me lightly again, not hard enough to hurt, just to send those sparks shooting along my nerves to my throbbing clit. "Remember what I said to you on the dance floor?"

Dipping my chin so I can see him, I rack my foggy brain for a recollection of anything other than this moment. "Th-that you'd make me come until I was exhausted, and then you'd give me your... your cock."

From between my parted thighs, he pierces me with a feral look. "You don't look exhausted to me, butterfly. You look needy. You're not ready for my cock yet."

A whimper escapes me as my muscles flex and quiver in response to his words.

"I'll take care of you, Violet. Make sure you're ready for me." His tongue traces a line along my other thigh. "You taste so fucking sweet."

My skin flares hot when it hits me—the insides of my thighs are wet from my arousal, and he's tasting me with every swipe of his tongue. A hint of embarrassment prickles through me, but it dissipates quickly, because he leaves no doubt as to his enjoyment. He sucks and licks my inner thighs, stopping every time he gets close to where I'm desperately aching for him.

"Please," I beg.

He looks up, eyes blazing. Holding my gaze, he slowly lowers his face and presses a soft kiss just above my clit. My sex clenches. "Is this what you want, Violet? You want my mouth on you again?"

"I need you inside me."

"Soon, butterfly. Soon I'll fill this sweet, hot cunt. When you think you're done, when you think you can't take any more pleasure, I'll bury myself deep inside you and make you come one more time."

His words make me that much more desperate. I've never felt so hot, so ready to implode in my life. In this moment, I'd happily do whatever he wanted.

He focuses between my legs again and lightly blows against my overheated skin, making my back arch. "So beautiful," he growls. "Such a pretty fucking pussy." He parts me with his thumbs, and I slap my hands to the table to keep from squirming.

Finally, he pushes one finger inside me, and even that small stretch has my nerve endings coiling in anticipation. He eases out slowly. "So tight," he says, expression almost pained. "I can't wait to give you my cock. See how well you take me."

"Yes." My voice is a shredded whisper.

He adds a second finger, burying them deep, twisting his hand until the heel of his palm makes contact with the top of my sex. Finally having pressure where I need it the most has the breath rushing from my lungs. I push myself up to my elbows so I can watch. The sight of him pulling his fingers out of me, then replacing them with his tongue, sends an electric thrill flaring up my spine. When he spears it inside me, my mouth opens on a silent gasp and my head falls back between my shoulders.

Tate doesn't give me time to adjust to the new sensation, pushing his fingers back into me and licking from where they're filling me to my over-sensitized clit. I almost sob as my legs shake. He's working me up and holding me on the edge until I'm desperate for relief, but never giving me enough to push me over.

I whimper and writhe under him, begging for more. Finally, with two fingers pumping in and out of me, he curls his tongue and flicks. I cry out and clamp down around him as heat and pressure build hard and fast in the pit of my stomach.

My hands grip his hair and pull as he sucks on my throbbing clit and presses his fingers against a spot that rips a gasp from me. With my eyes squeezed shut, I flex up, pressing myself harder against his face.

I'm on the precipice, ready to shatter, when he pulls his hands from me and stands. A cry wrenches itself from my lungs. I'm so desperate for release. Of their own accord, my hips buck, seeking friction, pressure, anything that will send me hurtling over the edge. He doesn't leave me empty for long. His fingers are there, filling me again while he circles my clit with his other hand. The dual stimulation has me writhing under his touch, crying out as he works me back up.

I'm so needy, so desperate to come, that I'm rolling my hips, pressing up against his hands. This time, he quickens his pace, relentless, until the heat and pressure inside me detonate, and ecstasy crashes over me.

"Fuck, you're so beautiful when you come, Violet."

I force my eyes open and get lost in the depths of his as he watches me fall apart.

The moan that escapes me is deep and unfamiliar as my body pulsates around him. But instead of slowing his movements as my orgasm ebbs, he keeps working his fingers hard and fast. When he leans over and adds his tongue, I grab a fistful of his hair and try to push him back. He doesn't budge.

My head lolls from side to side. "I can't, Tate. I can't so soon."

"You can," he insists, picking up his pace. His mouth moves in tandem with his hand, and somehow, an almost painful ache is building inside me. And then he adds a third finger and sucks hard on my clit.

Impossibly, another orgasm crashes over me. With my hand still in his hair, I hold him against me as my back bows and I'm racked by wave after wave of pleasure.

Even then he doesn't stop, fingers thrusting, mouth and tongue working. My core spasms again, bringing on a third climax right after the second, forcing tears from my eyes and a hoarse cry from my throat. I clench uncontrollably around his fingers, writhing and gasping until I'm breathless and spent. Only then does he slow. With a tender kiss to my swollen, sensitive clit, he stands.

I'm still shaking and panting when he unzips his pants and pulls out his erection. It's long and thick and straining for me.

My head spins, and need tightens into a hot knot deep inside my belly. This man got me off in the limo, the elevator, and three times here on his dining room table, and with all that pleasure, I still haven't had his cock in me. I'm exhausted, just like he said I would be. But still, I want it, I want *him*, so badly, that I press my thighs together in anticipation.

He pulls a condom out of his pocket, and I try not to let the thought that he was prepared for this distract me from what I'm feeling. I'm just glad we don't have to stop to find one. He sheathes himself quickly, then presses his thick, broad crown against my entrance.

I brace myself for the pressure, the stretch, because he's so damn big. But it doesn't come.

He looms over me, one hand planted next to my head, the other wrapped around the base of his shaft. The corners of his lips curl up. "Let me hear those pretty words, butterfly."

My whole body flushes hot. I'd forgotten what I promised. But after the way I came all over his pants in the limo, and on his mouth and fingers in the elevator and just now, there's no room for embarrassment. Now all I can think about is him pushing his way into me. "Please, Tate. Please fuck me. I need your cock. I need you to fill me up. I need—"

He spears into me, two, maybe three inches, wringing a gasp out of me.

"Jesus Christ, Violet." His voice in my ear is like gravel.

He's big. Even having seen him and felt him against me, I underestimated how big he is. He's nowhere near halfway in, and already, I feel the stretch. He yanks the bodice of my dress down and sucks a nipple between his lips, alternating between slow and gentle, then deep and hard. In response to the sensation, I buck up toward him, forcing him deeper.

He curses, then his lips are hard and urgent on mine as he works his hips until he's finally buried inside me.

My breasts are bared, and my dress is bunched up around my waist. Tate's shirt is still buttoned, and his pants are only pushed down far enough to free his erection. We're fully clothed, but somehow, that makes the moment hotter. Because we were so desperate for one another, we couldn't wait to be joined like this.

I run my hands over his shoulders and down his arms,

but he grips my wrists and stretches them over my head. Between his hold on me there and his cock impaling me, I'm pinned.

Helpless.

CHAPTER THIRTY-SEVEN

TATE

Nothing has ever felt this good.

Being inside Violet is like being encased in hot, wet silk. Her wide blue eyes are locked on mine, and her body ripples around me. Making her come, watching her fall apart, has left me on edge. I'm addicted to the look in her eyes when pleasure takes her over. The sounds she makes, the way she gives herself so trustingly. I can't get enough of it.

But now I need her. I need to lose myself in her. She's exactly where I wanted her, held down and helpless beneath me. Flames lick along every inch of my skin, and if I don't move, I'll lose my mind.

Upright and hovering over her, I grip her hip with one hand and tilt her so I can watch myself slide in and out. Revel in the way she's stretched around me, at the way her arousal coats both of us. "You're taking me so fucking well, butterfly. Just like I knew you would."

I pull back and pump into her, fucking her with long, sure strokes. The delicate muscles inside her flutter and clutch at my cock as I angle to hit that sensitive spot that will make her shatter for me. Her hands twist in my grip, and she meets my every stroke by raising her hips.

This view is pure heaven, but I need a taste of her again. I lean over her and suck on her nipples, her pulse point, the soft skin below her ear. I have to tighten my hold on her hips, because the way she's writhing against me has me too close to losing it.

"Tate," she cries out. She's teetering on the edge of overstimulation. She's come so many times, and now I'm forcing her body toward one more.

"Come on my cock, butterfly. Squeeze me so hard you force the orgasm out of me."

Back arching and desperate, she wraps her legs around my hips and tugs me impossibly closer. I can't wait any longer. I let go of her wrists and palm her breasts. Every time I pinch her nipples, her pussy spasms around me. It's too much. I'm already close to exploding. "Touch yourself, Violet. Make yourself come for me."

Sweat dews her flushed skin, and she whimpers. I know it's a lot to ask of her. But I need this. I need her to give me this, to give herself over to me completely. I've never wanted it before, but I want it with her.

She grips my bicep with one hand and glides the other between us. The moment she makes contact, her channel flexes and tightens around me, making sweat break out on my brow as I fight for control. With every one of my strokes, her knuckles bump against my pelvis. And fuck if having her touch herself like this, having her grind against me in her desperation for relief, fingers slipping and sliding over her clit, isn't everything I imagined.

"Tate," she moans. She focuses on me, pupils blown wide and sweat dampening the curls at her hairline. With her flushed skin and plump, swollen lips, she's the sexiest fucking thing I've ever seen. "I'm... I'm c-coming."

I can feel it happening, her body gripping me like a vise, her frantic breaths. When her lashes flutter, threatening to close, I grip her jaw. "Keep looking at me, Violet. I want to see it in your eyes at the same time I feel it on my cock."

She blinks hazily, then forces herself to hold my gaze. The pleasure drunk expression on her face has my climax clawing closer. I wrap my hand around her throat and squeeze lightly, not to choke her, just to hold her here in this moment with me, to feel her pulse beat against my palm, the clutch of her pussy around me, to know her eyes are on me when I possess her in every way.

"Tate," she almost sobs. "I need... I need..."

I know what she needs. I pull almost all the way out, then drive into her hard and fast. Once, twice. That's all it takes. Her body draws tighter around me, and her back arcs off the table. With a shudder, she convulses, her internal muscles pulsing, pulling me impossibly deeper. It's too much. Too good. I chase my own release even as the aftershocks ripple through her. I'm cursing now, low and deep and urgent, slamming into her over and over. Heat and pleasure rise up from my balls, signaling my impending release. With a long, guttural groan, I bury myself as far into her as I can get and let it explode out of me.

The force of my release is so strong I have to brace my palm on the table next to her head while I ride it out. Each throb of my cock sears through me as my orgasm seems to go on and on. When it finally eases and my muscles unlock, I gather her up against me and crash my lips down on hers.

Her body trembles against mine, and when our mouths finally separate, our ragged breaths fill the air between us.

I pull back a fraction and stroke her face. "You okay, butterfly?"

She lets out a shaky laugh. "I've never... that's never... I don't even know what to do with myself."

With my mouth pressed to the crook of her neck, I hum. "Luckily, I know exactly what to do with you."

She stares at me in shock. "You can't possibly think I have any more orgasms in me."

I chuckle. "I'm sure I could drag one or two more out of you, but I'll give you a break. For tonight, anyway."

Gently, I ease out of her. If I wasn't certain I could have her again tomorrow, I'd be tempted to slide straight back in. But her body is spent. So I tuck myself back into my pants and zip them up. I should have taken the time to undress her and shed my own clothing. Though I don't regret how it happened. How could I?

"Wrap your legs around me," I tell her.

When she does, I grip her thighs and pick her up.

"What are you doing?" She laughs, a soft, sleepy sound.

"I'm taking you to have a shower, and then to bed."

She lays her head on my shoulder, and a surge of tenderness rocks me. And when she curls a hand around my neck, I swear I can feel a cool touch from the band of her engagement ring. The engagement ring I put on her finger. As I carry my fiancée toward my bedroom, one thought runs on a loop through my head. Violet is mine. My fiancée. My future wife. This might have started out as fake, but that doesn't mean it has to stay that way.

When I push the door to my bedroom open, Violet raises her head. "I thought you were taking me to my shower?"

"My shower. My bed tonight."

She's silent for a beat, then her lips brush the skin of my neck. "Okay."

I let her down and lead her across the huge expanse of my bedroom to the bathroom. My shower is massive, with four rain showerheads. I don't let go of her when I turn on the water. As steam begins to billow around us, I tug gently on her zipper, then slide the straps off her shoulders so the dress pools at her feet.

She allows me to turn her so we're facing one another. I can't help but drop another kiss to her lips. Then I guide her toward the shower. While she stands under the spray, I quickly strip my clothes off as well. I'm hard again by the time I join her, my dick standing to attention, but I ignore it.

"You're fucking beautiful, Violet. So damn gorgeous."

I frame her face and tip it up to mine. With a soft smile, she wraps her fingers around my wrists. The movement makes the bathroom light reflect off the gemstones in her ring, drawing my attention. Heat surges through me, and this time when I kiss her, it's pure possession.

When we come up for air, she looks down at where I'm hard and throbbing. "That looks painful."

"I'll survive," I say.

She reaches for me, but I grasp her wrist lightly to stop her.

"This isn't a quid pro quo thing, Violet."

She peeks up at me through her wet lashes. "You made me come so many times, and you only came once."

I chuckle. "If you think I didn't get incredible pleasure out of making you come, then you're seriously mistaken."

"It's not the same though, is it?"

"We have time." I brush a wet strand of hair from her cheek. "I told you once you said yes to this, that was it. I intend to explore every inch of your body, and I'm more than willing to let you explore mine. But let's not do it when you're half asleep."

She tilts her head, a little crease forming between her brows. "You're not who I thought you were, Tate King."

For once, I let my walls down, even if just a little. "That's the way I've always wanted it."

I turn off the water, step out, and grab one of the big fluffy white towels from the stack on a bench in the corner of the bathroom. I wrap it around her, pull her close, smile down at her. "Come on, butterfly."

With the covers pulled back, I guide her onto the bed, and once she's settled, I join her and roll so we're facing one another.

She blinks sleepily at me, studying me from beneath heavy lids. "Why did you say that?"

"What?"

"That you've always wanted it that way."

A hollow ache forms behind my ribs. It's one I've ignored for so long I rarely notice it these days, yet there it is. "Not sure this is the best time to get into that."

She traces patterns over my chest with her fingers. "I'd like to know."

I let out a sigh. Not of frustration. More the kind that takes with it some of the weight that's been pressing down on me for most of my life. Violet's trusted me with all of her. She deserves the same from me. I curl my fingers around her waist. "Do you have any idea what it's like to grow up a King?"

She takes it as the rhetorical question it is and doesn't answer, only watches me with eyes full of compassion and encouragement.

"The name automatically brings power, wealth, respect. Except, that's not who I am. Not really."

A line forms between her brows. "What do you mean?"

I've never shared the full truth about this with anyone. It's an open secret in my family—ignored by my mother, relentlessly alluded to by my father, and only ever subtly acknowledged by my brothers—but never, *never* discussed. There are rumors in our social circle, but it's never been publicly commented on either. No one would dare. But for the first time since I learned the reality of who I am—or rather who I'm not—I want to talk about it. I want to talk to *her* about it.

"When I was seven, we were at a birthday party," I start. "Some of the other boys were whispering behind my back. They'd started doing that more often that year. I didn't understand what the whispers meant for a long time, because of course I was Cole and Roman's brother. We lived together, played together, fought like brothers. But at this party, one of the boys said it to my face. Called me the bastard son. I'm guessing they were just copying what their parents gossiped about behind closed doors, because there was no way their parents would ever have said that to my face. Or to any of my family."

The sleepiness dissipates from Violet's eyes. "Why would they call you that?"

The smile I give her lacks any humor. "Because it's true."

CHAPTER THIRTY-EIGHT

VIOLET

I lever myself up onto one arm so I can look down at his face. "What do you mean?"

He gives me a half smile, although there's a tightness around his eyes that belies the relaxed act he's going for. "My dad isn't the man who fathered me."

"Tate," I breathe, understanding breaking over me. It makes sense. His brothers share most of their physical attributes, yet he looks so different. Still, I never would have assumed.

Wariness shadows his gaze, and his whole body tenses almost imperceptibly. Does he think I'll judge him for it?

I want him to keep talking, to feel comfortable sharing his truth with me, but I don't want to force him, so I don't ask directly. I'll let him work up to it. Instead, I brush my fingers along his jaw. "What happened with the boys?"

"I froze. I didn't understand that term. Bastard," he continues. "But by the way he sneered the word, I knew it was a bad thing. Roman and Cole overheard. Gave them all a few bruises."

I stroke over his chest, hoping to imbue a sense of

comfort, a little peace, as he talks. "Did your mom or dad ever say anything to you about it?"

He lets out a humorless laugh. "They ignored the issue, even more than they ignored me. Or each other. I imagine admitting it would mean they'd have to do something about it. And neither of them was interested in rocking that boat. Appearances were always more important to them than any hurt or confusion I might be feeling."

"What about Cole and Roman? Did they know?"

He nods. "Even after that first fight, I didn't understand what a bastard was. But when it happened a couple more times, it started to sink in that there was something different about me. Then I overheard Cole and Roman discussing it. Not in a bad way. Just speculating about who my father could be. They talked about it as if it were true. For a long time, I resented them. Yes, they'd stood up for me, but now there was a gap between us that wasn't there before. And the two of them were on one side of it and I was on the other."

"Although," he sighs, surveying my face. "I'm starting to realize a lot of that was of my own doing. Because of my own insecurities. Growing up the way we did took a toll on all of us. I don't think Dad wanted us to be close the way we were when we were young. At that point, Roman was in boarding school and had already started to close himself off. Something happened with Cole too, though we've never talked about that either. He changed, became more cynical. But I was so sensitive about what I'd learned, I saw them pulling away from me as a rejection, when really, they were dealing with the shit show that our family is in their own way. When Cole started high school, Mom and Dad sent him to the same boarding school they sent Roman. Dad decided I should be shipped off at the same time. But not to the same place. He said he wanted to *diversify* our learning."

The blood pumping in my veins is hot, feeding the already brewing hatred I have for Tate's dad.

"After that, I really only saw Roman and Cole during school holidays. And by that stage, it was easier to believe I was on my own. I'm pretty sure that's exactly what Dad wanted."

Tears sting my eyes. Tate's cockiness, his charm, his flirtatiousness, make complete sense in light of this new knowledge. He hid the hurt and loneliness with a devil-may-care attitude.

"I'm so sorry. For all of it." I press my hand to his heart, savoring the strong, steady beat against my palm. "You shouldn't have had to find out that way. Your parents should have talked to you. Your brothers should have talked to you. Your Dad should..." I shake my head. I don't have the words for what Tate's father should have done. Been a different man? A better man?

Tate shrugs, though it doesn't come across as casually as he probably intended. "I came to terms with it. After a few more fights, it didn't take too long for the boys who were taunting me to realize it was a bad idea to use that word around me. And I soon realized that the only thing most people care about is my last name and everything that comes with it."

"Did you ever try to find your real father?" I ask.

He clears his throat and twirls a strand of my hair between his fingers, his eyes focused on where he's touching me, not on mine. "That first night you stayed with Mark..."

Pain lances my chest at the memory that I wish I could wipe from my head.

He clasps my nape and holds my gaze, tension radiating

from him again. "I got smashed out of my head that night because the private investigator I'd hired to find my biological father had emailed that morning to fill me in on what he'd found. My real father died in a car accident almost ten years ago."

A rock forms in my gut and my throat aches, but before I can tell him again how sorry I am, he continues.

"It hit me hard, knowing I'd never get answers. Not from him, not from my parents. I'll spend the rest of my life not knowing who my real father was. I know his name, but I'll never know what he was like. What kind of man he was. What kind of man that makes me."

This time I can't stop the tears that fill my eyes. The memory of that first morning with Tate comes rushing back. Except this time, I watch the replay through a different lens. He'd gotten terrible news, and he'd spent the night drowning his sorrows in whatever way he could. And I'd sat there judging him for it.

I close the distance between us and press my lips to his, hoping he can sense my genuine remorse for my behavior. He immediately deepens the kiss, pulling me closer and letting his hands roam over me until we're both breathless and panting.

When we finally break apart, he looks deep into my eyes. "I'm sorry that's how we met. I'll always regret—"

I shake my head. "*I'm* sorry. I shouldn't have judged you. I shouldn't have let it influence my opinion of you for so long."

A muscle leaps in his jaw. "If I had to live with a memory of hearing you with another man, I wouldn't handle it well." He brushes a thumb over my lower lip. "I'd want to track him down and do grievous bodily harm to him."

I press my mouth to his chest. I don't know how to respond to that.

He pulls me until I'm draped over him, my bare pussy dangerously close to the erection I can feel pressing against my inner thighs. I'm sore—how could I not be when I haven't had sex in well over a year?—but that doesn't stop the slow wave of heat that rolls over me at the feel of him.

Tate strokes my hair back from my face. "Nothing compares to what we just did."

My heart stalls. "You don't have to say that. I know you—"

He shakes his head. "You don't know. I've never once experienced anything that even came close to what I felt with you tonight. Every encounter was about proving something to myself, to the world. It was easy gratification, validation that, bastard or not, I was wanted, even though I knew it wasn't me as a person they wanted. I had no desire for a connection with any of them. I gave the minimum amount of myself every single time. I didn't want to hold them. I didn't want to breathe them in. I didn't want to press myself so close they'd become part of me. And I *never* wanted them to stay."

My lips are on his again, my hands stroking his skin. He wraps his arms around me, holding me tighter. I don't care how sore I am, I need him. I roll my hips, causing the head of his cock to press against my entrance.

He tangles his hands in my hair, tilting my head back so our gazes clash. "You don't have to, butterfly. I didn't take it easy on you before. You must be sore."

"I want to," I say. "You'll make me feel good." It's true. I trust him to take care of my body. How can I not when he's proven himself so definitively?

"Condom, top drawer," he grits out.

Despite the need growing inside me, a tiny niggle of jealousy works its way between my ribs, but I quickly push away the thought of him being with other women in this bed. That doesn't matter. The only thing that matters now is this moment.

As if he can read my mind, he gives me a grin. It's that cocky one I'm somehow starting to love. "Since you moved in, I've made a habit of keeping a couple in there. Always an optimist, I guess."

I can't help but laugh. The lightness infused in his tone after such a heavy conversation makes my heart ache in the best way. Maybe talking to someone about it has helped.

I stretch across the bed and fumble around, then pull out the little square. With hasty fingers, I roll it over his straining erection. He drags me down to him for a kiss, then lets me go so I can reach down and slide the head of him through my slick folds.

I lower myself down on him, hissing at the stretch.

And then he makes me feel good all over again.

CHAPTER THIRTY-NINE

TATE

"The VR tours are a hit," I say. "We've sold 25 percent more apartments than projected."

When Cole doesn't respond, I look up from the data. He's turned slightly away from his desk and staring out the window at the skyline. Has he even heard me?

"Cole?"

My brother jerks his head around. "Yes, sorry. Twenty-five percent. That's great. You stuck to your guns with the VR tours, and it's paid off."

I raise my brows. "Is something up? You seem distracted."

Cole shakes his head, a smile flickering on his lips. "The numbers look great. I'd still like to get the third penthouse sold, but other than that, we're looking good." He clears his throat. "Listen, Delilah and I would like you and Violet to come to dinner on Friday."

I lean back in my chair. "Dinner? This is a first. Normally, you like to keep Delilah all to yourself."

"Yes, well." Cole frowns. "Delilah likes Violet. *And* you, for some reason."

I smirk at that.

"And she'd like to do more things as a couple."

"Well, well. Who would have ever thought Cole King would turn out to be so domesticated?"

"Who would have ever thought Tate King would be engaged and living with a woman?"

"Except that's not real." As soon as I say it, my stomach clenches. It's a lie, one I wish I could take back.

Cole tilts his head, then braces his forearms on his desk. "There's nothing fake about what's going on with you and Violet. You and I both know it. Hell, we all do."

I pick imaginary lint off my pants and avoid his gaze. "I don't know what you're talking about."

He scoffs. "You've never looked innocent a day in your life. Don't try it now. Are you sleeping with her?"

I narrow my eyes at him. "None of your business."

He shakes my head. "That tells me everything I need to know. Why hide how you feel? I'm happy for you. Delilah is too."

I finally allow myself to smile. Because I'm happy too. It's been two weeks since Violet used her pretty words and finally asked me to fuck her. The connection forming between us isn't cooling off. It's just getting more intense. Having her living with me is... incredibly satisfying. Waking up with her body curled up next to mine every morning has filled a hole inside me I didn't even know was there. On the mornings I wake up before her, I can't stop myself from stroking my fingers gently over her satin soft skin, tracing the dip of her waist, curving my hand around the swell of her hips until her eyelashes flutter open and her beautiful blue eyes focus on mine. The softness in her expression when she looks at me makes it impossible not to roll her over, spread her legs, and sink into her. Or lick her until she screams. And the mornings when she wakes up thirsty for my cock and takes me into her mouth?

Jesus. I'm getting hard just thinking about her.

We've been out to a few more formal events and once to a nightclub opening. Every day, I'm more addicted to having her by my side, to watching her smile, to talking about our days over dinner, to feeling her come on my dick every night. And to seeing that ring sparkling on her left hand.

But I'm not ready to talk about what I feel for her or what it means, even with Cole.

I know Violet feels something too. She wouldn't have given herself to me if she didn't—there's not a single part of her that cares about the money, or my name, or the thrill of fucking a King brother. But one concern lingers in the back of my head, tripping me up each time I get close to admitting the truth. Violet was forced into this situation out of desperation. She didn't choose to be my girlfriend. Or my fiancée. She didn't choose to live with me. The only choice she's made is to share her body with me.

And I can't help but wonder if whatever she feels will be strong enough to survive once the pretense is over. Once the contract ends, will she go back to her normal life and realize that she doesn't want any part of being in mine?

I won't know her true feelings on that front until our contract ends in a couple of weeks. So I'll let our arrangement run its course and enjoy every moment of having her with me. Then, once it's done, once she's free to make a real choice, I'll ask her to choose me. And I fucking hope to God she will.

I stand and smooth my tie. "Violet and I would love to join you for dinner." I answer his original question while pointedly ignoring his last comment.

If anything, his grin gets wider.

"Send me the details, and we'll be there to give Delilah a break from you following her around the house like a lost puppy."

Cole laughs, and I'm smiling as I leave his office. Sophie hands me a small stack of messages on my way past her desk, and once I'm in my own office, I settle in my chair to get through the never-ending piles of work. But not before eyeing the clock and calculating how soon I can leave so I can make it home in time to cook dinner with Violet. It's become a habit I enjoy. Especially when I can taste her lips, and sometimes other parts of her, between chopping ingredients.

I shake my head at myself. All this time making fun of Cole about his obsession with Delilah, and now here I am, just as obsessed over Violet.

And I don't even care.

"WOW," Violet says, head tipped back as she looks up at the high-rise bordering Central Park.

"Don't tell me you think Cole's building is more impressive than mine."

She glances back up at the towering structure, then shoots me a smirk. "It *is* an impressive erection. But not as impressive as yours."

With a laugh, I hook my arm around her waist and drag her into me. I tunnel my fingers into her hair and press my lips to hers. I kiss her until we're both breathless and I'm wondering if we can skip this dinner so I can take her back home.

As if she senses my intentions, she pulls away and smiles up at me. "Hold that thought until after dinner."

I grumble but take her hand and guide her toward the front door. The doorman tips his head and greets me by name as he holds the door open for us.

Like my building, this one has an elevator dedicated to the penthouse, and when the doors open into the foyer, I'm hit with a delicious smell that instantly makes my mouth water. With a hand on the small of her back, I lead Violet farther into the apartment and stop alongside her so she can admire the view, which I refuse to believe is any better than mine, even if Cole's penthouse is two stories higher. Then we continue on to the huge kitchen, where Cole and Delilah are preparing dinner.

I never would have believed the domestic sight in front of me if I wasn't looking right at it. Delilah is standing at the island, slicing tomatoes while Cole stands behind her with his arms wrapped around her waist and his chin resting on her shoulder.

When she catches sight of us, Delilah beams. Cole, on the other hand, looks mildly annoyed that we've interrupted them, even though he was the one who invited us.

Delilah wipes her hands on a cloth, then rushes out from behind the counter and hugs us both. "I'm so glad you could make it."

"Can I help with anything?" Violet asks as we follow her deeper into the kitchen.

Delilah's green eyes are warm. "Thanks, but I think we've got it covered."

"From the look of things, the only thing Cole has covered is you," I say.

Delilah laughs. "He's been very helpful, I promise."

"It smells delicious," Violet says. "What are you cooking?"

"I'm no Michelin chef, but I make a decent lasagna. We have salad and garlic bread as well," Delilah says.

Violet smiles. "My favorite."

"Grilled cheese is mine," Cole murmurs, and Delilah's cheeks flush pink.

Interesting. "I didn't take you for a grilled cheese fan."

Cole's expression turns sly. "You'd be surprised how well it goes with a good bottle of wine."

Delilah chokes at what is obviously a private joke. "*Cole,* do you mind getting me some water?"

With a kiss to her head, he turns to the fridge and pulls out a bottle. As he's pouring it into a glass, he offers us drinks. Once we're set up with glasses of red wine, we sit at the island and chat as Delilah and Cole finish cooking and plate our meals.

The food is absolutely delicious. As is the wine. The conversation flows freely, and the four of us chat about various topics. It's impossible not to talk about work, and we discuss Genesis-1, the opening of the King Group's most recent chain of hotels—the one Delilah was working on when she met Cole—and how Violet's hard work with True Brew is paying off.

Delilah peppers Violet with questions about the shop and her upcoming tasting night. Violet's eyes are bright and her smile is wide as she explains the details. I love watching her talking so easily to my brother and soon-to-be sister-in-law. I reach over and rest my hand on her thigh, just below the hem of her dress, my thumb rubbing slow circles over her warm skin.

Her lips tip up in a hint of a smile as she covers my hand with hers. And fuck, I think I'm in love. No, not think. *Am.*

I can't even pinpoint when it happened. Maybe part of me always sensed this was inevitable. From the moment I saw her at Onyx, I was drawn to her. And yes, maybe there was a subconscious part of me that recognized her, but I don't think even that explains it. All I know is that I love her. I love her, and I don't want to let her go. The minute our agreement ends, I'm going to make this real.

Cole catches my eye and arches one dark brow while that same too-knowing smile lifts one corner of his lips. I smirk back at him, but my brother isn't stupid. He knows.

After dinner, Delilah produces an apple pie with ice cream that's just as delicious as the meal.

We're just about finished when Cole clears his throat. "We had another reason for inviting you here tonight."

Beside me, Violet straightens, focusing expectantly on Delilah, who's now biting her bottom lip and fidgeting with her napkin.

I look between her and Cole, doing my best to read the situation, but coming up with nothing. What is going on?

Cole cups the back of Delilah's neck and angles his head down to hers. "Do you want to tell them, kitten?"

With a deep breath, she looks up at us and smiles. "Well, it turns out, I'm pregnant."

What? I stare at her, then at Cole.

"Congratulations! That's so exciting!" Violet says, practically vibrating with excitement in her seat.

My brain finishes short-circuiting, and I clear my throat. "Congratulations."

"How far along are you?" Violet asks.

Delilah splays a hand over her flat stomach. "Twelve weeks." There's so much happiness emanating from her, she's practically glowing.

The way Cole watches her, with a love and protectiveness that's almost fierce in its intensity, hits me hard in the chest. I should be asking questions like Violet is, but I'm finding it hard to focus, my brain fixated on that expression on my brother's face. There's no way Dad ever looked at my mom like that. God knows if my real father did. It's hard to imagine. If he had, would he have been in my life? Would he have wanted me?

Those intrusive thoughts steal some of the joy of the moment, pulling me down like a weight in my chest.

Violet puts her hand on my leg and squeezes, a question in her eyes. As if she senses the strange disconnect vibrating through me.

I pull myself together. "I didn't expect to be an uncle so soon. But I think we all know who mini-Cole or mini-Delilah's favorite is going to be. Roman doesn't stand a chance."

Delilah smiles over at me. "You and Roman will both make wonderful uncles."

Cole turns his head, his eyes narrowed. "You'd better learn to be." Then he pulls Delilah on to his lap and murmurs something to her that makes her smile.

Violet glances at me, her lips twisting to hold back her own smile. "Maybe we should go," she whispers.

I smirk at her, even though it doesn't feel right on my face. "Maybe someone needs to explain to them that it's impossible to conceive baby number two before number one is out."

"I'll let you do that," she says with an eye roll. But when I pull her to me, press my nose to her hair and breathe her in, she wraps her arms around me as if she knows how much I'm craving her touch. When I let her go, she searches my gaze, smiles softly, then turns back to Delilah. "Would you like help cleaning up?"

Delilah climbs off Cole's lap and brushes down her dress, her chin tucked and her cheeks pink with embarrassment.

"Thank you so much, but no, we'll take care of it."

"The bare minimum," Cole growls in her ear, unfortunately loud enough for me to overhear. He smirks at me. "We might not be able to conceive number two yet, but we can practice."

I take Violet's hand. "And that's our cue to leave."

Delilah hides her face in Cole's chest while he arches his brows at us. "Hurry up and leave, then."

Violet smothers a laugh, smiling up at me, but my eyes bounce away from hers. My chest is still strangely heavy, and I don't have a clue what I'm feeling right now. Happy for Cole and Delilah, of course, but that happiness is mixed up with a host of other conflicting emotions.

"Congratulations again," Violet calls over her shoulder as I lead her toward the elevator, but Delilah and Cole are too absorbed in each other to hear her. She laughs again, completely unoffended that the two of them have lost interest in us.

I'm silent as the elevator doors open and we step in.

"That's wonderful news," she says when the doors close again.

"It is. I'm happy for them."

From the way Violet watches me in the car on the way home, a little crease between her brows, she's concerned about my lack of conversation. But the pinch behind my ribs that accompanied the news that my brother is going to be a father hasn't abated. In fact, it's twisting, expanding, spiraling outward until it's an inescapable pulse in my veins.

I can't look at Violet. If I do, I won't be able to keep my hands off her. I'm pretty damn certain this isn't how normal people react to hearing they're about to become an uncle. It's as if a door in my chest has swung open, and a craving I've never experienced before is driving me to claim Violet, mark her as mine, in a way I never have before.

"Are you okay?" Violet asks as I take her hand and stalk toward the elevator.

"I will be." The door opens, and I pull her in with me. As soon as I swipe my fob to take us up to the apartment, I turn, sink my fingers into her hair and crash my lips down on hers.

I swallow her startled gasp as I invade her mouth with my tongue. She tastes like apple pie and *Violet*. If I could savor that flavor for the rest of my life, I would. She's driving me insane, and I want the insanity. I crave her in a way I never knew was possible. The sex I used to seek out is nothing but a shadow, a pale imitation of what I have with her.

I need her. Before the doors are fully closed, I drag the straps of her dress down over her shoulders, leaving her completely bare to her waist.

Dipping my head, I suck one of her high, tight nipples into my mouth, making us both moan. I grasp her hips and lift so she can wrap her legs around my waist. When her heat hits me, I grind my erection into her.

The elevator dings, and I stride out with her still wrapped around me. "Fuck," I mutter, hefting the weight of her full breast in my palm. "I can't wait, butterfly. I need to be inside you."

"Yes, Tate," she breathes, rolling her hips and rubbing her pussy against me.

I manage to make it to the bedroom this time and lay her on top of my bed, pulling her dress down her body and over her thighs to reveal a tiny red thong. I hook my fingers in the fragile material, and with a snap of my wrists, rip it right off her. Then I step back and make quick work of stripping off my shirt and letting it fall to the floor.

Her gaze drifts over me, a beguiling little smile on her face as her hands go to her breasts and she rolls her nipples between her fingers.

I have no idea what I'm doing right now, my control stripped from me by this woman lying naked in front of me.

"Are you on birth control?" My voice is nothing more than a rasp.

The movement of her fingers ceases, and her eyes dart to mine. "Yes."

"Can I fuck you bare, butterfly? I've always used a condom. Always."

"Yes," she whispers. "I want that with you, Tate."

My chest tightens, even as my cock throbs. So fucking trusting. So fucking mine.

I shed the rest of my clothes, stopping for only an instant to wrap my fist around my cock and squeeze in the hopes of relieving some of the pressure. Then I lie next to her on the bed and drag her over me so she's straddling my hips. Gripping hers, I rock her against my throbbing shaft. "Get yourself off on me like this. I need you dripping before I fuck you."

Her body is hot and slick against me, every glide up and down the length of my cock the most incredible torture.

"That's it, beautiful." A groan works its way out from deep in my chest. "You feel so good."

Her chest and face are flushed, and her eyelids are heavy as she works herself over me.

I push my hand into her hair and drag her lips down to mine. The taste of her in my mouth, the feel of her against my cock. It takes all my concentration to stop myself from exploding. But I manage. Tonight, the only place I'm going to come is in her perfect little pussy.

I press kisses along her jaw, then lick and suck my way down her throat and chest until I reach her breast. She arches into me, and I swirl my tongue around her nipple, flicking it, then pinching it between my teeth, hard enough that she inhales sharply and her hips stutter against me.

With a desperate little cry, she splays her hands on my chest to push herself upright, forcing me to release my hold on her. "I'm going to come, Tate," she says, rolling her hips. "I'm so close."

The sight of her—cheeks pink, lips parted—makes every one of my nerve endings coil tight. "Make a mess of me, Violet. I want to be covered in you."

With a final erratic jerk, she starts to tremble. She screws her eyelids shut, but I'm not having that. I grip her hair at the back of her head, startling her eyes open again.

"Look at me, butterfly. Look me in the eye as you come rubbing your needy little clit all over my cock."

Her pupils blow wide, and her mouth drops open on a long moan as her body shudders against me. She keeps going as she rides out her orgasm. When it finally wanes, she sags against me.

I take her mouth again, demanding, claiming. But I need more. Heart pounding, I grip her hips and pull her up until she's hovering over my mouth. Her pussy is soaked from rubbing against me and from her orgasm. Fuck. I want every last drop.

"What are you doing?" Her breathy question is almost inaudible over my pulse pounding in my ears.

"I want all of you tonight." I lick my lips and drag her down.

"Oh my god, Tate," she cries out as I press my tongue

against her clit. When I flick it, her body jerks. "I can't. It's too soon."

She should know better by now. I flick again, then suck. Despite her protest, she clutches the headboard and widens her legs to allow me greater access. There's my good girl. She trusts me. Knows I'll always look after her. Give her what she needs.

She whimpers as I drag the flat of my tongue slowly up her sex. When I reach the swollen bundle of nerves at the top, I give it a flick. Then I start over. It only takes a few more swipes before she starts to tremble. When I draw her clit into my mouth and stroke it hard and fast, she sucks in a harsh breath and her thighs shake. An instant later, her arousal coats my lips and chin.

"You're so fucking sexy." I pull her down and roll out from under her so she's sprawled, boneless, on her stomach. One hand splays across her back, then smooths down over the mounds of her ass. There's no stopping the urge to give one of her cheeks a sharp slap. She moans in response, and my cock grows even harder as her skin turns pink.

With both hands, I spread her, being sure to brush my thumbs against the tight little pucker. "I'm going to fuck you here one day, butterfly. I'll fill both holes. One with my cock and one with a toy. Make you come so hard you'll pass out. I'm going to claim you everywhere, beautiful. But not tonight." I drag my thumbs farther down, spreading the lips of her sex to reveal her dripping entrance. On a groan, I dip the tips of both of my thumbs into her. "Tonight, I'm going to fill this beautiful little cunt up."

She turns her head to the side so she can watch me over her shoulder. "Yes," she hisses. And fuck if it doesn't drive me crazy that she wants that too.

I want one more thing from her tonight. I haven't asked

before because, although I love pinning her down and fucking her, I love her hands on me even more. But tonight, pure primal desire pumps through my veins. "Can I restrain you, butterfly?"

She blinks at me, a sweep of dark lashes over pools of blue. "Do you mean sh-shibari?"

I smile, even through the need that's threatening to drown me, as an image of that first night at Onyx flits through my mind. "No, not shibari. I want to tie your arms. Just with neckties. No ropes, no restraints. Just enough that you can't make the pleasure stop. Okay?"

"Okay," she whispers.

My heart swells at her trust in me. I get off the bed and grab two ties. If I had proper restraints, I could tie her legs as well. But this will be more than enough.

"Don't move." I wind one of the ties around her right wrist. It's just tight enough to hold if she tugs a little. Then I wrap the other end around her left wrist. I make quick work of using a second tie to loop around the one stretching between her wrists, then I tie it to the headboard.

Her breaths are coming deeper now.

"Still okay, butterfly?" I ask.

She nods, her eyes fixed on me. "Do I need a safe word?"

I lower my head until my lips hover over hers. "It's stop, butterfly. The word is stop."

"Isn't it supposed to be something I won't accidentally say?"

"Not for this. The minute you say stop, that's what I'll do. Got it?"

After she's given me another nod of understanding, I trail my finger down the dip of her spine and over her ass, closing my eyes and inhaling sharply as her muscles tremble under my touch.

Then I open my nightstand and pull out an item I bought just for her. A magic wand, like the one she seemed intrigued by as she walked past the windows at Onyx.

I switch it on, then slide my arm under her hips and pull her up so she's on her knees, with her ass in the air. With her arms stretched out in front of her, she's forced to keep her chest flat on the bed. Like this, her beautiful pussy is bared and open for me.

I run the buzzing head of the toy over her swollen flesh, eliciting a startled gasp from her. Her thighs tremble as I move it back and forth, getting it slick with her arousal.

"Oh my god," she whispers. "Tate, that feels... God, that feels amazing."

I slap her ass again, savoring her breathy little cry before circling her clit with the toy, never touching it directly. Violet whimpers, and her hips twitch in response to the indirect stimulation. My dick is so hard I swear it throbs in time with my pulse.

"You're dripping down your thighs, butterfly. You're going to leave a wet spot on my sheets before I've even fucked you."

"Tate," she moans. Fuck, she's so close, and I haven't even touched her where she needs it the most. I graze her clit with my fingertips, then tease her opening. When I slide two of my fingers inside her, she jolts forward. But a heartbeat later, she's pushing back against me, seeking more as I twist and curve them.

I run the toy over her again, still avoiding that swollen bundle of nerves, and a series of frantic pants spill from her mouth. Her thighs quiver, as if she's on the precipice of losing the ability to hold herself up.

I drag my fingers from her channel and bury my tongue in her beautiful pussy, lapping at her and teasing her clit with gentle flicks against it. The taste of her makes the throbbing in my cock almost painful. There's no way I can drag this out as much as I'd like. Not this time, anyway.

I pull back and lick her taste from my lips, then plunge two fingers back into her.

"Tate." Her cry is music to my fucking ears.

I work my fingers inside her, teasing her front wall until I find just the right spot.

Violet rocks back onto me as best as she can with her arms in front of her and unable to brace herself. "Please," she begs. "Please, touch me, Tate."

"Does your pretty little clit want this?" I press the toy just above where she wants it.

She jerks again. "Yes, please. Make me come, Tate. Please."

"Take three of my fingers, and I'll let you come," I say.

She shudders. "Okay."

I pull my fingers out just far enough to add a third and work them slowly back into her tight wet heat.

Her breaths are coming in gasps now, and I'm too close to hold off any longer. I'll let her come, but I won't use the toy to do it. Not yet.

I pull the wand away and switch it off, then drop it on the bed next to us. With my other hand, I reach around her and roll my fingertips over her clit, using the same rhythm as my fingers inside her. When her legs start to shake and she pushes back against me, I increase my tempo, thrusting deep while rubbing over her in tight, hard circles. She bucks against my hand, crying out as she clenches around me in a sharp, quaking orgasm.

As she comes down, I notch the head of my cock against

her soaked entrance. Fuck. I can't wait another second. The kiss of her wet flesh against me almost makes me lose my mind. I've never wanted to be bare with anyone. Never wanted to risk getting a woman pregnant. But right now, with Violet giving herself to me so beautifully, I can't think of anything but filling her with my cum. She already wears my ring. We could get married, have a baby, one we'd both love—one we'd raise together.

My thoughts aren't completely rational. But I'm not rational right now. I feel fucking reckless.

Violet makes me feel reckless.

I thrust into her, letting out a strangled curse. She's always tight, but at this angle, it's like forcing my dick into a heated vise. I only make it an inch or so before I have to stop, drop my head and breathe. "Relax for me, beautiful. You're so damn tight. I don't want to hurt you."

"I'm trying," she says, clutching at my comforter.

She closes her eyes and exhales, and I slide in another inch. "Oh God," she breathes. "More. I need more."

Fuck. My dick is so hard, I wouldn't be surprised if she can feel the tip inside her pulsing with every pounding beat of my heart. I'm worried I'll lose it before I'm all the way in. "Rock against me, butterfly. You're going to take every single inch of me, but I need you to fuck your way onto my cock."

She bucks back in jerky motions, and I curse again. Sweat breaks out on my forehead as she takes me deeper. Finally, her body loosens enough that I can take over, working myself the rest of the way into her until I bottom out. Every muscle tightens to the point of pain, and I'm so fucking ready to explode that I'm almost lightheaded.

I've never felt anything as good as having my bare cock buried all the way inside Violet's hot, wet pussy. I'm pressed so tightly to the end of her channel I'm worried I'm hurting her. "You okay, beautiful?"

"More than okay. You feel incredible. Nothing's ever..." She clenches her eyes shut. "Nothing's ever felt so perfect."

I stroke my hand up the curve of her spine until I can wrap my fingers around the back of her neck. "Tell me to stop if it's too much."

"Okay."

With one hand pinning her down and the other wrapped around her hip, I pull almost all the way out of her before burying myself to the hilt again.

She hisses out a breath, but before I can check that she's okay, she tilts her head and meets my gaze again. "More."

That's all it takes for my control to snap and my mind to go hazy. I drive into her, over and over. Her pussy is clenched so tight around me that I know it won't take long before I'm emptying myself inside her. The sound of our skin slapping only amplifies the need coursing through me. It's raw and real and dirty. It only makes me thrust harder.

There's no way I'm coming without taking her with me. I curl over her and quickly undo one end of the tie linking her wrists. "Use the toy. I'm not going to fill you up until your hot little cunt is gushing all over my cock."

Immediately, she releases her death grip on the comforter. With a shaky hand, she gropes for the wand. As soon as she finds it, she turns it on and slips it between her legs. Her initial gasp morphs into a moan as she presses the buzzing end to her clit. I'm rewarded too, when her delicate internal muscles immediately spasm around me. A faint echo of the toy's vibrations ripple around my shaft, and it's almost enough to send me over the edge before I'm ready. But I want to make sure this night is imprinted in her memory the way it will be in mine. So I release my grip on her hip and part the cheeks of her ass.

For a moment, I get distracted by the way her pussy is stretched so tight around me. "Fuck, butterfly. Just look at you."

But electricity is sparking at the base of my spine with such intensity that if I waste any more time admiring the perfect way she's taking me, I'll regret it. I'm balancing on the precipice, and based on her increasingly loud gasps and whimpers, she's there too. I tip my head and spit, then swirl my thumb over her tight little hole. My saliva lubricates it enough that I can work the tip inside her.

"Oh my god, Tate," Violet cries, clamping down around me.

"Look at you taking me in both holes," I growl. "Just a little more, beautiful, and we can both come."

"Give me more," she begs. "I want you to fill me everywhere."

Fuck, this woman. She's perfect in every way. I ease my thumb out, then push deeper until I'm in to my knuckle, my fingers pressing into the roundness of her ass.

Violet shudders. "I'm going to come, Tate. I can't... I can't..." Her voice breaks as the sensations from the wand on her clit, my cock in her pussy, and my thumb in her ass send her free-falling.

That's all it takes. "Fuck, butterfly. You're going to make me come so"—I thrust deep—"fucking"—I reach forward, wrap my free hand around her neck and tilt her head back so I can see her face when her orgasm hits—"hard."

Her lips part on a cry, and wet heat floods over my cock as her cunt clenches around me and her ass strangles my thumb.

The pressure at the base of my spine detonates, a blaze

of heat and electricity arcing up my shaft until it explodes out of me. I come so hard that a shout is ripped from my chest and my abdominal muscles spasm. I swear I almost black out as spurt after spurt jets out of me, filling her so full of my cum that it starts leaking out around my dick with every thrust.

She's dropped the toy and is gripping the covers again as she rocks back against me, riding out her orgasm and extending mine.

Finally, the almost agonizing pleasure eases, and I can take a full breath again. When my vision comes back into focus, I pull out of her, then flip her over so I can kiss her. "Fucking mine," I mumble against her lips. "You're fucking mine, Violet."

She kisses me back, just as desperately, and when I've finally gorged myself on the taste of her, I kiss my way down her body, then grip her thighs and press them wide open.

Violet's perfect pussy is pink and swollen from her orgasms and my exertions. My cum is still leaking out of her. The cum I filled her with. The cum that if she weren't on birth control could get her pregnant. The thought of Violet with her belly filled with my baby makes my dick twitch, even though I've just come harder than I ever have before.

I slide my fingers along her sex, gathering it up and pushing it back inside her.

She threads her fingers through my hair, the end of the tie still trailing from her wrist. When I look up, the understanding brimming in her eyes makes my chest squeeze tight. I've spent my life avoiding this kind of vulnerability. I put on a mask and showed the world only what I wanted them to see. I hide behind the façade of a man who's unaffected, unfazed. But Violet sees the real man through the pretense, and as fucking scary as it is, I love that I don't have to hide anything from her.

With a final, soft kiss to her clit, I lever myself up over her and cage her in with my arms. She cradles my face, her hands warm against my skin, and pulls me down to her lips. We don't say anything. No words can do justice to what I'm feeling. To what I hope we're both feeling.

Once this arrangement has run its course, I'm going to propose to my fiancée. And after I've married her, when we're both ready, I'm going to put a baby in her. Until those things happen though, I'm going to enjoy having her here. By my side and in my bed.

CHAPTER FORTY

VIOLET

I sit on a stool in the back of the shop, stretching my legs out and rotating my ankles. Marie, the new waitress, smiles at me as she bustles past. "Busy today, huh?"

"It is." I grin. "It's a great problem to have."

True Brew has been bustling all morning. I couldn't be more delighted that the hard work we've been putting in is finally paying off. Well, hard work and the money from Tate.

Tate.

When he looked up at me from between my thighs last night, his eyes were so full of emotion, it made my breath catch. He was thinking about being a father. I don't know how I knew that, but I did. And maybe he was thinking about his own father, the one who never claimed him. Or the one who did claim him but didn't want him. Either way, it broke my heart a little.

But it also gave me hope. Surely he wouldn't show that kind of vulnerability to someone he didn't care deeply for.

The thought fills me with a mix of excitement, happiness and fear. Nothing about last night felt fake. In that moment, I believed I was his. I wanted that. I wanted him to claim me and to keep me. Even this morning, when I woke up after passing out next to him, there was something new flickering in the depths of his golden eyes as he looked at me.

And now I'm here, wondering what it all means. I need to ask. I know that. The chance of falling hard and getting hurt if I don't understand these new rules is too high. But I can't bring myself to do it just yet. I want to enjoy whatever this is a little longer before I force myself to ask for the truth.

I sigh and heave myself upright. Rebecca, our part-time baker, left pastries in the fridge for restocking, so I pull the trays out and shove them into the oven. I set the timer on my phone so I don't lose track, then head back out to help Jarrod and Marie.

A couple of hours later, after the rush has died down, I'm sitting at one of the empty tables with my phone in one hand and my planner in front of me, working on the details of True Brew's inaugural tasting night. Jose has supplied a selection of single origin beans from family farms in Columbia, Brazil and Sumatra, as well as several specialty blends. Every one of them is incredible. Now I'm focusing on the menu to accompany them. I rule out anything too sweet, since that will overwhelm the subtler flavors of the coffee, but dark chocolate always pairs well. I jot down some ideas.

The bell above the door jingles, and I look up and smile like I always do at the sound. But the smile falls, and oxygen leaves my lungs in a rush.

Eric stands in the doorway, his hands tucked into his pockets, and surveys the shop, his pale blue eyes taking in the space. He doesn't notice me at first, since I'm tucked into the corner. My first thought is that if I stay here and put my head down, maybe he'll leave. Then I realize how silly that is. He's here to see me, so he'll ask Jarrod, and Jarrod won't know to put him off.

On the other side of the shop, Brad, today's Pinnacle bodyguard, is sitting with an open laptop in front of him. He's typing away as if he's an innocent, bulky businessman working at his local coffee shop.

His presence calms the anxiety that flared when Eric stepped over the threshold. I don't expect him to cause trouble. He cares too much about appearances, and his job, to do anything to draw untoward attention to himself, but on the off chance I need help removing him, Brad is here.

I take a deep breath and stand, drying my damp palms on the backs of my cutoffs.

The motion catches Eric's attention, and the smile he gives me makes my jaw clench. It's the same one he hit me with the first time we met. The one that's all perfect white teeth and sparkling eyes. As if he's never been so delighted to see someone.

When he starts toward me, I move his way to avoid being cornered, then usher him to the side of the shop.

"Violet, sweetheart, it's so nice to see you again. I've been looking forward to visiting True Brew. I remember how fondly you spoke of it."

I cross my arms over my chest. "What are you doing here?"

He doesn't let his smile drop at my terse tone. "The senator's campaign for reelection is heating up. I'm in town to get financial support from some high-value donors."

"And you thought you'd track me down to what, reminisce about the good times?" I arch one brow. "Like the day I walked in on you screwing your intern?"

His smile remains, but it warps into something far less

charming. "I told you back then, Violet, that was a mistake. I'm sure you've made those before."

"Uh-huh." It's as believable now as it was back then. Especially since, after he swore it was a mistake, he turned around and accused me of not being sexual enough to satisfy him. "Why are you in my shop, Eric?"

"Can't I just want to catch up with an old girlfriend while I'm in town? I thought we could go somewhere and chat." His words are mild, but he's giving off a weird vibe. I was never scared of Eric when we were together. He wasn't the type to use violence. He was more likely to manipulate and make false promises to get what he wanted. But his face looks strained, and there's a sheen of what almost looks like nervousness in his eyes. My hackles rise, and a voice inside me whispers to take a step back from him. But I don't want to give him the satisfaction of knowing his presence is affecting me. I just want him gone.

"Eric, you treated me like shit while we were together," I say, keeping my voice low. "You lied to me, manipulated me, and cheated on me. I have no desire to go anywhere with you, and I certainly have nothing to say."

In the space of a heartbeat, that hint of nervousness I sensed transforms into blatant anger. His brows slam down and his nostrils flare. "How does it feel being engaged to a billionaire?" The question comes out of left field and leaves me reeling. "Does he spoil you? Give you lots of gifts? I bet he'd be willing to give quite a bit if you ask the right way."

I jolt. This is about Tate? But he doesn't look jealous. Not like he did when we would go out and he'd watch any man I spoke to with narrowed eyes and a sneer. Not that it matters. I'm beyond caring why he's here. I step toward him, hoping the action will encourage him to move toward the door.

"You need to leave. I wasn't interested in what you had to say back then, and I'm not now. You took advantage of me after Dad died, but I learned my lesson, and I have no interest in rehashing the past. And I'm definitely not interested in discussing my current relationship with you."

Eric's face blanches, then reddens alarmingly.

My pulse kicks into high gear. "You need to leave," I reiterate. As casually as I can, I look for Brad. It seems as though I may need his help after all.

"I have more to say to you," Eric says. "And you're going to want to listen."

When I find Brad, he's already moving. But he's only halfway across the shop when Eric grips my wrist and yanks so hard it feels like my bones are grinding together.

"This was supposed to be the easy way," he hisses. He gets in my face, but a second later, he releases me and holds up his hands. "I'm leaving, I'm leaving," he says as he backs away.

"Yes, you fucking are," Brad, who's suddenly at my side, snarls. With his hands clenched into fists, he continues on, looming over my ex as he rushes for the door.

As Brad follows Eric, I cradle my wrist and stare dazedly after them. When the door shuts behind them and the shop falls silent, unease and embarrassment prickle my skin. I scan the customers around me. Every one of them is focused on me. Before I can find the words to apologize for the disturbance, Jarrod's at my side.

"Jesus. Are you okay?"

Shaking, probably from adrenaline, I duck my head and examine my wrist. It's ringed in red and slightly swollen, but other than the irritation and a dull ache when I flex my hand, it's okay.

Jarrod is holding my hand now, inspecting the injury.

He peers up at me, concern shadowing his gaze. "Who was that guy? Should I call the police? You could file assault charges."

I force myself to focus. To imagine what would happen if the press got wind of it. The whole point of this arrangement with Tate was to dissuade the tabloids from writing scandalous things about him, and to make True Brew a staple of the community again. Pressing charges against Senator Rawlins' nephew would have the opposite effect. And by the look of the fear on his face as Brad chased him out of here, I don't think he'll be back. I still don't understand why he came in the first place.

So I shake my head. "I'm okay. He just got carried away. It won't happen again." I'm glad that I sound calmer than I feel. Having Eric here, in my shop, where he never should have stepped foot—putting his hands on me in a way I never believed he would—is beyond disconcerting. He belongs in my past, not inserting himself into my new life.

Jarrod frowns. "You're going to tell Tate, right? He needs to know."

The bell over the door chimes, and Brad appears, heading straight for me. "Are you okay?" He takes in my wrist, and his expression darkens. "I should have beaten his ass."

I let out a shaky breath. "I appreciate the sentiment. But he's just a bitter ex. He doesn't even live in New York, so I doubt he'll be back."

He pulls his phone out. "I need to inform Mr. King."

I put my hand on his arm. "Can I be the one to tell Tate?"

He frowns but nods reluctantly and slides his cell back into his pocket. It's his job to inform Tate of any incidents, so I appreciate him letting me do this myself.

"You need to do it now though," he says. "He won't be happy if he hears about it in my end of shift report."

"Of course. I don't want you to get into trouble." I turn to Jarrod. "Can you cover the rest of the afternoon?"

He nods, concern still creasing his brow. "Absolutely. And now that I know what he looks like, I'll make sure he doesn't try creeping back in."

"Thank you. I'll be back tomorrow." I look up at Brad. "Can you take me to Tate?"

CHAPTER FORTY-ONE

TATE

I'm in the middle of my call to the UK when Sophie buzzes me. She knows I'm in a meeting, so if she's interrupting it, then the reason must be important.

I excuse myself, put the call on hold and hit the intercom. "What's the problem?"

"Sorry for the interruption, sir. Your fiancée is here to see you. You told me to let her in if she ever came to the office, so...?"

My stomach drops. Not because I don't want to see Violet, but because she should be working at True Brew. She's never come by before, and I'm hit with the uneasy feeling that the reason behind her visit isn't a good one. "Send her in. Thanks, Sophie. Can you reschedule the UK meeting for tomorrow?"

After hanging up, I close out of the call. Sophie will soothe any ruffled feathers for me. I'm more concerned about my fiancée. Itching to lay eyes on her, I push my chair back and make my way around my desk. I'm only a few steps from the door when she knocks, so I swing it open myself.

Violet takes a step back, her hand pressed against her chest as if I've startled her.

The red marks on her wrist practically jump out at me, and my heart slams into my throat. I reach for her hand and cradle it in mine as I scrutinize the injury. It's already bruising.

"Who the hell did this?" I bite out. When I focus on her face, needing an answer, her lips are parted and her eyes are wide. I gentle my tone. "Violet. Who hurt you? Was it a reporter?"

She peeks over her shoulder at Sophie, who's doing her best to not look like she's listening in, and turns back to me. "Can I tell you in your office?"

Still holding her hand, I lead her inside. I close the door quietly, and when I turn back, she's standing in the middle of the room, taking in the space. The part of me that isn't consumed with finding out what happened to her is frustrated, because I should have brought her here weeks ago. She's my fiancée. She should be familiar with my office. She should feel like she can drop in at any time, not just when something is wrong.

I shove my hand through my hair. "How did you get hurt? Was it at True Brew? I didn't get a call from Pinnacle."

Her blue eyes meet mine. "I asked Brad not to call. He drove me here so I could tell you myself."

Jesus Christ. If she doesn't hurry up and explain, my chest might implode. If she wanted to tell me herself, then it likely wasn't an accident. Someone hurt her. "Sit down, butterfly." I grasp her elbow gently and guide her to the couch in the corner of my office. "Tell me who I need to deal with."

She sits, and I take my place next to her, grasping her

hand again and brushing my thumb over the bruises. Now that I've gotten a good look, the places where the fingers pressed into her tender skin are obvious. Someone grabbed her hard enough to mark her. Anger is building hard and fast inside me, heating my blood to a simmer. "What happened?"

Her teeth press into her lower lip. "Eric came to the shop."

In an instant, my heated blood goes ice cold. "What did he do?"

"He wanted to talk. I honestly don't know why. When I asked him to leave, he got angry and grabbed my wrist."

"Where was Pinnacle while this was happening?"

"As soon as he grabbed me, Brad was there and got rid of him. He wasn't negligent, Tate. Don't blame him."

I don't blame Brad. I blame myself. It was probably the publicity around our relationship that caught Eric's attention, that told him where to find her.

It's my fault he hurt her.

"It's not your fault," she murmurs, as if she can read my mind. Or maybe it's my frozen expression.

"We'll press charges," I say.

She shakes her head. "I don't want to."

"Why the hell not? He ambushed you at your place of work and hurt you."

"It's not that bad," she says. "And he was never violent when we were together. I don't think he meant to hurt me. He just seemed a little... desperate, I guess."

"People can change. I don't care what state of mind he's in; he put his hands on you. I can make a call, get the police here right now, and you can press charges."

"Tate. The whole point of this relationship was to get the tabloids off your back. If the press finds out about me pressing charges against the nephew of a state senator, you'll be right back—"

"I don't care about that. He's not going to get away with hurting you."

"I care," she says softly.

I clench my jaw, holding back my frustration, when all I want to do is make sure he never comes near her again.

"And it's not just that. This arrangement has helped me bring True Brew back. I don't want the kind of publicity this will bring when we're just getting traction again. I don't know what Eric wanted, but I doubt he'll be back. If he is, then I'll go to the police. I promise."

Tension knots at the back of my neck. I pull my hand from hers and run it through my hair. I didn't think this whole thing through. From the minute I found out she was the woman I was with at Onyx, I've been careless with her, from convincing her to fake date me, to announcing that we were engaged, to deciding I wanted all of her, my moves have been based on my wants and desires. Now she's asking me to do something for her. It goes against every instinct that's screaming at me to track Eric down and threaten his life, but I'll give her this.

"Fine. But Violet, if he tries anything else..."

"He won't," she says, relief shining in her eyes. "He'll be back in Maine soon. And he knows I have security now. He won't want to risk his job and reputation, believe me. Eric is all about appearances."

I nod, swallowing down the frustration that's urging me to do it anyway. She doesn't want to press charges, and I'll give her that. But I will put in a call to the investigator I had track down my biological father and ask him to dig up all he can about Eric. I should have done it after she told me he'd commented on her True Brew post. I'm not letting it go this time.

Violet smiles at me. "Thank you. I know you want to help, but this is for the best."

"Come here." I gently lift her until she's straddling me. Framing her face with my hands, I tug her down until her lips are against mine.

She sighs against them and presses closer.

My thumbs trace over the soft skin of her cheeks. "I hate that you're hurt because of me."

"It's not your fault," she whispers again.

Guilt pinches behind my ribs and I trail my fingers down her back so I can wrap them around her waist. "It is."

"Maybe you could make it up to me when we get home." With a wicked little smile, she rolls her hips.

Heat flares up my spine. I'm suddenly too aware that I have her here, alone in my office. I ended my meeting early, and the next doesn't start for half an hour. There's a lot I can do in thirty minutes.

"I can make it up to you right now."

Her cheeks turn pink, and she looks at the door.

"Sophie won't come in," I say. "And she won't let anyone else in. She knows better."

Violet's muscles go taut in response. Dammit, her interpretation of that comment couldn't be further from the truth. She won't ask if I've had other women in here because she doesn't think she has the right. She still hasn't figured out that she's the only one who does. The only one who's ever been mine in every sense of the word.

"You're the only woman I've had in this office, butterfly. And I've spent far too long imagining you spread out on this couch or bent over my desk."

Her breath catches and then she drifts her fingers down

my chest until they curl around the leather of my belt. "What about on my knees? Have you imagined that?"

My pulse leaps, because of course I fucking have. I don't let myself react to the visual searing through my mind though. "You're hurt," I grit out.

She looks down at the red mark on her wrist and runs her fingers over her skin. "Not bad enough to stop me."

I tip her face up to mine. "The idea was for me to make it up to you."

"Why should making it up to me only involve *you* giving *me* pleasure?"

My thumb draws a line under the curve of her lower lip. "You don't think making you come gives me pleasure?"

She cocks her head. "I know it does, Tate. The same is true for me. And I want this. Maybe I've had fantasies of my own that involve your office. Maybe my ex being an asshole shouldn't take that away from me."

Fuck. My dick is rock hard at the thought of Violet on her knees for me right here. But the desire wars with my need to take care of her. There's something in her tone of voice though. Something that tells me maybe Eric turning up out of the blue shook her more than she's admitting. Maybe a little control is exactly what she's craving right now.

Or maybe there's a part of her that wants to claim me exactly the way I always want to claim her.

The war is lost when she slides off my lap and drops to her knees between my legs, looking up at me with wide, imploring eyes. She knows exactly what she's doing to me. "Fuck, Violet. How am I supposed to say no to you when you look at me like that?"

She gives me a smile of pure female satisfaction. "You're not."

Giving in to the inevitable, I inhale deeply, palming my erection to ease some of the ache. She watches me do it, her pupils dilating.

Reaching out, I trace my fingers over her collarbone and down to the swell of her breasts, tugging on the neckline of her tank top. "Show me."

Maintaining eye contact, she drags the straps of her tank top and bra off her shoulders, tugging them both down until she's fully exposed.

I lick my lips. "Play with those pretty nipples."

Without hesitation, she pinches them, rolling them between her fingers,

My dick throbs against my fly. "Such a good girl," I say. "Do you like showing yourself off for me?"

"Yes." Her voice is breathless, and I'd bet her panties are already damp.

I lean forward and pull the tie out from her ponytail, sifting my fingers through the length of her hair so it falls loose around her shoulders. "Stick out your tongue." When she does, I run the pad of my thumb down it. "Do you know what I'm going to use this for?" Goose bumps break out over her skin, but she doesn't answer. "After I fuck my fiancée's pretty mouth, I'm going to come all over it."

"Tate," she breathes.

I hold her gaze, giving her one more chance. "You know I just want to make you feel good, don't you?"

Her smile is soft. "Yes. And right now, what will make me feel good is you giving me what I want."

The last of my concern dissipates. She wants this. I unbuckle my belt, drag down my zipper and pull myself out. "Then use that beautiful mouth to make me come."

I wrap my fist around my shaft and stroke it, then guide it toward her. She keeps her eyes on me as I rub the already weeping crown over her lips. When I press against their softness, she opens for me, and I push inside. Then I let go so she can take control.

Her fingers circle my base, and fuck if my heart doesn't stop at the sight of her like this—mouth wrapped around me, hair brushing my thighs, beautiful bare breasts thrust out toward me, and my ring glittering on her finger. I'm never going to be able to get this moment out of my head. When I enter my office from now on, this will be all I can think of—Violet on her knees for me.

She runs her tongue along the underside of me before sinking all the way down until I'm at the back of her throat.

I groan. "Fuck, butterfly." I stroke my hand over her hair. "You look so pretty sucking my cock."

She whimpers around me, then redoubles her efforts. Her head bobs as she alternates between swirling her tongue over the tip and drawing me as far into her mouth as she can.

When she presses even farther down, I curse and fist her hair. "Are you going to take me down your throat, butterfly?"

"Mmm," she hums, desire shimmering in her gaze.

For a moment, my restraint slips and my hips jerk, driving me a little deeper.

She chokes and involuntarily tightens around my tip, sending a lance of pleasure up my spine. I force myself to pull back. To let her take me the way she wants.

But when she closes her eyes, her hips squirming. I know what she needs. "I want you to come while you suck me."

That has her focusing back on me. In the next moment, her hand slides down her stomach, and she fumbles with the button of her cutoffs. Once she has them open, she dips her fingers under the top of her panties, moaning around me as she circles her clit.

My own fingers itch to be the ones touching her there, to rub over her slippery, swollen flesh until she falls apart. I'm officially addicted to making her come.

That will have to wait, though. Because she's still working her mouth over me, flicking her tongue over the tip, then sucking hard as she sinks back down even deeper than before. When she gags, tears springing to her eyes, I have to take a deep breath to stop myself from spilling into her mouth right then and there.

Maybe she senses my struggle, because her gaze fixes on me and she speeds up, gagging whenever she goes too far or too fast. Her tears glitter like diamonds on her lashes before dripping down her cheeks, and I cup her jaw and wipe them away with my thumb. My breathing is getting harsher as heat claws at the base of my spine. I'm close.

She is too. Her eyelashes flutter, and her fingers move faster inside her panties. I wish I could see her working that pretty clit of hers.

I grip her hair tight. "I'm going to take over now. Concentrate on that beautiful pussy, because the minute you come, I'm filling your mouth."

Her enthusiastic nod is consent enough.

Using my hold on her hair to keep her still, I thrust into her. Her pupils dilate, and her cheeks flush as I fuck her mouth. I'm swollen, throbbing, desperate for release.

But I need hers first.

Dragging her down onto me until she gags one last time, I growl, "You look so fucking perfect with my cock in your throat and your fingers in your pussy."

Her eyes squeeze shut, her hips jerk, and a moan vibrates through me. That's all it takes for the dam to break.

A tidal wave of pleasure hits me so hard it feels like every muscle in my body seizes at the same time. I groan long and deep as my cock swells and the first stream of cum hits the back of her throat. Two more pulses, and I tug her head back so my dick rests on the tip of her tongue and I can paint it with my release.

"Open up, butterfly. Let me see."

She does, staring up at me with glazed, pleasure-soaked eyes as I throb again and again, filling her mouth.

"Fuck, fuck, fuck," I swear. The minute my muscles release and I can do something other than come like a damn freight train, I let go of her hair and wrap my hand around her throat. "Swallow for me."

The way her delicate muscles work against my palm as she does what I ask has my dick twitching again. I ignore it, because now I need something else. "Lie back."

"But—"

"Violet, I need you to lie back." My voice comes out shredded.

She complies, and now it's me dropping to my knees between *her* legs. I hook my fingers in her shorts and panties at the same time, dragging them down her thighs and off, before spreading her wide, exposing her gorgeous cunt. She's pink and swollen and wet from her orgasm, and I'm desperate to taste her. Using the flat of my tongue, I take long, luxurious licks from her dripping entrance to the still-pulsating bundle of nerves at the top of her sex. I suck it between my lips as I push first one, then two fingers inside.

"Tate," she gasps, her hips already starting to move against me.

I slide my free hand up her body and roll her nipple between my fingers, pinching it until it's hard and peaked. "Come for me again, butterfly."

She whimpers, still sensitive from her first orgasm. It doesn't take me long to work her up again though. When her channel tightens, I pull my fingers out, use my thumbs to spread her wide and lick her hard and fast from her tight little asshole to her swollen clit.

She arches her back. "Oh my God, Tate."

"Use my face to come," I growl against her slick flesh.

With a needy moan, she buries her hands in my hair and tugs. Then she grinds herself against me. I push two fingers back inside her and curl them, then suck hard on her clit while she thrusts against me. The first sign of her impending orgasm is the sudden gush of liquid heat that coats my palm, and then her muscles clamp down, and she chants my name as she holds me tight against her. Only when her thighs stop trembling around my ears do her hands drop away, and then, finally, her whole body relaxes.

I pull my drenched fingers from her and lick her off me, craving every last drop.

Still splayed out in front of me, she watches my every move, eyes hooded, skin damp with sweat, and a sweet, sated smile on her lips.

And fuck if that isn't the view I'm going to enjoy looking at for the rest of my life.

CHAPTER FORTY-TWO

VIOLET

Jarrod hands me a cup of steaming hot coffee. "What do you think of this one?"

I give it a small sip. "It's got a really bold flavor. It might be too much for the tasting night."

"Maybe balance it with that milder one we liked."

"Good idea." With a nod, I make a note on my pad. I stick the end of the pen in my mouth and consider how to best describe the flavor of the single origin coffee. I jot down *a hint of caramel with a bold finish.*

Jarrod and I are working on the tasting menus, choosing the right flavors to showcase what True Brew does best. We also need to pair pastries and desserts with the different coffees as well. Ones that complement the single origins and specialty blends we end up selecting.

We're in the middle of discussing how to position the tables to ensure the best flow for the event when the bell on the door jingles and Anna walks in.

When she sees me, her face lights up. "Hey, guys." She strides over and plonks herself down in the seat next to

Jarrod. "Thought I'd see if you need help getting ready for your big night."

"Your presence is always appreciated." I grin at her.

Jarrod stands up. "I'll brew that last blend and pull those brownie bites out of the oven."

As he walks away, Anna homes in on me, and her friendly smile turns into a sly one.

"What?" I ask.

"You're glowing."

Without thinking, I touch my face. "I have no clue what you mean."

She leans forward and lifts a brow, her inky black curls spilling over her shoulder. "You look like a woman who's been well, ahem, taken care of." The exaggerated wink she gives me makes my eyes roll.

I glance over to make sure Jarrod is still busy behind the counter, then back at my best friend. "Um, Tate is... incredible. I've never felt anything like I do with him."

"That's great, Vi. And I'm assuming he feels the same way about you?"

My heart stumbles just a little. "It feels like he does. But I'm not sure—"

"Hold on." She lifts a hand. "He hasn't said anything about how he feels?"

I bite my lip and regard her. "I think he feels the same as me. He says all the right things."

She frowns, her brow creasing. "So why the doubt?"

"Because sometimes, between swooning, when I think about all he's said and done, I wonder if it's too good to be true. Tate was such a natural at pretending to be my boyfriend at the start. I can't help but worry that maybe he's just good at pretending with *all* this relationship stuff. That maybe I'm falling for the patented Tate

King charm. That it's, like, concentrated in this situation."

Anna's eyebrows shoot up. "Concentrated charm?"

"Yeah, you know, because we've been put in this crazy situation, and he's got nowhere to focus all that intensity and charisma except on me."

"You can't really think that, Violet. You're a beautiful person. There's no reason Tate wouldn't fall for you."

"I know what we have *feels* genuine, but I keep wondering if he would still look at me this way if the agreement didn't exist."

My concern goes so much deeper than that, but the details aren't mine to share. Tate's felt like an outsider in his own family for most of his life. So what if his feelings aren't based on me as a person but on our proximity and the roles we've been playing? What if I'm merely a temporary embodiment of something he's been craving for so long—having someone to care for and to care for him in return.

Anna squeezes my hand. "You should talk to him. Tell him how you feel."

I sigh past the dull ache in my chest. "If I do, it's going to have to be soon. Our agreement is supposed to be over at the end of the week, so..."

Her eyes widen. "I didn't realize it was so soon. And neither of you have brought up what's going to happen when the date comes?"

I fidget and try to push away the apprehension bubbling up inside me. "I thought I might wait until it ends and see if he still acts the same way."

Anna stares at me for a long moment, her jaw slack. "Do you really think that's the way to handle this?"

"No," I whisper. Then I cover my face with my hands. "I'm such a coward."

She grasps my forearms and pulls my hands away from my face. "Being scared and being a coward are two different things. It's okay to be scared, Violet. Telling someone you're falling for them is a big deal, particularly considering your situation. But if you let fear hold you back from what has the potential to be an amazing love story, I think you'll regret it for the rest of your life."

"You're right. I know you're right," I say. "He hasn't mentioned the end date either. He would have if he didn't want to keep things going, right?" I shake my head. It's a rhetorical question. Anna doesn't know the answer any more than I do. I take a deep breath to settle the nerves that rattle through me. "I really hope he wants to, because I think I might already be in love with him."

Anna lets out a little squeal.

With a wince, I glance at Jarrod to make sure he can't hear our conversation. From his look of concentration as he cuts up the brownie bites, he seems unaware.

"Shh. Don't forget, everyone thinks we're in love already."

"I know, I know. But I'm so excited for you."

"So, you think I should tell him?"

"I think you should. If he doesn't feel the same way, then your agreement will be over anyway. You'll walk away with brand-new equipment, new staff, new décor and enough money to keep True Brew going for a long time, considering how many more customers you're bringing in these days."

I let out a sigh. "But I'll have a broken heart to go along with it."

She squeezes my hand. "I hate to say this, but if Tate doesn't feel the same way, it doesn't matter when you tell him. It's going to hurt. But if you talk to him before the contract ends, he'll at least know you're interested rather than believing he's releasing you from a situation you don't want."

The idea that Tate might walk away never knowing he was loved the way he deserves to be loved is all it takes for me to decide. I went into this with the sole purpose of restoring True Brew, but now, the thought of walking away with only that and not with the man I've fallen for makes my stomach drop sickeningly.

In my periphery, Jarrod approaches with a tray full of cups and a plate of brownie bites.

"Okay, I'll say something tonight," I tell Anna.

She gives me a sneaky thumbs-up before Jarrod appears next to the table. He hands us each a cup, and we sip the rich, aromatic brew. Paired with the sweet, dark chocolate brownie, it's absolutely delicious. As we discuss the options and I note down my final choices, my mind can't help but wander to what I have to do tonight. My stomach rolls over. I'm nervous, but I won't let that stop me.

I'll be brave and trust what Tate has shown me of himself these last couple of months. And then I'll ask him about the future of our relationship.

Our real relationship.

CHAPTER FORTY-THREE

TATE

"You've got an unscheduled visitor, Mr. King," Sophie advises me as I pass her desk on my way back to my office.

"Who is it?" Occasionally, we get crazies who think they can show up unannounced and get in to see one of us about whatever issue they think we're responsible for. But normally security deals with them without calling up to the PAs.

"His name is Eric Evans. He says he's an old friend of your fiancée and needs to talk to you urgently."

At the sound of his name, my hands clench at my sides, and anger floods me. For a moment, I don't move. I could tell security to escort him out of the building. In fact, I should. But I want to know what he's after. If he showed up here, then he isn't giving up easily like Violet expected. If I refuse to see him today, he'll probably come back tomorrow or track me down another way.

Regardless of that, I need to face the asshole who abused Violet's trust and tried to manipulate her. I need to look him in the eye and make sure he knows exactly who's standing next to her now. Let him know that he'll never get a chance to hurt her again. "Send him up," I say. "But tell security to remain on standby."

Her brows rise, but she nods and presses the button to call down to security in the foyer.

I stride into my office and close the door a little harder than necessary. My mind races as I round my desk, sit down and log onto my computer. I reread the email my PI sent me last night. It's only an initial assessment of Eric, which means it gives me little insight into who I'm dealing with. He has a bachelor's degree in public administration, has been working for his uncle since he graduated and is still working as Senator Rawlins' fundraising manager. So he hasn't earned the promotion Violet said he was after since they were together. His relationship with his uncle doesn't seem particularly close, although, according to the investigator, Eric is more than happy to play things up to make it look that way.

I don't have time to review more before there's a knock on the door. Sophie sticks her head in. "Eric Evans here to see you."

"Send him in, please."

I make sure to look as though I'm working on my computer when he enters, only glancing up to say "Take a seat," before turning back to the screen. As Eric sits in one of the chairs in front of my desk, I type out an email to the investigator with instructions to step up his digging on the asshole, ignoring the man himself the whole time. This power play is one of the oldest in the book, and I'm sure Eric knows exactly what I'm doing. But how he reacts will still give me insight into his character.

He's silent for a few minutes, but then he shifts in his seat. Another minute later, and he's clearing his throat.

That's all it takes to know he's not patient enough to play the long game. He wants instant gratification, and I have no doubt he's prone to acting rashly to get what he wants. Only once I've listed specific instructions and hit send on the email do I lean back in my seat and take him in.

His expression is cool, but irritation simmers in his eyes. "Mr. King," he begins, trying to sound casual. "I happen to be in town for some meetings on behalf of Senator Rawlins and thought we should meet."

I nod, giving nothing away. "And why is that, Mr. Evans? As far as I know, the King Group doesn't have any ties with the senator."

He's donned a confident demeanor, but his eyes shift around, never staying in place for more than a few moments. He's nervous. "You don't. But you have a tie to me, and I have a business proposition for you."

I ignore the tension building at the base of my neck as best I can. Keeping my cool and figuring out what his angle is so I can get him out of my office and out of Violet's life is my priority. "I'm listening."

He drums his fingers on the arm of the chair. "Let's just say I'm in a situation. A tight spot that requires a bit of... financial lubrication."

I raise an eyebrow. "And you think I can provide you some... lubrication?"

His mouth twists. "I need a substantial amount of money, and I need it fast. I believe we can help each other out."

Leaning forward, I rest my elbows on my desk. My hackles rise, and everything inside me is screaming that I need to be wary. "You want me to give you a substantial amount of money? And in return, what do I get? Because believe it or not, I'm not known for doling out cash to complete strangers, ties or not."

"What you get is the chance to maintain the reputation of your lovely fiancée."

The muscles along the length of my spine draw tight with tension. This fucker came here to threaten Violet? My instincts shout at me to make very sure he regrets it, but until I know what's at risk, I'll continue with the façade of calm, giving nothing away.

Eric pulls his phone out of his pocket, unlocks it and slides it across the desk.

My gut lodges itself in my throat as I smoothly pick up the device. But as the picture on the screen registers, fury unlike I've ever known roars through me. I clamp down on the urge to reach across my desk, grab him by the tie and smash my fist into his nose. I'm only able to restrain myself by calling on every second of practice I've had hiding how I really feel from the world.

The photo is a little out of focus, but it's clear enough: Violet, naked on a bed, eyes closed, head angled toward the camera, while a man, his face obscured, hovers over her. Her breasts are visible and her legs are spread. The man, who I assume is Eric, rests between them. Rage twists and turns inside my chest, struggling to escape. I grapple to control it as I flash through every possibility of where to go from here, every scenario and its consequences. If there's ever been a time to act as if I don't care, now is it. And the thought makes me feel sick to my stomach.

"Okay," I say, stripping every ounce of feeling from my voice.

Eric frowns and glances at the phone, then focuses on me again. "Feel free to scroll."

Dread churns through me as I swipe to the next photo.

Fuck. This one is taken from behind while she's on all fours. Nausea hits then. I swallow it back and continue to flip through the images just for show, unwilling to focus on them. I want to kill him. I want to launch myself across the desk, wrap my hands around his neck and squeeze.

The hardest thing I've ever had to do in my life is slide the phone back over to him, raise a brow and say "And?"

Shock flashes across his face for a second before he schools his expression. "I assume you don't want these photos of Violet uploaded to the internet."

A pulse throbs in my temple. I can only hope it's not visible. I would take him down right now, but the implications of his actions are clear. He didn't hesitate to give me his phone. He's not worried about me deleting them, so he has copies.

Even if I were to call security right now and have him detained, even if I accused him of attempted extortion, I have no evidence to back it up. He and Violet used to date, so on the surface, he has a reason to have those photos on his phone. Even though, from the images I saw, it doesn't look like Violet was aware the slimy motherfucker was taking them, which is a crime in itself. Regardless of my actions, he has access to copies, and the shiftiness of his gaze tells me he's desperate. And desperation makes people do stupid things, like uploading these photos to the internet as an act of revenge if I don't give him what he wants.

Or something even worse.

Whatever situation Eric's gotten himself into, he thinks my money is the way out of it. And Violet is his leverage to get it. There's no way I'll allow these photos to be put up online or let Eric get away with threatening Violet in any capacity. No fucking way.

There's only one solution I can think of to fix this.

Though just the thought cracks my chest open. I hate it with every fiber of my being, but I'm going to do it anyway.

"I don't give a fuck," I say, leaning back in my chair, affecting a bored expression.

Eric opens his mouth, snaps it shut, then scoffs. "Don't bother bluffing. There's no way a man like you wants photos of his fiancée having sex with another man spread all over the internet. With one press of a button, these will be uploaded to thousands of porn sites for millions to enjoy. Every time you're in public, and you see the stares, and hear the whispers and laughs, you'll know it's because those people have seen what she looks like when she's being fucked. And not by you."

"No, I won't." I lean forward and hit him with a careless grin that tears out my fucking heart. "Because she's not going to be seen out with me much longer." I laugh coldly. "Our relationship is fake. And time is about up on our arrangement. In fact, if you leak these photos, you'll be helping me out. What better reason could I have for ending our engagement?" My stomach rolls, but I keep my focus locked on him.

Eric's face turns red, and he sputters. "I-I don't believe you."

With a smirk, I open the top drawer of my desk and pull out the contract. I throw it down in front of him, then lean back in my chair and lace my hands together behind my head. I keep my mouth shut as he skims the pages.

As he continues, his face goes from red to purple, then it goes ashen.

"As you can see, the end date of our agreement is in four days' time, and I have no need to keep her around longer. So again, I don't care what you do with those photos. And considering you just attempted to extort me, I'd suggest leaving now, before I decide to get the police involved. I doubt Senator Rawlins would be happy about bailing you out of jail."

A muscle pulses wildly in Eric's jaw. I have no idea what he thinks he's doing, but there's no doubt he's in trouble. Maybe he has a gambling debt. Maybe he pissed off the wrong people. Whatever it is, he's desperate.

He shoves back his chair and stands in a rush. "Come after me, and I'll tell everyone your engagement is an act."

I force another laugh, channeling Roman's iciness. "I have no interest in coming after you. You took your shot, and it didn't work out. Now, if we're done, I have a meeting."

His eyes narrow. "If I find out you're screwing with me, I'll make sure these photos get the audience they deserve." He spins on his heel and storms from the room.

As soon as the heavy wooden door swings shut behind him, I snatch the phone from my desk. "Roman," I bark. "I need to talk to you and Cole. Right now."

"I'm in the middle of a meeting with—"

"This can't wait." Silence fills the line between us. He's going to tell me to fuck off, but right now, I don't care. I need my brothers' help. "It's about Violet." Those three words are full of all the anguish and fury coursing through me right now.

"Fuck," he says. "I'll be there in a minute." Then he hangs up.

Cole is next. Thankfully, he's between meetings and says he'll come straight away.

Thirty seconds after I hang up with him, my door swings open and Roman stalks in. He stands in front of my desk, hands on hips. "What's the problem?"

I scrub my hand over my face. "Wait for Cole. I only want to say this once."

He studies my face, brows pulled low, then jerks his chin and settles into one of the chairs.

A moment later, Cole walks in wearing a frown. "What's going on?"

"Sit down," I tell him.

He raises his brows but doesn't argue.

As soon as they're sitting, I'm on my feet, pacing the room. The cyclone of rage I've been suppressing is tearing through me, fighting to be released. "Violet's ex was just here. He tried to extort me by threatening to release private photos he took of her when they were together."

Roman frowns and leans forward, his elbows on his knees. "How private?"

"As private as they get. And from the look of them, she didn't know he was taking them." Even now, the thought of Eric having those photos on his phone, of how he abused Violet's trust so reprehensibly, has my blood pressure spiking.

"Fucker," Cole swears. "What did you tell him?"

The nausea that hits me is so intense I worry I'll vomit. "That I didn't care. That our engagement was a lie and about to end anyway."

Cole nods, a thoughtful look on his face. "You managed the narrative."

I choke back my self-loathing. "And I've never felt dirtier."

His scowl is full of admonishment. "You did what you needed to do to protect your fiancée. Now, how are we going to take him down?"

"I'm working on it, but I'll only do it if I can make sure Violet doesn't get hurt."

"Do you have a plan?" Roman asks.

I look from him to Cole, hit with a shot of gratefulness. Because my brothers have my back. "We need to visit Onyx."

AN HOUR LATER, we've descended on Reid's office. With four big men crowded in, the moderate-sized space is almost stifling.

"What's going on?" Reid asks. "I never thought the day would come when I'd have three billionaires in my office."

Cole and Roman sit back while I force myself to repeat Eric's threats. By the end, my hands are shaking with rage.

Reid narrows his eyes in thought. "You did the right thing. Going to the police would likely get messy, and it wouldn't guarantee the photos would disappear. Or that he wouldn't resort to more extreme measures. If he's really in trouble and thinks he can use her, there's a chance the threats against her could get physical."

I give him a jerky nod. "I already have a PI looking into him, but I need more. Can you help?"

Reid's dark eyes glitter with understanding. "I know someone who knows someone who can hack into his accounts and find those photos. As well as anything else he might be hiding."

It's illegal as hell, but I don't give a shit. I look at my brothers. I know what I'll see on Cole's face. He'd do anything for Delilah, so I have no doubt he'll back me up. But I have no idea what Roman will think. He's CEO of the King Group, and that's his only priority. But when I turn to assess him, there's an emotion I haven't seen in a long time burning in the icy gray depths of his eyes.

It looks an awful lot like protectiveness.

He nods, a grim jerk of his head.

That's all the confirmation I need. I turn back to Reid. "Do it."

He reaches for his phone, but before he unlocks the screen, he regards me with a frown. "If we do this, Tate, you shouldn't tell Violet."

I hang my head and taste the acid burn of defeat at the back of my throat. I've already figured this part out myself. If we get caught paying someone to hack into the accounts of a senator's employee, there will be hell to pay. And the only way to keep Violet from getting caught up in that is to keep her ignorant of it all. I won't implicate her in my illegal actions, and I won't put her in a position where she might have to lie to the police.

Reid makes the call, and we set the plan in motion. Then we spend the next few hours talking through various scenarios. But as Jeremy finally drives me home, my sole focus is on Violet. I'm doing this to keep her safe, but at what cost?

Keeping her in the dark, lying to her, is for her protection, but it feels an awful lot like betrayal. And I can't help but wonder if she'll ever forgive me for what I have to do next.

CHAPTER FORTY-FOUR

VIOLET

I listen to the message Tate left on my phone an hour ago. "I won't be home until late. Don't wait up."

When he called, I was busy cooking, and I've only just noticed the message notification.

I shouldn't be disappointed. It's the nature of Tate's job. He has to work late sometimes. But I was looking forward to sitting down to dinner and showing him the finished details of True Brew's first tasting night. Afterward, I hoped to celebrate with him in the best possible way. And then... then I planned to ask him. About us. About our future.

Instead, I eat alone and try to distract myself with a movie. It's no use. I spend the evening checking my phone and looking at the elevator, hoping to catch the display ticking up to show it's moving. But nothing. It's getting late now, and I'm tired. For the first time in weeks, I question if I should sleep in Tate's bed like I have been or go back to mine. Uncertainty weighs heavily on me, but eventually, I decide to sleep in his bed, since he's given me no indication that he doesn't want me to when he's not around.

It hits me then exactly how much we've both ignored

our situation. How we've let ourselves topple headfirst into this relationship that isn't a relationship, while ignoring all the rules that fell by the wayside and avoiding discussing the potential consequences. Burying my head in the sand seemed like a good idea at the time, but after my talk with Anna today, I'm desperate for some clarity. I need to know the truth of what Tate's feeling.

And I need him to know how *I* feel.

I take a shower, hoping it will relax my tense muscles, brush my teeth, then slide into bed. Despite my exhaustion, my mind races, and I struggle to fall asleep. Eventually, I must doze off, because I'm woken what seems like only a short time later when a body slides into bed behind me.

"Tate?" My voice is thick with sleep. "It's so late. What were you doing?" I hate how needy that sounds.

His body stiffens almost imperceptibly against me. "I was at Onyx."

The fog clears from my mind, and I sit up. I focus on him, taking in his features in the moonlight that floods through the large window. My stomach bottoms out at the thought that he spent the night at his sex club instead of at home with me. "You went to the club?"

He scrubs his hand over his chin. "Just to talk to Reid. That's all."

Foreboding unfolds in my chest. For weeks, he's made a point to come home and cook dinner with me. He's been affectionate and open. Yet suddenly, as we're approaching the end of our agreement, he's staying out late, going to Onyx, and giving me vague answers to my questions. Yes, he co-owns Onyx, but considering what happened between us last time he went to talk to Reid, I can't help but worry.

His fingers brush my arm. "Go to sleep, Violet. It's been a long day."

His voice is all wrong. It's flat, distant. In this moment, my plans to confess how I feel for him fly out the window. I can't do it when everything feels so off. And it's late. This is not the time to press the issue.

I lie back and stare up at the ceiling. Normally, we'd be wrapped around each other, but instead, we're lying here barely touching. I listen to his breathing, waiting for it to even out in sleep, but I still haven't heard it by the time my eyelids are too heavy to keep open and the world finally fades away.

When I blink awake the next morning, the space next to me is empty. The memory of last night comes rushing back, and I curl up under the covers, filled with doubt about what the day might bring. But eventually, I force myself up. I can't hide in here forever.

I get dressed quickly, then search through the apartment until I finally find Tate in his office.

He glances up at me where I stand in the doorway and smiles, but there's something missing in his expression. It takes me a second to realize what it is. His eyes are shuttered against me for the first time in a long time. I can't read him—he's as unknowable to me now as he was the first night I saw him at Onyx. Alarm bells go off in my head.

"I made dinner last night," I say.

A muscle jumps in his jaw, and he averts his gaze. "I'm sorry. Something came up at work, and then I had to talk to Reid."

"Okay." Why does it feel like he's shutting me out? I'm not sure what else to say, but I don't want to leave things like this. "What are you doing in your office so early?"

Tate keeps his attention fixed on his computer screen for a long moment. Eventually, he clears his throat and speaks. "I asked our PR department to write up a statement about the end of our relationship. I'm going through it now."

A lance of pain steals my breath. As if a frozen knife has pierced my chest, ice spreads from there to my limbs. "When... When are you...?" I can't even get the words out.

"The contract expires Friday, so we should plan for you to move home then. We'll release the statement the next day."

A sudden rush of tears blurs my vision. "I thought... I thought maybe things had changed."

There's a flicker in the depths of those golden eyes of his for just a second. Then he presses his lips together, stands and approaches me.

My heart tells me to run, but I'm frozen to the spot as he pushes my hair behind my ear, his fingers lingering on my skin.

"I won't lie, Violet. I've enjoyed this arrangement. I even considered extending the contract so I could spend more time with you. But when it comes down to it, I've never been interested in settling down permanently, and that hasn't changed. I don't want to drag this out and risk anyone's feelings getting more involved than they should be."

"Too late," I whisper as a hot tear drips down my cheek.

He catches it with his thumb and stares down at it, his throat bobbing as he swallows. "I'm sorry, butterfly. I should never have let it go so far. This is for the best though. You'll realize that soon enough."

He seems genuinely remorseful, and I think maybe that's worse than if he'd been uncaring. Though it doesn't matter. Either way, the result is the same. He doesn't want me anymore.

I won't let him see me fall apart. I wish I could go back

and handle the last minute differently, hide all evidence of my pain. Since I can't, I drag in a heavy breath of air, gather every ounce of strength I possess, and lift my chin. Then I force myself to meet his gaze. "I'll get started packing."

Emotion flashes across his face, but it's gone so quickly I can't name it. Maybe relief that I'm not making a scene? In the end, he nods silently and returns to his desk.

I put one foot in front of the other, headed toward the guest room, where the bulk of my belongings still reside.

But before I get far, he calls out to me, and I turn.

"It goes without saying that everything you've been given during the agreement belongs to you. Keep it all."

With a thick swallow to choke back my tears, I turn and leave. My heart is fracturing, and I can't get out of here fast enough.

The moment I'm inside the guest room with the door shut, I call Anna and ask her to pick me up. Then I shove the things I brought with me into my bags. I leave the designer dresses. Their presence would only remind me of Tate.

Then I go into his bedroom and collect the few things I left in there. When Anna messages me to tell me she's waiting outside the building, I quickly respond, then consider one last thing. For a long, painful moment, I study the ring glittering on my finger, struggling to swallow past the hard rock that's formed in my throat. It never meant anything, not if Tate's words and distance this morning are anything to go by, so why does it feel wrong to remove it? I can't wear it anymore. Maybe I could sell it, invest the money into True Brew. No. Just the thought makes the tightness in my chest start to burn. But, even as my heart cracks open wider, I slip the ring off my finger and set it on the side table. Blinking back tears, I take a final look around the room, shoulder one bag, grab the others, and walk out. As tempting as it is to just salvage my pride and leave the penthouse, I stop by Tate's office.

He doesn't notice me at first, so I take the opportunity to study him. His head is bowed, though the deep line between his brows is hard to miss. With the way he rubs his temple, he's clearly bothered by something. Is it an issue with Genesis-1? Whatever it is, it seems to be taking a toll on him. I have to fight the urge to walk in there, smooth my fingers over that crease in his brow and do what I can to ease his tension. He's made it clear he doesn't need or want that from me anymore.

Suddenly, he lifts his head, his eyes clashing with mine. When he spots the bags I'm carrying, he stands in a rush. "Where are you going?"

"Home, Tate. I'm going home." I'm too tired, too emotionally wrung out, to beat around the bush.

"You're leaving today?" He sounds almost panicked.

"Yes." I give him a small nod. "You don't need me anymore, and I... I just want to get... get back to my normal life."

He squeezes his eyes shut, and something like pain creases his face. When he looks at me again, the Tate I thought I knew—the real man behind the mask—is gone. He's back to the Tate I never would have fallen for. The careless playboy who lets everything slide off his back. I have to wonder if that's the real him. Maybe all along, I've been fooling myself into thinking I knew who he really was.

"Of course," he says, a practiced smile tilting his lips as he emerges from behind his desk and approaches. "You must be looking forward to getting back home. I'll make sure you still have security until any interest in our breakup dies down." His chin dips for the briefest of seconds. "I want you to be safe, Violet. Always."

I nod. I'm not going to argue with him. The last thing I want is to have reporters or paparazzi in my face when I'm trying to get over this... whatever this was. "Thank you."

He steps closer and lifts a hand, as if to touch my cheek.

But I can't. I just can't. I'm too close to crying again as it is. "No," I say.

He flinches and drops his hand to his side. Maybe he didn't do anything wrong—make me any promises—but I can't handle his touch right now.

With an audible swallow, he rakes a hand through his hair. "I'll get Jeremy to drive you home."

"That's okay. Anna is waiting for me downstairs. Can you arrange to have the rest of my things brought to me?"

"Of course." He regards me, his eyes bouncing between mine. When he speaks again, his voice is low. "Thank you, Violet. For all of this. Everything. I wish," he clears his throat, "I wish things could be different."

My throat is so tight I can barely talk. I force out a "me too," then turn to leave.

"Let me take you downstairs," Tate says.

I shake my head. "Please don't. Let's just end this the way it started. The way it should have stayed. Businesslike." I don't wait for his response. I whirl away and rush to the elevator. As it travels down, I touch the bare skin of my left ring finger.

And then the tears come.

CHAPTER FORTY-FIVE

TATE

I never knew how fucking empty and soulless this apartment was until Violet filled it with her warmth, then cleared her things out and left. Now that she's gone, being here is almost unbearable. She moved out three days ago. And for every minute since, I've argued with myself. Am I doing the right thing? Maybe I should tell her the truth. But if there's even the slightest risk that she could suffer the consequences of what I'm doing—what *we're* doing—I can't take that chance.

With Violet's engagement ring between my fingers, I slump into a dining room chair. I was too broken up when I realized she was leaving early to notice she wasn't wearing it. But when I forced myself to walk into our bedroom, I spotted it immediately, sitting on the side table.

I hoped she would keep it. But why would she after I ended things? I close my eyes and am once again hit with a memory of the look of devastation on her face when I told her it was over. Fuck. My chest compresses so acutely it's a struggle to take my next breath.

Maybe this is why my parents didn't care about us—

why my biological dad didn't stick around. Love fucking hurts. Loving someone and being forced to hurt them to protect them is a pain like no other. I tighten my hold on Violet's ring until one of the diamonds cuts into my palm. That sting is preferable to the ache in my chest.

Tonight, I'm set to attend my first public event without Violet since this thing between us began. Inside, my heart is in shards, but I have to put my game face on. I'll be photographed, and I can't look like I'm falling apart without her, just in case her asshole ex is watching. I don't doubt he's desperate enough to threaten me again if he catches on to my lies.

After shrugging on my suit jacket, I slip Violet's ring into my pocket, hoping like hell that keeping it with me will make what I'm about to do feel like less of a betrayal. At the very least, it will be the reminder I need to get me through tonight.

Halfway to the elevator, my phone rings in my pocket. Slowing, I pull it out, and my pulse spikes when Reid's name flashes on the screen. I swipe to answer it. "Hey, man. Please tell me you have good news."

"Too early for that," he says, and I do my best to force down my disappointment. "Thought I'd give you an update. My guy has tested the waters and thinks he'll have full access to Eric's accounts by the end of next week."

I rub my forehead and breathe deep, keeping my annoyance suppressed along with the disappointment. "That long? I thought you said he was good."

Reid grunts. "He is. He also doesn't want to leave any traces. If he gets caught hacking into Eric's work accounts, the blowback on all of us would be huge. And even taking into account his job, his security is disproportionately high. Which hopefully means he's got something to hide."

"So good and bad news, then?"

"Something like that." He huffs a sigh. "How are you holding up?"

"Not well. It's only been three fucking days, and I want to go over to her place, throw her over my shoulder and haul her back here."

He chuckles. "I never thought I'd see the day that Tate King would go all caveman over a woman."

"It's funny what love does to you."

"Love? Is that what it is?" Reid's voice is pitched high in surprise.

"That's exactly what it is." I may have to hide how I feel from the public, but that doesn't mean I have to hide it with my friends.

"Does she feel the same?"

I blow out a long breath. She hasn't said the words. Though neither have I. But her actions and her openness with me over the last few months make it possible to believe that she does. "I fucking hope so. Otherwise, I'm going to end up hurting like a bitch at the end of this."

When he speaks again, his voice is gentler. "I guess I better light a fire under my guy's ass, then. So you can get your girl back and ask her the question."

Squeezing my eyes shut, I shove my hand through my hair. "I'd appreciate it. I've got to go out tonight and pretend I actually want to socialize with people who would turn their backs on me in a second if my last name wasn't King."

"I get it, man. That's why you'll never see me at those events."

"Maybe when this is over, I'll retire. We can co-manage Onyx."

"If I thought for one second you meant that, I'd get an office set up for you right now. But we both know your relationship with your brothers will keep you on the top floor of that monstrosity for as long as they're there."

One corner of my mouth ticks up. He's right. Cole and Roman stood beside me without question while we made this plan with Reid. Hell, Roman didn't even hesitate to offer his help when I explained the situation to him. That simple act soothed something inside me that has craved a better relationship with my eldest brother for most of my life.

Now as long as I can ensure Eric can never threaten Violet again, I can turn my efforts to getting her back. If, by some miracle, she forgives me, then I'll have everything I never knew I wanted.

That thought sobers me. "I've got to go show my face. Keep me updated."

"You'll know as soon as I know."

Twenty minutes later, I climb out of the car and shove my hands into my pockets, steeling myself for what happens next. The press are lined up on either side of the entrance, so I make sure they get a good long look at me walking along the red carpet by myself.

"Tate! What happened to your fiancée?"

"Mr. King! Over here, Mr. King. Did you end it, or did Violet?"

This is what I want, but it's like rubbing salt in an already open wound. I ignore them and keep up my stride until I'm inside and working my way through the glittering crowd, heading directly to the bar. A drink is definitely needed if I'm going to get through this night.

I order a whiskey from the bartender and scan the space, looking for Roman. Instead, I spot a photographer working their way around the room, and as they near, I look for a likely target and quickly catch the eye of a familiar face. Perfect. Missy Myers, the daughter of a hedge fund manager. She's a socialite with a strong social media presence. Despite the way my stomach roils as I do it, I give her a thorough once-over, then let an inviting smile crook my lips. Just as I hoped, she returns my smile and makes her way over.

"Tate," she purrs as she reaches my side. "I'm surprised you're here all alone."

I'm surprised she hasn't heard the news. After taking a slightly too-long sip of my drink, I shrug. "You'll see a lot more of it going forward."

Her eyes widen. "What happened to your little shop keeper?"

I clench my whiskey glass in my hand at her tone. "Things didn't work out."

She affects a pout that isn't remotely sincere. "What a shame. Can I ask why?"

If this story were true, I'd let her know exactly what she could do with her curiosity. But since I want news to get out, I go along with it. "Unfortunately, this life isn't for everyone. And I suppose I didn't prepare her well enough for the pressure that comes along with being a King."

The sincerity in my voice is partially real, since there's a hint of truth to the statement.

Missy's mouth forms an O of surprise. "So, *she* left *you*?"

"It was a mutual decision."

She rests her hand on my arm, squeezing a little. "Well, her loss is our gain."

I force myself to give her a flirtatious smile. The fact that it's a shadow of my previous one is hopefully explained by my disappointment over my failed engagement.

With a long sip of my whiskey, I survey the area again.

When I catch sight of the photographer heading our way, I take a deep breath and turn back to Missy. Then, in a slow, casual move, I brush a strand of hair behind her ear. "I'm sure I'll eventually find a way to get past my disappointment."

Her eyes flare, and she wets her lips. "Maybe I could help you with that."

I tip my head low so it's close to hers, hoping to God I'm giving the photographer enough of an opportunity. "If I ever get over Violet, I'll be sure to let you know."

The seductive smile falls from her face as disappointment clouds her gaze. Then she steps forward and brushes my hip. "Maybe you just need a helping hand."

I angle away and smirk. "I have hands of my own."

She pouts, but I'm done with this act. If the damn photographer hasn't gotten the shot by now, he should be fired. It's hard to miss the irony that the attention I'm courting from the press now is exactly what I was trying to avoid by fake dating Violet in the first place. It would be funny if it wasn't so damn fucking heartbreaking.

"Well, it's been nice... catching up," I say. "But I need to find my brother. Have a good night."

"But Tate..."

I walk away, scanning the crowd for Roman. All I want is for this pretense to be over so I can have Violet back in my arms. But I'll attend a hundred of these events to make sure Eric doesn't win. That he'll never threaten her again.

I force a smile to my face and disappear into the crowd.

CHAPTER FORTY-SIX

VIOLET

The earthy aroma of freshly roasted coffee beans wafts through True Brew as I straighten chairs and wipe down tables. Tonight is our first tasting night, and I'm a jumble of excitement and anxiety. Worries about whether people will show up and what they'll think of our samples have haunted me all day.

I'll gladly soak in the trickle of panic those concerns bring, because beneath that is a deep well of pain. I haven't heard from Tate since I left my engagement ring at his apartment and walked out two weeks ago. Not only that, but I've seen the photos. Tate at various events with beautiful woman after beautiful woman. The last image I was confronted with flashes through my mind. A magazine spread open to the society pages: Tate standing too close to a stunning woman in a red dress that plunged nearly to her navel. They looked striking together. If I thought my heart couldn't break any more than it did when I left Tate's penthouse, then I was wrong. Seeing him so completely unaffected, as if he's forgotten about me already, has tears flooding my eyes at random times throughout the day.

I push those painful thoughts aside once again. I lost focus on True Brew for a while, let myself get distracted. But I won't allow myself to lose track of what's important ever again.

When I've finished setting out the tasting cups, I make my way to the counter. Despite my heartache, I can't help but smile at the sight of the variety of coffee blends in decorative labeled urns.

"Chin up, boss." Jarrod emerges from the back room. "Everything looks great. Tonight is going to be amazing."

I force a smile. "You think so?"

He squeezes my shoulder, his eyes warm with understanding. "I know so. Now, tell me what else I can do to help."

I breathe deep, letting the aroma of coffee and Jarrod's confidence bolster me. I've worked too hard—*we've* worked too hard—for this night to not be a success.

Tate be damned, I'll do my best to enjoy this moment.

"I'm here!" Anna dashes in from the back. "Tell me what I can do."

I rush to her and wrap my arms around her. "Thank you so much for coming."

"Always, Vi. I'll always come." She grasps my upper arms and holds me away from her to study my face. "Are you doing okay?"

Tears form on my lashes, but I blink them away. "I'll be fine." It's the same thing I've been telling her since she picked me up from Tate's.

"I know you will. You're going to be more than fine. Now, point me in the direction you need me."

"Help me arrange the pastries?"

"As long as I can steal one."

My laugh is watery but genuine. "You can have two."

I dive into setting out the pastry bites and pot after pot of rich, aromatic blends, forcing all thoughts of Tate and my broken heart out of my head. Tonight is about True Brew and Dad, not my tangled emotions. This is my chance to honor his legacy and prove that I can rebuild my life on my own terms.

When I stop in to check on Jarrod, he's finishing brewing the last few blends. "Almost done." He winks.

I pat his arm and give it a friendly squeeze. "What would I do without you?"

"Lucky you, you won't have to find out." His grin fades as his expression turns serious. "I'm here for you, Violet. Whatever you're going through, I've got your back."

My throat constricts. "Thank you, Jarrod. That means so much to me."

He watches me for a beat longer, then gives me a gentle smile and turns back to what he's doing.

Finally, we're ready. I unlock the door and wait, checking my watch a few times as my anxiety ramps up. But finally, the first customers trickle in. My nerves flutter, then turn to excitement as the initial arrivals greet me with smiles and enthusiastic comments.

A few minutes later, Mark and his girlfriend, Ashley, walk in. I give both of them big hugs. "Thank you so much for coming."

"As if we'd miss it," Mark says.

"It smells amazing in here." Ashley closes her pretty brown eyes as she inhales deeply.

With his hands in his pockets, Mark lifts his chin and peruses the shop, which now features matching seating, new artwork on the walls, and twinkle lights hanging from the ceiling. "You've really transformed the place, but it still feels the way it always did." He turns his warm gaze on me. "You did it, Violet. Dad would be so proud."

I look around, hit with a swift burst of happiness. I can picture Dad here, a smile stretching from ear to ear as he talked about the coffee beans he loved so much, his big booming laugh filling the room. "I think so too."

Mark leans close to his girlfriend. "Want to get started? I need to talk to Violet about something, then I'll join you."

Once she's headed to one of the tasting stations, Mark turns to me, his brows furrowed.

"So, how's it going being a free woman again?"

I try very hard to control my expression, but my chin wobbles, and for a moment, I'm not sure I can speak without breaking down.

Mark's frown grows deeper, and he takes a step closer. "Vi, he didn't hurt you... did he?"

I force my shoulders back. I have no interest in ruining Mark's friendship with Tate, or worse, giving him a reason to risk his job. After all, it's my fault for falling for a man I knew wasn't interested in settling down. No matter how much he might have enjoyed the few months of pretending. "He didn't hurt me. I'm just tired, that's all."

His frown eases a little, though it doesn't disappear completely. "You're sure? Because you know I'll kick his ass if he—"

I shake my head. "No ass kicking needed. I promise." I give him a kiss on the cheek. "Go join Ashely, have fun and tell me what you think of the coffees we chose."

Finally, the tension eases from his expression. He rubs his hands together. "I'm looking forward to it." When he spots Ashley, a soft smile tips up his lips.

With that look in his eyes, I can't help but wonder when he'll propose. The thought brings with it mixed emotions. I'm thrilled that he's found someone who makes him so happy, but even as the warmth of that sentiment spreads through me, a hard lump forms in my chest. I push it down. I'm happy for Mark, and tonight shouldn't be about Tate. It should be about True Brew and my family.

An hour later, the event is in full swing, and the atmosphere inside the shop is buzzing. Patrons fill the space, sipping samples of our carefully curated coffees while chatting and sharing their favorites. I flit from table to table, answering questions and soaking up their enjoyment, pouring out samples and explaining the origins of each blend as well as the process we go through to source them.

When I drop into a seat between Anna and Mark, I let out a deep sigh. My feet ache, but my heart is full.

"These tasting cards are a great idea," Anna says, waving the small booklet in front of me. "I love that I can easily compare the flavor profiles."

Slumped back in my chair, I fan my hot face. "I thought it would be nice to make it interactive."

As the earthy fragrance of the coffee tickles my nostrils, I'm filled with genuine contentment—a reminder of the simple joy that True Brew brought to my life, to my whole family.

Half an hour later, after I've made another round, I stop to take a deep breath and take the shop in again. The place is alive and vibrant, filled with conversation and laughter. We did it. We made Dad's dream a reality again.

I blink rapidly, willing the tears not to fall. He would have been so proud. Tonight is bittersweet, tinged with sorrow and joy in equal measure. I've found my purpose in the place he loved most. This is as much a new beginning for me as it is for True Brew. My chest aches with how much I wish Dad could be here to see it. But deep down, I know the truth. He never really left. His memory, along with Mom's, lives on in these walls, and in my heart as well as Mark's.

Despite the pride filling me, I can't shake the hollow ache that lies just underneath. For weeks, I've envisioned Tate here, sharing this moment with me. Yet while I'm here, pouring everything I have into this place, he's out there, back to living the life of a carefree playboy. The thought makes my stomach churn.

Jarrod catches my eye from behind the counter and gives me an encouraging smile, as if he senses my turbulent emotions. I nod at him, grateful as always for his support, then turn my attention back to the customers eagerly awaiting more samples. Keeping busy will help me get through this.

As the night draws to a close, I'm surrounded by the remnants of the successful event—empty cups, used napkins and crumbs from the pastries we offered. A feeling of accomplishment washes over me, but it also brings a wave of tiredness. I sag against the counter, exhaustion seeping into my bones. "We did it."

"We did." Jarrod steps up beside me, bumping my shoulder with his. "Your dad would be really proud of you, Violet. I know I am."

His words make my nose sting and my chest tighten. "Thank you. That means so much to me."

He flashes his dimples at me. "The turnout was even better than I expected. And the feedback was fantastic. All night, people asked when we were planning the next one."

Several customers asked me as well. It's incredible to

think they enjoyed the event so much they're already excited for another. With a smile, I survey the now-empty shop. What a mess, but oh so worth it. "Thanks again for all your help. I couldn't have pulled this off without you."

Jarrod grabs a damp cloth and gets to work wiping down tables. "We're a team, right?"

I nod, pulling out a garbage bag and clearing the leftovers.

As we clean up together, I'm grateful for the easy camaraderie we share. When we're finished, we step out of the shop together, and I lock the door behind us.

I let out a tired sigh, exhaustion really kicking in now that it's all over. And with the exhaustion comes the pain I've mostly been able to distract myself from for the last few hours. I don't want Jarrod to see it though. Not when I should still be on a high from the night. I muster another smile. "Thank you again, Jarrod. For everything."

He studies me, his mouth thinning as he sees straight through me. "I'm sorry you're hurting, Violet. You deserve better."

I've tried not to let on how sad I've been since things ended, particularly considering the short statement that Tate released to the press said the split was amicable, but there's only so much pretending I can do. "Thanks, I appreciate it."

"I was surprised when you told me it was over," he says thoughtfully. "Especially since he was so possessive of you. Even before you started dating."

I frown at him. "What do you mean?"

"He was jealous of me," Jarrod says, a small, slightly smug grin curving his lips. "I could sense it every time he came in."

I give my head a disbelieving shake. "Why didn't you say anything?"

He snorts. "It was amusing. And to be fair to him, it's not like I'm not attracted to you. Maybe if we'd met under different circumstances..." He shrugs, still with that half smile on his face. "But I'm well aware there'll never be anything more than friendship between us. So yeah, he never had anything to worry about when it came to me."

I stare up at him, struggling to take in what he's saying, not only about him being attracted to me, but that apparently Tate was jealous of him. I'm not sure if I believe it. Tate was protective while we were together, but nothing more than that. Then again, does it really matter if he was jealous? Being jealous doesn't mean you want the thing you're jealous over. Sometimes it just means you don't want anyone else to have it.

My mind flashes to Eric and how he used to quietly seethe if I spoke to other men, taking it out on me later in passive-aggressive arguments I could never win. That was never Tate though. Maybe he was jealous, maybe he wasn't, but he never took it out on me. He never blamed me for how my relationship with Jarrod might have made him feel.

I inhale shakily. Jarrod is still watching me, his brows drawn together. "I didn't mean to upset you."

I shake my head, tasting the tears I refuse to shed. Moved by his genuine care for me, I wrap my arms around him, finding comfort in the warm bulk of him. "Thank you. For being my friend. For being here for me."

He hugs me in return, a hard squeeze, then lets go. "Any day, boss." With a wink, he shoves his hands into his pockets and takes off down the sidewalk.

I sigh and head in the opposite direction, toward home, my mind drifting back to Tate—his smoldering eyes, his cocky grin, the way he made me feel so incredible. For a short time, I felt like the center of his world, and it was... beautiful.

But in the end, it was clear. Tate may be prepared to risk a lot, but never his own heart. He was only prepared to be reckless with mine.

CHAPTER FORTY-SEVEN

TATE

"Please fucking tell me you have good news this time."

Reid looks up at me, a grim smile crossing his face. "Sit down, and I'll fill you in."

I drop into a seat with a grunt and brace my elbows on my knees. "What did he find out?"

Reid taps on his keyboard. "Looks like our boy Eric has sticky fingers, and he dipped them into his uncle's honey pot."

Satisfaction rips through me. "He's been embezzling?"

Reid smirks. "To the tune of one million dollars. The bastard has been funneling money from campaign donations for ages. Until about two months ago, when the transfers suddenly stopped."

I study him, my mind working. "Do you think he got nervous?"

Reid nods slowly. "My guess is that someone got suspicious, and Eric's panicking, looking to replace what he took. Which is where you come in."

"He saw press coverage of Violet and me and figured he could use her to force me to give him the money." Maybe that's why he went to see her first. Maybe he thought he could convince her to ask me for the money. When that didn't work, he came straight to the source.

"Except you threw a wrench into his plan when you told him you didn't care." Reid's dark eyes meet mine. "Quick thinking there."

Pretending not to care about Violet is the last thing I should be praised for. "Now we need to remove the photos from Eric's possession and take him down. But in a way he can't trace to us or Violet. I don't want him catching wind of what's happening and releasing the photos as some form of twisted revenge."

Reid rubs his chin. "The timing has to be right. We can minimize links to you, but that doesn't mean Eric will write it off as a coincidence. But we could set things in motion so he gets arrested, and if we do things right, we can wipe all evidence of the photos from his system simultaneously."

"Can your guy do it?"

"If anyone can, he can."

"Okay." I lean back in my chair and take my first deep breath in weeks. "We leak it to the senator through a third party. From what I know of the man, he won't overlook this kind of betrayal. It'll be discreet, quick. He'll take care of informing the police about Eric's activities. Then the moment we get tipped the arrest is going to happen, your guy goes in and scrubs every digital footprint of those photos from Eric's system."

"And once the asshole is arrested, he'll be too busy dealing with legal hell to think about you or Violet. Everything will be tightly contained. There shouldn't be any blowback to you or the King Group."

As much as I want to look Eric in the eye when he's

taken down, I won't risk drawing attention to myself or my brothers. I let out a breath. "I owe you one, Reid."

"Considering you took a chance on me and helped me get this place up and running, I'd say helping to keep the future Mrs. Tate King safe is the least I can do."

Fuck. I hope she'll agree to be the future Mrs. Tate King again once this is all over. But I may have destroyed any chance I had with her, so there's no point in dwelling on that now.

I incline my head. "Let's get this done."

FORTY-FIVE MINUTES LATER, Jeremy's driving past True Brew. I can't be seen anywhere near Violet until Eric has been arrested, the photos are gone for good, and Reid's hacker is in the clear. But fuck if I don't want to see her.

Every evening since she left, I've asked Jeremy to drive past the shop. Most days, I'm not lucky enough to catch her leaving work. I savor the days I am. Tonight, we're driving past later because it was Violet's first tasting night. The thought causes a screw to tighten in my chest.

I should have been there.

Jeremy slows, and I straighten in my seat as Violet and Jarrod come into view. They're standing close to one another at the front door. A sharp pain lances my chest at the sight. I have no right to be upset, considering I announced to the world that we're not together anymore, but I don't fucking like it.

A moment later, they embrace, and tension ratchets my back.

Fuck.

It takes all my willpower to remain where I am. More

than anything, I want to burst out of the car, claim her and remind her and the world that she's mine. Only she isn't mine, and she never really was. Not in the way I wanted her to be. And maybe she never will be.

Jarrod gives her a lopsided grin, and Violet tilts her face up to him, expression warm.

My fingers curl into fists, even as bands tighten around my chest. She has no idea about the position she's ended up in because of me. I took what I needed and exposed her to the world. My selfishness put her back in the path of a man who already hurt her once and was prepared to do it again to protect himself.

Maybe she's realized she's better off with a man like Jarrod. A man who can work side by side with her. A man who won't take over her life and then crush her. After all, True Brew is thriving now. She doesn't need me anymore. And she definitely doesn't need the shit that comes along with my family name.

"Keep driving," I tell Jeremy. Once we've passed, I slump back in my seat and stare out the window. Maybe I'm reading too much into what could be a casual sign of affection between them. But being with me thrust Violet into a world of chaos. My world. One where others will use you for what you have and the press pries into every corner of your life. Jarrod represents the opposite—stability, safety, a life away from the relentless scrutiny that follows me.

I close my eyes and will away the what-ifs and maybes that haunt me.

From the beginning, my plan has been to win Violet back after Eric was taken care of. Selfishly, I was only considering what I wanted, not what was good for her. But I can't think about that now. Regardless of what happens between us after this, keeping her safe from Eric's threats is the priority, and that's what I need to focus on.

"Should we go home, sir?" Jeremy asks.

I tap my fingers on the armrest, then shake my head. "Take me back to the office, please."

Without a word, Jeremy turns the car around and heads back to King Plaza. I'm not sure what I'm looking for, but the only person I can think of to talk to about this is Cole. Hopefully, he'll still be at work.

When I step off the elevator on the fifty-third floor and mindlessly make my way down the hall, I find Samson at his desk outside Cole's office. "Is my brother in?" I ask him.

Samson's brows rise up in surprise. "No, he left early to take Delilah away for the weekend."

Damn it. I scrub my hand over my face. If I was thinking straight, I would have called ahead.

With a half-hearted thanks, I head back to the elevator. As I approach, Roman's voice stops me.

"I thought you'd gone for the day."

He's standing in front of the stainless-steel doors, hands in his pockets, expression stony as always.

"I had. Just came back to talk to Cole about something." Head down, I hit the button for the elevator.

"Is it something I can help with?"

With a long breath out, I survey him. "It's not work related."

He rocks on his heels, his brows drawing together as he studies me. He clears his throat. "I'm game if you are."

What the hell. Maybe Roman will have some words of wisdom for me.

I give him a small nod, and when he turns on his heel, I follow him back to his office. I expect Roman to take a seat behind his desk once we enter, but instead, he heads to the couches facing each other in the corner.

He settles on one, so I drop into the other. "I'm going to take a guess and assume this is about your fake fiancée," he says.

"She's not any kind of fiancée anymore."

"There's a reason for that though." His gray eyes assess me. "You're not making this permanent, are you?"

I tap my thumb on my thigh. "I'm wondering if I should."

Roman arches a brow and crosses his ankle over his knee. "Why would you think that?"

"I don't know if I'm what she needs." The confession tastes bitter on my tongue.

His eyes narrow slightly. "You're a billionaire. Who better to give her what she needs?"

The vise squeezing my chest tightens further. "*I* want to be what makes her life better, not my money. But I can't help but think she'd be better off with someone else. Someone normal."

"From what I've seen, Violet makes her own choices. And unless I'm misreading what I saw of your interactions when you were together, she chose you, complications and all."

"Did she really choose though?" I voice the uncertainty out loud for the first time.

Roman leans back and crosses his arms, his expression thoughtful. "What's brought on this doubt?"

I clear the emotion from my throat and rough a hand down my face. "What if it's like Stockholm syndrome? She's been forced to be with me, to pretend she loves me. She didn't even like me before this whole thing started. And it's not just about that. I saw her with Jarrod outside her shop. They seemed... comfortable. Normal."

Roman's lips tilt up with the hint of a smirk. "So you think she's better off with someone like that? Someone without the King baggage?"

"Isn't she? We're not exactly the poster family for loving relationships and emotional stability. And with Dad—"

Roman cuts in. "Dad's actions are his own. Don't let his actions define you."

"It's more complicated than that."

"Complicated because you're making it so. You're a King. You can make things as easy or as complicated as you want them to be."

"Am I though? A King, I mean." It comes out more challenging than I meant it to.

Roman sits up, a flicker of understanding in his eyes. "Ah. So this is about your place here. I wondered if you were ever going to broach the subject."

Annoyance sparks in my chest, and I sit straighter as well. "And you had no plan to, did you? I've lived with this knowledge hanging over my head for almost all my life. And no one has ever brought it up with me."

His brows pull together. "You closed yourself off to us, Tate. Stopped sharing the real you. Became this playboy who didn't care—"

"Easier to be the playboy than to risk being unwanted."

"You've never been unwanted. Not by Cole and not by me. To us, you've always been our brother."

I lean back, swallowing against the tightness in my chest his words trigger. "I've spent my life feeling like I was on the outside looking in. Trying to live up to a name that I'm not even sure is mine to claim."

"It's not the name that defines us. It's what we do with

it. You're more than just a title, more than Mom's secrets and Dad's resentment."

I scrub my hands over my face. "But what if I've made that who I am? The playboy, the flirt, the charmer, the one who always walks away."

"You have the power to redefine yourself. You need to see yourself through your own eyes. Not Dad's, not the tabloids', not even Cole's or mine."

I nod slowly, my heart lodging itself in my throat. "You're right." I've spent my whole life letting my uncertainty over who I am and where I fit in my family define me. Seeking validation from those women who only cared about my name, while never letting anyone close enough to see the real me. In case the real me wasn't someone worth knowing—or loving.

But I let Violet see. Letting her in was as effortless as breathing. She saw who I really am, and she still wanted to make this relationship real. And that's worth something. It's worth everything. *She's* worth everything. And I won't take this choice away from her because of my own issues.

"Deal with the past, in whatever way helps," Roman says. "But don't let your history dictate your future. Not who you want to be or what you want to do with your life. And definitely not who you share it with."

I sit in silence, letting his words sink in. This is more than just making sure I'm what Violet needs. It's about confronting the demons that have haunted me since that boy first sneered the word bastard at me when I was seven.

"I need to resolve this once and for all." With a nod, I stand and tug at my cuffs. Before I go to Violet, I need to talk to someone else. Someone I should have confronted a long time ago.

Roman stands too, a glimpse of understanding crossing

his face. "Do what you have to do. Talk to who you have to talk to. But remember, you're not defined by anyone else's actions. You never were."

The small smile I give him is genuine. "You've been holding out on me."

He cocks his head. "What do you mean?"

"You're not bad at this big brother stuff when you put your mind to it."

I expect him to brush me off, but instead, a faint smile softens the harshness of his usual expression. "Maybe I should put my mind to it more often, then."

CHAPTER FORTY-EIGHT

VIOLET

"Another glass?" Anna waves the almost-empty bottle of champagne at me.

I swallow the last of my first glass, the bubbles tickling the back of my nose, and hold it out for a refill.

She fills it halfway and drains the dregs into her own glass, then holds it up to me. "Cheers to you, Vi. For turning True Brew around and making your family and friends proud."

I give her a smile, though it's not as big as it should be.

She quirks a brow and brings her champagne to her lips as she waits.

I let out a sigh. "I'm thrilled with how things are going, but..." I pick at a loose thread on the couch. "It doesn't feel like just my success. It feels like Tate's as well. I couldn't have done it without him."

With a frown, Anna gets up on her knees. "He may have provided the money—for a *service*—but it was your hard work that brought it back, that got people in the door and reintroduced customers to your amazing coffee."

"You're right." I firm my spine, willing myself to accept

those truths. "I'm not going to let a broken heart take away from what I've achieved." Even though it doesn't feel the way it should without Tate here. Even though it feels like something's missing.

"That's what I like to hear. I—"

She's cut off by the sound of her phone pinging. She picks it up to check the notification, and her mouth drops open.

"What is it?"

"Eric," she says. "He's been arrested."

"What?" I snatch the device from her hand and skim the news report.

Senator's Nephew Arrested Amongst Accusations of Embezzling.

The headline is accompanied by a photo of Eric, looking smug and arrogant, alongside a photo of his uncle. Underneath are a few paragraphs spelling out the minor details that were discovered about Eric's crimes at the time of publication.

"I can't believe it," I whisper.

"I'm not sure why," Anna says. "He's proven himself to be a grade A piece of narcissistic shit. He probably thought he was too smart to get caught."

I shake my head, but it's true. I can imagine him thinking exactly that. "Why did you get a notification about this?"

"After Eric confronted you at True Brew, I set up a Google alert. He was obviously up to something."

I shake my head, stunned. My first instinct is to call Tate. He was so upset about what Eric had done to me, he'd probably be happy to hear that the jerk has been arrested. Except, maybe I'm wrong. Maybe he wouldn't care. A hard lump forms in my throat. I still can't reconcile the man in his office that afternoon, the one who was so tender, so protective, to the one who watched me walk away without any protest whatsoever.

My heartache must be written all over my face, because Anna leans in and gives me a hug. "If he doesn't see what he let go, then he doesn't deserve you."

Tears sting my eyes. "I have you, and Mark, and that's the most important thing."

"You know." Her expression brightens. "You still have your Onyx membership. Maybe you should—"

"Oh no," I say. "I don't think sex clubs are for me. I've crossed it off my bucket list now, so I'm good."

Anna laughs. "Along with dating a billionaire? Not many can cross that one off."

"You're right. I should appreciate the experience. How many people can say they've lived in a penthouse over-looking Central Park?"

"And you have so much more to look forward to."

I nod. I wish I could get past this pain slicing through me so I could truly believe it myself.

An hour later, after Anna has gone home, I'm sitting on my couch staring at my phone. I brush my thumb over the screen, and before I can second-guess myself, I tap the Call button, waiting with bated breath as it rings.

A click on the other end makes my pulse leap, but it's quickly followed by a recording. The sound of Tate's deep voice, holding that thread of amusement, makes my chest squeeze.

I consider hanging up, but instead take a deep breath to bolster my courage. When the phone beeps, I clear my throat. "Hi, Tate, I'm not sure if you saw the news, but it looks like Eric's been arrested. I thought you might like to know, but I guess... I guess you're busy." My chest constricts, so I wrap the call up quickly. The last thing I want to do is embarrass myself by bursting into sobs. "I hope you're well. Bye."

I hit the End Call button, throw the phone onto the couch, and cover my face with my hands. God, I probably sound clingy. Like all those women dying for another night with him. I wrap my arms around myself. He's probably with some leggy blonde right now.

I lie down, curling myself into a little ball on the couch, and let the tears I can't seem to escape fall once more.

CHAPTER FORTY-NINE

TATE

I pull up outside the house I grew up in, taking in the huge expanse of brick. Roman probably assumed I was planning to confront Dad. But Dad is a cold, petty man who resented having to raise a son who wasn't his, nothing more. If I want answers to my questions about who I am, then there's only one person I can ask.

The door swings open before I have a chance to knock, and I'm confronted by the familiar face of the estate's steward. "Good morning, sir," he says, his tone as disapproving as always. I don't take it personally. He sounds that way regardless of who he's talking to.

"Morning, Peters. Is my mother in?"

He nods and steps back. "She's in the solarium."

I pass by him, not bothering with small talk. Peters would find it distasteful.

The sound of my footsteps on the marble floor echoes as I make my way through the huge, empty house to the solarium. For the first time, I wonder why Mom still lives here. Now that Dad's in prison, she's all alone except for the staff.

I shouldn't care. And maybe I wouldn't have in the past,

but loving Violet, being loved by her, has changed things. There's a tinge of sadness that wasn't there before. What must it be like to rattle around in this mansion knowing she has no one who cares enough to be with her?

I shrug off the thought. I'm here for answers, not to empathize with a woman who doesn't want it.

Mom is sitting at the table in the solarium, her ash blond hair swept up off her face. She's sipping tea from a delicate bone china cup and staring out through the glass to the flat green grounds of the estate.

The sound of my shoes on the three steps leading down draws Mom's attention.

Her brows arch. "Tate? I wasn't expecting you this morning."

"Apologies for not calling ahead," I say, taking a seat at the table.

She puts her cup down and regards me with a small, wary frown. Is she anticipating the questions I'm about to ask her? Has she spent years waiting for this day to come?

"How have you been the last few weeks?" she asks, shocking me.

"Fine." I say a little stiffly. "Why do you ask?"

She tilts her head and assesses me with those icy blue eyes. "Your normal... spirit... has been missing."

"My spirit?"

"Yes. That," she waves her hand in the air, "flair for living you've always flaunted."

Flaunted? "You mean the 'not acting like a cold fish at all times' type of flaunting?"

The corner of her mouth twitches infinitesimally. "Yes. Something like that. I thought it might be related to the end of your... arrangement."

The lancing pain that hits me in the chest at inopportune times returns. "It stopped being an arrangement a long time ago."

"Apparently so." She eyes me.

With a deep breath, I push away the pain. I've let myself get distracted. "I'm not here to talk about Violet. I'm here to finally find out the truth."

One pale brow arches. "The truth?"

"My father."

She keeps her composure but looks away. "If you have questions for your father, you could visit him in prison and ask him yourself."

I don't bother to reply, just wait her out.

Finally, she sighs. "There's nothing to say, Tate."

Anger burns through my veins. "You might have nothing to say. But I have plenty. Do you know what it was like growing up in this house? How fucking cold and empty it was? You and Dad didn't care about the three of us. We only had each other. And then I found out the truth, and suddenly I didn't have that anymore. At least it didn't feel like I did."

She's frowning at me. "Why should the situation with your father have any effect on your relationship with your brothers?"

I throw my hands up in the air. "Because I didn't know who I was anymore. They were the legitimate sons. The wanted sons. The true heirs to the King name. And who was I? I had no clue because I had no clue where I came from—who my real father was. And now that he's dead, I'll never get a chance to find out all the things I was desperate to know."

Mom's face blanches. "He's dead?"

I pause, studying her expression. "You didn't know?"

She shakes her head mutely, her lips pressing together

for a moment before she takes another sip of her tea. When she sets it down again, the cup rattles against the saucer. Then she inhales deeply, composing herself. "No, I didn't know. After he left, I never saw him again. I did my best to... to forget."

"Forget?" The word is bitter in my mouth. "How convenient for you. But what about me? What about the son he left behind?"

The icy composure she's hidden behind for as long as I can remember falters, revealing a hint of emotion. "I concealed the truth to protect you."

"To protect *me*?" I scoff, leaning forward. "You mean to protect yourself. Your image. The family name."

She keeps her chin high as she regards me, though there's a shadow of something that might be vulnerability in her eyes. "Yes, those things too. I defied your father when it came to you. I didn't know what it would mean for me."

"Why did you bother? You've never given any indication you care about me. Or my brothers."

What looks suspiciously like pain flashes across her face. "I was twenty-one when I was married off to your father. Twenty-two when I had Roman. I was scared, but I hoped... I *had* hoped that I would be a good mother, different from my own." She focuses on the table in front of her, brushing a hand over the spotless tablecloth. "But after he was born, I didn't know what to do with him, how to hold him, to soothe him when he cried or make him happy. My maternal instincts were... not what I wanted them to be. I realized then that I was just like my mother after all. Watching my baby smile and laugh when the nanny held him only solidified what I already knew. I was never made to be a mother."

I've never seen this side of her before, the human side.

It's hard to know what to make of it. I don't comment, hoping she'll continue. Give me insight into my own childhood.

"But your father wanted another son. He was... persistent. Five years later, Cole was born. And once again, it became clear that I wasn't the motherly type. I thought I was done then. Your father had what he wanted. But when I found out I was pregnant with you, Ted was... very unhappy. It was only then I realized I did have some modicum of motherly instinct after all."

"You kept me," I state.

She nods, expression impassive.

"Why? Why go through all that if you weren't interested in being my parent?"

She traces the rim of her teacup, her attention fixed on the liquid within. "I couldn't bring myself to do what your father wanted. But I still didn't know how to be a mother, not in the way you needed. The best I could do was keep up the façade. Ensure you received the same benefits as your brothers."

It's hard for me to wrap my head around that, so I file it away for later.

"And my real father, did he ever know about me?" I ask. Maybe after all this time, I'm still seeking some connection to the man who was half of who I am.

She looks away. "No. He left before I found out. There didn't seem to be much point in tracking him down."

"So I was an unplanned consequence of a fleeting affair that meant nothing."

"You're more than a consequence, Tate." Her tone is as close to gentle as I've ever heard it.

I stare down at my lap, my throat tight as I pick at an

invisible speck on my pants. "Can you tell me about him? My father?"

"I don't know much. Christian worked here for a few months. As a gardener, and he was..." She looks out the window. "Kind. He was kind to me. Polite, even at the start, when I wasn't." A faint smile tilts her lips. "And funny. He managed to make me laugh when not many things could."

She sighs and meets my gaze, her blue eyes a shade warmer than I'm used to seeing them. "You look like him. You have the same smile, the same wit. I wish I could tell you more, but we didn't share many personal details. Why would we? He was passing through, and I was married."

I nod woodenly, racking my brain for other questions I'd like answered and coming up with nothing. When I arrived, I assumed my mother wouldn't tell me anything. Though what she's told me isn't much, it's enough to loosen a screw in my chest that's been tight for too many years.

And maybe that's all I need.

I stand and push my fingers through my hair. "Thank you." I turn to leave her to her tea, but her next words stop me.

"I'm sorry, Tate. I wasn't meant to be a mother. I don't have that kind of selflessness." She swallows. "I wish that I did."

For a moment, I consider that, consider her. "The time when we needed a mom is long gone. But you can still be part of our lives. A real part, if that's what you want. No one's asking you to start baking cookies, but you have a choice. You might not have felt as if you could love us the way a mother should love her sons back then, but nothing's stopping you from caring for us as the men we are now. Because at the end of your life, all of this"—I gesture around at the solarium and the estate beyond—"isn't going to matter one fucking bit. What will matter is knowing that you cared and were cared for. That your life was well lived, that your family will remember you when you're gone. And all you need to do to have that is to show up for us."

Her normally cool gaze is shadowed. "Distance has always been my armor. It was how I grew up, how I dealt with your father—" She winces. "I mean Ted. It's the only way I knew how to make it through."

It's hard to get a grip on the emotions that rush through me as I look at her—resentment, hurt... sympathy. A part of me wonders how things might have turned out for her—for all of us—if Dad had been different. If he'd shown her what it was like to be cared for rather than treated as a means to an end. After all, look at how I've changed, how Cole's changed, since finding love.

For the first time, regret washes over Mom's face. "I can't change the past, Tate. But I want you to know that, despite how it might have appeared, I am proud of the man you've become. Of the men all three of you have become."

Her words, so unexpected, cause an ache deep in my chest and leave me momentarily speechless. I came here wanting answers, perhaps even a confrontation. But instead, I've been given a glimpse into my mother's struggles, her reasons, flawed as they are. While this conversation hasn't healed old wounds, it has helped shed some light on the shadows of my past.

"And I'm," she clears her throat, "I'm glad."

"About?"

"I'm glad you found someone. Violet seems... kind. You and Cole. I'm glad you have people who... care about you."

I bite back the automatic response. That she should have been one of the people who cared about us all along.

What's the point? I'm sick of looking back. All I want now is to look to the future. To *my* future. "I don't have Violet."

A shadow of a smile touches Mom's lips. "If I know anything about you, once your mind is set on something, you'll find a way to do it. And I think perhaps you've set your mind on that young woman."

I smile back, perhaps the first genuine smile I've given her in years, then start for the door, determination lengthening my stride. "I think you're right."

CHAPTER FIFTY

VIOLET

With a sigh, I curl my feet up under me on my small but comfy couch. Work was busy once again. While that makes me incredibly happy, coming home to my quiet, empty apartment, which never used to bother me, now just twists the knife in my heart a little harder.

I'm in my pajamas and flicking through the channels, looking for something to distract me from the hollow that seems to live permanently behind my ribs now, when there's a knock on my door.

I sit up, nerves prickling down my spine. Who's visiting this late at night? Anna would message me if she was coming over.

After tossing the remote on the cushion, I make my way to the door. When I peer through the peephole, my heart spasms and I lose my breath. His broad chest and wide shoulders have become as familiar to me as my own reflection. The chiseled jaw I know so well is currently clenched tight, a muscle twitching in it.

Instead of opening the door, I take a step back. I'm not sure I'm ready to hear what Tate has to say. Whether he's here to reaffirm the current non-state of our relationship or to maybe tell me he misses me as much as I miss him, I can't allow myself to be vulnerable again. He let me go so easily. What's to say he wouldn't do it again?

"I know you're in there, Violet," his deep voice comes through the door. "I don't blame you for not wanting to talk to me, but you need to hear what I have to say. If you want to kick me out afterward, I'll go. Although I can't promise I'll stay gone."

With my hands pressed to my chest, I heave in one deep breath, then another, willing my pulse to steady. I realize then that I'm touching the bare skin on my left ring finger and drop my hands in a rush.

"Violet." His voice is lower now, rougher. "Please."

The tension in his tone forces me forward. With a shaking hand, I unlock the door and swing it open.

For a moment, we stand like that, one on each side of the threshold, staring at each other.

Tate's throat moves in a swallow. "Can I come in?"

The nod I give him is jerky, but I step back to allow him to pass. I try not to inhale as he does, but the familiar fresh, masculine scent of him reaches me anyway. My fingers tighten around the handle, and I close the door a little harder than I intended to.

I move around him, not sure where to position myself in the small space where we won't be too close. When I meet his gaze, his golden eyes have darkened to bronze.

"I left a message for you." The moment I utter the words, I cringe. Why bother reminding us both that he didn't bother to answer or return my call?

"I know." His muscles bunch as if he wants to move, to come closer, but he keeps his feet planted where they are. "I needed to make a decision before I let myself speak to you."

"Let yourself?"

He nods slowly. "I hurt you, Violet, and it killed me to do it. I wanted to make sure I wasn't going to inadvertently do it again."

My chest is so tight it's hard for me to speak. "So you needed to go back to your old ways to make sure you were really okay with giving that up?"

His jaw clenches. "I never went back to my old ways. There's no going back to that. Not now that I've had you."

I cross my arms to fortify myself and hide my trembling hands. "I saw you, Tate. I saw the photos of you with those women. They made it very clear that you'd moved on without any difficulty."

This time he does step toward me, but I hold up my hand to stop him. Allowing him to get too close is what caused this heartbreak to begin with.

He rocks back on his heels and grips the back of his neck. "You believing I'd moved on was exactly what I needed. It's what I needed everyone to believe. Particularly Eric."

Shock reverberates through me, and I drop my arms. "What does Eric have to do with this?"

With a heavy exhale, Tate scrubs his hand over his mouth. "You know Eric was arrested for embezzling. What you don't know is that he tried to extort me in order to replace the money he stole."

Now it's me rocking back. "What? When? *How*?"

"The day I went to Onyx. Eric came to see me at my office that afternoon. After I got him to leave, I needed to talk to Reid. I needed his help handling the situation."

I shake my head. "But what could he possibly have to hold over your head? You've never even met before."

This time when Tate moves toward me, I'm too shocked

to keep space between us. He cups my shoulders, holding me gently in place. There's a line between his brows, and for the first time, I notice the shadows under his eyes.

"What did Eric do?" I whisper.

"He had compromising photos."

I blink. "How would he get photos of you?" A sudden thought occurs to me, and it's followed by a slow roll of nausea. "Were they during our arrangement? Did he catch you with... with another woman?"

"Fuck, no," he says, pain flashing across his features. "I haven't touched another woman that way since you came into my life again, Violet." He sighs. "They were photos of you."

I stare at him blankly. "Me? But I didn't do anything while we were together."

"They were taken when you were with him."

My insides twist sharply. "What?" It comes out with hardly any breath behind it.

He rubs my shoulders soothingly. "He took photos of you without your knowledge when you were being intimate. I'm so fucking sorry, Violet. He's a piece of shit who deserves everything he's got coming to him."

"No." I shake my head. "No. He wouldn't." I search his face for a hint of doubt. For any inkling that he may be wrong. But the rigid set of his jaw and the fire in his eyes tells me the truth, and a stone settles in my gut. "I can't believe it," I whisper. "I can't believe he'd do that." Tears spring to my eyes. God, I'm so tired of crying. It's exhausting.

"There was no way I'd let him hold those photos over your head and risk the possibility that he'd use them later when he needed something. Or, God forbid, threaten you with something worse. The only way I could think to handle it was to tell him the truth but lie through my teeth at the same time."

Understanding hits me. "You told him about the arrangement?"

He nods, worried eyes scanning mine. "I told him I didn't care what he did with the photos because our arrangement was temporary. He left, but I knew he'd be watching. So Cole, Roman, Reid and I removed any threat he might pose in the future. Him and those fucking photos. But it took time."

"The photos are gone?" My voice shakes as I ask the question.

He nods. "Every copy deleted."

The relief I should be feeling is dulled by shock. How could this have happened? I wrap my arms around myself, as if I can hold myself together. "Why couldn't you just tell me? Why did you have to make me feel so unwanted?"

Tate steps back and pushes his hand through his hair. "What we did wasn't legal, and I couldn't risk you getting caught up in that if it went wrong. If things went to hell and the police got involved, you couldn't be implicated. If you knew, you could be charged with conspiracy or as an accessory."

I stumble to the couch and sit as his words sink in. "So you ended our engagement and kept me in the dark to keep me safe?"

His only response is a simple nod.

I don't know what to think. My head is rattling so much I can barely process everything he's telling me. Eric turning out to be a criminal and someone who would betray me even more than he already had. Tate protecting me by breaking my heart. Everything that's happened over the last few months. The last few *years*. Even True Brew finally turning around. It's all too much.

A chill settles in my chest, and my body shakes. Tate sits beside me, and I let him gather me in his arms. I'm desperate to wrap my own arms around him and hold tight, to let him anchor me when I feel so untethered, but I can't do it. My thoughts are whirling around my head, and my muscles are taut. I can see Tate's reasoning. How he thought he was doing the right thing. I can't fault him for that, but the last few weeks have been devastating. I've cried almost as much as I did when Dad died. My heart has been torn to shreds. I fought so hard to protect myself against Tate, only to fall for him anyway. And then the rug was ripped out from beneath me just the way I feared.

"Violet," he murmurs. "I'm sorry. I'm so fucking sorry that I hurt you, that Eric hurt you."

There's no stopping the tears that overflow. Before I can wipe them away, he brushes his thumbs over my skin. The tender move only sharpens the pain. He watches me, his eyes swimming with so much emotion. Grief and regret and a pain of his own mingle in his gaze.

I grasp his wrists but don't remove his hands from my face. "What are you doing here, Tate? Why did you come?" My voice wavers as I ask the questions.

"Isn't it obvious? I never wanted to let you go, Violet. I wouldn't have if it wasn't for Eric. Now that he's out of the picture, and there's no risk to you, I want you back. And not a fake relationship this time. I want it to be real. I want you in my apartment, in my bed. I want my ring back on your finger."

My heart flip-flops, as if struggling to beat the way it should. "What are you saying?"

"I want you to be my fiancée. I want to marry you.

Having you, loving you, it's opened my eyes to all I've been missing."

Those words should stitch this tattered mess inside my chest back together. I should be throwing myself into his arms right now, but I feel so bruised and so battered that I'm practically numb. "I don't know what to do with that. You broke my heart, and now you're telling me you love me, and it was all to protect me. This, all of this, has moved so fast. Nothing that's happened between us has been normal."

His brows draw down. "And is normal what you want?"

I pull his hands away from my face and press my fingers to my temple. "I don't know. I just don't want the rug pulled out from under me again. Dad, Eric, you." Doubt and confusion churn in my mind. "How do you know you really want *me* and not just the first woman you've let yourself get close to? What if we make this real, and you realize I'm not actually the right one, I'm just the right now? That it was just this situation that made you feel this way about me?"

He presses his lips together, but surprisingly, his eyes seem to dance with a hint of amusement. "You mean like Stockholm syndrome?"

"Yes, like that."

He smiles softly. "It's not Stockholm syndrome, I promise. And I'm more than happy to show that to you. I understand if it's hard to forgive me. I understand if the idea of a relationship with me, a real one, is overwhelming. If you need time, take it. I'll be here. I won't leave you again, Violet. I won't hide how I feel. Take the time, but I won't let you convince yourself I don't care, that I want anyone but you."

With a brush of his fingers over my jaw, he's gone, and I'm left alone with a heart full of too many emotions. I slump back against the couch and close my eyes. The room feels emptier, the silence louder. Tate's words echo in my mind, a chaotic mix of questions I have no answers to.

Deep down, I know this isn't about Tate. It's about me. I love him, I do. Seeing him today, it felt like the first time I could take a deep breath since we ended. But I'm paralyzed. Frozen somewhere between hope and fear. In the last few weeks, I've done my best to rebuild the walls he tore down, and now he's asking me to let them fall again.

I just need a moment, space to breathe and find my feet after being buffeted around.

I hope by taking time to think, I'm not making a terrible mistake.

I STEP out of the front door of my apartment block, ready to head to work, but my feet stutter to a halt at the sight of the black town car waiting at the curb. Jeremy is propped against the passenger door, arms crossed and a smile on his face.

I peer into the back of the car. The windows are tinted dark, but it doesn't look as if Tate is waiting inside. Even so, my pulse kicks into high gear as I approach. "It's lovely to see you, Jeremy, but I'm not sure what you're doing here."

"Mr. King wants to make sure you get to and from work safely every day."

"But if you're driving me, then how is he going to get to work?"

The corners of his eyes crinkle. "He claims he was getting too lazy being driven around all the time and wants to drive himself from now on."

My heart swells, and I blink back a sudden rush of tears. I'm honestly surprised I have any left by now. "Thank you.

And thank Tate for me too. I'd tell you not to worry about driving me, but I have a feeling he won't take no for an answer."

"You know him well," Jeremy says, opening the door for me.

Maybe I should be annoyed that Tate isn't leaving me alone to think, but I'm not. After the last few weeks and after seeing reports of him with woman after woman, even if I know now it wasn't real, I've been left shaken. But knowing he's thinking about me floods my chest with warmth.

As I slide into the back seat, my hand brushes a folded note lying on the black leather. On top of it is a single violet.

I pick up the delicate little flower and twirl it between my fingers. For a moment, I close my eyes and let myself think back to the first time he showed up at my door. Back then, I never could have guessed how things would turn out. My lips tremble up into a smile, and I tuck the flower behind my ear like he did that night.

As Jeremy starts the car, I unfold the note.

Violet,

The very first time I saw you, you were eating Cheerios at the breakfast bar in the apartment Mark and I shared. You were wearing a blue tank top that matched the color of your eyes. Trying not to stare at my friend's little sister was damn near impossible. I made a terrible impression on you that day, and you made a lasting one on me. I didn't know then how much you'd change my life.

Always yours,
Tate

I wipe more tears from my cheeks. I can't believe he remembers what I was wearing the first time we met. Never once did I think I'd made even the tiniest impression on him back then. Clutching the note in my hand, I stare out the window at the people and cars we're passing.

When Jeremy lets me out in front of True Brew, I'm still in my own world. As I go about opening the shop, I run through what Tate said last night and even pull his note back out for a reread, but when I flip the sign on the door to open, and customers start to stream in, I push aside my chaotic emotions and confused thoughts and focus on work.

But that afternoon, when I step back out of the shop and lock up, Jeremy's there, a smile on his face. I can't help but smile back, my heart lightening. When I slide into the back seat, my pulse flutters at the sight of another folded note, another violet.

I pick up the flower, tuck it behind my ear and open the note.

Violet,
The third time you visited Mark, my friends had invited me to a party. I turned them down because even though I wouldn't admit it to myself, I enjoyed verbally sparring with the girl who couldn't stand me. The thought of it was far more appealing than having another meaningless one-night stand. When I sat next to

you on the couch to watch a movie, you wrinkled your nose at me, but I couldn't stop thinking about how good you smelled.

Always yours,
Tate

I press the note to my chest, and once again, tears wet my cheeks. If Tate's trying to prove this isn't a case of him falling for me due to proximity, he's going about it the right way. I had no idea he remembered our earliest interactions at all, let alone in such detail.

That night, I lie in bed and run through the last few months. I relive every touch of Tate's hand, every kiss, every whispered secret, the way it felt to be his. With each memory, my worry, my distrust over the unconventional nature of our relationship, is dissolving, and little by little, my heart is putting itself back together.

The next day, Jeremy is there and so is another note.

Violet,
When you and your dad came for Mark's graduation, I watched the three of you and wondered what it would be like to have that kind of close bond with my family. When you hugged your brother after the ceremony, I imagined for just a moment that you might hug me too. Spoiler alert: you didn't.

Always yours,

Tate

I can't help but laugh, even as my chest constricts at the thought of Tate watching my small but close-knit family from the outside. Regret pierces me that I didn't hug him that day. Or all the days between then and now.

The note that's waiting for me that evening talks about when he saw me that first time at Onyx.

Violet,

I'll never forget the moment you walked into Onyx. You weren't just a masked face in the crowd; you were the only person in the room. Maybe I sensed who you were even then. If so, my subconscious was one step ahead of my conscious mind in recognizing who you'd become to me. That night was the start of something I didn't even know I was looking for.

Always yours,
Tate

On the third day, when I see Jeremy waiting outside, I've already realized I'm being foolish. I've doubted Tate because I've been scared to risk my heart again. But he's risking his. He's risked more than that, and the least I can do is throw myself as recklessly into this relationship as he has.

When I slip into the car, I tuck the violet behind my ear and unfold the note.

Violet,

The night we went to Trio's and you told me the truth about Eric is seared into my memory. You trusted me with something deeply personal that night, and all I wanted to do was to feel worthy of that trust. I wanted to be the kind of man who could give you everything you needed.

Always yours,
Tate

My heart flutters in my chest, and a smile I can't contain breaks over my face. I'm desperate to see Tate, to touch him and tell him how I feel. But I can't leave the shop short-staffed, as much as I'm tempted to. So I force myself to go in to work.

It isn't until Jarrod comments on my good mood that I realize I'm smiling and humming as I wipe down the espresso machine Tate bought for me.

"Tate and I are... I think we're getting back together."

He stops what he's doing to scrutinize me, his hazel eyes bouncing between mine. Then he smiles. "I'm glad to see you happy again. He'd just better do right by you this time."

"Turns out, he never did wrong," I say.

He arches a brow, curiosity simmering in his gaze. But all he says is "Glad to hear it."

The rest of the day doesn't pass quickly enough. I'm desperate to leave work to see Tate, so when I finally lock up, I rush over to where Jeremy is standing next to the car. "Can you take me to him?"

His smile drops. "I can't, Miss Sinclair. He had to fly to LA for business."

My heart sinks at the news. "How long will he be gone for?"

"Until Friday."

"Oh." I swallow down my disappointment. "Okay. Thank you."

He opens the car door for me, and I climb in, finding the note I knew would be waiting. I hold it between my fingers for the span of a few heartbeats. If he's not in New York, then he must have written these before he left with instructions for Jeremy to place them in the car. I touch the violet I've tucked into my hair. Did he stockpile these as well?

After taking a deep breath, I unfold the paper and read.

Violet,

The moment I slipped the ring onto your finger, I knew I wouldn't want you to take it off. I already loved that you didn't care who I was or what I had. As soon as you were wearing my ring, I knew I'd never put one on anyone else. I just needed to make sure you felt the same. I'd like to think you do. I'd like to think that, soon, you'll come back to me. I'll be forever grateful you said yes to being my fake fiancée.

One day, I hope you'll say yes to me again.

Forever yours,

Tate

It's hard to believe I have any tears left at this stage. And yet I'm still forced to wipe away the strays that trickle over.

Anticipation floods through me in a rush. I just have to get through the rest of the week without losing my mind, and then I'll ask Jeremy to take me to Tate. Because what I need to say to him has to be said in person.

I sit back in my seat and close my eyes as I imagine being back in his arms, where I should have stayed, and finally, finally telling him how I feel.

CHAPTER FIFTY-ONE

VIOLET

My alarm goes off what feels like only a couple of hours after I fell asleep. I blink awake to the hazy gray of early morning.

Too early.

I push my hair out of my face and reach for my alarm, wondering why it's gone off, when I realize it wasn't my alarm that woke me up. It was my ringtone.

Rubbing my eyes, I fumble for my phone, my pulse racing when I see Tate's name flashing on the screen.

I stab the answer button. "Hello?"

"Butterfly, you need to let me in."

My stomach free-falls at the sound of his deep, husky tone. "You're here?" I ask, even as I'm pushing my covers off and climbing out of bed.

"I didn't want to bang on the door and wake all your neighbors up."

I want to ask him what he's doing here when Jeremy told me he was in California, but I need to see him even more, so I rush to the front door and unlock it.

My heart stutters and leaps in my chest. His blond hair

is mussed, and there are shadows under his eyes. His shirt is wrinkled and half-pulled out of his pants.

"Tate? What's wr—"

He doesn't give me time to finish the question before he's on me. His big body crowds close, his hands framing my face. Those startling golden eyes of his sweep over me as if he hasn't seen me in months rather than only a few days. I'm pretty sure mine are doing the same to him.

He strokes over the arches of my cheeks with his thumbs and tilts his head down. "Yes or no, Violet? And please, for fuck's sake, say yes." His voice is rough and threaded with emotion.

There's no possible way I could say no to what he's asking.

"Yes," I breathe.

His mouth is on mine before my lips have finished forming the words. The taste of him has my eyelids drifting shut in relief. I've missed it. I've missed him. So much. All my reasons for telling him I needed space crumble like ash and float away. I don't beat myself up about them though. I'm too busy twisting his already wrinkled shirt in my fists and pulling him as close to me as I can manage.

His tongue surges into my mouth, the kiss growing deeper, more frantic, and I swallow the groan that escapes him at the contact. He drops his hands to my ass and drags me against him, so his erection presses hard against my belly. It has need crashing over me in a wave. I tug at him and take a step back, urging him to follow me to the bedroom so we can strip out of our clothes and he can imprint himself onto my body again.

He pulls back and grasps my wrist, stopping me before I can put my plan into action. "We need to talk."

Wariness creeps through the fog of need clouding my

head. *We need to talk* doesn't usually end in sunshine and rainbows. I swallow. "Okay."

I turn, prepared to take a seat at the kitchen table so I can hear him out, but he gently grips my shoulders, stopping me.

He cradles my face again and brings his in close. "I didn't ditch my meetings and fly all the way back from California overnight to talk politely at the table. This conversation will only take a few minutes."

It hits me then why he looks so rumpled. He flew all night and came here straight from the airport. "Why did you come home?"

"Jeremy told me you asked to see me." His beautiful lips curve up at the corners. "I hoped that meant you'd forgiven me."

My throat constricts so hard I can barely breathe, even as sorrow that I put him through that weighs heavy on my chest. "Tate, there was nothing to forgive. I'm sorry that I made you feel that way. I know everything you did was to protect me. That means... so much." How could I not have seen the truth when he first came back to me? How could I have pushed him away when what he did proves just how much I can trust him to keep my heart safe?

"I hurt you." Remorse shadows his eyes.

I smooth my palm over his stubbled cheek. "It hurt thinking you didn't want me. It hurt thinking you'd moved on without a second thought. It hurt so much I couldn't pretend anymore. I love you, Tate. I love you so much that thinking of spending my life without you tore me up inside. And that was... scary." I suck in a shaky breath. "I was scared and overwhelmed and terrified that none of what we had was real. But those notes, Tate." I stare up at him, consumed by the intensity of his gaze. "I had no idea."

The tension in his jaw eases, and one corner of his mouth turns up. "Neither did I. Not back when we first met, anyway. And not at the start of all of this. Not consciously, anyway. All I knew then was that being around you made me happy. Our relationship may have started out as fake. But this connection, what I feel for you," his throat works on a swallow, "nothing in my life has ever been this real."

My heart pounds almost painfully in my chest. "I feel it too," I whisper. "It just took me a little while to admit that it could be true. I didn't trust my own judgment."

He threads his hands through my hair and cradles my skull, his thumbs ghosting over my jaw. "You trust it now?"

"Yes." I look into his beautiful golden eyes. "And I trust you. Every part of me feels how right this is."

He drops his forehead to mine and inhales, a faint tremor vibrating through his fingers where they're cupping me. "You trust me?"

I let my lashes flutter closed and breathe him in. This man kept everyone at bay with his devilish smirk and cocky attitude, when all along, he just needed someone to be his. Someone to see him for exactly who he is and to trust him to be the kind of man who won't walk away.

"I trust you." I brush my mouth against his. "With keeping me safe. With my heart. I trust you to be mine."

This time, his kiss is hard and urgent. I wrap my arms around his chest, arching up against him. Too soon, he pulls away. I whimper in response, my body humming with the need to feel his skin under my fingers. But it's only a second before his lips brush, soft and sweet, across mine again. Then he takes my hand in one of his, holding up his other one.

Between his fingers, my engagement ring glitters in the

light. I can barely speak past the rock that forms in my throat. "Did you go home to get this before you came here?"

He shakes his head. "I've been carrying it with me." A smile plays at the corners of his lips. "It made it easier to believe I'd be putting it back on you soon."

He brushes his thumb over my bare ring finger as he searches my face. The question shines in his eyes, burning so bright the answer bursts from me before he can even ask it.

"Yes. Tate. Yes. All the yeses."

One corner of his mouth curls up, but it's so easy now to see past that arrogant smirk that used to drive me crazy. I see a man who was desperate for someone to love him for who he is. Not for his last name or his family. Not for the money in his bank account or the power he wields because of those things. Someone who loves him just for him.

"We can take as long as you need," he says. "We can wait until you're ready to get married. I just need my ring back on your finger."

Emotion threatens to choke me. "Put it on me. Please."

With no hesitation, he slides it on, and the cool touch of the band launches a flurry of wings in my stomach.

"You're mine again." His voice is all gravel, sending sparks arcing through me.

When I look down at the ring, it blurs into a rainbow. I blink the tears away and meet his gaze again. "I was always yours. I always will be."

He presses his face to the crook of my neck. "Fuck, butterfly. I've missed you."

I slide my arms around him. Breathing him in. Feeling the reality of his big body against mine. "It's been too long, Tate. I need you. I need you right now."

He pulls back, that gorgeous, cocky smile that I love

breaking over his face. "Well, if my fiancée needs me..." His hands go under my ass, and he lifts me so I can wrap my legs around his hips. "Who am I to refuse her."

He carries me that way to my bedroom, where I proceed to show him exactly how much I need him.

But not just that. I show him how much I want him, how much I trust him, how much I *love* him. And I plan to keep on showing him those things.

Every day for the rest of our lives.

EPILOGUE

TATE

I can't stop the smile that crosses my face at the sight of the woman walking down the white aisle runner toward me. The lush greenery of the botanic gardens forms a bright backdrop behind her. Her expression is full of love, and the swell of her stomach is barely visible beneath the beautiful high-waisted white gown she's wearing.

Next to me, Cole has gone completely still as his wife-to-be approaches.

"Breathe, man," I mutter from the corner of my mouth. "It might give the wrong impression if you pass out just as she gets to you."

"Fuck you. I'm breathing," he says. But there's a catch to his voice. His eyes are glossy as he keeps his gaze pinned on Delilah.

My own chest tightens at his display of emotion. Seeing his happiness, how complete Delilah has made him, makes me incredibly grateful. Not just that he found love, but that, along with Roman, *I'm* standing next to him as he takes this step.

And I'm beyond grateful that I can relate to how he feels about his soon-to-be wife.

I find Violet where she's sitting in the front row of guests, the white of the chairs bright against the green lawn. She's not looking at me. She's watching Delilah being escorted down the aisle by Beth, her mother. I take my fiancée in, from the elegant updo that shows off the slender curve of her neck to the pretty blue off-the-shoulder dress she's wearing that matches the color of her eyes.

She's perfect. And she's mine.

My ring has been back on her finger for the last three months, and things couldn't be better. Violet moved back into my penthouse the day after I got back from California, and instantly, it felt like a home again.

My brothers barely blinked when I told them Violet and I were officially engaged. Cole gave me a rough slap on the back and a manly hug, while Roman shook his head, a wry smile on his face. "Falling like damn dominoes" was all he said.

I raised my brows at him. "I've heard the last domino falls the hardest."

He snorted. "I've been down that road before. I have no desire to repeat the experience."

Cole and I shared a look but didn't comment further.

Call me a romantic—and I can guarantee no one ever has—but I'd like to think there's a woman out there who will be up for turning my brother's world upside down.

Delilah reaches us, gives her mom a kiss on the cheek and hands off her bouquet. She smiles softly as Beth takes her place next to the only other bridesmaid, Alex, her best friend. Then she turns to face Cole, her green eyes shining as she looks up at him.

There's a sharp tug behind my ribs when I imagine the moment a pair of blue eyes will look up at me the same way.

Not that Violet and I are in a rush to get married. I'm happy to wait for the moment Violet is ready. It's not that she doesn't love me or trust me, but the whole start of our relationship was a whirlwind, and after what happened with Eric, I don't blame her for wanting to settle into a calmer life with me before setting a date and getting swept up into the craziness of planning a wedding.

Although when Delilah and Cole decided not to wait until after their daughter's birth to get married, they got theirs sorted in a short amount of time. While the King Group has any number of hotels that could have hosted a huge society wedding, Delilah wanted something outdoors and far more intimate. And here, with a wooden arch adorned with ivy, white roses and peonies behind us, and the subtle fragrance of the flowers filling the air, feels much more her than any glittering ballroom.

We've all seen the inside of enough ballrooms to last us a lifetime.

Cole and Delilah hold hands as the officiant leads them through their short, simple, but emotion-filled vows. There are sniffles from the guests, and tears shimmer on Beth's cheeks as she stands behind her daughter. But it's the emotion on my fiancée's face that steals my focus. When she catches me looking at her, she gives me a wobbly smile. I get the feeling there'll be tears on her cheeks before too long as well.

I realize I've gotten distracted from the ceremony when I hear the words "you may now kiss the bride." Maybe missing the end of their vows makes me a bad best man, but I think Cole will forgive me. Not that he looks like he'd care right now, anyway. As the guests erupt into cheers, he cups

Delilah's cheeks and kisses her like there's nobody watching. When they break apart, I don't think I've ever seen my brother smile so broadly. Roman, standing next to me, clears his throat.

"Keep it together," I say, trying to hold back my smirk. "I know it's emotional, but what will people think if the big bad CEO of the King Group breaks down into tears at his brother's wedding?"

He narrows his eyes, then, surprisingly, cracks the slightest of smiles. "About the same as they'll think when the playboy CMO falls to his knees at the top of the aisle when he sees his bride for the first time."

I chuckle, watching as Delilah takes her bouquet from her mom, then clasps Cole's hand. "Maybe one day we'll get to see how you react to marrying the love of your life."

Unsurprisingly, his response is merely a derisive snort, and I grin to myself as I take Alex's arm so we can follow Cole and Delilah back down the aisle. As we pass the front row, I give my fiancée a wink, and she smiles that beautiful, wide, unguarded smile that I love so much.

Two years ago, I couldn't have imagined a day like today. Cole marrying a woman he loves and my ring on the finger of a woman who feels like she was always meant to be mine. And in a few months' time, there'll be a new member of the King family. This time, she'll be brought up with all the love and affection her family can give her.

A short while later, I wind my way through the tables on the lawn until I find Violet talking to Delilah's mom. I sweep my fiancée up in my arms and plant my lips on hers. As always, her taste explodes on my tongue, and I fight the urge to let the kiss get more heated. I'd love nothing more than to slide my hands up under her skirt and grip her ass, but I'll restrain myself until we get home. Then all bets are off.

When we surface from the kiss, Beth is laughing. "I think I'll leave you lovebirds alone."

Violet protests, but Beth waves her off with a warm smile. "I think it's about time I hugged my daughter and new son-in-law again anyway."

After she moves away, Violet looks up at me. "You looked so handsome standing up there in your tuxedo."

"I couldn't take my eyes off you," I say. I kiss her again, and I don't want to stop. But I'm forced to when the food is served.

Instead of a formal sit-down dinner, there are several gourmet stations set up around the area serving a variety of cuisines. There's also a bar stocked with fine wines, craft beers, premium spirits and specialty cocktails. The small tables scattered throughout the space mean guests can move around and mingle during the meal, continuing the relaxed atmosphere of the wedding.

An hour later, after we've eaten and taken photos with the happy couple—although happy might overstate Cole's mood at having to share his bride with so many other people—I find myself standing next to Roman at the bar while Violet talks to Alex and her rockstar husband, Jaxson.

"Having fun?" I ask him, after the bartender serves me my whiskey.

"Beats going to another gala."

I let out a surprised laugh. "It does. Maybe we could tone it down a bit. We've shown the world we're not like Dad. We shouldn't have to keep parading ourselves around, trying to prove something."

He nods slowly. "I think you're right."

It's a relief. While having Violet by my side has made

attending formal events more enjoyable, I'd much rather be at home with her, making her scream my name.

"I heard Eric was convicted," Roman says.

I shoot him a look. Since Eric's arrest and the removal of the photos, we rarely talk about what we did.

"Yeah, six years' jail time in a federal prison. Maybe he'll end up in the same one as Dad. That would be fitting."

A smile lightens Roman's usual severe expression. "It would."

Warmth fills my chest. One which has become familiar since Violet came into my life. The warmth of belonging. I study my brother. Does he feel it too?

He meets my gaze, one dark brow arching. "What?"

I shake my head. "Nothing."

He stares at me for a moment longer, then clears his throat, as if deciding not to press the issue. "Have you spoken to Violet about your idea?"

I take a sip of my drink before answering. "Not yet. I'll see what she thinks tonight."

"Let me know what her decision is."

"I will." I'm hoping Violet will be interested in expanding True Brew. We need a coffee shop for the foyer of Genesis-1, and I don't just want True Brew because it's Violet's. I genuinely believe the sustainable, community-minded feel of it fits within the purview of Genesis-1, while the quality of the coffee will keep the wealthy residents happy.

I also plan to broach the subject of stealing Jarrod to run the place now that she has plenty of help at the shop. Not that I'm trying to separate them. Violet told me what he said the night I saw them hugging, and I admitted he was right. I may not like his confession about being attracted to her, but I can't exactly blame him either. And I don't have any concerns over Violet having more than friendly feelings for him. How could I when she shows how much she loves me every single day? No, jealousy isn't the reason I'm considering offering Jarrod management of a potential new True Brew. He's more than proven his dedication to Violet's family and the shop. He helped her when she needed it, and for that, I'll be forever grateful. But most of all, I know he's the person Violet would trust the most to keep the spirit of True Brew alive, even if it's in a different location.

That's a discussion for later though.

When I catch Violet's eye, she wanders our way, a smile on her pretty lips.

She slips under my arm and looks up at Roman. "Are you having a good time?"

His eyes are dark as he watches us. "I like seeing my brother happy." Then he gives her the ghost of a smile. "Both of them." He downs the rest of his drink and puts the glass down on the bar. "Have a good night, you two." And then he's gone, wandering off with his hands in his pockets.

Violet sighs. "Do you think he'll ever open himself up to meeting someone again?"

I set my own glass down and wrap her in my arms. "I don't know. He's pretty hard-headed, and he's stuck on the idea that he's done with love. I'm not sure anyone can convince him otherwise."

She nods sadly, but before she can respond, we're summoned so the toasts can begin. After mine, where I only *subtly* emphasize my role in Cole and Delilah's current happiness, it's time for the couple's first dance.

Strangely enough, Violet and I end up standing next to Mom as we watch the newly married couple float around the small wooden dance floor set up on the lawn. I'm surprised to hear a quiet sniff from beside me, and not from the side Violet's standing on. I turn just in time to see Mom blink away a faint sheen from her eyes.

She catches me looking and pulls her shoulders back. "I told Cole he should consider an indoor wedding. So much dust and pollen floating around outside."

I can't stifle the laugh that escapes me. "Mom, you know the old 'must have gotten some dust in my eye' excuse doesn't fool anyone, right?"

Her lips purse, but a moment later, the tension seems to leave her. "Yes, well." She looks back at where Cole is staring down at his bride with so much adoration it's almost painful, and her cool expression softens, just a fraction. "It's a beautiful wedding. Much lovelier than mine."

Next to me, Violet squeezes my hand. I know what she's telling me. I could let this moment slide, make a smart-ass comment and walk away, or I could find some forgiveness for a woman who was the product of her upbringing and her marriage. A woman who I hope may be beginning to learn the value of love and family.

"You have plenty of time, Mom. Maybe one day you could have a wedding of your own like this."

She shoots me a startled look, and I grin back. I've been shocking her my entire life, but this suggestion seems to have taken her by surprise more than most of the things I've said over the years.

When she turns back to where Cole is kissing Delilah, I think she's going to ignore me. Then the corners of her mouth turn up just a bit. "If I do, I hope it will be with a man who makes me laugh."

Then, with a tight, self-conscious smile at Violet and me, she glides off, her posture as stiff as always.

I watch my mother's retreating back, then shoot Violet a bemused look.

Her gaze is warm. "I joined team 'leopards can change their spots' a while ago."

I pull her to me and nuzzle my nose into her hair. "Would you like to dance, butterfly?"

"I'd love to."

I lead her to the dance floor, then pull her against me.

"Your mom is right. It is a beautiful wedding," she says.

"It is. They did a good job of pulling it together so quickly."

She lifts her chin and assesses me, the love in her eyes making my chest squeeze tight. "Do you think we could do a good job of it too?"

I cradle her cheeks and search her face as my heart beats wildly in my chest. "Are you saying you're ready to marry me, butterfly?"

She looks at me through her lashes. "Maybe?"

I lightly grip her hair and tug until her chin tips up a little higher. The way her eyes slip half-closed sends a rush of heat up my spine. I know how much she likes it when I do that, and when I pin her down and hold her with my hand around her slender throat. It makes my beautiful fiancée go wild. Her lips part, but I won't kiss her until she gives me an answer. "Yes or no, butterfly?"

"Yes," she breathes. "I'm ready. More than ready. I can't wait to walk down the aisle and see you waiting for me at the end."

I kiss her, long and hard and hungry, the way I'm always hungry for her. When I pull back, she's flushed and breathless.

"I love you, Violet. In a way I didn't know was possible to love someone. I think about what you said months ago. When you know, you know. I used to question the feelings I had. How could it happen so quickly, so surely? And I kept coming back to that. Deep down, I knew from the moment I saw you at Onyx that the whole trajectory of my life was going to change."

Tears glisten in her eyes. "I love you too, Tate. So much. My parents would be proud that we've made True Brew successful again, but they'd be even happier knowing I have you to spend the rest of my life with. I'm so grateful you asked me to be your fake girlfriend." She grins then. "I'm even grateful you were my brother's roommate."

A laugh escapes me. I'll forever hate the impression I first made on her, but she doesn't hold it against me anymore. She understands more than anyone the headspace I was in that night—and for so much of my life. I brush my lips across hers. Our journey to get here might be anything but conventional, but it was what we both needed to get past the barriers we had in place. And soon, soon, I'll get to call her mine forever.

I kiss her then, holding her to me, the softness of her body molding to mine. When I come up for air, I lift her up in a hug. "I can't wait to call you my wife."

"Tired of calling me your future-wife already?"

"Just looking forward to dropping the future part." I press my nose to the crook of her neck and breathe in her peaches and cream scent.

When I pull back and look at her, a smile breaks across my face. I wasn't joking about looking forward to calling her my wife. We've already had the kids discussion, and she wants them too. As much as my desire to be a father took me by surprise, it hasn't ebbed over the intervening months. I'm determined to be the parent to my children that I never had. I want to teach any sons or daughters we might have that there's so much more to them than their last name or the blood that runs in their veins. That who they are inside, and the love they share with those around them, will mean more than anything else in this life.

I'd like to think that my biological dad would have loved me if he'd known about me, but I've realized it doesn't matter either way. Because there are others that do. My brothers, although they may never say the words out loud, and my sister-in-law, because Delilah has a lot of love to give. Maybe even my mom, deep down. And best of all, my now very-soon-to-be wife. Violet's love is strong and bright enough to fill the rest of my days.

She presses her body against mine, definitely feeling how ready I am to take her home and make her feel good. "I'm looking forward to calling you my husband."

I groan. The feel of her and the way she purrs the word husband are driving me crazy.

"When we get home, I'm going to make sure you practice saying it. Just so you're ready for the big day."

Her pupils flare. "I could use the practice."

"How much longer do you think we need to stay?" I ask.

She laughs. "We're going to stay right to the very end. But if you want, I can tell you exactly what I want you to do to me when we get home."

I growl, then kiss her again, hard and then gentle and then hard again. I can't help myself when it comes to her. I've never been able to. From pushing her buttons when she visited in college to touching her at Onyx to making her my fake girlfriend and then my fiancée. I never had any control, and I doubt I ever will.

I tip her face up so I can look into her beautiful blue eyes. "You're always going to be mine, aren't you?"

Her eyes darken, and her lips part, but she's not quick enough to give me what I want. I slide my fingers under her hair and cup the back of her neck. "Yes or no, butterfly?"

She presses her palm against my heart. “Yes, Tate. When it comes to you, my answer will always be yes.”

As I hold her close to me, I know no matter what happens in my life, there will always be one place I belong.

With this woman in my arms.

THE END

ACKNOWLEDGMENTS

There are so many people to thank, starting with my husband and children, for putting up with my endless preoccupation with the people in my head. Thank you to my editor, Beth, for helping make this story shine. To Linda and the team at Foreword PR, thank you for not giving up on my disorganized self. To my PAs, Tricia and Mikaela, for making beautiful graphics and videos and for helping me connect with my readers. Thank you to Bobby K, for sharing his wisdom so generously. And to the bloggers, bookstagrammers, booktokkers, and everyone else who has shared my books with their friends and followers.

And lastly, a massive thank you to you, the reader, for taking a chance on my books. I hope you loved Tate and Violet's story. If so, please consider sharing. Word of mouth is an incredible thing for an author.

L.M. x

ALSO BY L.M. DALGLEISH

Empty Kingdom Series

Coldhearted King

Reckless King

Fractured Rock Star Series

Fractured Hearts

Fractured Dreams

Fractured Trust

Fractured Kiss

Box Set

Fractured: The Fractured Rock Star Romance Complete Four Book Series

Crossfire Rock Stars

The Promises We Make

Novellas

Wishing for Always

ABOUT THE AUTHOR

L. M. Dalgleish is a life-long book lover who, as a child, used to shut herself in her bedroom with a good book and a packed lunch so she could spend all day reading. Her passion for romance novels began in the long sleepless nights following the birth of her first baby. Two more babies later and she's still in love with strong, sassy heroines and sexy, but emotionally unavailable (at least to begin with) heroes.

She lives in Canberra, Australia, with her husband, three kids, and a very large, very fluffy cat. In her spare time, she enjoys hanging with her family, reading, eating too much pasta, and watching horror movies.

Made in United States
North Haven, CT
18 October 2024